W9-BYK-061

Eternity's Mind

KEVIN J. ANDERSON

Eternity's Mind

THE SAGA OF SHADOWS · BOOK THREE

TOR

A TOM DOHERTY ASSOCIATES BOOK

NEW YORK

This is a work of fiction. All of the characters, organizations, and events
portrayed in this novel are either products of the author's
imagination or are used fictitiously.

ETERNITY'S MIND

Copyright © 2016 by WordFire, Inc.

A Tor Book
Published by Tom Doherty Associates, LLC
175 Fifth Avenue
New York, NY 10010

www.tor-forge.com

Tor® is a registered trademark of Tom Doherty Associates, LLC.

The Library of Congress Cataloging-in-Publication Data
is available upon request.

ISBN 978-0-7653-3301-8 (hardcover)
ISBN 978-1-4299-6649-8 (e-book)

Our books may be purchased in bulk for promotional, educational, or business
use. Please contact your local bookseller or the Macmillan Corporate and
Premium Sales Department at 1-800-221-7945, extension 5442,
or by e-mail at MacmillanSpecialMarkets@macmillan.com.

First Edition: September 2016

Printed in the United States of America

0 9 8 7 6 5 4 3 2 1

For more than twenty years, Tom Doherty and Linda Quinton at Tor Books have been supporters of my work—as cheering section, sounding board, and business partners. *Eternity's Mind* is the end of the Seven Suns universe, for now, and this novel is dedicated to them.

ACKNOWLEDGMENTS

When I write a big book like this, I dictate chapters at a furious pace, sometimes as many as four per day, nearly overwhelming my typist, Karen Haag, but she keeps up with me and I owe her a special thanks. Also, my gratitude for the work of my editor, Pat LoBrutto; my agent, John Silbersack; test reader, Diane Jones; and, as always, my wife, Rebecca Moesta.

Eternity's
Mind

THE STORY SO FAR

Even as the mysterious and deadly Shana Rei attack random colonies throughout the Spiral Arm, industrialist Lee Iswander expands his operations to extract stardrive fuel from clusters of bloaters—enigmatic nodules that drift in the dark spaces between the stars. Bloaters seem similar to plankton in space, and since they are filled with the valuable fuel ekti-X, Iswander considers them a treasure trove. He keeps his operations completely secret, to prevent competitors from producing great quantities of cheap stardrive fuel, which would glut the market and cause prices to crash. But many Roamers are desperate to know the secret.

Aelin, the green priest who serves Iswander at the bloater-extraction field, suspects the nodules are something very important. He can tap into the immense verdani mind and all the knowledge there, and he also senses a powerful presence among the bloaters. Occasionally, unpredictable energy discharges ripple through the nuclei of the nodules. In an attempt to understand them, Aelin flies a stolen scout pod out among the bloaters with his treeling and is inadvertently caught in one of the discharges—which sends him into a coma of overloaded thoughts and revelations. He claims that bloaters are filled with the "blood of the cosmos" and that the Iswander operations are causing great harm. Iswander and his hardline deputy, Elisa Enturi, believe Aelin is mad. The green priest tries to escape the extraction field to sound a warning, but he is captured and held, considered a threat. Since the bloater outburst destroyed his treeling, Aelin has no way to communicate with other green priests on Theroc.

Back on the worldforest planet, the green priests are intrigued by the newly arrived Onthos, the remnants of a nearly extinct race of "Gardeners," who once tended another worldforest in a distant star system. The Onthos and their worldtrees were wiped out by the Shana Rei long ago, and now the last hundred of them request sanctuary on Theroc. With the blessing of the green priests and the worldforest, King Peter and Queen Estarra grant them permission to stay.

Their daughter Arita, who failed in her attempt to become a green priest, is fascinated by the Gardeners. She hovers close and listens to the Gardeners talk about their lost homeworld and how they cared for their immense but now extinct worldforest. Though she is not one of them, the green priests tolerate Arita's presence. More surprisingly, the leader of the Onthos, Ohro, takes an interest in Arita, telling her she is more special than the green priests, that she can connect with something else. Indeed, she has heard strange whispers of thoughts in her head from a distant and immense consciousness, but she never understood them.

Arita's brother, Prince Reynald, suffers from a debilitating disease which will soon cost him his life, a rare illness he contracted from the worldforest itself. The King and Queen have spread the word to all worlds in the Spiral Arm and the Ildiran Empire, searching for a cure, but they have been unsuccessful. Osira'h, daughter of the Ildiran Mage-Imperator and the human green priest Nira, has befriended Reyn and now stays with him on Theroc as his condition continues to worsen. He collapses on the tree canopy, and Osira'h tends him but feels completely helpless.

Meanwhile, Osira'h's father, Mage-Imperator Jora'h, deals with crises in the Ildiran Empire. The Shana Rei and their black robot allies have attacked Ildiran colonies, but the shadows have also infiltrated the Ildiran telepathic network of the *thism*. Though he tells no one, even his green priest lover Nira, Jora'h fears the shadows are inside him as well. A mob of possessed Ildirans recently wiped out an enclave of human settlers in the capital city of Mijistra, and Jora'h announces he will go to Theroc to personally express his regret to King Peter and Queen Estarra. With the Shana Rei continuing their depredations, Jora'h hopes to strengthen the Ildiran alliance with the human Confederation.

Jora'h departs Ildira with an entourage including two warrior women as bodyguards: Yazra'h and Nira's halfbreed daugher Muree'n. The Mage-Imperator leaves his eldest son, Prime Designate Daro'h, in charge, with Nira's halfbreed son Rod'h as his friend and adviser. Rod'h resents the fact that he has become irrelevant since the Elemental War; born as part of the Dobro breeding program to be a savior of the Ildiran Empire, he never got the chance to fulfill his destiny, and feels like he has no purpose. Rod'h tries to help Daro'h in his duties, and saves the Prime Designate when a shadow-possessed Ildiran mob tries to kill him. If the Shana Rei can infiltrate anyone, anywhere, then no place is safe. Fortunately, all of Nira's halfbreed children—Rod'h, Osira'h, Muree'n, Tamo'l, and Tal Gale'nh—seem to be immune.

Adar Zan'nh, the leader of the Solar Navy, works with Ildiran factories to produce sun bombs and laser cannons, the only weapons that have proved effective against the Shana Rei. Tal Gale'nh, the protégé of Adar Zan'nh, still struggles to recover from the horrific experience of being captured by the Shana Rei. When Gale'nh was held prisoner in a Shana Rei entropy bubble, the creatures of darkness could not penetrate him, and he does not know why he was ever freed. After checking on the sun-bomb production, Zan'nh takes Gale'nh to a Lightsource shrine on the planet Hiltos, where the young tal hopes the lens kithmen can give him insight.

The Adar's counterpart in the Confederation Defense Forces, General Nalani Keah, has also set the CDF weapons industries at Earth to work at full capacity. Dr. Jocko Krieger modifies old Ildiran sun-bomb designs to create even more powerful sun bombs, but the the new bombs are produced in such a rush that safety routines are not followed, and an unfortunate accident destroys one of the major factories in lunar orbit. Back to square one.

Mage-Imperator Jora'h and Nira meet with the King and Queen on Theroc, cementing their alliance. Prince Reyn's health is declining, and Osira'h asks her father to send a message to Tamo'l (also one of Nira's halfbreed children), who tends the "misbreeds," misfit survivors of the now-defunct breeding experiments on Dobro. The misbreeds are often deformed, barely able to survive, and are considered sad mistakes of the program, but Tamo'l believes that they are not just discards, but possess some special worth. Receiving her sister's plea to help find a cure for Reynald, Tamo'l investigates some of the rare kelp strains on Kuivahr, the ocean world where her sanctuary domes are located.

The only facility that might possess the medical information Reyn requires is Pergamus, a secret library of diseases and cures owned by the wealthy recluse Zoe Alakis, who built the secure facility on a poisonous planet and has no intention of sharing her treasure of data or her cures with anyone. Zoe stays sealed in a sterile environment, afraid to be infected by the outside universe. Her loyal majordomo Tom Rom provides everything she needs and often risks his life to acquire new specimens for her collection. He just recovered from the deadly Onthos space plague, which he accidentally caught when forcibly obtaining a blood sample from Orli Covitz, who was herself infected. The researchers on Pergamus finally found a cure for Tom Rom, and now he continues to complete whatever mission Zoe gives him.

Orli was cured of the plague, too, by immersing herself in the protoplasm inside the bloaters—which the green priest Aelin called the blood of the cosmos. Once she recovers enough, Orli goes with her new companion Garrison Reeves and his young son Seth to settle on the quiet colony planet of Ikbir. As their relationship deepens, Orli and Garrison realize that Ikbir is just too dull for them, and they set off to the Roamer capital of Newstation, where Seth will go to school. On their way out of the Ikbir system, though, they see an astonishing number of bloaters drifting in clusters and chained together like breadcrumbs across vast reaches of space. Because she was once immersed in a bloater, Orli feels a strange connection to them. . . .

Iswander keeps producing ekti-X, and the main distributors are Xander Brindle and Terry Handon, pilots for Kett Shipping. Rlinda Kett has made huge profits from all the new stardrive fuel, but she, as well as Xander's parents Robb Brindle and Tasia Tamblyn, remains suspicious about where the ekti-X comes from. It seems too cheap and too easy. Xander and Terry make the unpleasant discovery that some of the medical treatments they deliver for Kett Shipping have horrific consequences. The treatments come from Rakkem, a biological black market with an extremely dark track record and a string of corpses in its wake. Concerned, they decide they need to know more about the suppliers who hire Kett Shipping and the products they deliver—which include ekti-X.

Lee Iswander refuses to tell anyone his source, and Rlinda is sure Iswander is hiding something. Xander and Terry do some subtle spying on their own, even deciding to place a tracker on Elisa Enturi's ship the next time they receive a delivery. For his own part, Lee Iswander has been treated with suspicion by the Roamer clans, who snub him and claim he is not a real Roamer. He makes overtures, offering to help, but they simply don't see eye-to-eye. He feels disrespected.

Shareen Fitzkellum, a spunky and ambitious teenaged Roamer, gets assigned with her friend Howard Rohandas to Fireheart Station, where they will become research assistants for Kotto Okiah, the legendary but eccentric Roamer genius who is building a gigantic experiment in the middle of a nebula. Kotto doesn't want any apprentices, especially teens, but Shareen's grandfather, Del Kellum, uses his political clout to get them the position. Del, a former Speaker for the Roamer clans, runs a distillery on the ocean world of Kuivahr with his daughter Zhett and her husband Patrick. They make exotic liquor from the same kelp extracts that Tamo'l uses to treat her mis breeds. Del thinks Shareen has so much potential, he wants her to learn from the best: Kotto. Del delivers Shareen and Howard to Fireheart, and they get to work with the famous but eccentric scientist.

Kotto gives them busywork projects of half-developed ideas or designs that he never completed. Thinking it's a test, Shareen and Howard work on the problems and find innovative solutions. Kotto compliments them, but is secretly disturbed, since he himself was never able to finish those problems. In fact, though he used to be a great genius, he hasn't produced anything significant in many years and fears he no longer has the talent. He is constructing a gigantic high-energy experiment, the Big Ring, in the middle of a blazing nebula, banking his entire reputation on this concept, and he secretly fears it might not work. He won't show Shareen and Howard the detailed plans, worried that they would find something wrong with it, and he doesn't want to know.

At the isolated Hiltos Lightsource shrine, Tal Gale'nh and Adar Zan'nh meet the lens kithmen who have devoted their lives to developing their mental abilities and studying philosophy. There, they are alarmed to discover Rusa'h, the mad Designate who nearly brought down the Ildiran Empire with his destructive alliance with the faeros and his civil war against Mage-Imperator Jora'h. After his defeat, Rusa'h was exiled to Hiltos and has caused no trouble for twenty years. Now, knowing the incredible threat of the Shana Rei, Rusa'h insists that the only way to fight the creatures of darkness is to renew the alliance with the fiery elementals—a shocking proposal, considering how much destruction the faeros caused before. Zan'nh and Gale'nh refuse to consider the suggestion.

Then the Shana Rei and their swarms of black robot battleships strike Hiltos, drawn by all the lens kithmen's connection to the Lightsource. Led by the black robot Exxos, the ships devastate the shrine as Adar Zan'nh evacuates as many of the lens kithmen as possible, as well as the disgraced Rusa'h. The Solar Navy battles the Shana Rei in orbit, and the Ildiran warliners barely escape, suffering great damage. Rusa'h insists on going back to Ildira and presenting his plan to the Mage-Imperator.

As their diplomatic mission to Theroc finishes, Mage-Imperator Jora'h and Nira join a meeting in which General Keah debriefs the King and Queen about CDF military preparations against the Shana Rei. Ohro surprises them by revealing the location of the lost Onthos star system, which shows up on no star charts. The leader of the Gardener refugees explains that the Shana Rei swallowed up their sun and all its planets. Eager to learn anything about the shadows, General Keah proposes a mission to the dead star system, and Jora'h agrees to let Adar Zan'nh and a group of Solar Navy warliners join the expedition.

Ohro and the Onthos refugees do not want to go along, though; they are too frightened of the creatures of darkness. Instead, the aliens ask permission to settle on the isolated continent of the Wild, where they can live in peace. The only others in the Wild are a group of isolationist green priests (including Arita's friend Collin) and Queen Estarra's estranged sister Sarein, who lives as a hermit. King Peter lets the Gardeners pack up and go.

Before he can depart for home, the Mage-Imperator suddenly senses catastrophe in the Ildiran Empire: the Shana Rei attack on the Hiltos shrine, and the mob assassination attempt on Prime Designate Daro'h. He and Nira rush back to Mijistra, bringing their daughter Osira'h. There, they learn that Rod'h saved the Prime Designate from the possessed mob, and they meet the ragtag Solar Navy returning from Hiltos with mad Designate Rusa'h, who is very unwelcome after his crimes against the Empire. When Jora'h expresses grave reservations about joining forces with the faeros, Rusa'h claims that the Mage-Imperator is too weak to do what is necessary to save his people. As a contingency, Osira'h and Rod'h—the most talented of Nira's halfbreed children—seek out contact with the fiery elementals. The two encounter the faeros, but the sentient fireballs flee, refusing to communicate. Osira'h and Rod'h realize the faeros are *afraid* of the Shana Rei.

Back at his bloater-extraction facility, the powerful Lee Iswander feels snubbed and disrespected by the Roamer clans. He discusses with Elisa Enturi how to restore his reputation. Loyal and defensive, she agrees to do what she can when she delivers a large shipment of ekti-X to the trading hub of Ulio Station, where she will meet with Xander Brindle and Terry Handon.

The desperate green priest Aelin escapes from the Iswander facility by hiding in Elisa's ekti shipment. At Ulio Station he slips away to spread a warning about the bloaters. When he sees the ambitious Roamer traders, though, he fears they won't heed his warning, but might instead rush off to begin extraction operations of their own and cause even more damage to the bloaters! He inadvertently blurts the information to clan Duquesne and hunkers down at Ulio Station, not sure what to do.

Elisa Enturi delivers her stardrive fuel; a large stockpile will remain at Ulio, and the rest is sold to Kett Shipping. Xander and Terry place a tracker on Elisa's ship, so they can follow her movements and know where the ekti-X comes from. Elisa flies off, unaware that her trading partners are spying on her.

Terry and Xander receive a mysterious message to meet a ship out in deep space and are surprised to find the wandering vessel of old Maria Ulio, founder of Ulio Station, who vanished years ago.

Maria was a mentor to Terry, and she surprises Terry by transferring to him all of her wealth, which is locked in Ulio Station accounts. Stunned, Xander and Terry fly back to Earth to report to Kett Shipping.

Orli Covitz and Garrison Reeves, along with Garrison's young son Seth, travel to the Roamer capital of Newstation. On the way, Garrison stops at Rendezvous, the abandoned site of the former Roamer capital. For years, Garrison's stern father attempted to rebuild the asteroid cluster, but eventually gave up. Leaving Rendezvous, they arrive at Newstation, where Garrison learns of Kotto Okiah's Big Ring experiment, which is exactly the sort of work he wants to do. Although he and Orli are very close, both have been through difficult relationships, so they decide to spend a month apart to assess their feelings for each other. Leaving Orli, Garrison heads to Fireheart Station to join the Big Ring work crew.

At Fireheart, Shareen and Howard continue to amaze and intimidate Kotto Okiah. The two young assistants secretly get their hands on detailed plans for the Big Ring and are dismayed to see flaws in Kotto's calculations. The experiment won't work! Indignant, Kotto refuses to listen. He insists the Big Ring will be completed shortly and the experiment will proceed as planned.

As Prince Reyn's health declines further, one of Zoe Alakis's former medical researchers comes to Theroc, selling information about the secret Pergamus library to the King and Queen. With new hope, Peter and Estarra dispatch Rlinda Kett to negotiate for any relevant data Zoe might possess. But Rlinda is angrily rebuffed and chased out of the system. Tom Rom is upset to learn that one of Zoe's former researchers betrayed them, so he finds the man, incapacitates him, and sells him to be used as an experimental subject in the biomarkets of Rakkem. Knowing that Pergamus has been revealed, Tom Rom and Zoe have to decide how to proceed.

Meanwhile, in the sanctuary domes on Kuivahr, Tamo'l and her researchers develop possible treatments for Prince Reyn, based on exotic strains of kelp from the oceans. Tamo'l sends the good news to her sister Osira'h. Glad to have this chance, Reyn travels with Osira'h to Kuivahr, where Tamo'l will attempt to treat him.

Elisa Enturi learns that clan Duquesne has formed competing

bloater operations, after Aelin blurted out the secret source of ekti-X to them at Ulio Station. Determined to protect the livelihood and profits of Lee Iswander, Elisa tracks down the Duquesne operations and shows no mercy: she detonates the entire cluster and wipes out every person there. Then she returns to Iswander, confident that she has done what was necessary.

Without Garrison, Orli joins Tasia and Robb on a trip to Ulio Station, accompanied by Xander and Terry to retrieve spy data from the tracker on Elisa's ship. In the *Voracious Curiosity* Orli, Tasia, and Robb track Elisa, while Xander and Terry remain on the station to retrieve the fortune that Maria left Terry.

A shadow cloud appears outside of Ulio Station, and thousands of black robot fighters emerge to attack the complex. Xander and Terry barely escape, while the green priest Aelin is killed along with thousands of others. One of the Confederation's busiest trade depots is entirely wiped out.

Following Elisa's trail, the *Voracious Curiosity* comes upon the destroyed Duquesne ekti fields. In one of the wrecks they find a log recording that clearly shows Elisa intentionally causing the destruction. Orli, Tasia, and Robb are sickened as they follow the tracker to Iswander's main industrial operations. Iswander himself has gone to Newstation to regain his reputation among the Roamers, leaving Elisa in charge. When Orli, Tasia, and Robb discover the highly secret operations, Elisa races out in her ship and blasts the *Curiosity*. Even Iswander's other employees are horrified to see this over-the-top reaction. Tasia and Robb do some fancy flying to escape, though their ship is damaged. In empty space, they make repairs before limping back toward Newstation.

Meanwhile, General Keah and Adar Zan'nh launch their expedition to the Onthos star system, carrying Nira's halfbreed sons Rod'h and Tal Gale'nh. Their ships discover that the *entire star system* is sealed inside a vast black shell composed of hexagonal plates of dark matter. The expeditionary ships break through the shell and explore inside, finding dead planets and a snuffed-out sun. On the Onthos homeworld itself, they retrieve some blackened shards of long-dead worldtrees.

Outside the black shell, their sensors detect a gigantic verdani treeship, dead and drifting. Rod'h takes a small solo craft out to investigate and learns that the dead treeship is full of dead Onthos bodies—it was an arkship trying to escape the Shana Rei. As Rod'h's craft explores, a shadow cloud appears in the Onthos system: the Shana Rei and their black robot attack fleet. General Keah, Adar Zan'nh, and Tal Gale'nh unleash their arsenal of sun bombs against the enemy, but Rod'h is stranded. Sensing another one of Nira's oddly resistant halfbreed offspring, the Shana Rei engulf Rod'h's craft and take him prisoner. The devastating space battle continues, and the human and Ildiran ships have no choice but to retreat, leaving Rod'h behind. . . .

Zoe Alakis and Tom Rom consider Prince Reyn's disease, and knowing that Pergamus has been discovered, they decide to negotiate on their own terms. Encased in a protective suit, Zoe leaves her sterile dome for only the second time in years. Tom Rom takes her to Theroc, where she speaks to King Peter and Queen Estarra. In exchange for their data on the Onthos plague, as well as the King's promise to destroy the vile biological black markets on Rakkem, Zoe gives them all the information she has on Reyn's illness. She also extracts a promise that the Confederation will leave Pergamus alone. Since Reyn has gone to Kuivahr to be treated by Tamo'l, Tom Rom volunteers to fly there and deliver the records personally, because he also wants to get Tamo'l's research data on the misbreeds for Zoe's collection.

Rod'h finds himself held inside an entropy bubble that isolates him deep within the shadow cloud, where he is interrogated horrifically by Exxos. The Shana Rei use the dark matter from the hex plates around the Onthos system to rebuild their own ships as well as many more robot battleships. Scheming against the Shana Rei, Exxos is using the linked processors of all his robots to run extremely complex calculations for an entropy-crystallization device that will destroy the creatures of darkness, but the calculations will take a very long time. Meanwhile, however, he is pleased to torture Rod'h to extract information. The Shana Rei demand to know why Nira's halfbreeds can somehow resist them. Under constant torture Exxos gets Rod'h to reveal that his halfbreed sisters

Tamo'l and Osira'h are on Kuivahr with the misbreeds—and so the shadow clouds decide to conquer that planet.

On Theroc, after the Onthos settle in the Wild, Arita goes to visit her aunt Sarein, who lives alone there. She also finds her friend Collin, who lives among Kennebar's isolationist green priests. Distressed, Collin takes Arita to see a large swath of worldtrees that are dying from a mysterious blight. In the forest, they also come upon the alien Gardeners, but far more of them than the original hundred refugees. After Arita departs, Sarein investigates the dying trees and discovers that the blighted areas are infested with hundreds and hundreds of Onthos, which reproduce by killing the worldtrees. Before Sarein can reveal her terrible discovery, the Onthos kill her.

Later, Collin comes to see Arita in the fungus-reef city, extremely disturbed. He thinks the worldforest is losing part of its connection, and that Kennebar's isolationist priests have withdrawn. Collin asks her to come with him to investigate, but when they arrive in the Wild, they find Kennebar's entire tree settlement abandoned. Then Kennebar himself comes to confront them: he is no longer a green priest, but entirely contaminated by shadows, as black as the void. He captures Arita and Collin. . . .

The damaged *Voracious Curiosity* limps back to Newstation, arriving just as Lee Iswander is challenging the Speaker for his position. Iswander expects to regain his power and importance, to change the leadership of the Roamers . . . but Orli, Tasia, and Robb announce their dramatic news: the valuable fuel ekti-X is easily extracted from the common bloaters. They also show proof that in order to keep that secret, Iswander's deputy destroyed all of the clan Duquesne operations, killing dozens, and when the *Curiosity* discovered the Iswander extraction fields, Elisa tried to blast them out of space. The Roamers are furious to hear of Iswander's crimes. The ruined industrialist is unable to understand what has happened to him, since he didn't know what Elisa was doing in his name. More importantly, Roamers now know how to extract stardrive fuel, and they rush off in droves to form their own operations.

At Fireheart Station, Garrison and the Roamer workers have finished constructing Kotto's Big Ring in the middle of the nebula, and it is ready for a full-power test run. Despite Shareen and Howard's reservations, Kotto is anxious for the demonstration. He hopes the Big Ring will be the high point of his already illustrious career. The gigantic ring is activated in the intense flux from the nebula's core stars, but the power escalates, caught in a feedback loop, and the experiment runs out of control. The Big Ring collapses under its own forces with such titanic energy that it tears a hole in the fabric of the universe—like a doorway into another dimension that no one knows how to close.

On Kuivahr, some of Tamo'l's experimental kelp extracts prove effective in treating Prince Reyn, and Osira'h is pleased to see him gaining strength. Tom Rom arrives with the Pergamus data on Reyn's illness in exchange for Tamo'l's research on the misbreeds, which she happily shares.

Then the Shana Rei arrive with their shadow cloud and black robot fighters, to capture the two halfbreeds Osira'h and Tamo'l. In orbit, the Shana Rei send out countless hex plates, building up an opaque shell that begins to grow around Kuivahr. Soon, the entire planet will be swallowed up. Reyn and Osira'h immediately evacuate, joining the fleeing personnel from the Kellum distillery. But because Tamo'l won't leave her misbreeds, Tom Rom helps her get them to the Klikiss transportal, so they can escape to another world.

Inside his entropy bubble prison, Rod'h desperately tries to warn his siblings using his telepathic connection, and just as Tamo'l is about to escape Kuivahr through the transportal—which the misbreeds have just gone through to the planet Gorhum—Rod'h links with her. She is stunned, as the shadows hijack the link. Tom Rom forces Tamo'l through the transportal, but changes the coordinate tile so that they arrive on a different planet, beneath the Roamer complex of Newstation. Behind them, Kuivahr is entirely englobed.

The station attendants at the transportal are surprised to receive the two bedraggled escapees. Tom Rom and Tamo'l hurry to his ship. Curious to know where the strangers came from, the station attendants foolishly open the transportal coordinates back to Kuivahr. A gush of insidious shadow floods out, overwhelming the station. Seeing this as he lifts off in his ship, Tom Rom circles back around and uses all his firepower to destroy the transportal and cut off the shadows. Relieved, he takes Tamo'l away, but she is strangely unresponsive. He doesn't see that she has a dark taint of shadows behind her eyes. . . .

Adar Zan'nh and Tal Gale'nh race with a large Solar Navy force to defend Kuivahr. They battle the black robot ships while the shell completes itself around Kuivahr. Even though the planet is lost, the Solar Navy unleashes a substantial arsenal of sun bombs and laser cannons. Those weapons damage the Shana Rei and prove devastating to the black robots. Seeing an enemy they can defeat, Adar Zan'nh gives orders to use sun bombs in an all-out effort to wipe out the black robots once and for all. The robots are completely exterminated except for three, which follow the Shana Rei shadow cloud as it retreats into its own dimension. Not victorious, but still alive, the Solar Navy force returns to Ildira, bringing Osira'h, Reyn, and the Kellums from their ordeal.

Hearing news of the tremendous battle against the Shana Rei, mad Designate Rusa'h again demands that Jora'h try to make an alliance with the faeros. When the Mage-Imperator refuses, Rusa'h takes matters into his own hands. Following an example from the Saga of Seven Suns, Rusa'h goes to the top of the Prism Palace and immolates himself under the open sky. As he is burned alive, his agony rages through the *thism* strongly enough to summon the fiery elementals. Mage-Imperator Jora'h and his companions see numerous faeros fireballs gather above the Palace like threatening suns overhead. . . .

In the dark void after the disastrous battle at Kuivahr, Exxos is in despair. Nearly all of his original robots are gone, a once-invincible swarm of fighters. He cannot possibly succeed now. Almost as an afterthought, the Shana Rei offer to use the dark matter from the Onthos system to create duplicate robots, just as they build battleships. Exxos accepts their offer, and the creatures of darkness oblige by manifesting a million copies of Exxos, and all of the black robots are ready to attack the Spiral Arm.

1

MAGE-IMPERATOR JORA'H

The sky was full of fire.

Crackling balls of flame hovered above the crystalline towers of the Prism Palace. The faeros—elemental entities that lived within stars—had arrived in all their chaotic destructive glory, summoned by the agony of a madman who believed the fiery creatures would protect the Empire against the Shana Rei.

Mage-Imperator Jora'h stood among his awestruck people in the plaza, looking up at the entities that blazed brighter than the seven suns. He wished he had been able to stop Rusa'h from making such a deadly summons. Jora'h could feel the throbbing terror that emanated from his people . . . terror that he himself felt, but he quashed it so the reverberations would not tremble out through the *thism*. Every Ildiran could feel what their Mage-Imperator felt, and now more than ever Jora'h had to feel strong, brave, confident.

It seemed impossible.

Jora'h had led the Empire through many disasters, including the previous invasion when the faeros had destroyed cities, incinerated countless people. And Rusa'h had just called them back, blithely assuming the Mage-Imperator could control and guide them against the creatures of darkness.

The fireballs clustered high in the Ildiran sky, but even here down in the Foray Plaza Jora'h could feel the blistering heat. Many people had fled into buildings, while others gathered outside to share their strength with Jora'h, a strength that he sorely needed.

Beside him, his consort Nira shuddered but controlled herself.

She grasped his hand. "We have to do something before they attack."

Their daughter Osira'h, who had once controlled the faeros at the end of the Elemental War, said, "Rusa'h's death-agony summons has made them listen—for the first time." She shook her head, still staring upward. "Rod'h and I tried to ask for their help, but the faeros fled. We cannot control them. They are terrified of the Shana Rei."

Her friend Prince Reynald of Theroc also stood close, along with the Kellums, a Roamer family rescued from the planet Kuivahr. The refugees had come here to be safe from the Shana Rei, but now they might all be wiped out by a different enemy.

The faeros pulsed in the sky, flames crackling around their incandescent cores. Waiting. Jora'h stared at the fireballs until his eyes ached. He knew that mad Rusa'h had called them here for *him*. "They are waiting for me. I have to go."

"But I am the one who can communicate with them," Osira'h interrupted. "Let me do it."

Alarmed, Prince Reynald grabbed her arm. "It's too dangerous."

She shook her head, and her face was drawn. "It is *all* too dangerous! But we have to survive."

"How will the Empire survive, unless I can make this work?" Jora'h said, exuding a confident determination he did not feel. "The faeros are waiting for me, the Mage-Imperator. I will go."

His heir, Prime Designate Daro'h, stood in the crowd. The faeros had burned his face during their previous conquest of Ildira, and his voice reflected his tension. "They will burn you, Father, steal your soulfire—the *Ildiran* soulfire. That is what they want. They are hungry!"

"No," Osira'h said, sounding uncertain. "They are . . . terrified."

"As we all are." Jora'h embraced his beloved Nira. "As destructive as the faeros may be, the Shana Rei are worse. They mean to wipe out all life." He paused. "If there is any chance the faeros will help us, I must be the one to face them. Rusa'h may not have been wrong."

In his Solar Navy uniform, Tal Gale'nh looked grim, recalling his own recent military battles against the creatures of darkness. His unnaturally pale skin flushed under the blazing heat. "The Shana Rei want to erase the Galaxy—perhaps the universe itself."

Jora'h stepped away from his loved ones. "If I do not succeed . . ." He let his words hang for a long moment, before turning to Daro'h. "Then you will become Mage-Imperator sooner than you expected. Lead the Empire well."

As he strode toward the Palace, he could feel threads of hope from the crowd woven together into a lifeline through the *thism*. Everyone watched him, believed in him . . . and Jora'h had to believe in himself. He would face the fiery elementals, knowing they shared an even more fearsome enemy.

Entering the Prism Palace, he climbed staircases that brought him to the highest pinnacle. He stepped out onto the wide rooftop that had once held a botanical garden including small worldtrees that Nira herself had planted. The light and heat from the faeros were blinding.

The air crackled, and he sensed the elementals' hot and blazing presence reaching out to him. The air smelled of smoke and death— but not from the elementals. This was where Rusa'h had set the greenhouse on fire and immolated himself amid the burning trees so that his agony issued a summons that even the faeros could not ignore.

As the Mage-Imperator stepped through the crumbling ashes of the greenhouse and past Rusa'h's blackened bones, he called out. "I need your help! We all do. The Shana Rei will destroy us, and they will destroy *you*—unless we fight."

In ancient history, Mage-Imperator Xiba'h had also allied with the faeros and saved the Empire from the Shana Rei. This time, though, the creatures of darkness were attacking more than just planets. Their black nebulae oozed through space; their hexagonal ships struck the Solar Navy and tore apart colonies, and they were infiltrating the *thism* network itself. Jora'h had felt the darkness inside him, and he had seen possessed Ildiran mobs wreaking bloody havoc. He could not predict or control the shadows, but as the center of the entire *thism* network, Jora'h knew that their taint had reached into him as well.

The swirling faeros dropped closer, their pulsing flames like a wall pressing him down, trying to intimidate him. When he called upon the *thism,* he saw the shadows there. Despite the blazing light of the faeros fire and the seven suns in the Ildiran sky, the Mage-Imperator felt cold inside.

2

CELLI

Like a great polished jewel, the Roamer terrarium dome drifted against the background of ionized gases. The Fireheart nebula was a canvas of color, its gases illuminated by the clump of hot supergiant stars at its core.

Inside the greenhouse, the green priests Celli and Solimar monitored the crops that provided fresh produce for the Roamer workers at Fireheart Station. The two green priests also tended the pair of huge, groaning worldtrees trapped under the dome. Touching one of the nearby branches, Celli stared through the crystal panes, and shielded her eyes from the nebula glare. This place was so different from her home in the worldforest. . . .

Roamer industrial operations were scattered across the nebula like pebbles in a cosmic stream. Giant scoops harvested rare isotopes and exotic molecules that had been cooked by the central blue supergiant stars. Energy farms captured the solar flux in vast thin films that would be packaged into power blocks.

Fingers brushed Celli's face, and she turned to see Solimar standing close, looking intently at her. He was handsome and well muscled, his head completely hairless like hers, his skin the rich green of the healthiest plants. The two were connected by their thoughts and their love, and their shared concerns. The enormous worldtrees pressed against the curved terrarium ceiling, hunched and stunted, and still growing from the flood of energy that poured in. But the trees had no place to go.

Solimar did not need telink to know Celli's heart. "I can feel them, too. My joints and back ache—and it is their pain, not ours. They want to burst free."

The worldtrees were part of the verdani mind, a vast intercon-nected organism that spread across the Spiral Arm. As Celli stroked the gold-scaled bark of a suffering, cramped tree, she felt that these two were more than just insignificant trees like millions of others. "Sometimes I find it hard to breathe. I feel trapped and claustrophobic—for them. The trees know we can't save them."

When she connected her mind through telink, all other green priests knew her thoughts and concerns. For their sake Celli tried to hide her despondency about the doomed trees, but it did no good. Despite their best efforts, they could think of no way to save them. By now, it was too late. So much else was happening in the Spiral Arm that few people were concerned about two trees.

Celli placed her fingers on a transparent pane, looking out at the expansive nebula, and Solimar placed his hand over hers. "Do you see any change where the Big Ring was?"

She shook her head. "It's still just a giant hole in the universe."

"Because of the accident, more scientists will come to study that rift. One of them might have an idea of how to help the trees."

Celli looked at the black gash across the nebula field. "They'll come only if it remains stable. The rift might tear open wider, and the void could swallow Fireheart Station, along with the terrarium dome and our trees. I wonder what's on the other side."

Kotto Okiah's Big Ring research project, which had taken years to build and cost an immense fortune, had failed catastrophically during its first test. From inside their dome, Celli and Solimar had watched the giant torus collapse, tearing a hole in the fabric of space itself. No one quite understood what had happened, or what sort of threat the gap might pose. The idea sent a chill through Celli's heart.

In response, the twisted worldtrees shuddered with dread. She could feel pain coiled inside the enormous trunks, and the trees could not escape, could not grow anymore inside their crystalline cell. . . .

She said, more to reassure Solimar than herself, "I'm sure some-one will figure out how to rescue our trees."

Kotto's two young lab assistants, Shareen Fitzkellum and How-ard Rohandas, arrived at the greenhouse in a small shuttle from the admin station. Once presented with the problem of rescuing the trapped worldtress, Kotto had delegated these two to find a possible solution.

Celli and Solimar went to greet the two teenagers and immediately saw that they did not bring any miraculous solutions. Celli drew a deep breath, smelled the rich dampness of the bottled-up worldforest. Shareen and Howard were young, but Kotto insisted they were brilliant. Celli continued to hope. "Have you made any progress?"

"We've tested the materials of the dome, the underlying structure," Shareen said.

"And the trees themselves." Howard presented a pad filled with unfathomable calculations. Celli could have dipped into the verdani mind and combed through the engineering expertise compiled over many years, but instead, she said, "What did you find?"

"We thought there might be a way to tow the whole greenhouse to a nearby terrestrial world, using Ildiran stardrives. That way the trees could take root, grow as large as they like," Shareen said, then looked away and lowered her voice. "But this structure was never designed for stresses like that."

"Also the bow shock of dust at the edge of the nebula would offer too much turbulence." Howard looked pained at not having a better answer for them, but he pointed to the calculations as if to give himself strength.

Shareen straightened, crossed her arms over her chest. "The greenhouse wouldn't survive being moved out of the Fireheart nebula, so your trees are stuck here. Sorry. The option of taking them to a planet is off the table."

Celli looked up at the stirring fronds. Soon—very soon—the dome would no longer hold them. The trees would either break and die, or they would burst through the crystalline prison walls . . . and die.

"Thank you for trying," Solimar said as the two left, dejected and guilty.

"We'll keep thinking," Shareen called. "We might still come up with something."

"We will," Howard said.

"We know you will," Solimar answered.

"I won't leave our trees," Celli said after the two were gone. She felt a stinging burn in her eyes and a gap in her heart that seemed as empty as that black gateway in space.

As green priests, their duty was to tend the trees and preserve them. She and Solimar had given up so much when they'd left Theroc to come here, because the Roamers needed green priests for communication. And now Celli's duty might be to die here with the trees.

"We will find a way to save them." Solimar released one hand from the golden-barked trunk to caress her arm. "And us."

"We have to," Celli answered, determined.

In the middle of the blazing nebula, the black dimensional gateway throbbed with shadows.

ARITA

The worldforest had never seemed so threatening. Arita and Collin felt trapped as they confronted a manifestation of darkness that they had never imagined.

Collin challenged the ebony figure in front of them. "You are no longer a green priest, Kennebar."

The leader of the isolationist green priests faced the two of them in the empty dwelling high up in the branches of a dying worldtree. Kennebar's skin was flawless obsidian instead of a vibrant emerald, like Collin's. Kennebar was a humanoid figure entirely infused with night, his eyes as dark as the void between the stars. Even his mouth was just a hollow opening.

"I am more than a green priest, now," Kennebar said, "for I have seen into the void. The thoughts of the Shana Rei are like a shout, and the thoughts of the verdani are a mere whisper by comparison."

Collin stood his ground before the dark voidpriest. "You betrayed the worldforest. Look at the damage you caused—it's all around you!"

"The worldforest is insignificant." Kennebar's voice was cold and hollow. "There is so much more. . . ."

Arita stood firm beside Collin, who raised his voice in defiance. "You are nothing!"

She had gone with her friend to investigate the sudden disappearance of the isolationist priests, as well as the gulf of silence that had appeared in the telink network. With the sprawling worldforest and the connected verdani mind, there should have been no place to hide, yet Kennebar's followers had vanished.

Although Arita was not a green priest, Collin had told her about the alarming gaps. Entire sections of the forests were dying off—he and Arita had seen them with their own eyes—yet the other green priests seemed oblivious to the disaster. Overconfident in their connection with the verdani mind, they couldn't conceive that such a tremendous secret might be able to slide past them.

"We should have brought reinforcements with us," Arita said to Collin in a low voice.

They stood side by side, in the upper boughs of the large worldtree, where the isolationists had lived and slept high off the ground. Collin's former companions were gone now. Had they been captured and contaminated by the shadows that infiltrated the worldforest mind—just as Kennebar had been?

"The void is nothing," Kennebar said in a ponderous voice, "and the emptiness is everything. The Shana Rei wish to bring back entropy, chaos . . . nothing and everything. And the voidpriests will assist them by unraveling the worldforest mind."

More tainted green priests emerged from the interwoven fronds or climbed down from higher branches: the rest of Kennebar's followers. The priests were also as black as oil, moving with the silence of shadows.

Arita felt a fresh jolt of alarm. She and Collin had no way to fight the ravenous darkness, and she was sure Kennebar would not let them go.

"Collin will join us, as will all other green priests." Kennebar turned his frightening ebony face toward Arita. "But this one has been found wanting. She must be discarded."

A shudder passed through her, partly from her own fear . . . but partly from surprise. Deep inside her mind, she heard a distant voice, yearning, intense and mysterious . . . something that was not of the trees at all. A call? It was not connected to the telink communication network, and she had to find what it was, hoping it might be some unexpected ally.

"I don't need to be reminded that the trees rejected me," she said in a voice that shook with anger. But what had Kennebar meant about discarding her?

When they were younger, she and Collin had both tried to become green priests. The trees had tested them, accepted and converted her friend—but not Arita. Nevertheless, the trees *had* altered her mind somehow, before sending her away. Arita had always regretted her failure to become part of the green-priest community. Did these traitorous voidpriests mean to kill her now?

"You will not touch Arita," Collin said.

Kennebar said, "When you are a voidpriest, we will let *you* kill her."

Fourteen black silhouettes of once-faithful green priests pressed closer, moving as if they had all the time in the world. They prevented Arita and Collin from fleeing.

In her head, Arita heard that distant whispering again, but it passed along no discernible thoughts beyond alarm and foreboding. She knew it was not the voice of the trees, but a different entity entirely.

She heard the fronds rustling, saw movement above. The black voidpriests glanced up as a swarm of figures appeared—diminutive humanoid creatures with smooth gray skin and large eyes. They moved so quickly and nimbly that they reminded Arita of spiders. The Onthos.

"Help us," she cried out. "Stop them!"

The refugee aliens had once tended another distant worldforest that was destroyed long ago by the Shana Rei. The last hundred Onthos survivors, the only remnants of their race, had come to Theroc seeking sanctuary. Because the green priests and the verdani vouched for the aliens, King Peter and Queen Estarra had granted them sanctuary, letting them make a new home here in the uninhabited continent of the Wild.

Arita counted at least a dozen aliens emerging to join the ominous voidpriests. They squatted on the fronds above; they swung down from the branches; they came close while Kennebar and his companions stood like shadow people, imprisoning Arita and Collin.

"Help us," Collin said to the Onthos.

Arita's hope upon seeing the Gardeners changed as the aliens merely stared at them, as if they were insects. She had always thought of the Gardeners as friendly and cooperative, unquestioned allies, because they too had been victims of the Shana Rei. Ohro, their leader, had said that he sensed something in Arita, a connection with that strange voice in her mind, but he had offered no explanation.

Now, the aliens just regarded Arita and Collin as if they were lacking somehow.

Then, as if content with what they'd seen, the Onthos skittered away, climbing along the worldtree branches and disappearing high above, leaving Collin and Arita painfully alone.

The voidpriests closed in.

CHAPTER

4

LEE ISWANDER

Unfortunately, Lee Iswander was familiar with losing everything. Ruined, disgraced, nearly bankrupt—he had all too much experience with that.

He boarded his private space yacht to leave Newstation, not bothering to issue either a defiant or defensive statement. He felt like a thief in the night. As the head of Iswander Industries, he had changed commerce across the Spiral Arm . . . yet now he ran from the Roamer center as soon as he received clearance. Until recently, Iswander had been one of the most influential, and arguably wealthiest, men in the Confederation.

Operative words: *Until recently*.

He left the clans in an uproar. Now that they knew that the ubiquitous bloaters were his secret source of cheap and easy ekti-X, the greedy clan members were so excited that they hadn't yet begun howling for his blood. Soon enough, though, they would demand justice and strip him of even more than they had already taken.

Iswander had been through it all before.

Always, he clung to his determined and triumphant mantra: *A successful man fails more times than an average man bothers to try.* It gave him little comfort, though, as he raced back to his isolated industrial operations. The bloater-extraction field had remained secret until Tasia Tamblyn, Robb Brindle, and Orli Covitz exposed it, uprooting yet another pillar of what had made Lee Iswander great.

He activated the stardrive, leaving Newstation behind—good riddance!—and raced off into the emptiness. They would come for him sooner or later, and he had to decide what to do.

He was furious that his secret had been revealed. Tamblyn and Brindle, the acting managers of Kett Shipping, had reaped great wealth by being his primary distributors for stardrive fuel, yet they had stabbed him in the back. For her own part, Orli Covitz had been cured of an alien plague by immersing herself in the protoplasm of a bloater in his first extraction field. That woman was alive *because of* Iswander's operations. And she, too, had stabbed him in the back.

On top of that, he was angry with Elisa Enturi. Iswander valued efficiency, but he regarded loyalty even more highly. All too often, he overestimated the good in people. Although Elisa was unfailingly loyal, and would do anything necessary to serve and protect Lee Iswander, she had also gone disastrously overboard. Now everything was unraveling. . . .

But of all those who upset him, Iswander was most disappointed in *himself.* He should have paid better attention, planned for disaster. He knew disasters so well. . . .

He brooded as he flew back to the bloater-extraction field, which would be—for a time, at least—a last sanctuary for him. Normally, he found the solo trip to be a pleasant journey, time to review business matters without being interrupted. On his recent flight to Newstation, he had been filled with brash confidence. He had compiled indisputable evidence of corruption and outright incompetence against Speaker Sam Ricks. The man had cost the Roamer clans a great deal. Armed with such information, Iswander had expected to walk into the convocation, overthrow Speaker Ricks, and send him off to prison. And then the clans should have placed Iswander in the Speakership, by acclamation. He had been so sure.

Instead, that victory had been snatched from his hands, and he was knocked to his knees . . . disgraced yet again, forced to flee. How many times could one person pick up the pieces and start from scratch?

He had always been a bold man, espousing the philosophy that made the Roamers great. Innovation required taking risks, and sometimes risks were dangerous. Sometimes accidents happened. Sometimes it couldn't be helped.

Iswander made his first fortune by manufacturing prefab modular habitats, widely used during reconstruction after the Elemental

War. When distributing so many modules, it was inevitable that a few would suffer construction flaws. Four orbiting habitats had failed catastrophically when imperfect hull seams had split, exposing inhabitants to explosive decompression. Those lawsuits cost him a small fortune, but he had paid off many people to keep those failures quiet. Considering how many thousands of habitats he had manufactured, the failure rate was minimal.

After that, Iswander invested heavily in the lava-processing operations on Sheol, extracting exotic metals and unusual alloys. He had found treasure in the molten seas, right there for the taking. But Elisa's former husband, Garrison Reeves, had raised questions about the dangers of the unstable planet, warnings that Iswander foolishly ignored. And the geological instabilities triggered a complete disaster: one thousand five hundred and forty-three people had lost their lives during the collapse of Sheol.

Iswander had been ruined then, too. His entire fortune and an even more valuable commodity—his reputation—completely gone.

Then Elisa discovered the bloaters out in space, each one filled with a potent form of ekti, the stardrive fuel that powered Ildiran engines. Clusters of the greenish nodules wandered aimlessly from star system to star system, like space plankton, all that ekti just there for the taking . . . another fortune.

When Iswander had rebuilt himself this time, though, he was smarter. He realized that as soon as the source of his ekti-X was revealed, countless other Roamer clans would rush out to drain bloaters and glut the market. Easily obtained stardrive fuel would drive down the price. He knew he had a limited time to rebuild his vast fortune, and the secret had to be kept as long as possible.

But he had never imagined Elisa would take it upon herself to murder any rivals to protect the source of ekti-X. She was a hard, determined, and efficient woman—and more importantly, a completely *loyal* woman—but she had killed so many, destroyed the entire Duquesne complex, and tried to shoot down the *Voracious Curiosity.* Iswander would never have believed her capable of such violence.

Or at least, he wouldn't admit that to himself. All alone in his space yacht, though, his inner doubts grew. . . .

* * *

When he finally reached his bloater-extraction field, Iswander saw that business continued as usual. The people here didn't even know yet about the dramatic turn of events and how their operations would be forever changed.

Pumping rigs drained ekti-X from the mottled nodules, filling tank after tank for distribution. Scout ships and inspection pods flitted among the operations and subsidiary depots. Small tugs with oversized engines hauled away the flaccid husks of empty bloaters, discarding them in a disposal area outside the ever-moving cluster. Illumination rigs looked like tiny star systems throughout the operations, and the central admin hub hung like a bright jewel in the midst of the operations.

As he guided his yacht in, Iswander noted that one array framework was nearly filled with harvested ekti-X, ready for delivery . . . but even that was now questionable. Ulio Station, one of Iswander's primary distribution hubs, had been wiped out by the Shana Rei and their black robots. Even without Ulio, their main distributor, Kett Shipping, had plenty of alternative ways to deliver stardrive fuel to an always hungry market . . . but Kett Shipping had torn up their commercial agreement with Iswander, thanks to Elisa's foolhardy actions. He had to find some other way to sell his fuel, because soon, very soon, those Roamer jackals would rush out and begin extracting stardrive fuel themselves.

Maybe it was time for him to just shut down these operations and move on. Iswander was horrified that such a thought even crossed his mind. An Iswander did not give up. Shaken, he landed in the admin hub and disembarked.

He was immediately met by his deputy, Alec Pannebaker. The man had long hair and a salt-and-pepper goatee; Pannebaker had an avuncular personality and a cocky daredevil air. "Chief, we're so glad you're back! Or do we now call you, Speaker Iswander?" He grinned. "How did it go?"

Iswander dropped the news like an asteroid impact. "Complete failure. Our ekti-X operations have been exposed, and all the

Roamer clans know about the bloaters. We need to go into full damage-control mode, and I don't know if even that will be sufficient for this company to survive." His throat went dry. "I need to see Elisa Enturi, right now."

Pannebaker looked uncomfortable. "Chief . . . about Elisa and what she did while you were gone . . ." He shook his head, and his face grew dark. "Her behavior was unacceptable. We had an incident. An outside ship managed to make it past the perimeter, and our security attempted to detain them. I thought we were going to figure out how best to retain confidentiality, but Elisa . . ." His face reddened. "I think she really meant to kill them!"

"That was indeed her intent," Iswander said, "and there can be no forgiveness for it. That's what turned all the clans against us."

He entered the main control center, where his technicians and admin staff studied ekti-production statistics, mapping the cluster, and compiling extraction logs so that the large pumping rigs could be moved efficiently from one bloater to the next.

The staff turned to see him, but he looked around with a sharp gaze. He controlled the anger boiling up inside him while he searched for Elisa. As a businessman, he was good at masking his emotions, displaying anger only at the appropriate time—and when he spoke privately with Elisa, *that* would be the appropriate time.

Answering the intercom summons, she arrived on deck, flushed from hurrying to present herself. "Mr. Iswander, sir—I have my report ready for you, and I'm eager to hear what happened at the Roamer convocation." She had a shine in her eyes, seemed so eager to earn his appreciation.

He fired his words at her like bullets. "In my private conference room. Now." He strode to the adjacent chamber, and as soon as the bulkhead door was sealed, Iswander took his seat. He felt cold. His hands were trembling.

Elisa sat across from him and clearly sensed that something was wrong. "Did you oust Speaker Ricks as planned, sir?"

"No. You've destroyed us."

Her dark eyes flew open. "What do you—"

"You know damn well what I mean!" he said, then raised his voice even further. "We always knew someone would eventually discover the source of ekti-X, and I took precautions to mitigate how that would affect us. But you blew up an extraction operation, murdered dozens of clan Duquesne workers." She stiffened, paled, but he kept talking. "Their video log survived, and it's come to light. Now all the Roamers have seen it. There is no doubt in anyone's mind—including mine! And then, while I was on my way to present an airtight case to the clans, you were attempting to shoot down an outside ship that stumbled upon these operations—right in front of our people! The *Voracious Curiosity* got away and flew straight to Newstation to report us. I was completely humiliated in front of the entire convocation."

She stood like a stone pillar, letting his words buffet her.

He rose to his feet and faced her, only inches away. "What the hell were you thinking? You murdered those people."

She stopped him cold. "It's what you would have wanted."

"How could you even think that?"

"Because I'm thinking of Iswander Industries, sir. Because I'm thinking of you, and of our future together. Clan Duquesne stole our process and were profiting from it. I had to stop them, so I did it in the swiftest, most efficient way possible. I regret that I left evidence behind." She didn't seem ruffled. "You put me in charge of security here, and I reacted accordingly. As soon as the *Voracious Curiosity* came upon our operations, I knew they would expose us. I tried to intercept them before they could report our industrial secrets to the general public, but more aggressive measures became necessary."

"They were never necessary," Iswander said.

Elisa looked at him as if she were heartbroken. "Yes they were, and you know it, sir. I was always aware of your goals and priorities. You told me I needed to protect us. After the disgrace we suffered on Sheol, I would not allow such a disaster to happen to you or to Iswander Industries again."

"I never meant for you to murder anyone."

Her eyes glittered, and she stood straight. "Are you sure of that, sir? I can recall our conversations, and your implications were quite clear. You knew full well what I might have to do. Your orders were implicit."

"You misunderstood them," he insisted.

She refused to back down. "Maybe you misunderstand yourself, sir. I've always been loyal to you, and I've never done anything that didn't put your needs or interests first."

"And now I'm ruined again. You murdered those people, and the Roamers will come after me—but even more important, they will come after you. I'll tell them that you took your actions without my knowledge or approval. I have to make sure that you face justice." He forced himself to sit down again, pretending to be calm and rational. "And I am sorry about that, Elisa. I know all the positive things you've done for me, but this . . . this is unforgivable."

Her face darkened as she wrestled to control her fury. "You would throw me to the wolves in order to save yourself?" She paused but didn't give him enough time to respond before she gave a small nod. "Yes, that's your best play. I agree."

Iswander felt guilty to hear her response, and a heavy weight of conscience pushed down on him. He tried to recall everything he had said to Elisa, all the business discussions. Had he really led her to believe that she should kill anyone who uncovered his secret? Deep inside, was that what he really wanted? He refused to admit it to himself, but his inner hesitation told him much about what he needed to know.

He sighed. "Thanks to Tamblyn and her companions, everyone knows the location of our bloater operations. Someone will come here sooner or later. If you are here, they will arrest you. I want you to take some private time, Elisa; contemplate how you wish to respond to this. I will leave you alone so you can consider the consequences. Take all the time you need."

She was surprised. "Are you saying you'll look the other way if I just flee?"

"I didn't say that at all, but you seem to be proficient at extrapolating my implied wishes. Go!"

Elisa stared at him for a long moment, then departed. Even after she left the conference room, though, Iswander wasn't sure whether he had done the right thing.

5

ORLI COVITZ

After learning how easy it was to extract ekti-X from the bloaters, clan leaders rushed away from Newstation on "urgent business." Roamers would scramble to modify old water tankers or cargo ships so they could harvest stardrive fuel. Within a day of the clan convocation, every vessel or piece of equipment that could conceivably be converted to pumping operations had been purchased from the Newstation salvage dealers.

Orli Covitz wanted no more involvement with bloaters and ekti, though. She and her compy, DD, settled into temporary quarters, still trying to decide what to do with themselves. The clans were well known for seizing new opportunities, but she hadn't expected them to move so *fast*.

A year ago, when she had happened upon Iswander's original operations, she hadn't grasped the value of the knowledge she had obtained. Of course, she had been dying from the Onthos plague at the time, but now Orli was surprised that Lee Iswander had let her go, rather than eliminating her as an inconvenient witness—just as Elisa had tried to do. Maybe the industrialist hadn't been thinking far enough ahead.

The Iswander facility was also where she had met Garrison Reeves, and the more she thought about it—and about *him*—the more she decided that the benefit was well worth the cost. She and Garrison had been apart for the better part of a month now, by mutual agreement. While he was at Fireheart Station working on the Big Ring project, Orli had joined Kett Shipping for the time being, but she missed Garrison. Taking some time had seemed like a good idea when she had suggested it. . . .

Now, from her temporary quarters on the station, she looked out the windowport at the busy ships flying around the trading center. DD stood beside her, filing away details. "There's quite a bit of traffic, Orli Covitz. The Roamers seem very excited about the new method of ekti extraction. Isn't it a good thing we told them?"

"I'm sure not everyone will be as happy, DD," she said. "Now that their Iswander distribution contracts are out the airlock, Kett Shipping is losing a huge amount of business."

"But Iswander Industries was an unpleasant and dangerous partner. Is it not likely that many of these new operations will hire Kett Shipping for distribution?"

"I'm not a business visionary. What I like is fixing compies, and I should figure out how to get back to that. I'd be happier. We both would be."

"We could return to Relleker," DD said. "We had a very efficient facility there for rehabilitating unwanted compies."

Relleker had been a nice world, civilized, comfortable, a temperate climate; Orli had spent quiet years there with her husband . . . and some of those years had even been happy ones. But now that Matthew had left her and she had disbanded the compy facility, there was nothing for her there. She had to find somewhere else.

She shook her head. "We should try a fresh start, DD, but there's a point where personal independence crosses the line into being just plain lonely."

In a remarkably astute observation, DD said, "Does this mean we will return to Garrison Reeves?"

She smiled at the Friendly compy. "Let's see if Tasia and Robb will give us a ride to Fireheart Station."

The *Voracious Curiosity* had been repaired after being attacked by Elisa Enturi. On their retreat to Newstation, Robb and DD had completed the most urgent fixes. After they reached Newstation, Tasia had used Kett Shipping accounts to book a spacedock and maintenance techs to finish all the repairs their beloved ship needed.

When Orli found the two in the assigned maintenance bay, they were fending off questions from inquisitive clan members about the bloaters. The workers wore jumpsuits with decorative embroidery marking different clan symbols. Tasia sounded impatient. "We already made the ekti-extraction information available. Go look it up yourselves—you won't get any more details by pestering me."

"And you're all losing time," Robb said, trying to shoo them out of the bay. "Better do your homework en route—otherwise, you'll be the last ones to market."

The clan members hurried off in different directions.

Robb stood beside the *Curiosity*, wiping his hands. "Ship's refueled, and all systems check out. We've finished our business, so it's time we head back to Earth. Rlinda must be worried about us."

Tasia crossed her arms over her chest. "I'm worried about Xander. He got away from Ulio Station, but a lot of excrement has hit a lot of waste-recycling fans in the past few weeks." She looked up and greeted Orli and DD, smiling. "Shizz, we were about to summon you! Enough frivolous adventures—let's get to work."

"Oh, I've had enough adventures," Orli agreed. "Of course, I've said that plenty of times before."

Robb had a look of concern on his face, as if something had just occurred to him. "Orli . . . have you heard what happened down on Auridia?"

She frowned. "Not much ever happens down there. What's on Auridia besides the Klikiss transportal and a handful of people?"

"Exactly. The transportal and the whole outpost were wiped out by a single ship. The guy just destroyed everything and flew off."

Orli blinked. "Why would anyone attack Auridia? It's barely even a way station." Few Roamers or Confederation customers used the Klikiss transportal wall, preferring to conduct their business at the giant orbiting station.

Tasia said, "It was the man who hunted you down when you had the plague. Tom Rom."

Orli could not control her shudder. "I thought he was long dead." DD had sabotaged Tom Rom's ship after the ruthless man attacked her, making it explode out in space. She controlled her panic. "He was . . . here?" He could have easily found her, if he'd wanted to. What in the world was he doing down on Auridia, so close to Newstation?

That was all the nudge she needed. "Suddenly, I want to be out of here—and DD and I want to see Garrison. He's at Fireheart Station, where they just had that Big Ring accident. I really need to see him. I . . . I miss him."

Tasia and Robb simultaneously rolled their eyes.

DD interrupted. "I miss him too, and young Seth Reeves."

Orli patted the compy on his polymer shoulder and spoke to Tasia. "When you two go back to Earth, give Rlinda my regards and my thanks. But we're looking for a ship heading to Fireheart."

"Shizz, you found one—we can do a cargo run from Newstation to Fireheart, and it's important that we study our markets," Tasia said. "We'll take you there as soon as we finalize the load."

The *Curiosity* easily arranged for a lucrative cargo of goods that Fireheart had requested. The facility personnel were so isolated inside the nebula that they needed all basic supplies, not just luxuries.

As Orli rode in the ship, feeling anticipation build, she studied the pastel cauldron of the Fireheart nebula, the expanding gas lit from within by a clump of bright hot stars. The ship shuddered and shook as they passed through the shock front at the dust boundary.

Orli had seen spectacular sights across the Spiral Arm, but she could hardly contain her excitement as they approached Fireheart. "It's amazing."

"And a good place to do business," Tasia said.

Most important of all, Garrison was there.

6

XANDER BRINDLE

"Good as new," Terry said when he watched the *Verne* emerge from the Kett Shipping dock after more than a week of around-the-clock repairs, maintenance, refurbishments, and improvements. Since he didn't have the use of his legs, the young man kept his balance by resting a hand on their compy's shoulder.

With a chuckle, Xander clapped his partner on the back. "Far better than new. By the Guiding Star, the *Verne* is better than any other Kett Shipping vessel, better than any vessel in its class across the Spiral Arm. We've installed every available upgrade."

Terry looked embarrassed. "Even the unnecessary ones."

"If it's available, it's not unnecessary. Besides, 'spare no expense' is going to be our motto from now on. You deserve it."

Repair techs used the *Verne*'s antigrav engines on low thrust to bring the gleaming ship forward into the open bay, where it settled down on the reinforced floorplates for their inspection.

Rlinda Kett strolled into the maintenance hangar, hands on her generous hips. "Now that's a beautiful spacecraft—new, shiny, and an excellent hull job. I think you're showing off."

"Maybe a bit," Terry admitted.

"We are *definitely* showing off," Xander said. "A lot."

"I knew it. But with a ship this fancy, you'd better take her out and earn a few bumps. Right now the *Verne* has everything except for character. You've got to earn that."

Xander lounged with an elbow against the hull and sniffed. "We've made enough runs for Kett Shipping to earn a standard amount of character. In fact, I'd say that escaping the destruction of

Ulio Station and running away from the bugbots earns us extra credit."

Rlinda pursed her lips. "Maybe, but you've rebuilt the whole thing. You need to start over."

"Ready to get started on that, ma'am," Terry said. "I don't like sitting around. We're eager to get back out and do some cargo runs."

The big trader walked beside them as Xander inspected the *Verne*'s exterior. Wearing his antigrav belt to support him, Terry held OK's shoulder and let the compy tow him around the vessel. While studying the ship, OK filed away all the improvements and accessed the detailed maintenance and test results.

Rlinda gave the two young men a frank look. "You were among my best earners at Kett Shipping, and I'm glad to hear you want to fly again, but . . . do you have any conception of how *wealthy* you are, Mr. Handon? 'Filthy rich' doesn't even come close."

Terry nodded nervously. "I've seen the numbers."

"Numbers are one thing, but do you *understand*, dear boy? You could buy my whole company several times over. You could buy your own planet."

Xander interrupted, "*Planets*. Plural."

"Well, not any good planets," Rlinda said. "You should be thinking bigger. That money from Maria Ulio is not just a life-changing amount, it's a *Confederation*-changing amount. You can form your own businesses, travel anywhere you want, give a bunch to charity. Be a philanthropist. Be everybody's favorite friend. Maria collected so much profit from Ulio Station that just spending it is going to be your new full-time job."

Terry blushed, which Xander found endearing. "Do you need any money, Rlinda? You helped us so much, and I'd like to pay you back. Can we maybe invest in Kett Shipping? Or help you build another restaurant?"

Rlinda gave a hearty laugh. "My dear boy, I may not be as fabulously rich as Maria was, but I've done quite well for myself. I could've retired ten times over, and I've already got restaurants on Relleker, Earth, and Theroc. Kett Shipping is doing just fine."

When they paused behind the *Verne*'s new main engines, she held out a stern finger. Her words echoed against the wide thruster cones. "That's your money, Mr. Handon. A *lot* of money. Don't do anything foolish, but you need to think seriously about what you want."

Xander nodded. "Exactly what I've been telling him, but it hasn't sunk in yet. I'll keep Terry in check, just in case he goes overboard. If he wanted to have a whole asteroid carved into an orbiting likeness of his face, I'd stop him. Maybe."

The other man flushed again. "I would never do that!"

"Of course you wouldn't. So far, the only way you've splurged is by ordering more expensive meals and better wine."

"Now that's a good use of the money," Rlinda said. "A wise investment."

Xander grew serious. "I know where I mean to spend part of it, and this is one case where I truly intend to spare no expense. I'm going to dig into all available medical research. Terry's had medical studies done on his spine, and nobody's been able to help. With all of these resources now, there's got to be a way we can give him the use of his legs again."

Terry sounded exasperated. "I get along just fine."

"'Just fine' doesn't mean you can't do better," Xander said. "With all the doctors in the Confederation and the Ildiran Empire, someone will be able to make you walk again."

"In zero gravity it doesn't make any difference," Terry insisted.

The two had talked around in circles many times; they'd even gotten into arguments, which resulted in memorable apologies. Xander had held his partner, explaining that he just wanted what was best for him.

"It's just not the highest thing on my priority list," Terry said.

Xander knew when to be quiet, and he decided to keep doing research on his own. He would find an answer and present it to Terry—and then he wouldn't back down so easily.

Rlinda's big brown eyes moistened as she looked from one man to the other. She said in a chastising tone, "You don't have to hold out unreasonable hope, dear boy, but that doesn't mean you should give up hope entirely." She reached out with her big beefy arms and swept the two into a generous awkward embrace that made Xander stumble while Terry's antigrav belt kept him balanced. OK remained silent, standing there like a long-suffering observer.

"You can fund medical research, you know," Rlinda said. "You could buy any laboratory, create a think tank, found a university, devote countless hours to it—and you wouldn't be the only one to benefit if you did find a cure. Think of the others who suffer from a similar condition."

Xander knew that response might have more of an effect on Terry. He was a selfless person, didn't like to be pampered, but all those other people . . .

Awkwardly, Terry looked at them and quickly changed the subject. "Look, I have been thinking big, and I have a new idea that'll keep us happy. I think even Xander will be impressed."

Xander raised his eyebrows, waiting.

Terry explained, "Maria founded her station, and countless thousands of traders relied on it over the years. Ulio Station was a pivotal center of commerce."

"Until the Shana Rei obliterated it all," Xander said.

"So, what's to stop us from *rebuilding* Ulio? Or building a whole new trade center from scratch?" Terry smiled at them. "I've got the money, and it's not a need that'll go away anytime soon. At the moment, where do Roamer traders go? What happens to the ships that need massive repairs? And how do we deal with all the decommissioned wrecks just floating out there? They need a central place."

Xander looked at Terry with building excitement. "Somebody's going to start their own supply and repair depot . . . so why not us?"

Rlinda blinked. "With all the money in the Spiral Arm, you want to build your own . . . junkyard?"

"Repair yard," Terry corrected. "And trading depot. Like Ulio Station, but better! Maria's facility coalesced by accident once she started gathering wrecked ships after the Elemental War. We can make ours bigger and better—with a little bit of planning."

Xander wanted to hug him. "That sounds exciting—and right up our alley. With my parents, our connections to Kett Shipping and all the Roamer clans . . . it'll be perfect!"

Rlinda warned them, "Take it from me, running your own business is not as glamorous as it sounds. You'll need help."

"I don't need anything glamorous," Terry said. "But it sounds like fun, and it is something I want to do." His lips quirked in a smile, as he gave Robb a nudge. "And I think I'll be able to find some help."

CHAPTER 7

SHAREEN FITZKELLUM

Emptier than emptiness. Blacker than blackness. The giant hole in the middle of the Fireheart nebula made Shareen uneasy.

"Hmm, this wasn't at all what I expected when I activated the Big Ring test." Kotto Okiah managed to sound both distracted and troubled. "Nevertheless, it is very interesting."

"That's one word for it," Shareen said with a sigh. She didn't point out that she and Howard had warned Kotto that something might go wrong with the experiment, because they had reviewed his calculations, against his orders.

Kotto was such a revered, even legendary, engineer that few Roamers ever questioned his assertions. By delving into his plans, Shareen and Howard hadn't been trying to challenge him, just to understand what the project was all about. But the more they analyzed the plans, the more they suspected that even Kotto wasn't sure of what he was doing. No wonder he hadn't wanted his two assistants probing for details.

With everyone watching the test, eager to see a spectacular scientific breakthrough, the Big Ring had been brought to full power. The thrumming ring spun up, vibrating in space, draining the countless chained power blocks, thus creating a titanic electromagnetic tug-of-war. The Roamers got their spectacular result all right, and a giant rip in the universe to boot.

Since one of Kotto's postulated outcomes for the Big Ring was to create a new interstellar transgate doorway, the scientist claimed the result was not entirely unexpected, but Shareen knew he was just waving his hands. Even if it worked, Station Chief Beren Alu, a practical businessman, quickly realized that any transit system requiring such a massive investment of time, money, and effort to open even one end was utterly unfeasible.

The Roamers might have indulged Kotto once, but they would not do so again . . . especially if the results of the Big Ring experiment turned disastrous.

His technical compy KR said, "We have been monitoring from a distance. The opening has not grown noticeably in the past two days."

"So it's stable," Kotto mused. "That's a good thing."

GU, his other compy, added, "The boundaries are indistinct and difficult to measure, however."

"We can all agree it's a good thing the gap has not torn wider . . ." Howard said in his usual quiet voice. He sounded reticent.

"Definitely better than the collapse of the universe," Shareen agreed. The void where the Big Ring had been was like a hole in the nebula, where streamers of wispy gas poured down into nowhere like the diaphanous veil of a colorful waterfall. It made her stomach queasy.

And she had thought solving the problem of the green priests and the trapped worldtrees seemed difficult. . . .

For two days, the tense Roamer workers at Fireheart Station had waited for answers. Completing the Big Ring had required so much effort that they felt adrift now that it was over. The complex had not yet gotten back to normal manufacturing levels, despite Chief Alu's urging. Many workers had fled immediately after the Big Ring collapsed, afraid that the tear in the universe would swallow the nebula whole. Fortunately, that disaster hadn't happened. Yet.

Garrison Reeves, one of the Roamer crew leaders, had established a conservative safety perimeter by placing warning buoys far from the edge of the void. A web of sensor packages provided instant telemetry closer in, but the sensors revealed no useful information. Long-distance sensors just weren't able to do the job.

Very soon, Shareen knew, Kotto would be pressured to provide answers about what the void was and what dangers it posed, but so far he had not yet offered even preliminary hypotheses.

When Shareen and Howard first came to Fireheart Station to be his lab assistants, she had been excited to learn from such a famous figure, a genius in every sense of the word. Despite working at Fireheart for years, Kotto had produced nothing remarkable, until he invested his entire reputation in the Big Ring project.

Shareen was ambitious and intelligent, and Howard was eager to learn. When Kotto asked his new assistants to comb through old notes and half-finished projects, the two dove into the work with great enthusiasm. They solved problems that had stumped him for years, and Kotto had seemed pleased with their work, even a little astonished at what they figured out. Afterward, the great scientist had been even more determined to prove that his Big Ring would work.

That hadn't turned out as planned. Shareen and Howard refrained from saying "I told you so"—they had not wanted to be right. Now, in the aftermath, Kotto didn't tear his eyes from the view of the void. "I wonder where it goes."

"We should send probes," KR said. "That would be the best way to map the anomaly from within."

"Naturally we'll send probes," Kotto said. "I was planning on it. That's our next step."

Chief Alu entered the observation deck to join them at the windowports. Alu was a small, wiry man with a long ponytail that extended down to the middle of his back. Long hair was not practical for anyone working in space, which was why Shareen kept hers short, but Alu was more of a manager than an actual space worker; he rarely donned an exosuit.

"I have to start reassigning work teams, Kotto," he said with a long-suffering sigh. "By the Guiding Star, we need to get back to manufacturing power blocks and harvesting isotopes again. Fireheart will still provide the support you need to assess the results . . . but we've got to get to work. Fireheart Station isn't a charity operation. I'm accountable to seventeen major clans."

Kotto sounded baffled. "But I'm not stopping you from doing anything."

Alu frowned. "We've been waiting to find out what that void is."

"It is something very interesting, with a great deal of potential," Kotto said firmly. "It may take some time to get the answers, but by all means don't stop the business of Fireheart. Shareen and Howard here can help me collate the results. We'll keep ourselves busy."

The Station Chief looked confused but also relieved. "So, you think we can start isotope skimming again, stretch the films to make more power blocks? You're sure the void doesn't pose any danger?"

Kotto gave a dismissive wave. "Garrison Reeves marked out a safety perimeter. So long as your operations stay outside the boundary, you'll be fine."

Shareen turned away so no one would see her doubts. Kotto had no basis for making such a statement.

"All right, I'll inform the teams. They'll be glad to get Fireheart back to normal." Alu glanced through the windowport at the black void slowly drinking the nebula gases. "Your experiment was a big setback for us, Kotto. By the Guiding Star, I'm amazed by what you accomplished here, and it was the greatest show I've ever seen . . . but once the experiment was over we were hoping to repurpose the superconducting magnets and strip out thousands of power blocks. Now they've all been sucked down the cosmic drain, gone forever. We have to start from scratch."

The chief's tone had only a hint of scolding, but Kotto did not seem bothered. "Starting over from scratch, Beren—that's what Roamers do. Depending on what it turns out to be, that void could make Fireheart Station into a major tourist attraction."

Shareen and Howard both shot a surprised glance at him.

The Station Chief blinked and let out a nervous chuckle. "I highly doubt that."

"One never knows. Right now there are too many unanswered questions, and a lot of theoretical physicists will be on their way to have a look. Feel free to have your teams start generating income in the traditional way. As soon as I have answers for you, I'll present them."

Since it wasn't her place to interject, Shareen waited for Alu to leave. When he was gone, she started to ask her questions, but Kotto rubbed his hands briskly together. "There, that's the impetus we needed," he said, as if trying to sound certain. "We have to find some answers—and that will involve asking more vigorous questions.

We can't just stand here at a distance and look. I'm going to take the next step."

KR said, "We have standard probes ready for immediate deployment, Kotto Okiah. They will give us a first look into the gap."

Kotto was impatient now. "Not good enough. Everything about my project was big and bold. We can't be shy now—this calls for a scientific adventure!"

Unsettled, Shareen looked at Howard, but she could tell that Kotto had made up his mind.

"I'll outfit a survey craft and prepare for an expedition," he said. "I'm going to go inside that void."

CHAPTER

8

OSIRA'H

The faeros were like a sunstorm in the Ildiran sky. Her father had gone up to face them.

The gathered people were terrified, their uncertainty thrumming through the *thism*. Osira'h could feel it. In the crowd, the human historian Anton Colicos frantically took notes. Nira wept, tears trickling down her emerald cheeks as she gazed up at the Mage-Imperator's small figure high on the tower. "What if they incinerate him, just like Rusa'h?" she whispered.

Osira'h put a comforting arm around her mother. She felt a call of her own, though. She had been bred to command the elemental hydrogues, and her powers also extended to the faeros. She and her half-brothers and sisters—Nira's children—were successes of the Dobro breeding program, just as the remaining misbreeds were the failures.

She knew she still had the strength within her.

Even from here, Osira'h felt her father struggling with the faeros, and knew that she had to help him. If he failed and the elemental beings careened across Mijistra, tens of thousands of Ildirans would be turned to ash. Breaking away from Nira, she grabbed the arms of her siblings Gale'nh and Muree'n standing next to her. "The Mage-Imperator needs us! I can connect with my father, and if you connect with me, we'll be stronger together. Maybe strong enough."

They pushed through the crowd, some of whom were too young to remember when the fireballs had scorched the city and laid waste to other Ildiran colony worlds. But many of them knew that horror and realized that their future balanced precariously on what the

Mage-Imperator did next. Osira'h wouldn't let him do it alone. "We have to hurry!"

Athletic Muree'n bounded ahead and cleared a way to the entrance arch. Tal Gale'nh, in his military uniform, wore a commanding expression as they hurried past the throngs. He had been fighting self-doubt ever since the shadows had engulfed the *Kolpraxa* and absorbed his hapless crew. Thanks to his halfbreed genetics, Gale'nh was able to resist the Shana Rei, and Osira'h now hoped that he could also find the inner strength to help forge an alliance with the fire elementals.

The three of them ran up the steep spiraling staircases to the apex of the main tower. Osira'h could see the flickering backwash of faeros light through crystalline structural blocks. When she, Muree'n, and Gale'nh finally rushed out onto the high platform, the atmosphere was like a bonfire. Hot air seared Osira'h's mouth and nose as she inhaled, and she could feel a crackle on her skin. She and Gale'nh reeled from the onslaught of heat, but Muree'n bowed her head and marched forward like a soldier about to take a strategic hill.

Mage-Imperator Jora'h stood with his arms upraised before the fireballs, his glittersilk robes flapping in the fiery breezes, the edges singed brown. His sinuous hair flew loose, writhing around his head like a corona. He stretched out his hands and squeezed his eyes shut as he concentrated. His face was tight, his lips drawn back. He shouted into the thermal white noise. "You must help us. The pain of Rusa'h brought you."

The faeros loomed in the sky, rotating ellipsoids of flame as large as spaceships. The elementals throbbed as if they could hear him. Jora'h strained, but he could not make them understand.

Osira'h could feel the fireballs all the way to the core of her being, a looming presence that was familiar to her—defiant, yet frightened. Rusa'h had called them here, and she doubted that her father could control them himself. He needed her—just as she needed her siblings. Together, they could get through to the capricious fiery elementals.

Clasping hands with Gale'nh and Muree'n, she called out with her mind. Osira'h was the perfect combination of breeding: all the strength of the Mage-Imperator, and all the sensitivity and telepathy of a green priest. The Ildiran Empire had tried for generations, breeding and misbreeding, to create someone exactly like her. Muree'n and Gale'nh, similar attempts at developing just the right hybrid, each had a significant power, and Osira'h drew on them now.

Not long ago, she and her half-brother Rod'h had gone out to find the faeros and beg them to make an alliance. But even though they made contact, the faeros had been too afraid of the creatures of darkness. It was unnerving to think that even the fire elementals were intimidated by the Shana Rei.

Osira'h still did not understand what deep connection existed between the faeros and Ildirans that Rusa'h's agonized call could compel the elementals to respond. But they had come.

She shouted both with her mind and her voice. The words *burned* out of her mouth. "The Shana Rei are a great enemy, but we will fight—and we beg you to fight them as well."

The fireballs swirled as if in alarm, resisting her. She felt waves of uncertainty. If beings as mighty as these trembled before the creatures of darkness, then the Shana Rei must be far more powerful than any enemy they had fought during the Elemental War.

Jora'h drew strength from his mastery of the *thism*. "The blood and agony of Rusa'h called you—and I bind you by it. You must listen to me." His command sounded powerful, but Osira'h felt that his control was strangely slipping. She added her strength to his and drew more from Gale'nh and Muree'n.

Jora'h opened his eyes under the orange blaze of faeros, and she was startled to see that her father's normally bright irises were now obscured by an oily black sheen of darkness that seemed to well up inside him. Beside her, Muree'n saw it as well and recoiled, but Gale'nh's eyes were closed. Still recovering from the Shana Rei and now in the presence of elemental beings of pure fire, Gale'nh fought to focus on his inner strength.

Under the onslaught, the Mage-Imperator shuddered, ready to collapse, but then the blackness in his eyes washed away. Osira'h gave her father all the secondary strength and focus that she could summon, and her mental voice intertwined with his. "If you refuse to fight the Shana Rei with us, then the entire cosmos will be unmade. You cannot ignore this threat. Help us! We share the same enemy."

The Mage-Imperator's eyes were clear now; Osira'h had steadied him. He looked to her, and then all of them stared up at the fireballs. Together, their single voice rang out. "You cannot hide from the Shana Rei. We beseech you to fight them with us! Come when we call you. We bind you with the agony that brought you here."

The Saga of Seven Suns described how Mage-Imperator Xiba'h had set himself on fire to call the faeros, which held them in thrall long enough to battle the Shana Rei. That tactic had worked millennia ago, but perhaps the Shana Rei were stronger this time . . . or the faeros were weaker after the Elemental War.

Now the fiery elementals brightened under the demand, like stars ready to explode. Osira'h could sense how they fought against the command, and she was afraid they would lash out at anyone who tried to force their will upon them.

For a long moment the firestorm seemed to be approaching a critical state.

Then the faeros backed away and rose up from the Prism Palace. She couldn't tell whether or not they had agreed to anything. The fireballs hovered high above them, and all the Ildirans in the Foray Plaza below watched the ominous blaze in the sky. Osira'h could feel a pounding, thrumming mental turmoil of churning faeros thoughts.

The fireballs streaked away, rising up and out of sight.

ADAR ZAN'NH

Adar Zan'nh had assigned his battered warliners to stand guard over Ildira, because he knew the Shana Rei would return. He had hoped for time to strengthen the Solar Navy after the great battle at Kuivahr, but he never expected mad Designate Rusa'h to summon another enemy to Ildira.

The Solar Navy had been gravely damaged at Kuivahr. Even so, their laser cannons and enhanced sun bombs had wrought tremendous devastation on the Shana Rei and eradicated the malicious black robots—though at great cost. Now his warliners needed to be repaired, their laser cannons recharged, their sun-bomb stockpiles reloaded.

They were not ready for the faeros.

Perimeter sentries on the edge of the system had spotted the fireballs racing toward Ildira. The Adar had activated the guardian warliners to stand as a barrier, but the faeros were coming in fast. "Prepare all available weapons. Laser cannons first, but be ready with sun bombs and conventional projectiles." His throat went dry, but he kept his voice strong. "We will have to try everything."

He and all the Solar Navy crew braced themselves . . . but the burning ellipsoids dodged through the blockade like embers scattered from a fire, ignoring the warliners and plunging into the atmosphere.

"Should we pursue them down to the surface, Adar?" asked his weapons officer.

Below, the faeros converged above the center of the Prism Palace. The warliner's communications officer sounded tense and perplexed.

"The faeros have made no aggressive moves. The Mage-Imperator has gone to meet them."

"Stand ready," he said. "Let us not provoke them. Yet."

An agonizing hour passed. Whatever happened down on the surface, Zan'nh knew the faeros would come back. Rather than waiting in helpless dread, he used the time to prepare. All soldiers knew that if they were forced to hurl themselves into the path of the faeros, they would surely be vaporized—but it was a price they were willing to pay to defend the Ildiran Empire.

Again, alarms bolted through the warliners gathered in a tight cordon. "Faeros are withdrawing to orbit at full speed, Adar! They are heading directly toward our warliners."

The fireballs closed in, scorching a path through the outer atmosphere. "Stand ready," he said. He had to hope. "Report from the surface? How much damage to Mijistra?" *And is the Mage-Imperator still alive?*

In the past, the faeros had obliterated the city and melted the Prism Palace. Yet if there were substantial casualties, he would have sensed the death of so many Ildirans through the *thism,* especially Mage-Imperator Jora'h. Therefore, the faeros must not have attacked. So why had they come?

The sensor chief called in a voice that cracked, "No obvious destruction in Mijistra, Adar."

"If we wait any longer to launch sun bombs, Adar, we will also be destroyed in the detonation," said his weapons officer.

The faeros roared closer, clearing the atmosphere and rising up to orbit toward the Solar Navy.

"Adar?" the weapons officer pressed, ready to launch the sun bombs.

"No . . . this is not what I thought." Zan'nh stared at the oncoming fireballs until his eyes ached from the glare. What were they doing? Did he dare provoke them? If so, he knew the Solar Navy would lose.

The comm system crackled, and a voice came through—Tal Gale'nh on the primary command channel. "Adar, the faeros caused no harm down here. They did not attack!"

Zan'nh reacted immediately as the fireballs closed in. "Stand down. Do not fire sun bombs." His insides twisted, knowing what a gamble this was. The fireballs rushed closer.

Gale'nh continued to transmit from the surface. "The faeros communicated with the Mage-Imperator. We . . . we believe we were able to enlist their aid. Let them pass."

Through the *thism* Zan'nh's emotions broiled. The fiery elementals hurtled closer, showing no sign that they even saw the warliners lined up against them. The Adar clenched his hands on the rail of the command nucleus. The fireballs careened into the cohort of Solar Navy warships . . . and then soared past and headed out into deep space as if the warliners weren't even there. They simply rolled away into the universe.

10

COLLIN

The worldtrees could not help free them, Collin knew that. The forest here was tainted.

The sentient forest was one of the greatest forces in the universe, a power so vast that no one could comprehend it all. But now, when he needed them most, the verdani were silent, as if blind to the darkness that was devouring them from within. And that emptiness manifested itself in this hollow remnant of Kennebar and his followers, who had become human-shaped wells of darkness.

He tried to get through. "Maybe it's not too late, Kennebar. You were a green priest once. Maybe—" Fear stiffened his words, and his voice cracked.

The voidpriest's eyes were nearly invisible on his ebony face, and when he spoke, his mouth was even darker than the rest of him. "We all tended the trees, but now we know something more. No one can stop the fall of night. The darkness is coming, and we will usher it in."

Arita clamped her hands against her head, as if a loud noise roared inside of her. "Something is calling me, Collin—but not the trees."

"The trees are silent," Kennebar said.

Two more black figures came down from the fronds and stood with the other gathered voidpriests, all of the isolationists who had once been Collin's comrades. He couldn't even recognize them now. A sick chill flooded through him. If he hadn't discovered the groves of dying worldtrees and rushed to ask Arita for her help, he would have been here with Kennebar and his companions. He would be one of *them*, nothing more than a black emptiness.

Collin took her hand as the voidpriests pressed closer.

"Arita cannot hear us," Kennebar said. "The trees rejected her, and now the shadows reject her. She is . . . different inside. If we cannot engulf her, we will kill her, as the Onthos killed Sarein."

"No! Sarein is alive." Arita reeled, tried to lunge toward the void-priest, but Collin held her back.

"You are all dead," Kennebar said. "The worldforest is withering. Eventually, the blackness will be absolute . . . and all will be peace and calm."

"I refuse. I *am* a green priest, and the trees are still alive." Collin pressed backward against the thick, gold-scaled trunk of a comatose worldtree. They could retreat no further up here among the branches. Desperately seeking any help, he used his telink to pierce deep into the heartwood, like a hard projectile.

Always before, the verdani mind had enfolded him like a safety net. He had been able to sense their thoughts, their information, just by stroking a frond or touching a trunk. Now, though, it felt as if his mind had plunged deep into cold, still water. Where there had once been a cacophony of information, billions of lives, trees, and green priests, along with all the knowledge that human acolytes and green priests had fed them over the centuries . . . now there was nothing. Silence.

Refusing to give up, he sank deeper, sending his mind all the way down to the roots, searching for some spark of the intellect that had been there. The worldforest in the Wild was withdrawing, falling silent . . . growing senile.

Collin had to find something. The trees were all connected, and other trees on Theroc were alive and strong.

Knowing that he was leaving Arita and the voidpriests behind for a few moments, he made contact with the deepest heartwood—and there he did find a spark, a few confused and faint recollections. He awakened them, searching for answers, hoping those thoughts would give him a way to fight.

Inside the verdani mind, he found long-buried memories, alien memories, some of them restored by the Onthos when they came to Theroc asking for refuge. But the Gardeners had also brought with them an insidious taint of shadow that they themselves hadn't known they carried. Collin read the information there and found the answers.

In those lost, ancient memories he saw waves of Onthos rushing to escape from their homeworld as the enormous shadow clouds closed in, as the Shana Rei built an impenetrable black sphere around their star system. Many aliens, unable to flee, had been left behind to smother in freezing darkness.

Others had stayed behind to fight, fusing themselves with the great trees via the catalyst of wental water to become verdani battleships . . . lifeships that carried millions of escaping Onthos, who burrowed into the trees like parasites. Some of those lifeships were destroyed by the Shana Rei before they could get away.

A very few Gardeners had escaped, though, along with their rare spore mothers, but their race withered and declined, because they had no worldforest, and the last refugees spent thousands of years fleeing and wandering, trying to establish new colonies, doing anything to survive. Along the way, they were also hunted down and nearly eradicated by the Klikiss race.

And all along the Onthos had carried a blight hidden within their DNA, which they had now unwittingly brought to Theroc. They planned to thrive again, to become part of an ever-larger worldforest, which the blight was killing. The infestation would destroy the Wild; then it would snuff out the whole verdani mind.

Kennebar and the voidpriests intended to assist in that doom. They were entirely composed of dark matter now, a manifestation of the shadows.

Now only Collin knew the truth, and he and Arita were trapped here. Sarein must have discovered some part of the secret herself and been killed for it.

Through his probing, Collin had nudged the worldforest mind, awakened part of it here. And now he knew he needed to emerge, return to his body and to Arita. The two of them had to fight and survive. It was more important than ever.

I am a green priest! He came back to himself and although only a moment had passed, he saw the voidpriests closing in like slow ink-black soldiers. Collin and Arita stood together, ready to fight. "I am a green priest," he said aloud, his voice strong and clear.

He heard a rustling sound and realized that the fronds overhead were filled with Gardeners—not just the few who had come to watch before, but dozens of them crowded shoulder-to-shoulder, all identical and staring down with clinical fascination. As if anticipating death and blood.

Collin drew a deep breath. The first enemies he and Arita had to fight were the voidpriests.

ROD'H

The void around him was a lifeless purgatory that preserved his existence so the shadows and their malicious robots could toy with him, study him, excavate his mind.

Because Rod'h was a halfbreed, he could resist them to a certain extent, but he was no longer truly alive. The Shana Rei held him in an entropy bubble, a vague chamber apart from the real universe. He drifted in the blackness with no sensory input, except for pain. And the robots were extremely good at inflicting pain—almost as good as Rod'h was at preserving his secrets. The Shana Rei were growing frustrated with him.

During the battle at the Onthos home system, black robots had captured his scout ship, taking him as an experimental subject. Months earlier, the shadows had also seized his brother Gale'nh when they engulfed the *Kolpraxa*, but they let Gale'nh go—weakened and damaged—when they could not derive the answers they needed.

They took Rod'h instead, and he knew they would not make the mistake of releasing him.

Even in his bizarre isolation, though, he remained connected with Gale'nh and their three half-sisters, Osira'h, Muree'n, and Tamo'l. As he drifted, an unknown time after the attack on Kuivahr—because time had no meaning here—he reached out to make a connection with his siblings. He was surprised to sense Tamo'l more clearly than the others. She had devoted her life to tending the misbreeds in the sanctuary domes on Kuivahr, and she had escaped just before the shadows engulfed that planet. Now, he could sense that Tamo'l was vulnerable, susceptible . . . contaminated in a way. Somehow, the creatures of darkness must have touched her before she escaped Kuivahr.

Rod'h feared that the Shana Rei had found some way to break her innate halfbreed defenses. Was it because of something they had learned by torturing him? He was frightened for Tamo'l. If the shadows had inserted some insidious hook into her mind, what sort of damage could they do?

The frustration cut through him like a hot wire. Could he help his siblings? Could he learn anything useful from the Shana Rei? From the black robots? He had to accomplish something!

One of the shadow creatures appeared, a formless inkblot against the darkness in his prison cell of nothingness, but he could sense the presence because the stain of darkness seemed somehow more malicious than the background. The center of the blot manifested a bright glowing eye, useless and symbolic, perhaps only for the purpose of frightening the captive.

Rod'h had moved past fear, though his emotions were tempered into strength. He promised himself that he would disrupt them if he could not find some way to escape from this void. He was sure his siblings knew that he remained a captive among the Shana Rei. His thoughts were still active, his body alive . . . in a certain sense.

Nira's halfbreed children were connected by a mental bond that went beyond *thism*. That had been one goal that the Dobro breeding program had tried to achieve, and why Nira had been forced to bear children against her will by different mates. Rod'h and his mother had never been close, but because of the torture and deprivation he now endured, he could comprehend the torment she must have felt to be held prisoner, constantly abused. He hadn't treated her well, had even resented her for complaining about her duty. Not understanding her pain and helplessness, he had thought her weak. And now he doubted he would ever have a chance to tell her about the change in his perspective. . . .

Now, focusing his defiance, he glared at the throbbing Shana Rei inkblot. The glowing eye did not blink, nor did it show any expression.

Rod'h refused to acknowledge his helplessness. He pushed

outward with his mind, searching for contact with his siblings. They would know him when his thoughts touched theirs. Osira'h . . . Osira'h was strongest. When he reached out for a susceptible contact with his sister, he felt fire carried along with her bright mental light. Osira'h was with the faeros! The faeros were on Ildira, right now!

Muree'n was there, too . . . and he sensed Gale'nh, who had suffered much the same agony aboard the *Kolpraxa* as Rod'h was enduring here. Feeling the connection, Rod'h tried to open up to his brother. Gale'nh attempted to respond—but as soon as the bond was established, dozens of Shana Rei inkblots swarmed around Rod'h, pressing closer, swelling darker. They were trying to commandeer the connection, pushing through the bond to Gale'nh.

Rod'h scrambled to block off his thoughts, to sever the link. He felt Gale'nh also resisting on Ildira, despite his longing to connect with his lost brother. But when the shadows reached out through Rod'h, Gale'nh broke the connection with his own will and determination. So, his brother was stronger than Rod'h had thought.

Through that brief link, Rod'h saw a glimpse of fire, blessed light—the faeros! He and Osira'h had desperately tried to call the faeros . . . and now the fiery elementals had come to Mijistra.

The Shana Rei were angered, but Rod'h shut them out, walled them off to show they could do nothing further to him. Eventually, the creatures of darkness withdrew, but he didn't believe he had won. He would keep being defiant, because that was the only thing he could do, the only strength he could show.

As if petulant, the Shana Rei sent in the black robots to torment him again.

Exxos appeared in the entropy bubble, like a giant beetle with sharp claws clacking, threatening. Another ominous robot appeared, then ten more.

"You cannot frighten me," Rod'h said. "And you won't learn anything more from me."

"We know," said Exxos, as they closed in. "But we will continue, nevertheless." Their crimson optical sensors blazed, and they took pleasure in telling him, "There are many of us now—a million. And our large-scale attacks will begin soon."

12

SHAWN FENNIS

Although they had escaped from Kuivahr before the black shroud sealed off the planet, Shawn Fennis still faced a crisis on the other side of the Klikiss transportal. During the frantic evacuation, medical technicians had loaded group after group of the misbreeds through the dimensional doorway . . . but now the patchwork Ildirans could barely survive.

This backwater place was not adequate for their requirements. Gorhum was just a small, isolated outpost that did not have the medical facilities or sophisticated support equipment for misbreeds and their special needs. Fennis had realized that right away.

Fewer than fifty human workers resided at the transportal station, support personnel waiting for infrequent travelers who wanted to use the Klikiss transportal network. The outpost's medical facility was little more than a glorified first-aid station.

The sleepy personnel were understandably astonished to receive the sudden flood of refugees—and even more astonished by their physical appearance. Fennis had grown up on Dobro, accustomed to the unusual "mistakes" of the breeding program. He was a member of the first free generation after the breeding camp was shut down, and he had stayed behind to work with the program's leftovers. The former human prisoners and their former Ildiran masters had vowed to work together to heal the scars of their history. Fennis had even taken an Ildiran mate, whom he considered more beautiful than any woman he had ever seen. Together, he and Chiar'h had volunteered to work in Tamo'l's sanctuary domes on Kuivahr, tending the worst genetic flukes and helping them lead a somewhat comfortable life.

But the misbreeds wanted more than just existence—they wanted to be *useful*. These were the greatest outliers of the breeding program, and they needed their tangled lives to have some meaning, some benefit to result from all their suffering. They might have been bred as capricious experiments, but the misbreeds had their own worth. As Fennis got to know them, he wanted to help them find their worth, their purpose.

When the shadows attacked Kuivahr, they had tried to seize Tamo'l and Osira'h, to study the unlikely powers of those halfbreed sisters. But had the Shana Rei wanted only those two? Fennis suspected that the creatures of darkness might also have wanted to eradicate the misbreeds, in case they held some latent, undiscovered power.

Fennis, Chiar'h, and others had taken the misbreeds by boatload after boatload through the transportal wall to Gorhum. It should have been the safest way to escape. Tamo'l and Tom Rom should have been right behind them.

The stress of the fear and the evacuation, as well as the loss of their medical support equipment, had placed several misbreeds in crisis. After the groups passed through the transportal with a backwash of salt water from the stormy Kuivahr sea, some of the misbreeds struggled to survive. One in particular went into respiratory arrest, fighting to breathe: Mungl'eh was one of the most severely deformed misbreeds, with a sluglike body and atrophied flippers, but a sweet, beautiful face. When she began to sing, Mungl'eh could seize the heartstrings of a listener and weave them into any pattern she chose.

Just after the transportal was sealed and the crisis calmed down to held-breath tension, the Gorhum station chief stared at the sluglike misbreed writhing in the saltwater puddles on the floor, struggling to inhale. Chiar'h rushed forward with her medical pack and applied a respiratory enhancer across Mungl'eh's toothless mouth.

"We are safe now," she said in soothing voice, stroking the soft sloping shoulders. "Breathe slowly. We are far from the shadows."

Fennis, one of the last evacuees to come through the transportal, stood shuddering, looking around the complex as the well-trained

Kuivahr medical kithmen found places for the misbreeds to rest in the transportal reception area.

Fennis grabbed the attention of the Gorhum reception staff. "Do you have cots?" When they didn't move quickly enough, he raised his voice. "We need assistance! Don't just stare."

The facility chief blinked in disbelief at the freakish forms that had just stumbled through the stone trapezoidal wall. "Uh, we've got a station doctor. I'll get her."

"We need *equipment* more than we need another doctor," said Chiar'h. "Most of us are already medical technicians, and we are familiar with the infirmities of these misbreeds. Bring what you have."

Gor'ka and Har'lc, two severely deformed but otherwise healthy misbreeds, offered to help. The Dobro breeding program had mated kiths that were unlikely to interbreed under normal circumstances, just to see what might result. Har'lc was a combination of an otter-like swimmer and a lizardlike scaly kith. He possessed the correct number of limbs and eyes, but his skin was a constant nightmare of rashes, blotches, and peeling patches.

Gor'ka had three eyes, one located halfway down his cheek on a face that appeared to be made of melted wax. He reached out with a flexible, tentacle-like arm, wrapped it around a handle, and helped Har'lc pick up a levitating pallet that held a bedridden Pol'ux, whose body was a landscape of oozing boils. He seemed to be allergic to life itself, yet Pol'ux endured, as they all did.

As Har'lc and Gor'ka hauled the misbreed away from the salt-water puddles on the transportal room floor, the Gorhum facility doctor rushed in bearing first-aid kits. Chiar'h seized one and rummaged through the items. She didn't recognize the unfamiliar supplies, but she found a respirator and brought it to Mungl'eh. The misbreed singer cooed and relaxed, and soon her respiratory crisis was over.

In the arrival area, the misbreeds kept up a loud background drone of distraught conversation and noises. Fennis wiped perspiration from his freckled brow and turned to the station chief. "Thank you for your assistance. My name is Shawn Fennis. We just evacuated from Kuivahr—the Shana Rei destroyed our world. Everything there is gone, and we're the last refugees."

"Wait!" gasped Alaa'kh from a gaping open mouth, looking back at the blank transportal. "Where is Tamo'l?"

Fennis turned to look in distress at the now opaque stone trapezoid. He was surprised to see no sign of her. "I . . . was expecting one more group to come through."

Tamo'l and Tom Rom had organized the rushed evacuation, while numerous Ildiran swimmers had helped move the deformed patients across the water to the transportal wall. Many of the sleek swimmers now stood dripping in the Gorhum reception area, but there was no sign of Tamo'l or Tom Rom.

"What are we going to do with you all?" said the station chief in clear dismay.

"You're going to help us," Fennis said, and he stared back at the stone wall, willing it to open so that Tamo'l could join them, dreading that she and Tom Rom had been caught by the shadows on the other side.

"Where is Tamo'l?" Alaa'kh demanded, again.

On his levitating pallet, Pol'ux thrashed about so that two of his hand-sized boils burst, and he cried out in pain. "We need Tamo'l."

Chiar'h tried to reassure him. "We will take care of you. I'm sure Tamo'l is safe."

Stabilized, Mungl'eh breathed easier. She lifted her head on an uncooperative body and began to hum a beautiful melody that served as a lullaby for the others. Even Shawn Fennis felt his heart grow warm and calm. All the refugees also settled down.

"We'll care for these people and let them rest," Fennis told the station chief, "but we need to arrange passage to Ildira. We must go home to our Mage-Imperator."

Somehow, the chief managed to look relieved and alarmed at the same time. "We don't get a lot of traffic going into the Ildiran Empire, but we'll certainly help arrange the ships to get you out of here. Maybe we can divert the next trader who arrives." The man looked skeptically at the misbreeds. "I hope they have the facilities to transport your patients with all those . . . special needs." He seemed uncomfortable just looking at the strange patchwork people.

"Where is Tamo'l?" Alaa'kh said for a third time.

Fennis didn't have an answer.

The rescued misbreeds and swimmer kith gathered their strength for a day, but tension increased in the small, crowded station. Tamo'l should have come through long before now, and Fennis would not let anyone activate the Kuivahr coordinate tile, for fear of what might lie on the other side.

His hope was that Tom Rom had used a different coordinate tile to take Tamo'l to another planet, and that they were safe. But they had no way of knowing.

The shadows had swallowed the planet entirely, and it was far too dangerous to go back there. He didn't dare let anyone else return to the shrouded ocean world because of the risk. With a heavy heart, knowing he was cutting Tamo'l off, if she was indeed still trying to get through, Fennis took a heavy metal bar and destroyed the Kuivahr coordinate tile.

Now no one could get through from there . . . especially the creatures of darkness.

13

TOM ROM

The Pergamus medical library contained thousands of deadly pathogens and virulent diseases. The planet's atmosphere was poisonous, and all research domes were rigged with instant self-destruct systems.

Tom Rom considered it the safest place in the Spiral Arm.

After escaping from Kuivahr with Tamo'l, and destroying the Klikiss transportal on Auridia when the shadows tried to flood through, Tom Rom headed for Pergamus.

The half-Ildiran medical researcher seemed withdrawn. He was no expert on Ildiran psychology, but he thought Tamo'l's behavior indicated acute mental shock—for good reason. To help her recover, he offered the privacy of his personal cabin, and she slept for a good part of the journey. He could sleep later if necessary.

Tom Rom liked quiet time to think and plan anyway, to review mistakes made, and to frame his report for Zoe Alakis. He knew she would be waiting for him.

Per Zoe's request, he had gone to Kuivahr to assess the genetics of the Ildiran misbreeds. He had taken great risks to bring Tamo'l back with him, but he would downplay the danger so Zoe wouldn't worry. She always worried.

As soon as the Shana Rei began their attack at Kuivahr, Tamo'l should have listened to him and escaped. Prince Reynald of Theroc and the Mage-Imperator's daughter Osira'h had both fled with most of the Roamer distillery workers, but Tamo'l refused to leave before all of her misbreeds were safe. Logically, she should have cut her losses and gotten away, since the freakish anomalies could barely survive under the best of conditions and with constant care, but she had insisted.

And so Tom Rom helped evacuate the misbreeds through the transportal to Gorhum first. Once they were gone, it was a simple matter to change the coordinate tile so that he and Tamo'l arrived at the planet Auridia instead, beneath the Roamer complex of Newstation. During their escape, she had been stunned, resistant, practically catatonic, but Tom Rom whisked her away to his ship, along with all of her data about Ildiran genetics. His priority was to carry out Zoe's wishes. Always Zoe . . .

Now he flew into the Pergamus system along a precise flight path, broadcasting his authorization ID code so the mercenary security force wouldn't blow him out of space. Tamo'l rode beside him in detached silence.

After verifying his identity, the mercenary ships met the vessel and escorted it toward the planet. "Welcome back, sir," said the security team leader. "Any report on the situation in the Spiral Arm? We're cut off here."

"All hell is breaking loose," he said. "The Shana Rei and their black robots are attacking planets. The Confederation is in an uproar, the Ildiran Empire reeling." He stared hard at the captain's face on his comm screen. "You're better off here where it's calm and sensible."

He left the security team behind as he dove through the atmosphere toward the sterile main dome. Tamo'l became aware of her surroundings, as if awakening. She looked at the unfamiliar planet below, the misty atmosphere, the escort ships following them. "Where are we?"

"Your new research facility. My employer will be glad to have you as part of the team."

She showed no sign of alarm at the answer; in fact, she showed no reaction at all.

Although Zoe's interests focused primarily on human diseases, the intensive genetic knowledge Tamo'l had compiled over years of analyzing the misbreeds made her a profoundly talented researcher— one that Zoe could certainly use.

Though she asked no questions, he continued, "My employer has gathered cures and treatments for countless human diseases, and by adding your Ildiran work, Pergamus will contain the greatest collection of medical information anywhere in the Spiral Arm."

Tamo'l nodded distantly, not understanding the magnitude of what he was saying. "What about my misbreeds? Are they on Pergamus too?"

"You don't need to worry about them. I helped to get them away as I promised, and now you're with me. You have work to do here."

Alarm finally penetrated her expression. "But where are the misbreeds?"

"Safe," he said. "Not your concern at the moment."

"I need to let them know where I am. Shawn Fennis and Chiar'h are quite skilled, but if I am not there, the misbreeds will worry."

Tom Rom needed to stop the conversation. "If you like, I can check on them and bring you reports, but you'll be much more interested in the work my employer has for you."

Tamo'l didn't look convinced, and she retreated into herself again.

He guided the ship through the buffeting chemical mists. The fog lifted and the bright daylight revealed only a barren brown landscape blotched with black and gray lichens. The main hemispherical outpost was armored and reinforced, consisting of multiple nested domes leading into the protected central chamber where Zoe lived in sterile isolation. Clusters of satellite domes were separated widely enough that if any emergency fail-safe detonations occurred, the collateral damage would be minimal. Orbital Research Spheres conducted the most dangerous work in the perfect quarantine of space.

After docking, he and Tamo'l passed through the security interlocks into one of the outer-hemisphere rooms. He sat the halfbreed researcher in front of the large comm screen and activated it.

Zoe was waiting for them, her dark eyes eager. He could see her relief that he had come home again safely. He reassured her, "I was successful, Zoe. I've got all the genetic research, and I also brought the lead researcher from the sanctuary complex."

Zoe regarded her on the screen, and Tamo'l responded with a formal nod. "I have much more data, but I need to care for my misbreeds," Tamo'l said. "I have to be sure they are tended, that they are kept safe."

"Not my concern," Zoe said. "We intend to continue your

research. I will provide an entire dome for you to analyze the data you brought us."

Tom Rom cut in, "You can do more to help the misbreeds if you stay here, Tamo'l—develop treatments, maybe even a genetic cure. You won't need to worry about the Shana Rei or contamination or distractions here on Pergamus. You can do pure research, use equipment and facilities far more extensive than anything you had in the sanctuary domes."

"The Mage-Imperator always provided what I needed," Tamo'l said.

"But now you'll need more," Zoe responded. "Use our equipment to create a full genetic profile of all the misbreed specimens. We have modeling programs and biological-analysis capabilities that will help you obtain insights. Unravel the secrets, find every possible disconnect in their genes, and then use our methods to develop repairs that will help them survive."

Tom Rom was pleased to see how well Zoe understood the incentive that would drive Tamo'l. He expected the Ildiran researcher to resist what she might view as imprisonment, but instead Tamo'l wore her strange disoriented look. She averted her eyes, and her attitude changed. "Yes, I need to analyze the misbreeds. They all have interesting, undocumented strengths. The combination of kiths led to many unexpected results. I wish to understand them. I will use your facility and find the necessary answers."

"Then this will be a beneficial partnership for all of us," Zoe said.

14

GENERAL NALANI KEAH

Wiping out the horrific biological black market on Rakkem had been a satisfying mission for General Keah, but not satisfying enough. There were worse enemies abroad in the Spiral Arm—and she had a lot more ass-kicking to do.

"We accomplished a good thing there, General," said Admiral Haroun on the bridge of the *Okrun* as the CDF battle group returned to Earth.

None of the CDF ships had taken any damage in the Rakkem engagement. Not a scratch. The despicable biological black marketers and illicit medical researchers had offered no resistance when the Confederation Defense Forces had cracked down on the place.

"It's always good to clean up the neighborhood," Keah said. "But we shouldn't have had to bother with nonsense like that in the first place. The Shana Rei and the bugbots are raising hell across the Spiral Arm." She made a disgusted sound. "We've got more important things to worry about."

Haroun frowned at her. "What we did was important enough to anyone who was tricked or killed by those charlatans on Rakkem, General."

An unwanted flood of images passed through Keah's mind as she remembered the breeding warehouses, the organ-storage facilities, the horrific and ineffective "treatments" designed to prey upon desperate people, the embryos and newborns harvested for biological material.

"You're right, Admiral. That place was a noxious weed that had to be pulled from the Spiral Arm. But now it's time to get back to saving the human race for a better tomorrow."

The returning battle group cruised into the Lunar Orbital Complex at Earth, the CDF's main operations center, which had been constructed in the rubble of the destroyed Moon. Trading ships, delivery vessels, and construction crews flitted around the numerous spacedocks.

Keah was glad to see dozens of operational Mantas flying about in military practice maneuvers. Emergency repair crews had worked around the clock to reconstruct the ships damaged in the encounter with the Shana Rei and their black robots in the Onthos home system. The creatures of darkness wished to wipe out all intelligent life, and they weren't the sort of enemy King Peter and Queen Estarra could negotiate with.

That meant this war against the Shana Rei and their black robots was going to be a balls-out fight, and it wouldn't be over until either the enemies were defeated, or the human race was extinct. General Keah preferred the former outcome.

As the strike force returned to the LOC, the comm filled with a flurry of transmissions, including a long list of "urgent administrative matters," which General Keah ignored. Rakkem was horrific, but she had enjoyed being away from the paperwork, at least for a little while.

"I'm glad to have the *Okrun* back home, General," said Admiral Haroun, "but I admit, it felt good to be doing something active and important."

Keah felt a warm glow to hear him say that. Haroun was one of her three lead admirals, all of whom had been promoted for bureaucratic reasons during the decades of peace after the Elemental War. She would have preferred that officers be promoted because they demonstrated spectacular prowess on the battlefield—as she herself had done early in her career. Twenty years of peace had been a wonderful respite for the human race, but calm stability was not conducive to producing seasoned commanding officers.

Haroun, along with his colleagues Admirals Handies and Harvard, were collectively called "the Three H's." The emerging threat of the Shana Rei and the need for aggressive defenses had forced those three to step up to the plate, but General Keah wasn't sure they had it in them. At least Haroun had performed well during the recent Rakkem crackdown. Now if only she could see the same improvement in Handies and Harvard . . .

The returning Mantas separated to their assigned positions in the Lunar Orbital Complex, while the *Okrun* cruised to the headquarters spacedocks, where Keah saw a sight that gladdened her heart. She smiled to Haroun and said, "I like your Juggernaut just fine, Admiral, but I prefer mine."

Her flagship, the *Kutuzov,* hung there with running lights aglow. A bright patchwork of new repairs across its hull bore witness to the damage inflicted by the Shana Rei and the bugbots. The stardrive engines were new, the destroyed decks now restored. The *Kutuzov* looked absolutely beautiful. "Now that's what I like to see."

On the comm screen, jowly Admiral Harvard smiled at her. "Welcome back, General. You've noticed the surprise we have for you?"

"It's a pleasant surprise indeed. I wasn't expecting the *Kutuzov* to be finished for another week."

Harvard nodded. "We completed all inspections, but someone needs to take the flagship out on a shakedown cruise. We thought you might like to do it yourself."

"Absolutely." Keah was anxious to be back on her own bridge. "I'll come to LOC headquarters for a briefing—and the operative part is *brief.* What else has fallen apart in the Spiral Arm while I was gone?"

"There have been many disturbing reports, General," said Harvard. "Please keep your schedule clear. I'll set up a succession of briefings."

Keah frowned. "Brief, Admiral. *Brief.*" The Three H's seemed to think meetings could solve everything.

Despite her reservations about sitting in a room and talking, General Keah found the briefings informative and necessary. With reports of all the shadow cloud sightings and bugbot encounters, she could dispatch her ships—preferably loaded to the gills with enhanced sun bombs.

Admiral Handies presented his preliminary report with so much excitement she expected him to announce a substantial victory over the Shana Rei. Instead, he summarized the progress of ship repair and presented the dispersal of currently deployed CDF Mantas and Juggernauts, as well as full budgetary breakdowns for new battleship construction. The costs were offset by drastically reduced stardrive fuel costs, thanks to the reliable supplies and generous discounts from Iswander Industries.

When the main briefings were finished, a flustered Dr. Jocko Krieger appeared in the conference room. The weapons scientist was fifteen minutes late, but when he walked in and unrolled his projection pad on the table, he just started talking as if everyone had been waiting for him. "I'm pleased to report that we now have six fabrication stations in full operation throughout the LOC. Each station is producing enhanced sun bombs at the rate of five per day."

Keah was pleased. "Now that'll do some damage. Are they being deployed?"

"Since you departed for Rakkem, General, twenty-five Mantas have been fully loaded and dispatched on patrol. All they need is something to blow up."

Admiral Harvard spoke up. "I can give you the full mission plan, identify which systems they're visiting and what their patrol routes are. Sooner or later they're going to encounter a Shana Rei infestaton."

Keah set aside the lengthy document. "I'll review it later. Is the *Kutuzov* loaded with sun bombs, too?"

Krieger gave a vigorous nod. "Fully loaded, plus an extra ten percent, General. I thought you'd want that."

"Yes, Dr. Krieger, I definitely do."

The scientist kept talking about his accomplishments, patting himself on the back if no one else would. "The orbital labs are manufacturing at full capacity, ma'am." He quickly added, "With full safety systems in place this time."

"Good." Keah turned to Handies. "What else did you have to report?"

The other Admiral displayed a succession of starfield images; each one showed black blots, as if someone had smeared an ink-covered thumb across space. "Shadow clouds are appearing, dark nebulae that haven't been mapped before. They seem to be . . . leaking out of space." He shook his head. "I suspect it has something to do with the Shana Rei."

"No shit," General Keah said. She looked down at the images—swirling blobs of opaque smoke that seemed to be expanding from numerous origin points. "Are they threatening any star systems yet?"

"Some, but not directly. The shadow clouds seem to be moving, and we're trying to map them. Several Mantas have gone out to take images. The largest cloud is on the outskirts of the Relleker system."

Keah immediately made up her mind where the *Kutuzov* would go on the shakedown cruise. "We'll head out as soon as possible."

"But the shadow clouds have made no threatening moves yet," Admiral Harvard pointed out.

Dr. Krieger let out a loud snort—a snort that Keah agreed with.

"Their *existence* is a threatening move, Admiral," she said. "Now, if we're finished, here? Give me summaries of this data, and I'll take it back to the *Kutuzov.* I've decided to move up my launch. We'll be out of here before the end of the day."

15

ARITA

After dreaming of serving the trees, Arita considered the betrayal of Kennebar's voidpriests and the Gardeners the greatest treason imaginable. They meant to bring about the downfall of the verdani mind, and they wanted to watch her die.

As the threatening voidpriests came for her and Collin, the chittering Onthos swarmed into the fronds overhead. They stared down, no longer pretending to be innocuous survivors to elicit sympathy. These creatures were evil. The voidpriests were even worse. Kennebar wanted to kill Arita, and they intended to *absorb* Collin.

That sickened her—and made her angry. She looked within herself, cast about for any sort of strength, any unexpected hope.

Collin had sent his mind into the heartwood of the silent worldtrees; he had communed with them, demanded answers, and upon emerging, he seemed inspired by what he had learned. "I know what you are now!" he shouted to the voidpriests as he pulled Arita close. He glared up at the Onthos. "The trees told me."

Kennebar and his dark companions were undeterred. They reached toward their trapped victims, and Arita and Collin pressed back against the trunk of the huge tree behind them. "The worldtrees are not dead," Collin said. "They are aware of you!"

"The trees are weak," said Kennebar.

Then Arita felt the whispers stir in her mind again with a wordless urgency. Something *else* was awakening in the cosmos, something that sensed the danger of the growing shadows. Arita didn't understand it, but she reached out for it nevertheless.

She had despaired of ever knowing what it was like to be a green priest, to share thoughts with a mind so vast. But the trees had altered her, left her open for something more. It seemed impossible, but she realized that the inner voice also belonged to some grand sentience, different from the verdani. It was beyond the faeros, wentals, and hydrogues. Arita was connected to it, could commune with it the same way Collin connected with the trees.

As the voidpriests reached out to kill them, coronas of blackness shimmered from their hands. Arita felt Collin grab her like a safety net. "The trees know me," he rasped. "They remember me . . . and they have to remember themselves!"

Collin dug deep and touched the slumbering worldforest, while Arita called on that other presence. And the power of her plea joined with his, magnifying it, building, reverberating until it woke the trees at last, forcing the verdani to defend themselves.

Arita felt dizzy as the inner sounds became a roar in her ears. Her vision expanded, and she could see through the clustered trees, their thick fronds interlocked in a canopy that now began to stir. Leaves thrashed about, and vines twisted up from the forest floor.

Startled by the unexpected response, the alien Onthos skittered away, some scrambling higher into the fronds while others dashed across the branches.

Kennebar and his voidpriests froze as if in disbelief.

Collin shouted out to the verdani. "Save us! Save the forest."

The other voice inside Arita also thrummed out wordlessly, offering defenses against the spreading stain of the destructive shadow.

Alive, the thrashing fronds hurled dozens of fleeing Gardeners into the air, dashing them against the branches. Newly wakened vines and branches reached out to catch the Onthos and squeeze them like huge fists.

Fronds whipped about with the sound of a great windstorm. Branches wrapped around Kennebar, engulfing him. The voidpriest leader struggled with his ebony arms, soulless eyes wide on his blank, shadowed face. The other tainted priests made no sound as they struggled.

Arita felt as if her mind would burst from the surge of energy using her as a conduit. Collin's eyes were squeezed shut, his lips drawn back. He groaned at the strain of the impossible effort.

The trees shuddered with a last gasp of their own energy. Gold bark scales flaked away, and the tree trunks split open with a resounding crack. Gaps in the heartwood spread wider, yawning like dark and dangerous mouths in the thick trunks. The frond tentacles that held the struggling voidpriests scooped them into the gaps. Thrashing, the dark priests fell into the wooden maws of the angry trees, which swallowed them like predators devouring prey.

It took only seconds, but one by one, all of the tainted voidpriests were swept into the yawning gaps, and the openings snapped shut again with a loud crack.

Arita gasped, and Collin still clung to her. They collapsed, shaking, onto the tangled platform high in the trees where the isolationist priests had made their home. Arita didn't understand what she had just experienced, but now she dared to hope they might survive after all. The trees around them thrummed, shaking as if in great pain.

Collin rose to his knees. He touched the worldtree trunk again, as if for reassurance. The wood shuddered. The conjoined trunks that had swallowed the voidpriests now rumbled and spasmed. Alarmed, he grabbed Arita's hand. "Come on, it's not over yet. We're not safe!"

Where the heartwood mouths had snapped shut, a black stain began to spread as if from a fatal dose of poison. More golden bark scales fell off, tinkling down and leaving the wood blotchy, like the skin of a leprous lizard.

"The trees are dying," Collin cried. "We have to climb down."

They scrambled to the fronds and began to drop from one branch to another. The broad fanlike fronds fell off as if being ejected by the worldtrees. Arita and Collin were still high above the ground, and she felt the trees rocking. Loud shattering sounds echoed through the air as parts of the contaminated trunks broke apart in the spreading blackness. Consuming the voidpriests was killing the trees from the heartwood out.

"We've got to make it to the forest floor!" Collin yelled. "These trees sacrificed themselves, but they'll help us for as long as they can."

Taking risks, they jumped down to lower branches, clutching fronds and barely catching themselves in time. Arita had spent much of her youth climbing among the trees, and she remembered those skills now. As a green priest, Collin was in tune with the worldforest, even though the verdani mind was stunned and writhing now.

High above, heavy boughs cracked and broke off, tumbling down to smash through the thickets of dying fronds.

"Faster!" Arita risked a glance upward and saw that the tree trunk, branches, and fronds had all turned black, like pure coal, and the stain was spreading as fast as they could flee. With cracking and crumbling sounds above, more shards of the burned-out worldtree fell all around them.

She and Collin both let go of the last branch, fell the rest of the way to the ground, and tumbled into the underbrush.

"Run!" Collin said.

They bolted away from the thick trunk. The poisoned trees turned dark and each collapsed into a mound of razor-edged crystal shards like fossilized obsidian.

The shards cut their skin, but Arita and Collin got far enough away to check each other for injuries. They were both shocked, but safe now. Arita held him, and they stared at the black scars of shattered worldtree wood.

"Did we kill them?" Collin asked. "Did we cause all that destruction?"

"The trees were dying already," Arita said. "And we would be dead, if we hadn't summoned help. The best thing we can do now is get home and bring the rest of the green priests back here to fight the Onthos."

16

ZHETT KELLUM

The smoke from the departing faeros dissipated in the bright Ildiran sky, and Zhett Kellum shook her head. "A Shana Rei shadow cloud, a robot attack fleet, and a swarm of giant fireballs all in the space of a week. And I thought running a distillery would be a boring career."

Patrick Fitzpatrick slid his arms around her waist. "Don't forget the hydrogues and the shadows that destroyed our skymine on Golgen. That's why we had to go to Kuivahr in the first place."

"You two brought bad luck with you, by damn," said Del Kellum. With his barrel chest and potbelly, he was clearly the stockiest man among the Ildiran crowds in the Foray Plaza.

"I prefer to call it 'circumstances beyond our control,' Dad," Zhett said.

Her son Kristof and baby Rex were also with them. Toff, who had no sense of personal danger, was grinning up at where the faeros had vanished. He shaded his eyes against the dazzling Ildiran sunlight, but the fireballs were long gone. "That was the most amazing thing I've ever seen!"

Zhett raised her eyebrows. "You have a high bar."

"Let's hope the sight lasts you a while, boy," Del said. "We can't afford too many similar adventures."

"We can't afford adventures . . . or anything else," Patrick said. "We lost our skymine on Golgen, we lost the distillery on Kuivahr, and it's not likely we're going to set up new operations any time soon. Who would finance us?"

Del puffed up his chest. "By the Guiding Star, I'm a former Speaker of the Roamer clans! I can find credit. Someone will fund us."

Patrick frowned. "Nobody with any sense, once they look at our string of bad luck."

Zhett interjected, "Not bad luck. Circumstances beyond our control."

Thankfully, most of their distillery crew had escaped the shadows and black robots, fleeing in time, though her heart felt heavy to know that their operations manager, Marius Denva, had not gotten away. He was the last to leave the distillery, for reasons that had made sense to him, but which certainly seemed stupid to her in retrospect. He hadn't made it out before the black shell swallowed the planet. Even those ships that did make it to orbit had a difficult time evading the black robots. Fortunately, the Solar Navy had rounded up Zhett and her family, along with Osira'h and Prince Reynald.

Nearby, Reynald looked weak and sickly, but he kept himself steady. His face was drawn with concern rather than pain as he stared up at the towers of the Prism Palace. He muttered, "Please be all right up there, Osira'h."

Before long, the Mage-Imperator emerged from the arch accompanied by Osira'h, Gale'nh, and Muree'n. All of them looked scorched, their faces red, their hair singed, their clothes crisped. A resounding cheer broke out among the Ildirans, and Zhett found herself grinning.

"I am now convinced the faeros understand the danger of the Shana Rei," the Mage-Imperator announced. "Whether they will help us as they did in ages past . . . I cannot be certain."

"They will help us," Osira'h said, strengthening the crowd with her crystal-clear determination.

Reyn rushed to her. "You're safe!" He embraced her, looking rejuvenated, and she winced with pain from her burns.

"I do not think any place is safe until we defeat the Shana Rei," she said. She took Reynald's hand, addressing her father. "I brought Reyn to Kuivahr so that Tamo'l's research could help him. We still have the viable kelp extracts, but it is not enough. He needs to be back home in the worldforest."

Nira nodded. "The worldforest will share its health and give him strength. I certainly understand that."

"I need your strength even more, Osira'h," Reyn said. "Will you come with me?"

"Of course." She did not even look at her parents for confirmation.

"Let's not be left out of the party," Zhett said to Patrick, urging her family forward. Seeing no point in being shy, she spoke to the Mage-Imperator. "If an Ildiran ship is heading back to the Confederation, could we tag along?"

Mage-Imperator Jora'h looked at the Prince, but his gaze took in the Kellums as well. "We will see that you are returned to your own people."

"We can't pay for passage, though," Del grumbled. "We lost everything when the Shana Rei wrecked Kuivahr."

Jora'h gave a dismissive wave. Zhett knew that economics meant little to the Ildirans. "You helped rescue Osira'h. We will deliver you wherever you wish to go."

Zhett didn't have to consult the others. "Newstation is where we'll most likely find the help we need."

"And where we'll find the rest of our distillery workers," Del said.

"We don't have any money to pay them," Patrick pointed out.

Zhett said, "I'd rather be penniless at Newstation than anywhere else."

CHAPTER

17

GARRISON REEVES

Working in operations at Fireheart Station, Garrison couldn't help but stare at the ominous void in space. The black opening was a stark blot in the nebula sea.

As a Roamer, Garrison had wanted to be part of the Big Ring project, a part of history. He had accomplished what he set out to do. Kotto Okiah had done something spectacular, no question about it, but Garrison wasn't sure that the dimensional wound would lead to a new transgate network, as intended. The thing just seemed . . . dangerous.

Though not a superstitious man, Garrison didn't want to go near that void. None of the Roamers did. At the Iswander extraction fields, he had already seen a Shana Rei shadow cloud: a roiling black nebula emerging from its own doorway in space. This new hole in the universe reminded him too much of that experience. Once was enough.

Kotto would keep studying how safe—or unsafe—the vicinity was, but Garrison didn't want to take any chances. He took it upon himself to deploy danger buoys along a very conservative perimeter. Roamers often made up their own minds, getting cocky and feeling immortal. His perimeter buoys wouldn't prevent any determined pilot from flying too close, but he felt better just for having laid down a warning.

Station Chief Alu rallied his workers and set an ambitious production schedule to bring the complex back to profitability. Many of Fireheart's facilities, laboratories, and packaging habitats had taken a backseat to the Big Ring project, and now it was time to catch up. Alu appointed him a new team leader with increased responsibilities—although Garrison never promised he would stay.

Fireheart Station was like a wonderland for a Roamer, a facility for scrubbing isotopes, developing ionic catalysts, and cooking exotic raw materials in the extreme environment. But Garrison wasn't sure this was where his Guiding Star led him. His thoughts turned more and more often to Orli. . . .

Garrison now led other exosuited Roamers as they reeled out vast sheets of absorptive film to catch the furious stellar wind from the nebula's core. The racks and sheets would take advantage of the photonic bombardment, and when the film was saturated, it would be folded thousands of times and packaged into dense wafers as power blocks. A large power block could serve the energy needs of an entire colony for months.

Bowman Ruskin, his deputy, used a jetpack to maneuver the unwieldy frame. Garrison jetted to the opposite corner to orient it properly. The nebula looked like a turbulent place, but the gases were so thin they barely registered above a vacuum. Even so, maneuvering such a gigantic, delicate structure took great care.

"There we go," Ruskin said when he had stabilized it in place. "Halfway done rebuilding the energy-film farm."

Garrison said, "Chief Alu won't be happy until we start making shipments. We have a lot of ground to make up."

"Stay here another six months, Garrison, and you'll be running the power block division."

"I came out here for the Big Ring."

"You mean, the Big Hole?" Ruskin laughed into his helmet.

"I mean it's hard to be away from my son, who's at Academ and . . . I have other things dividing my attention."

Ruskin chuckled again. "Yes, you told us about her."

No one could see Garrison flush behind his faceplate. "I have to make up my mind about a lot of things, Bowman. Sometimes personal business takes priority over Roamer business."

"It wouldn't if she was a Roamer. There must be plenty of daughters who wouldn't mind marrying the head of clan Reeves." Ruskin paused, realizing what he had said, the reminders he had triggered.

Too many people were expecting Garrison to finish the work of his gruff father, who had wanted to rebuild Rendezvous. Garrison had no interest in it, especially now that Olaf Reeves and all of the self-exiled Roamers had died in deep space. Garrison was independent. He would make his own way, along with Seth—and Orli . . . if she decided to go with him.

After the shift was over, he went back to the habitation module with other workers to play games and watch entertainment loops. Garrison looked at the calendar: only one more day until their month apart was up. He decided to send a message to Seth through the green priests in the terrarium dome.

Before he could jot down his notes, an unexpected ship arrived in the nebula and headed toward the Roamer complex. The inbound cargo vessel carried a load of supplies for Fireheart and asked to pick up any power blocks or outgoing isotope samples.

Garrison recognized the *Voracious Curiosity*, and couldn't stop grinning when he received a message from the admin hub. "Garrison Reeves, you have a visitor."

He didn't even need to ask. He knew exactly who had come.

His reunion with Orli was everything a month apart had prepared them for. He laughed when he saw her face light up upon seeing him. She rushed toward him, overcompensating for the low gravity, and he caught her in his arms. "I thought we still had one more day!"

"I didn't need the extra day," she answered, and kissed him.

He swung her around. It felt so good to hold her again. "Neither did I."

Tasia Tamblyn didn't try to hide the roll of her eyes. Robb said, "We came to see the Big Ring in operation, but it looks like we're too late."

Garrison said, "It was spectacular, but . . . we seem to have damaged the universe."

"If anybody can fix it, Kotto can," Orli said, still holding him. "We've had a few adventures of our own. Taking a month's break from you was a lot more stressful than anything we ever did together."

Garrison listened with seesawing emotions as she told him how his former wife had attacked them when they accidentally found

Iswander's bloater-extraction operations. "Elisa always had a hard edge, but I didn't think she was a killer."

Then he remembered how she had also fired at his ship when he and Seth hid among the first bloaters ever discovered. The resulting explosion had nearly killed him, along with Seth and Elisa. He'd always thought it was an accident . . . but he couldn't be sure she would have held her fire even if she had known how volatile the bloaters were.

"Are you staying here at Fireheart, Garrison?" Orli asked. "I'll stay too if they can find some compy work for me."

"I'd prefer something closer to Seth," he said. Orli's report on Elisa's ruthlessness worried him more than he wanted to admit. "I still have the *Prodigal Son*. I'm not sure exactly where my next job will be, but I am sure I want to be with you."

Orli said, "In that case, when you wrap up your business here, we can figure it out together."

ELISA ENTURI

She couldn't stand it anymore. She no longer felt welcome at the bloater-extraction complex. Iswander's workers continued to drain the floating nodules, filling countless tanks with ekti-X and discarding the shriveled husks. To her eyes, the production crew just seemed to be going through the motions.

Elisa felt like a pariah. She had commanded these people, guided them whenever Iswander was away on business. Because she took her responsibility seriously, she was a far better administrator than Alec Pannebaker, who wanted to be everyone's friend rather than their boss.

The employees revered Iswander. That was why they had trusted him and followed him out to this new business venture after the Sheol debacle. Elisa had always been his most loyal deputy—every Iswander worker knew it. Her actions were driven by his best interests, and although she never asked Lee Iswander for credit or public acknowledgment, her discovery of stardrive fuel inside the bloaters had resurrected his ruined company. She had done it for him.

Now everyone here shunned her. In their eyes she saw the haunted looks, anger, fear, even disgust. Worse, though, was the fact that Iswander himself had cast her aside. That left a sharp wound in her chest. After everything she had done for him . . .

At first Elisa tried to justify it as a cool business decision that made practical sense. He needed a scapegoat, someone to take the blame in order for Iswander Industries to survive. But when he confronted her, she saw the cold reality in his face. He wasn't doing it for pragmatic reasons that he regretted. He was truly throwing her to the wolves, and that hurt more than anything.

At that point, her life had unraveled for her. Even as she watched Pannebaker command the work teams, directing the extraction tankers and the ekti arrays, she knew that Roamer clans were racing across the Spiral Arm to find untapped bloater clusters, which were growing more and more common. Roamers would have little difficulty finding them. Within weeks, dozens more operations could be harvesting stardrive fuel and rushing it to market.

Iswander Industries would fall apart—and it was her fault.

She didn't regret what she had done, because she knew it was necessary—and she knew damn well that Iswander had wanted her to do it. No matter what he said, her mind and heart were perfectly connected to his. But she'd been careless; she left evidence behind and let witnesses escape. If she had been more careful, the bloater operations would not have been exposed. Iswander could have continued to extract and sell ekti-X at great profit for quite some time. And he would have kept her at his side.

Now, though, the Roamer clans had all turned against him. Against *her*.

For a full day after Iswander returned and rebuked her, Elisa stewed, avoiding him. She wrestled with her memories, replaying their earlier discussions about the future of his commercial empire. He had talked about protecting his secrets. From the gleam in his eyes, the hard look on his face, she had *known* what he wanted. She had always been able to read him, and she understood the necessities of business, especially when the stakes were so high.

"By any means necessary"—how else was she supposed to interpret that?

But now he had abandoned her. He pretended he hadn't meant what he so clearly instructed her to do. When someone else broke the highly lucrative Iswander monopoly, had he really planned just to shrug and chuckle, "Oh well, you caught us!" She had tried to protect his empire, his legacy, his fortune.

I will leave you alone so you can consider the consequences. Take all the time you need. Clearly, he meant that he would turn a blind eye if she chose to dash away like some guilty criminal, if she went into hiding and never again showed her face in the Confederation. He had pushed her away and backed her into a corner.

She hated him for that. For her years of service, for her dedication, for spending her every waking hour building his empire, for the pain she had suffered, the blood she had shed . . . The only thing Iswander had offered her in return was the chance to run away. Was that all he thought of her? And he would rescind that offer the moment anyone from the Confederation came looking for her.

Elisa had to leave. She wouldn't even say goodbye, didn't want him to offer her an insincere wish for good luck. Elisa was too angry now, and she doubted she could even look at his face without seeing a betrayer.

She gazed out at the bustling complex. She knew these people, but she was alone in her heart. They had turned their backs on her, shut her out. They saw her as a murderer rather than as their protector. Well, with the imminent collapse of the ekti market, all of these workers would again find themselves without a viable existence. Iswander Industries would fall apart yet again, and this time, Elisa wouldn't be there to save it.

Damn them all. They were on their own.

After Garrison railed about an imminent disaster on Sheol and no one believed him, he had run away with her son—as well as an Iswander ship. She had never forgiven him for that, but now she would steal a ship of her own. Elisa had no qualms. It was the only way she could get away.

She briefly considered taking Iswander's private yacht; it would serve him right if she just took it. But that would be too petty, and Elisa Enturi was not childish. Whether or not Iswander recognized it, she was a professional, and everything she had done was for professional reasons.

She made her way from the admin hub to the docking bay. Most of the craft were small scout pods, never meant for long-range travel. Iswander workers were bound by confidentiality agreements and were not allowed to travel even on furloughs, for fear that they would reveal the company's secrets.

Elisa went straight to the ship she had selected. She discreetly checked its systems, made sure the tanks were filled with stardrive fuel—Iswander's fuel, of course, but she would take it, and he would allow it. She was sure he had even turned off some of the surveillance monitors. He probably thought he was doing her a favor.

Plausible deniability.

Monitoring the shift operations, Elisa watched industrial vessels moving among the bloaters. The nonstop operations here had managed to drain three-quarters of the cluster, but Iswander knew he could always find more. Elisa herself had scouted alternative clusters for when this field was played out. Now, though, she wouldn't be part of it.

She powered up the ship, drained the atmosphere from the launching bay, dropped the atmosphere-containment field, and drifted away from the admin hub—the place she had helped build, the place she had considered her home and headquarters. She filed no flight path, didn't authorize her own departure, but none of the systems locked her out.

Iswander Industries was *hers* in everything but name. Her eyes burned as she flew away, though she refused to believe it was from tears. She blinked several times and focused her vision on the innocuously peaceful bloaters that lumbered across space. Workers swarmed over the huge protoplasm-filled sacks. Drills and pumps drained the fuel—what the mad green priest had called "the blood of the cosmos."

They paid no attention to Elisa. She was sure that back in the control center, Iswander had noticed her departure. He could have transmitted a farewell, or sounded an alarm . . . or begged her to stay. But her comm system remained silent. No one contacted her, no one questioned her.

As she departed, she saw the bloaters sparkle as energy bursts traveled along a line of them in sequence. Everyone on site had experienced the strange flashes, some kind of bloater energy that linked them all together. Knowing the danger, the extraction crews retreated to a safe distance. The sparkles bounced around the dwindling cluster, then settled down again, and the pumping crews went back to work.

Elisa turned her ship about, looking forward instead of back.

In that very first bloater cluster, when she opened fire on Garrison's ship, she had only intended to frighten him. She had realized he was holding their son hostage in his ship, and she was astonished when all the bloaters exploded. She had never meant any harm to come to Seth. For a long time after the explosion she had believed the boy was dead—only to find out that it had been an illusion. Garrison had tricked her somehow. Another betrayal.

When she left her husband and devoted her life to Lee Iswander, she had felt no reservations. When Iswander forced her to choose between chasing after her son and being promoted as his second-in-command, Elisa had never regretted her decision—until now. Maybe she had made the wrong choice. Maybe she had trusted the wrong man.

Or perhaps none of them were trustworthy. She could rely only on herself.

She would go where she wanted, make up her own mind. As she thought of the debris that remained of her life, she needed to hold on to something she could call her own. Something she would not let anyone take from her.

She set the navigation systems and activated the stardrive, heading for the Roamer school at Academ. Where her son was.

19

JESS TAMBLYN

Four new Teacher-model compies came to assist at Academ, and Jess Tamblyn welcomed the help. The compies' instructional programming contained Roamer history and culture, along with scientific techniques, survival skills, and engineering exercises that could help clan children learn to solve problems, both in daily life and in emergencies.

Since joining the Confederation, Roamers no longer needed to live in difficult environments, as they had when they were outlaws. Clans were free to settle on hospitable planets and in space colonies. It was a much easier life for them, but even so, most Roamers were determined to make sure that their children did not lose those hallmark Roamer skills. Olaf Reeves had often said, "A knife loses its edge unless it is sharpened." Jess and Cesca had formed their school here inside a hollowed-out comet so that Roamer children would never forget their heritage.

The thick ice walls were riddled with passages, offices, classrooms, and laboratory vaults. During the construction of Newstation, much of the cometary ice had been excavated for water supplies, and over the years, the school had expanded as more clans sent their children here.

When Cesca greeted the new compies, the small figures responded identically. "We are glad to be here, Cesca Peroni and Jess Tamblyn."

Cesca led them from the hangar grotto, and the compies followed like robotic ducklings behind a new mother. "Our students are broken into seven classes, based on their abilities. We'll supply their educational portfolios so you can download the details and get to know each child. Some come from special circumstances, and some are so smart they can teach me." She laughed. "Our goal is to give each of them what they require."

The Teacher compies nodded in unison, as if she had thoroughly convinced them.

Jess added, "Rendezvous was our original home and government center, which was destroyed by the Earth Defense Forces. But it remains in our memories."

They made their way along the icy passages, past classrooms where students performed low-gravity chemical experiments and highly reactive tests inside shielded chambers. "As part of their studies, they are reproducing some of Kotto Okiah's early work," Cesca explained. The new compies trooped past the rooms while students gawked at them, distracted.

The tunnel walls were covered with opaque polymers alternating with transparent insulating films so the cometary ice could illuminate the passageways. The ice was infused with quiescent wentals, which glowed to light the way.

"The comet walls seem brighter today," Cesca noted.

"Maybe the wentals are restless," Jess said. He could sense something unusual inside his mind. "The energy level is increasing. I think they're becoming more aware." There could be no mistaking it now.

He and Cesca had both been infused with the water elementals during the great war. Since then, the wentals had mostly gone dormant, and at times Jess missed communing with the strange beings.

A few days earlier, however, the wentals had experienced a similar surge that caused them to reach out to Jess and Cesca to share the source of their agitation. A renegade named Tom Rom had attacked the Klikiss transportal outpost on Auridia below. While the Roamers were in an uproar over the destruction of the outpost, the wentals reacted to something else . . . recoiling from a cold shadow that reached through the transportal wall. Tom Rom had severed the connection by destroying the conduit and blocking the flood of darkness. Then, just as quickly as it had begun, Jess and Cesca's brief contact with the wentals faded again.

Jess wondered if the wentals might reach out to touch their minds again today. Just before their group reached the comet's central chamber, they came upon several students gathered at the opening into the great zero-G hollow. Three older Roamer boys—one of them a member of clan Duquesne, Jess noticed—crowded around Arden Iswander, who looked like a younger, thinner version of his father. Right now, he looked defiant and scrappy.

"It's your dad's fault," jeered the Duquesne boy, hanging among his companions. Punches had already been thrown.

Seth Reeves, who was even younger than Arden, launched himself in among the bullies, shoving the threatening young men who closed around Arden. "Leave him alone! You can't blame *him*."

"Arden's father is a murderer, so—" one of the bullies began.

"His father is *his father*," Jess said, startling the boys. "And Arden is his own person. He can only be held responsible for his own actions, not someone else's."

"Well, Seth's mother fired the shots that killed my family and destroyed our operations," the Duquesne boy pointed out. "No wonder they stick together."

"Seth isn't responsible for that either," Cesca answered. "I will not let you blame either of these young men for what their parents did."

Jess interrupted, "Don't you have better things to do? Exercises? Classwork? Or do you all need detention?"

The four new Teacher compies hurried forward. "We would be happy to assist in imposing disciplinary measures. We wish to make a good impression as new teachers."

Cowed for the moment, the bullies bolted into the cavernous chamber where students were doing zero-gravity exercises. Arden and Seth looked shaken. Jess felt compassion for the unlikely friends. "We want you to feel safe at Academ. We'll protect you."

Cesca added, "If you keep being harassed, we'll take strict measures."

Arden and Seth mumbled something, their faces flushed. The two boys also bolted away into the core chamber.

"Is this a daily occurrence?" asked KA, one of the new Teacher compies.

"I don't think so," Jess said, "but we better make sure it doesn't become one."

"Would you four please keep an eye out for problems?" Cesca

asked. The compies assured her with great enthusiasm that they would.

Jess felt the inner tingling again, a pull that grew stronger. Cesca gasped as the comet walls suddenly sparkled and glowed a bright icy blue. The wental light was more intense than ever, and Jess sensed a response from them that he had never experienced before. The wentals felt *afraid*.

20

NIRA

After the faeros had departed, Mijistra quietly fell back into a tense semblance of normal life.

Nira had experienced the threat of the Shana Rei reaching through the *thism* to possess Ildirans, and now she also felt the dark fear and emptiness that permeated the telink network. She had always drawn comfort from the worldtrees and her fellow green priests, but without that solace, she felt very alone.

Just as her son Rod'h must be terribly alone right now, lost among the shadows. Her other children could still sense him, but as a green priest, Nira had a connection to him that was tenuous at best. She ached to think of what he must be suffering. He had been captured while trying to understand the mysterious Onthos.

The Gardeners had told of their distant worldforest, which was obliterated by the Shana Rei in ages past. The recent expedition to the Onthos home system had yielded evidence of those long-dead trees and retrieved specimens of blackened wood. She hoped the petrified fragments would provide some answers. The ancient disaster had so thoroughly obliterated a part of the verdani mind that the worldtrees didn't even remember it. . . .

Nira went to the Prism Palace's laboratory annex, where members of the scientist kith were analyzing the preserved remnants from the Onthos homeworld. After Adar Zan'nh's expedition returned, the worldtree shards were delivered here, and the scientists had set the wooden samples out on a long analysis table.

As a green priest, Nira hoped to unlock some of the data frozen inside the crystallized wood. She didn't know if it would help Rod'h, but because it might add to their information about the shadows, she would do her best. She tentatively touched one of the fragments on display and immediately pulled her fingers back. Even though the fragments had been sitting at room temperature for weeks, the black wood remained cold to the touch.

The lead scientist came over to her. "The fragments remain several degrees lower than the ambient temperature, and we have been unable to determine why. It is one of many mysteries. We have already studied the samples, performed chemical tests and materials analysis, but the results are inconclusive. Our work here is finished. We will submit our final report to Mage-Imperator Jora'h."

"Your methods give only dry scientific answers," Nira said. "Not the sort of insights I can provide."

The scientists backed away to let her continue her inspection. In the bright chamber, Nira stood and studied the drained wood with quiet intensity. The shattered chunks were angular, like crystals made of night, showing the faintest whorls and swirls, like some mysterious code.

Nira remembered, decades ago, when she had tried to make contact with chunks of burned worldtrees taken from Theroc after the fires. Back then, she had been able to tap into hints of the verdani mind, and she had reawakened a spark of life even in those dead ashes. She hoped to do the same with these cold and ancient shards, to learn anything that these verdani cousins had forgotten.

Anton Colicos joined her in the laboratory, curious. He had gone on the expedition to the Onthos system, and now he looked at the black fragments with a chill, as if he did not like the reminder. He shook his head. "Their planet was a nightmare that hadn't woken up yet. I went along to chronicle the expedition, and I barely survived when the shadows attacked us."

Her heart felt heavy. "Were you with my son Rod'h at the end? Did you see him?"

The historian looked awkward. "I was with the Solar Navy battle group, yes, but Rod'h was off in a scout ship studying a dead verdani battleship when he was taken." Anton brightened. "He and I did go together down to the Onthos planet, though. Most of the Ildirans were uneasy about the darkness, but he was very determined and brave. He helped us gather these specimens."

Worried, Nira frowned at him. "Adar Zan'nh is about to go back to Kuivahr. Will you go with him this time?"

The historian shrugged. "The Mage-Imperator asked us to assess what's left there, if anything can be salvaged from the planet. I expect it will be the same as the Onthos planet, everything black, empty, and dead."

Nira felt a heavy chill. "No survivors? It's only been a few days."

Anton just shrugged. "We'll know soon. And I'll be there to record what we learn."

Nira looked closely at him. "Would you please search for any trace of my daughter? No one has heard from Tamo'l or the other misbreed evacuees, but Adar Zan'nh is sure most of them got away."

"We'll certainly look. We've been told that many managed to escape through the Klikiss transportal, so it could take a while for them to make appropriate connections and get back in touch, depending on where they went." He seemed to be trying to reassure her. "I wouldn't give up hope yet. Maybe Tamo'l is already safe."

Nira looked down at the blackened chunks of ancient wood. "Then I'll do my part. Maybe I can learn something, for the sake of Rod'h and Tamo'l."

"We already have our data." A male Ildiran scientist presented her with a crystal sheet filled with dry technical results.

She shook her head. "These tests can't tell you what those ancient trees endured, or what they learned before they perished."

The researcher looked at her, perplexed. "It cannot be learned."

After being the Mage-Imperator's consort for so many years, Nira was accustomed to Ildirans regarding her with a lack of comprehension—no hostility, just a distant separation. "I have to try."

Anton Colicos scolded the scientists. "The problem of the Shana Rei has not been solved. Let her try."

Just as Nira cleared her mind to plunge into the black shard, five attenders rushed in, leading Mage-Imperator Jora'h. A tired darkness hovered around his eyes. She smiled at him, but her heart ached. Since she could not share his pain through the *thism*, the best she could do was to share her love and confidence.

She held her green fingers over the cold lump of dark wood. "I was about to hunt for lingering memories in this Onthos worldtree wood. Your scientist kithmen claim they can learn no more."

The Mage-Imperator looked at his scientists. "Is this true?"

"Yes, Liege." The lead researcher bowed, looking shamed. "There is no more information to be gained from these fragments."

"Then we will let Nira do what she wishes."

Even Nira wasn't certain what she could accomplish. It was quite likely that this wood had been dead and drained for far too long, but what if it *did* hold ancient information? Or maybe the fragments would even let her touch Rod'h's mind . . . or find Tamo'l.

She ran her green fingertips along the sharp surfaces and flinched from the unnatural cold. She sent her thoughts into the wood, reaching out, searching for a link to the verdani mind. The trees would remember.

The cold Onthos wood contained ancient echoes. She felt lost and adrift. Her own thoughts vanished into emptiness rather than being caught in a safety net of interconnected trees and minds. Inside, there was . . . *nothing*.

Not giving up, she went farther into the blackness of an empty mind and she was answered only by the void of a universe before creation. These fragments of alien worldtree wood did not remember. Were they so terrified that every memory had been erased?

Anxious for answers, Nira dug deeper, explored farther, extending a wider web to see if she could sense anything of Rod'h or Tamo'l. The blackness became more absolute, the emptiness more disorienting. She began to feel cold inside, as if the darkness were seeping into her, pushing toward her, trying to empty her mind just as the wood fragments had been emptied.

Nira pulled violently back, feeling a surge of panic. She tore her thoughts away from the quicksand of the worldforest fragments. These were not the trees she knew! Whatever remained of this ancient forest was no longer part of the verdani mind. It was dangerous.

With a gasp, she broke contact and emerged, yanking her hands away from the blackened fragment as if it had stung her. When she reeled, both Jora'h and Anton caught her.

"There is nothing to be learned in there," she said, gasping. "That worldforest is . . . more than dead. I sense nothing but an absolute black emptiness so deep I almost drowned in it." She shuddered.

Jora'h gave orders for the scientist kith to gather up the fragments of blackened wood. "Seal them away, where they cannot contaminate anyone else." He dismissed the attenders and the scientist kith, then held Nira in his arms. She felt his strength, but also his uncertainty.

When they were completely alone, he whispered, "That black emptiness . . . I feel it inside myself as well."

KOTTO OKIAH

The black void inside the nebula both called to him and terrified him. Kotto had always known that innovative science might lead to unexpected and remarkable results—and this gaping hole in the universe was certainly unexpected and remarkable. And possibly dangerous.

Kotto muttered out loud to his two compies, as if they were privy to the silent conversation in his head, "An experiment that breaks the preconceptions of physics is worthwhile in and of itself. Now we just have to figure out what to do with what we've discovered."

"Of course, Kotto Okiah." KR scanned the boundaries of the dark trapdoor, mapping the indistinct lines and tracking the fluctuations. If not for the background pool of ionized gas, the tear would not have been visible at all. "Our studies will surely be beneficial, somehow."

GU added, "We would be happy to help you compile a technical report, Kotto Okiah, but we need more guidance."

"I'm not ready to write a report yet," he said. "We don't have enough answers."

"When will we have the answers?" asked KR.

"When we finish our research."

"When will we finish our research?" asked GU.

Kotto took a long breath. "That depends on what we find on our expedition." He raised his hand to cut off further questioning from the compies. He knew these conversation chains all too well, and if he got sucked into the successive inquiries, he might continue for an hour until the compies exhausted their curiosity. Curiosity was good, but they had work to do.

He finished reconfiguring a dozen different sensor packages. He wanted his survey craft to be completely outfitted, because he had no idea what conditions he might encounter, and once his ship entered that compelling and ominous void, he couldn't just turn around because he had forgotten something.

Down in the admin hub's launching bay, Roamer technicians helped him equip the survey vessel, adding shields and filters just in case. Kotto let them make all the modifications they could think of. KR and GU assisted with the inspections.

Kotto felt butterflies in his stomach. Despite his display of confidence and scientific bravado, he knew this journey would be dangerous. What if he was swallowed up in an alternate universe and never came back? What if his mere passage through the boundary disassembled the survey craft down to its component atoms, including himself?

He doubted that would happen, since they'd sent in initial probes, which had returned intact, although the readings were baffling and contradictory. The mechanical and electronic devices functioned in the void just fine, but Kotto couldn't say how his brain's biochemistry or his psyche might react to the change. On the other hand, the complex probe circuitry remained intact, and wasn't his brain just a sophisticated biological circuit board? It made sense.

He intended to take the two compies along. Even if the strange other dimension incapacitated him, KR and GU should still be able to pilot the ship back. He didn't want to risk anyone else.

Shareen and Howard entered the bay, looking both eager and concerned. Kotto was glad to have them working with him. They seemed more innovative, more mathematically adept than he himself had been in recent years. In fact, their youthful energy, imaginations, and enthusiasm intimidated Kotto, although he was careful not to let them know it.

He hadn't actually wanted lab assistants in the first place, and Shareen and Howard inadvertently reminded him of his own fading talent. For years, he had feared that his ideas were running out, that the great Kotto Okiah had served his purpose and should just rest on his laurels. But he wasn't resting—he was *restless*. He didn't want to retire.

Now, the teens studied his prepped survey craft, noting the modifications, watching the Roamer teams work. Nodding, Howard spoke in his crisp, polite manner. "Sir, Shareen and I wish to voice our concerns about this expedition. There are too many unanswered questions. We should collect more data via probes before letting you travel into the void. It would only be prudent considering the possible risks."

Shareen added, "Failing that, if you won't wait any longer, then Howard and I want to go along. You might need us."

Kotto blinked. "Absolutely not. It's too dangerous."

"Then it's too dangerous for you, sir," Howard said. "Your mind is a treasure for the human race, as you've demonstrated many times. We can't lose you. Let others go explore the other side of that gap."

"If my intellect is such a treasure," Kotto said, "then *I'm* the one who should go. It's possible that no one else would be able to figure out the sensory input and draw the proper conclusions. Maybe I'm the only one who can solve it."

"Now you're just making up answers," Shareen muttered.

"That's what scientists do," Kotto responded, "and then we find the technical basis for those answers. I intend to go into that void and have a look around. It's *my* void. I created it."

He had strung the Roamer clans along for years, convincing them to fund the outrageously extravagant Big Ring project. And because of his track record, the clans had believed in him, accepted his fuzzy explanations and vague promises of practical results. They had done it for *him*, not because of the rigorous scientific basis of his proposal.

And his science, his idea, had torn a hole in the universe.

"You two are staying here," he reiterated to Howard and Shareen, impatient for the discussion to be over. "The compies will come with me. They've been perfectly good research assistants for many years, long before you joined me."

"And we will continue to do our best," KR piped up.

"Howard and I came here to help you with your research," Shareen said. "We want to be explorers. Let us go with you."

"Maybe we could provide insights, sir," Howard added. "We've proven our worth at that, haven't we?"

Kotto didn't want to admit he was afraid of just that. This was his expedition and his risk. "Think about it. I need you two to stay here and monitor whatever telemetry I manage to transmit back out. What if I need rescue? Who else could I count on?"

Shareen grumbled, "You *would* have to offer the one compelling argument that would convince us."

"Besides, you still have my other projects to work on, prototypes to finish. You've done so well on my earlier designs—" He suddenly brightened. "Wait, isn't your priority working with the green priests? I asked you to find a way to transfer those giant worldtrees before the terrarium dome shatters . . . and from the looks of it, that could be within weeks or days." He nodded to himself. "Yes, I think that's an excellent use of your time."

Howard frowned. "We've been working on it, sir. We did structural tests and mapped possible routes for moving the greenhouse."

Shareen cut in. "The dome is sturdy—it's a Roamer structure, after all. But due to the energy requirements, time, and stresses incurred on the terrarium structure, it's not feasible to move it into a gravity well to replant the trees, and the dome was never built to withstand being accelerated by an Ildiran stardrive."

"And even if we could accelerate it to a habitable system," Howard said, "the terrarium would not survive the stresses of the dust boundary at the edge of the nebula."

"We also looked for a way to encapsulate the trees and transport them individually, but the process might be dangerous to the trees."

Kotto blinked as an idea occurred to him. The concept was fresh and exciting—he remembered the days when new ideas like this had occurred to him regularly. He brightened. "Why not build a bigger dome?"

"A bigger dome?" Shareen asked, frowning.

"Out in the middle of—?" Howard added.

"Of course. Have engineers build out the base of the current greenhouse, extend the support structures, then create another hemisphere over the top of the old one. Once it's sealed, dismantle the inner shell and give those trees some breathing room. It would buy them some time at least." Kotto rubbed his hands together. "Yes, that could work."

"But we don't have much time," Howard said. "It would take months."

"Not for Roamers," Shareen said. She wore a hopeful look as calculations seemed to click in her mind. She started talking faster. "You and I would have to start on the design right away, Howard. If we pulled the teams together and got Chief Alu to sign off on the resources we need, they could get it done in three or four weeks."

"There you go—your Guiding Star," Kotto said. "Keep yourselves busy while I'm gone."

A Roamer tech crawled out of the engine vault at the rear of the survey craft and called, "Aft sensor array is complete, Kotto. Do you want to check it?"

He gave a confident wave. "I trust your work." He turned back to his assistants. "Well, now that you have my idea, go implement the plan. You're pretty good at that."

"Yes, sir."

Raising his chin in a display of bravado, he said, "I'm going into the void, and that's that. We'll launch as soon as the survey craft is ready."

Shareen hesitated. "But if the void is a different dimension . . . what if the Shana Rei live there? What if you fly straight into one of their shadow clouds?"

"Well, then, we will see what we will see."

He tried to sound cheerful and optimistic, dismissive of the perils, but his voice cracked at the end, and his throat went dry. He touched the shoulders of his two compies. "Come on, KR and GU. Let's get ready for our adventure."

22

PRINCE REYN

Being with Osira'h had always given him energy and hope, but Reyn received an entirely different kind of strength when he returned to Theroc. Reyn was not a green priest, yet the energy of life, the energy of his *home* came to him regardless. As he stepped out of the shuttle, he inhaled the verdant scents of sun-warmed fronds, the pollens of epiphytes and sweet blossoms that wound among the worldtrees. He stretched out his arms on the canopy landing field. Reyn just closed his eyes and drank it in. Osira'h took his hand, and he could hear the smile in her voice. "The color has come back to your face."

He was home, and he was safe . . . for the most part.

Unfortunately, his relief was all too transient. With a malicious suddenness, a dark fog at the edges of his vision made him sway, and cramped signals of pain crackled throughout his nerves. Osira'h caught him, held him, before his knees could buckle.

Coming to him with a large reception committee, King Peter and Queen Estarra ran forward, their faces distraught. Reyn leaned on Osira'h and locked his knees so he remained standing straight. "I'm fine," he insisted. The strain in his voice belied his words.

"We brought the last kelp extracts from Kuivahr," Osira'h said, partly to Reyn and partly to the King and Queen. "They help a little, but we're starting to run short."

"Kuivahr is gone," Reyn said. "There won't be any more kelp extracts."

"Then we'll synthesize the best ones," Peter said, wrapping an arm around his shoulders and giving him a hug. "If there's a way, we'll manufacture a treatment."

Reyn wasn't so sure. "The kelp is extinct."

"We'll still try," his mother said, giving him a longer embrace to welcome him home. "We'll always try. With all the pharmaceutical operations in the Confederation, someone should be able to replicate it."

Though his legs trembled, and he felt frail and weak, Reyn insisted he was strong enough to walk. He hated to look like this in front of his parents; it wasn't the homecoming he wanted to have.

"The worldforest will help restore him," Osira'h said, taking charge. "The disease has drained him, and he needs to rest."

They took him back to his familiar quarters in the fungus-reef city. Reyn looked around his room, smiling at his bed, his belongings on shelves, his writing desk, the view out the window. It felt good just to be here.

His father gave him an optimistic report. "Zoe Alakis delivered a lot of raw data about your disease, and teams of Confederation researchers have been combing through it. Our studies have advanced ten times farther than they were a month ago."

"But is there a cure?" Osira'h asked.

"Progress," Estarra said firmly. "Progress that could lead to a cure."

Osira'h wasn't entirely reassured. "Maybe your researchers can combine their work with an analysis of the most effective kelp extracts."

Peter nodded. "The extracts, along with our recent progress, give us good reason to hope. And Reyn is home now, which will help, too. We should let him rest."

The King and Queen turned to leave, trying to shoo Osira'h out the door with them, but Reyn gave a wan smile. "It's all right. I'd rather Osira'h stayed here with me."

For all their concern over his health, his mother flashed a surprised smile at him, and his father grinned. "As requests go, that's a fairly simple one to grant," Peter said, and they left.

Reyn relaxed on his bed. The open windows of his chamber let in the sounds of the forest: the ratcheting buzz of a pair of condorflies in an aerial mating dance, the chatter of green combat beetles in blustering collisions in the sky. The familiar forest noises seemed so peaceful they almost lulled Reyn into a belief that the Spiral Arm was at peace, with no Shana Rei or black robots or faeros . . . a place with only fond memories and the company of beautiful Osira'h.

That illusion was false, but he clung to it nonetheless.

Osira'h rummaged in her possessions, unfurled an insulated carrier pack that held the carefully labeled sample vials. Shawn Fennis had insisted on giving them the rest of the kelp extracts when they evacuated from Kuivahr. She held out a nearly empty vial of brownish-green fluid. "We have only two doses of the one that worked best. Do you want to save it for a different time?"

Reyn shook his head. "Right now I want to feel strong—for my parents' sake if nothing else. We'll use the proven sample." He placed the vial against his triceps, and the self-injector applied the dose. From experience, he knew it would take an hour before he felt partially recovered again, and the benefits would last a day, maybe less. "Save the last dose for analysis. Maybe some Confederation chemists can synthesize more."

In shelf alcoves in the bedchamber's soft white walls, Reyn saw a piece of vine-strand artwork he had done when he was a boy, decorative polished burl nodules, a preserved insect cocoon, and a pair of gloves he had often worn when climbing the outer shell of the fungus reef.

His sister had always collected biological specimens: interesting beetles, moths, fluffy spore clusters, seeds. Arita planned to gather the entire worldforest, one species at a time. She was endlessly fascinated with nature and had tried to interest him as well, eager to show Reynald a mobile fungus or a spiny arachnid she had discovered. She knew early on that she wanted to be a naturalist, and he remembered how devastated she had been when she failed to be accepted as a green priest. She had tried to hide her sadness, but Reyn sensed it. He had comforted her and helped shore up her determination.

Now, he reminisced aloud for Osira'h. "When we were young, my sister and I would go out in the forest and climb the trees. She was better at it than I was, but I kept up with her." He lay back on his bed and looked at the curved white ceiling. "Remembering that makes me realize just how much I've slipped. I could never climb out there now. Day by day, I'm growing worse by degrees, and if I think about how I was then . . ."

He shook his head and felt discouraged all over again. He supposed Arita was off on some expedition. She often went to the Wild to gather new specimens for the vast naturalist encyclopedia of Theroc she dreamed of compiling.

Restless, he climbed out of bed and went to his wardrobe, where he removed his shoulder cape of overlapping preserved moth wings, one of the garments he wore as the son of Father Peter and Mother Estarra for performing local duties. "I don't need to rest. Let's go to the throne room. I want to be there."

Osira'h smiled at the fine exotic cape. "All right. It might be good for you."

When they reached the large decorated chamber, Reyn saw Confederation representatives, traders from other planets, government delegates, CDF officers, and green priests. Peter and Estarra sat in ornate chairs decorated with crushed beetle carapaces.

Admiral Handies was presenting a report, and when Reyn and Osira'h entered, the military officer looked flustered to have his well-practiced speech derailed. Reyn minimized the disruption by taking a guest seat at the side of the dais. "Continue please, Admiral. I want to listen in, so I can get caught up."

Handies cleared his throat. "I was discussing the black shadow clouds that our sensors have detected. Patrol ships report greater numbers of them appearing in open space. General Keah just went to investigate one seen near Relleker. Those shadow clouds are likely incursions by the Shana Rei, and we must be prepared for them."

Peter responded in a brisk voice. "How do you propose that we prepare, Admiral? What can we do beyond what we're doing now? If you have new suggestions, we need to get started."

Handies seemed flustered. "I wish I had a better answer for you, sire. All of our Mantas and Juggernauts are loaded with enhanced sun bombs, but we don't know where the Shana Rei will strike. Adar Zan'nh reports that the Solar Navy succeeded in eradicating all the black robots at Kuivahr, so they should no longer be a threat. If true, that significantly improves our defensive position."

"And the shipyards at the LOC are building new warships?" Peter asked. "Repairing the damaged ones?"

Handies glanced at his notes. "Yes, sire. As swiftly as possible. We are constructing and repairing at a pace not seen since since the height of the Elemental War. General Keah is quite a taskmaster."

"Yes," said Estarra. "It's one of the many reasons she commands the Confederation Defense Forces. Let's hope that we're prepared enough when we need to be."

After the Admiral departed, Reyn looked around the throne room, disappointed that his sister's chair remained empty. "Where is Arita? Off on another research trip?"

Estarra's forehead knitted in concern. "She and Collin left for the Wild several days ago, and they were very worried. They'd lost touch with Kennebar and his followers, and even our green priests weren't quite sure of the situation over there. Your sister and Collin went to investigate."

Peter frowned. "We haven't heard anything yet. Collin should have sent a message back through telink by now."

Reyn tried to sound confident. "Arita can take care of herself. She always has." But he felt uneasiness grow inside him.

CHAPTER

23

ARITA

They left the shattered black worldtrees behind and ran through the underbrush toward Arita's personal flyer that had brought them to the Wild.

Collin stumbled along. Now that they had escaped the voidpriests and the murderous Onthos, the reality of what Kennebar had done was catching up with him, and they were both in shock. Breathing hard, he said, "I don't know if any other green priests heard me when I called out through telink. I didn't feel anyone else inside there. The verdani mind in the Wild has been cut off, partitioned somehow. The trees aren't aware of what they've forgotten and what they're not seeing. Back at home, the green priests don't even notice."

"We'll tell everyone when we get there," Arita said. "I still don't know how to explain the . . . *immense* voice I felt when I was most desperate. It certainly wasn't the verdani."

They hurried to the aircraft. Arita feared that the rest of the Onthos—and there must be many more—would come hunting for them. They sensed the oppressive silence of the trees, as if the world-forest were either slumbering or unconscious, having expended all its energy to overthrow the voidpriests. Right now, the forest felt dangerous and threatening again, the close massive trunks pressing in. Having grown up on Theroc, Arita had danced through thickets all her life, dodged shrubs and vines, but now the forest seemed to be hindering them, intentionally. Even Collin struggled, and a green priest usually slipped like a summer breeze through the densest underbrush.

She let out a sigh of relief when they found the flyer in an open meadow. Exhausted, their bodies aching, they ran toward the craft. Even without telink, they could use the aircraft's comm system to announce the emergency, and when they returned home, Collin would tell the green priests the full extent of what was happening in the Wild.

With long-delayed dismay, Arita recalled something Kennebar had said. "We can't go back just yet. We have to stop by Sarein's dwelling first. If the Gardeners attacked her, she may need our help. And if they killed her . . ."

She activated the engines, expecting that at any second the trees or the Onthos would find some way to prevent their departure. But the craft rose unhindered above the meadow and skimmed over the treetops.

Beside her, Collin continued to heave large breaths, holding his head in his hands. After a minute, he straightened and explained to her what he had seen deep inside the trees. "Now I understand what's really happening. Thousands of years ago, the Shana Rei did wipe out the Onthos home system and killed part of the worldforest. Some of the Gardeners got away—but they carried a . . . spark of dark." He looked over at her as she flew. "And when the refugees came here, our worldforest didn't notice it. We welcomed the Onthos, but now they're spreading their blight and killing the trees. We have to stop them."

"How can there be so many?" Arita asked. "Only a hundred landed."

"Based on their relationship with the trees, we thought they were symbiotes, but they have become *parasites*. They use the trees, infest them. That's how they reproduce like spores—dozens of Onthos created from each worldtree—and that process kills the tree. The shadows destroyed their original grove of worldtrees back on their home planet. That's why the verdani mind has no memory of it, and now the same memory loss is spreading here."

Arita was horrified. "But if they always reproduce like that, how could the worldforest not know about it?"

"Normally there was a balance in the ecosystem. It started as a symbiotic relationship. Only older or damaged trees were used as incubators—that was how the Gardeners were born. Trees did die in the process, but the Gardeners tended the forest in exchange and the trees flourished. Because of the Shana Rei, though, the Onthos are nearly extinct, and they're desperate. They're now breeding far faster than the forest can sustain."

"They've got to be aware of the damage they're causing," Arita said, feeling the anger again. "They know damn well what they're doing. That's why they tried to kill us."

She landed their flyer in a small clearing near Sarein's isolated home, the hiveworm-nest dwelling where she lived as a hermit. As they climbed into the dry, silent structure, Arita called out repeatedly, holding out hope that her aunt would step onto the open balcony to scold them for causing such a ruckus.

But the place remained silent, as ominous as the too-quiet world-forest.

"I don't think she's here," Collin said.

Arita insisted on searching the dwelling for clues. Sarein's chambers were full of shadows and the beginnings of dust. Some cooking implements were still out, and the bed was unmade, as if she had disregarded any chance that anyone would visit. A cup of cold klee sat on a counter.

Sarein had been working on memoirs that chronicled her own activities and some sad crimes, back in the final days of the Terran Hanseatic League. She had told Arita she wanted to preserve an accurate history, without excuses. The bound, physical journals rested on a shelf, with a half-finished one still open on the table. Sarein had written some of her memories by hand because it served a cathartic purpose. The journals seemed so archaic, yet so appropriate. Arita picked one up, flipped the pages, then closed it. Tears pooled in her eyes.

"She's not here," Arita said. "Kennebar must have been telling the truth." She remained quiet for a long moment, not sure what to do, hoping like a naïve little girl that Sarein would simply return from an expedition of gathering food in the forest. But they both knew that wasn't going to happen.

Sarein was gone.

The Onthos had killed her.

She had been all alone here, with no one to hear her call for help, no one to be with her. Sarein was gone. . . .

Collin waited patiently, not pressuring her, but Arita realized they needed to go. The worldforest itself was at stake.

Before she left the empty nest dwelling, however, Arita gathered all the volumes of Sarein's writings. Her aunt had set them down as a kind of confessional, and they were historically important. Arita slid them into a satchel that Sarein kept near her shelves and slung the satchel over her shoulder. Once they got back to the fungus-reef city, she would make sure that her mother, Anton Colicos, and any interested historian would have access to them.

It was the best way to remember Sarein.

ADAR ZAN'NH

The septa of warliners arrived in the Kuivahr system, where Adar
Zan'nh expected to find nothing but a graveyard. He remembered full
well what he had left behind here after the battle with the Shana Rei.

His warliners spread throughout the system, all defenses alert,
scanning for any evidence of the ominous shadow clouds. The
Ildiran crew were uneasy, not because of something they sensed, but
because of what they knew.

Anton Colicos waited in the command nucleus next to the Adar.
Tal Gale'nh had been assigned to lead another warliner on the expedition. Now he transmitted from his own command nucleus,
"Sensors indicate significant debris in the vicinity, Adar. It may be
worthwhile to analyze the black robot ships that we managed to
destroy."

"If the sun bombs left anything worth studying," Zan'nh said,
but gave his permission for the scouts to retrieve any wreckage.
Fortunately, the space battle had completely eradicated the black
robots, so that enemy would no longer pose any threat. "Approach
Kuivahr."

One of the technicians frowned, the lobes on his face flushing
with consternation. "Nothing appears on our sensors, Adar. The
planet is gone."

"It is there," Zan'nh insisted. "But you might not be able to see it."

With careful study, the warliners located the black sphere that
had only recently been a vibrant ocean planet. Now it was a polished black ball, encased in a shell that allowed no light whatsoever,
in or out.

"We will have to break through," Zan'nh said. "I do not expect to find survivors but we may still learn something."

The seven warliners went into orbit around the black world, cruising over the shell of interlocking hexagonal plates. Just like the vastly larger barricade that had enclosed the entire Onthos system.

With a laser-cannon barrage, the Solar Navy ships targeted the vertices of the hexagonal plates. Back at the Onthos system, they had discovered the precise energy and impact point that could break the plates apart. Now the warliners hammered away at the opaque shell, and finally the hexagonal plates shuddered and broke apart like a disintegrating mosaic. Black pieces spilled into empty orbital space and drifted aimlessly; some plates remained intact while others evaporated into clots of nothingness and dark energy.

With part of the shell blasted open, the seven ships hovered at the opening.

Rememberer Anton pointed out, "It's only been a week since the shell was completed. Even if all sunlight was cut off, some of the deep ocean species might have survived, maybe plankton or dormant spores drifting in the waters. Do you think the oceans are frozen over?"

"If that was all that happened, something may have survived," Zan'nh said. "But I believe the Shana Rei darkness represents a complete absence of life as well as light."

Using caution, the Adar dispatched automated probes ahead into the darkness. As the deployed probes streaked toward the planet's surface, they shone inspection blazers down on the smooth surface of black water, but they found no sign of life, light, or movement whatsoever.

"Tamo'l is not there, but I know she is still alive," Gale'nh said. In his image on the screen, he seemed deep in thought. "It makes me glad. At least the shadows do not have her as they have Rod'h."

After the warliners blasted away an even larger equatorial swath of the hex plates, creating an obvious escape path, Zan'nh guided his flagship inside, followed by the other six warliners. The ships' combined running lights illuminated the inky nothingness ahead of them, and the interior blazers brightened to reassure them. They flew low over the oceans; there were no weather patterns, no tides, no waves. The darkness was absolute—not just an absence of light, but an absence of all things living.

Adar Zan'nh stood at the command rail, staring at the screens. He breathed slowly, focusing on their mission. Even knowing what he expected to find, he was struck by the hopeless emptiness, the black *erasure* of all that had been Kuivahr.

The warliners located thready remnants of what had been enormous kelp rafts in the oceans, now decayed and disintegrating. And then, using stored coordinates, they reached Tamo'l's sanctuary domes, which until recently had risen like blisters out of the water. They had been a safe place for the surviving misbreeds, but those domes had collapsed. The structures appeared to be thousands of years old, although only seven days had passed.

The Ildiran crew just stared. Anton Colicos took more notes. "It's as if chaos itself is reclaiming the planet."

On their expedition to the Onthos home system, when he and General Keah had breached the black outer shell and explored the smothered solar system, they knew that millennia had passed. Kuivahr, however, had been englobed only days earlier. There should have been hope. Zan'nh shook his head.

Rememberer Anton said, "There's no one alive and waiting for rescue, that's for sure."

Gale'nh said over the comm, "I wish Tamo'l had evacuated with us, but they must have made it through the Klikiss transportal."

"We will continue our survey," Zan'nh said. "We have come all this way. We will be thorough for the Mage-Imperator."

Finally, they reached the towers of the abandoned Kellum distillery, where the structures creaked and crumbled, the girders collapsing, the distillery platforms tumbling into the reefs.

Tal Gale'nh's warliner arrived first and circled slowly overhead to take images of the ruins. His voice sounded startled. "Adar, there is a ship down there—a small shielded craft. I am detecting a very faint energy signature."

The command nucleus fell into an immediate hushed silence. "How can that be?" Zan'nh asked.

Rememberer Anton looked intently at the Adar, struggling

to maintain optimism. "That's what we're here to investigate. We should have a look."

The rest of the warliners converged above the collapsing distillery towers, and under enhanced magnification, Zan'nh made out a small craft resting askew in the mudflats against the foundation reefs. Dazzling blazers from the warliners shone down to illuminate the derelict craft. Its hull looked corroded, darkened. Judging from the collapsed platform above, Zan'nh guessed that the vessel had landed on the distillery's deck, which had since crumbled, dumping the ship into the soft mud.

"The energy signature is barely detectable, Adar," said one of his sensor techs. "Not much more than one functional power block. If the rest of this world weren't so completely dead, I doubt we would have detected it."

Anton sounded excited. "Someone must have been trapped, unable to get away before the black shell was finished. The ship is small enough for us to bring aboard the warliner, isn't it? Can we retrieve the whole thing intact?"

Zan'nh nodded. "It is a personal craft. We can easily bring it into our landing bay. We will want the ship's log, if nothing else."

Anton licked his lower lip. "That would be a record we've never had before—an eyewitness account."

The Adar's flagship descended gently with its lower launching bay open. A tractor beam and secondary cables attached to the small derelict ship and uprooted it from the mud. As the craft was lifted into the air, however, it began to lose structural integrity. Obvious cracks in the hull split open. Wisps of atmosphere vented out.

"The ship is disintegrating," Anton said.

"Quickly," Zan'nh barked to his crew. "Whatever is inside will not remain intact for long." Extending shields to encompass the craft and taking intense care, the Ildirans lifted the derelict ship up into the warliner's lower hold.

Zan'nh and the historian hurried together down to the bay. "If nothing else," Anton said, "we'll find out who the pilot was and give him a proper memorial."

The retrieved Kellum ship rested on the bay deck, sagging under the weight of its decay. Hull plates slipped off and clattered to the deck, and the ship groaned as it settled.

Solar Navy engineers gathered around the vessel, taking readings but keeping their distance. Traceries of frost ran along the hull. Rememberer Anton put his hands on his hips and stepped forward. "We need to get inside."

The structural braces groaned, and part of the roof collapsed into the interior. Two engineers stepped up to the opening. When they tried to activate the main hatch, it simply fell off. The engineers lifted it aside.

"It is not safe," Zan'nh said.

One of the engineers studied readings from his scanner screen. "There is an energy signature inside, Adar, the last flickers of a power block . . . and a life sign."

"Someone's alive in there?" Anton pushed to the lopsided opening of the craft.

"Very low level," the engineer replied.

"Well, there won't be any life sign if this ship collapses around whoever it is." The historian turned to the nearest Ildiran engineer. "Come on, help me."

"You do not—" said the engineer.

The Adar snapped, "Do as he says. If there is someone to be saved . . ."

The ship continued to fall apart as the historian and Ildiran engineer ducked inside. Adar Zan'nh waited, quelling his worry so the others would not sense it through the *thism*. He swallowed hard, glanced at the other tense crewmembers. He heard movement inside the craft, then Anton's shout. "It's a survivor!"

"We are retrieving one human male," called the Ildiran engineer. "Please send for medical kith."

Moments later, the two carried out a limp, pale form—an unconscious dark-haired man in his late forties. "He powered everything down, wrapped himself in insulating blankets," said Anton. "Based on the medical kits out on the table, it looks as if he took a sustained dose of tranquilizers."

"He was trying to extend his resources, to last as long as possible," said Zan'nh. "A very resourceful man."

"A Roamer," said Anton. "I'm sure of it."

The medical technicians quickly brought their diagnostics. "He is cold, his metabolism at a bare minimum, but there is still brain activity." The lead doctor looked up. "This is most unexpected."

"It is indeed," said Adar Zan'nh. "Let us warm him, give him stimulants and nourishment—and we will see what he has to say."

The salvaged craft groaned, and its hull sagged further. Rememberer Anton wiped perspiration from his brow. "I suggest you send someone to retrieve the ship's log before it's too late, Adar."

The survivor's name was Marius Denva, facility chief of the Kellum distillery. Despite being terrified and constantly chilled, he was unharmed.

Adar Zan'nh stood at Denva's bedside in the medical bay with the human historian. Anton nodded to the food tray at the bedside. "The ordeal doesn't seem to have affected your appetite."

"Not at all," said Denva. "I've got time to make up for. It seemed like I was trapped aboard there for a hundred years."

"Seven days," said the Adar.

By now they had reviewed his log. Some of the files were corrupted, the audio filled with static, but Anton had been able to gather the gist of what the survivor had been through.

"The last of the Kellum ships got into orbit," said Denva, propping himself up in the sickbay bed. "I had only my small craft, couldn't carry any refugees, didn't even make it to orbit. I was stupidly protective of our operations. Guess I stayed too long."

He shook his head, then took a slow slurp of the hot broth in front of him. He shivered, pulled the blankets closer around him. "I can't believe how fast the shadows assembled that shell. I saw the sky dwindling, the mosaic building up piece by piece. I raced to the opening, but my ship wasn't fast enough. I watched the gap close in front of me, and then the whole planet was sealed off.

"I knew I was the last one at the distillery, so I flew to the sanctuary domes, but the Ildirans had evacuated, too. Most of them escaped through the Klikiss transportal, I think. No one answered my signal. The entire world was dark, the comm bands totally silent.

"I had only one chance to get away, so I raced to the Klikiss transportal." He leaned forward, looked up at Zan'nh with an intense and astonished expression. "Even that didn't work. The transportal was cut off. I couldn't get away. The darkness was strangling everything."

His eyes took on a faraway look. "It wasn't just emptiness—I've been out in deep space before. This was something different. The darkness was tangible and threatening. I'm not a little kid to be afraid of the dark." He swallowed hard. "But I was afraid of this."

"Now you understand how all Ildirans feel in complete darkness," Zan'nh said.

"I didn't think I'd ever get away," Denva said. "I flew back to the distillery again, figuring I may as well go home. I landed my ship on the deck, locked down all my systems, ate my fill of the supplies I had on board." His voice cracked. "I made sure my log was in order, and I increased shields, hoping they might help the ship last just a little longer.

"I combined all the power blocks I had left, buried myself under emergency blankets, and hooked up the slow-release tranquilizer. By my calculations, I figured I could last for a month, maybe six weeks. I'm sure glad you came when you did."

Zan'nh said, "We arrived in seven days."

Denva let out a nervous laugh. "A week? Did you see the condition of my ship?"

"Seven days," Rememberer Anton repeated.

Denva gulped the rest of his broth. "Then I'm doubly glad you got to me when you did." He looked up. "What about Del Kellum and the rest of the crew from the distillery? Did they get out?"

"They are safe," Zan'nh said. "We retrieved them."

"We'll take you back to them," said Anton Colicos.

Denva let out a long sigh. He seemed very weary, but his lips formed a wry smile. "Del Kellum will put me right back to work . . . in whatever new business he's come up with."

The Adar turned to leave the sickbay. "We have finished our mission on Kuivahr. We will return you to your people."

25

EXXOS

More and more black clouds appeared across the Spiral Arm as the Shana Rei broke through the walls of space, forming doorways through which they could slide their enormous hexagonal ships. The stain of darkness spread as if seeping through holes poked through the structure of the universe.

Exxos monitored the incursions of the creatures of darkness—like a thousand cuts torturing and killing the cosmos. The process would eventually lead to the obliteration of the human race, the Ildiran Empire, and the cacophony of sentient thoughts that caused the shadows such agony.

In this particular circumstance the robots' plans aligned with those of the Shana Rei, but Exxos never forgot his own priorities. Once the universe itself was erased, the shadows had promised to grant the black robots their own pocket universe that they could manage as they wished.

Exxos didn't trust the Shana Rei—he never had—and always remained alert for ways to manipulate them. Even though the shadows were incomprehensible and quite likely insane, they did not suspect treachery. And now they had created a million new robots with which Exxos could fight. Yes, that would be sufficient.

A tear opened in the back passageways of the universe, and a new shadow cloud spilled through like inky blood. It was time to attack again, and the robots would have free rein. Carried along in the gush of night, Exxos rallied his identical companions in countless battleships. The robot fleet boiled out, like infuriated stinging insects from a thousand disturbed nests.

The Ildiran colony of Wythira did not stand a chance. . . .

He and his million identical minds were exhilarated now, their thoughts synchronized, their goals in lockstep. Not long ago after the flood of sun bombs, Exxos had despaired, one of only three remaining original copies of himself. The black robots had naïvely felt invincible when facing their enemy at Kuivahr, but nearly *all* the rest had been eradicated by the Solar Navy weapons. All but three. Everything was ended, a complete failure.

But that all changed when the Shana Rei agreed to use the dark material they had created in millennia past, reusing those molecules to construct a new force of black robots, more than had existed during the height of the Klikiss swarm wars. Exxos had been surprised at how easily the shadows agreed to the task, and it opened up many new possibilities. He pressed them wherever possible.

With the near-limitless raw material from the black shell around the Onthos system, the Shana Rei had reconfigured that matter into not only all the duplicate robots but also thousands of well-armored warships. Exxos had the tools he needed to dismantle every conceivable enemy.

The Shana Rei's goal of obliterating all sentient life, then all star systems, and then the cosmos itself was magnificent, and Exxos looked forward to getting on with the project. But because the Shana Rei were chaos incarnate, they had no comprehension of plans; they could not build schemes extending from one end of the universe to the other. So, the robots handled that for them. . . .

When the angular black ships stormed in over Wythira, the Ildiran splinter colony throbbed with life. Although the robots could not sense *thism*, the Shana Rei felt it like hot razor wires. The robots would do their duty and erase that gnawing pain, not because he felt sorry for the chaotic creatures, but because it made the Shana Rei more manageable. And destroying Wythira would be a fine start toward avenging all the black robots the Solar Navy had destroyed at Kuivahr. He expected this attack to be enjoyable as well as efficient.

Seven bristling warliners orbited the Ildiran planet, a guardian patrol to protect the colonists against attacks from space. Seven. Ridiculously insignificant against thousands of robot battleships.

The emergence of the shadow cloud gave the Solar Navy enough warning to prepare their warliners . . . just enough time for them to know they would be annihilated. And when the helpless Ildiran colonists saw the multitude of enemies, they too would realize they were soon to be erased from existence.

From the lead warliner an Ildiran commander sent an urgent transmission. "I am Septar Dre'nh, assigned Solar Navy protector of Wythira. You will not harm these people."

His ornate Ildiran ships regrouped, sounding battle stations. Their solar-sail fins were extended, their weapons banks activated and hot. The septar's posturing was an absurd defense against so many robot battleships, but the Ildirans remained defiant. The Solar Navy warliners drove forward, minuscule attackers against an overwhelming wave. Their laser cannons slashed into the angular vessels, annihilating four of Exxos's identical counterparts. It didn't matter. Now that Exxos knew how to convince them, the Shana Rei could always create more.

Behind them, gigantic black hex cylinders slid out of the shadow cloud like blunt spears, rattling the Wythira system with disruptive bursts of entropy that caused technology to fail. Blurred waves like chaotic heartbeats rippled out, and glimmering city lights from the nightside of Wythira flickered out. Entire power grids died. It was just the beginning of the darkness about to fall on that planet.

Septar Dre'nh's warliners charged, reckless and suicidal. What other choice did they have? The robot ships opened fire, taking shots at the Ildiran vessels that careened toward them. Exxos did not bother to issue threats or communicate with the septar in any way. Thinking as one, the black robots decided to wipe them out like gnats while the shadows began the full-scale eradication of life on the planet.

Septar Dre'nh seemed to sense his imminent destruction. The seven attacking warliners launched a spray of glowing spheres that crackled and swelled as their plasma cores ignited. More than fifty sun bombs spread into the approaching cluster of tens of thousands of robot ships.

Exxos did feel alarm then. All robot vessels launched simultaneous retaliatory fire, and their blasts ripped the warliners apart. Within seconds, the septa was nothing more than spreading slag and debris.

The fifty sun bombs detonated. Wave after wave of small novas branched outward in combined shock waves. The rolling blast carved swaths of devastation among the robots, and many Exxos counterparts died in a flash. The expanding shock wave vaporized nearly two hundred black ships. Some of the outer detonations even gouged a divot in the black material of a Shana Rei hex cylinder that pushed closer to Wythira.

Countless sets of Exxos mental processors and optical sensors vanished as the nova waves flared, but once the energy dissipated, thousands of black robot ships remained. Undeterred by the setback, they rushed forward to the hapless planet. Exxos was angry.

This splinter colony had no interesting halfbreeds for the Shana Rei to capture and analyze, like Rod'h. The shadows would not waste energy building up a black shell to englobe Wythira. It was not worth the effort. Those Ildirans down there—loud sentient minds that hurt the Shana Rei simply by existing—they were all just victims. The remaining black robot ships would devastate the surface until no living thing remained.

Exxos guided his thousands of attackers as they swooped down and opened fire. It wouldn't take long, but Exxos would invest whatever time was necessary. Then they could move on to another world . . . a human world next time.

He was making good progress.

26

PRIME DESIGNATE DARO'H

Daro'h had never expected to be Prime Designate, next in line to lead the Ildiran Empire. He had only fallen into the position after his oldest brother Thor'h betrayed the Empire and was killed. In the Elemental War, Daro'h had fought against the faeros invasion, and he had burn scars on his face as proof.

During the last two decades of peace, he had lived the rich life of a true Prime Designate, studying leadership, while taking countless Ildiran lovers from the breeding index to spread his bloodline among the kiths. He knew and acknowledged all of his mixed-breed children, which made him different from previous Prime Designates.

But his peaceful existence had abruptly ended with the reappearance of the Shana Rei—and the terrifying faeros. Now Daro'h had to be strong again. The Mage-Imperator spent more and more time with him, ensuring that the Prime Designate was prepared to lead their race.

"There is a darkness in the Spiral Arm," Jora'h told him. "Its tendrils affect us all, in ways we cannot understand. The Shana Rei could kill me from within, or they could strike Mijistra from outside."

Inside the Skysphere audience chamber, surrounded by the majesty of the Prism Palace, the Mage-Imperator sat in his chrysalis chair with Daro'h standing beside him. Jora'h gazed up at the misty projections in the high upper dome, but his thoughts were far away. He spoke quietly. "I might reign for a long and happy life, as have many other Mage-Imperators." When he clasped his son's hand, he appeared strong and confident, but Daro'h sensed a trembling uncertainty there. "Or I could die at any time—and you must be ready at a moment's notice."

Daro'h caught his breath. "I will never be ready, Liege, but I am trying."

"Then you are ready. That is all any of us can do."

"Was *Rod'h* ready to face the shadows when they captured him? He protected me. He was my friend." His heart ached. "Gale'nh told me that the Shana Rei keep torturing him. Is there no way we can mount an expedition to rescue him?"

Jora'h shook his head and said in a grim voice, "None that I can conceive. He is deep inside one of their shadow clouds."

Listening to their conversation, Nira climbed the dais to take her place on the opposite side of the chrysalis chair. She looked distraught. "Rod'h is my own son. If there were any hope of success, I would beg Jora'h to devote all the resources of the Ildiran Empire to save him."

"And I would do it, too," the Mage-Imperator vowed. "But we have no way to reach him, and no way to free him even if we found him."

"But we know he is alive," Daro'h insisted. "Osira'h, Gale'nh, and Muree'n all say so."

"Knowing he is alive may be worse than knowing he's dead." Tears left glistening tracks down Nira's green cheeks. She lowered her voice. "My daughter Tamo'l is missing as well."

Daro'h said, "The Shana Rei do have vulnerabilities. We know we can harm them with our sun bombs and laser cannons, so why must we wait and only fight back whenever and wherever they choose to strike us?"

Jora'h's expression grew even more troubled. "We cannot track them, and we need far more weapons before we fight them again. Until then, we have to keep the Ildiran race strong and unified. To that end . . ." He raised his voice and called out to the courtiers who stood at a discreet distance. "Send in the supplicants. They have waited outside for too long."

Ildirans of all kiths came to the Prism Palace to see the Mage-Imperator. Daro'h watched, knowing that someday he would receive similar supplicants. Attenders flurried about, taking care of every possible subservient need.

But as the first pilgrims came forward with reverent eyes, Mage-Imperator Jora'h suddenly gasped and collapsed back in the chrysalis chair, his face wrenched with pain.

Nira rushed to him. "What is it?"

An instant later, Daro'h also reeled off balance. Waves of crisis pounded through the *thism,* amplified through the Mage-Imperator.

Supplicants, courtiers, attenders, and pilgrims in the Skysphere also shuddered as the shock wave passed through them; many collapsed, and a vibrant wail circulated around the hall, scattering the flying creatures in the terrarium mists above.

Jora'h convulsed. He closed his eyes, his lips drawn back in agony. "The shadows! Solar Navy ships—my people on Wythira."

The screams of innumerable Ildirans roared through the *thism.*

Daro'h felt the pounding terror and pain as so many people were slaughtered. Slaughtered! "We must help them."

Seven warliners were already stationed at Wythira, armed and ready to defend. But the creatures of darkness and their robot allies—the black robots that had supposedly been eradicated!—struck and struck, not content until they had turned Wythira into a wasteland.

Daro'h sensed when the Solar Navy ships were annihilated, but the attack was not yet over. He, his father, and every other Ildiran in the Palace endured the agony for hours as the Wythira colonists were methodically massacred.

A shadow cloud of despair engulfed his heart. No backup fighters, no rescue ships could ever get to Wythira in time. The fastest Solar Navy vessels were days away from the outlying splinter colony.

Neither Daro'h nor the Mage-Imperator could escape the *thism* shock as the deaths went on and on . . . until Wythira fell mercifully, and devastatingly, silent.

27

ZHETT KELLUM

Clan Kellum had lost everything—more than once—and they had only scraps of profits from skymining at Golgen or selling Primordial Ooze from their distillery. Zhett calculated that she and her family could afford basic expenses for a couple of days, but their future didn't extend much beyond that.

They would stay at Newstation until something better came up. After being evacuated from Kuivahr, she felt like she'd been cast adrift in zero G without a lifeline. Yes, the Mage-Imperator had welcomed them and graciously provided whatever they might need, but Zhett and her family did not belong in Mijistra.

Newstation, however, was full of loud conversations and the constant flow of ships coming and going, boisterous discussions among clan members, laughter, intense negotiations, and food—familiar flavors that she had missed for some time. Zhett did like being back here, even if clan Kellum didn't have much. It was their kind of place.

Word of their extraordinary encounter with the black robots and the Shana Rei drew great attention, and some skepticism. But they had images to prove their story, and reports began to trickle in from traders who had also escaped the Kuivahr attack. Dando Yoder, a grizzled Kett Shipping cargo pilot, came to Newstation, babbling about the shadow cloud and claiming that he was in possession of the very last cargo of Kellum's famous Primordial Ooze; he offered to sell it at a premium, but had a hard time finding takers. Zhett wished she had the money to buy it herself, for old times' sake if nothing else.

Fortunately, Roamers took care of their own. Kristof complained halfheartedly about going to the Roamer school, though he didn't have much justification. "I'm not cut out for school like Shareen. I'd be better off working here at Newstation. I can find a construction crew, or sign aboard a ship instead—think of how the experience would benefit me."

"Right," Patrick said. "But your education comes first. Academ is the best place for you."

Putting Rex in a free daycare group with other Roamer infants and toddlers, they sent word to Fireheart Station through a green priest, and learned that Shareen and Howard were well and in good spirits.

Through his old political connections, Del Kellum began meeting with other clan heads, proposing cooperative operations, leveraging his reputation because he had no cash. Del banked on tall tales of his adventures for drinks and conversation in Roamer public establishments. He also attended the daily clan business meetings and set up separate conversations with Speaker Sam Ricks.

But times had changed. Newstation was an exuberant chaos of people rushing about, with clan members buying unexpected equipment and components of all sorts. Every surplus starship and water tanker, any kind of space industrial apparatus had been snapped up and hauled away. New supplies were bought out as soon as they arrived.

Zhett kept hearing rumors of massive new ekti operations, but she and Patrick were too busy getting Toff settled at Academ, Rex taken care of by the Governess compies, and their personal finances in order (although their accounts were so low, there wasn't much organizing to do). They all stayed together in a single set of rooms; it was crowded, but they were family. After all, in years past the Kellums had lived in "rabbit holes," tiny hidden settlements in the rings of Osquivel.

One night her father burst in, slightly tipsy from his "information gathering." "I sampled three of their best orange liqueurs, had to compare them with what I used to make." He made a raspberry sound. "Nothing comes close. Maybe I should get back into that business."

"I'm sure it would taste better than your kelp liquor," Patrick said.

Del waved his finger. "Primordial Ooze will become legendary, mark my words. Now that they can't have it, people will want it more than ever." He slumped into the reclining seat that folded down as a place for him to sleep. Zhett wondered what the twinkle in his eye might mean.

"I found out what all the excitement's about," he said. "Ekti-X—Iswander's special stardrive fuel. It made him a fortune, but he wouldn't tell anyone where it came from. Now the man's been disgraced and his secret's out." He clapped his hands. "And it's the easiest thing in the world, by damn! We can make our fortune back in no time."

Zhett remained pessimistic. "Any time someone uses the words 'fortune,' 'easy,' and 'no time,' I've got a lot of questions. If it's so simple, why isn't everybody doing it?"

Del leaned forward in the chair. "Everybody *is* doing it, my sweet! Only a week's passed since the Roamer convocation when it all came out into the open." He described how simple equipment could pump stardrive fuel out of the bloaters, condense it, and store it in tanks.

Patrick said, "We've heard about bloaters, but nobody can explain what they are."

"Who cares what they are?" Del said. "They're full of ekti-X! We can go fill a hundred tanks and sell it on the open market. Everybody needs stardrive fuel."

Zhett pulled back her long, dark hair to secure it in a ponytail. "But if all the Roamer clans are harvesting ekti-X, will we be able to sell it?"

"That's why we've got to hurry, by damn!" He sounded exasperated.

"Dad," Zhett said, "we can barely afford this room. How are we possibly going to launch an operation like that?"

Her father stroked his beard. "You leave that to me. I've got an ingenious plan."

Zhett found the idea of his "plan" almost as frightening as the thought of another shadow cloud.

From his years serving as Speaker, with backroom deals and clan connections, favors passed back and forth, Del Kellum had more influence than Zhett realized.

He bullied Speaker Ricks, especially in light of all his awkward dealings—dealings that were being quietly ignored with the ekti-X rush and all the angry attention turned toward Iswander Industries. Del reminded Ricks that any Speaker could be ousted with a vote of no confidence if someone bothered to push—someone, say, as powerful and well-liked as Del Kellum. "In fact, I might even be interested in being Speaker again. I suppose I could challenge your leadership in an open session." After the offhanded comment, Ricks was very amenable to suggestions, and Del negotiated reparations for those clans that had been caught on the short end of Ricks's bribes and favoritism. As a result, he earned the undying gratitude of the Roamer Speaker—which translated into a very solid line of credit that clan Kellum needed.

Zhett joined her father in some of his business meetings, marveling at how adept he was at interpersonal negotiations and barter. Del was a master of the art of politics.

Now that they had a chance again, Patrick and Zhett were able to reconnect with their distillery employees who had fled to Newstation after Kuivahr. They didn't have Marius Denva, who had been lost in the shadow attack, but they had plenty of competent line managers.

Zhett asked if the crew would be willing to join another Kellum industrial operation. These workers had followed them from place to place, serving first on the great Golgen skymine—which the shadows had destroyed—and then at the Kuivahr distillery, which also ended in a disaster. Zhett was touched that all these people would stay with employers who faced so many "circumstances beyond their control." But they saw their Guiding Star, and she was glad they did.

Feeling flush and hopeful again, Del rented a banquet room in one of Newstation's eating establishments. He bought the crew dinner, and as the meal was served, Zhett, Patrick, and Del looked out at the optimistic group. She wasn't comfortable promising them something so uncertain and intangible, but Del was as blustery as ever while the eager crew ate their spiced noodles with a side dish of fresh fruit from the greenhouse deck.

Zhett tried to enjoy her meal. "I think you're promising them too much, Dad. You've got a line of credit, and we've got eager workers, but—in case you haven't noticed—other clans bought up every scrap of available equipment. A good plan isn't going to help us harvest ekti-X. We don't have the tools. How are we going to pull this off?"

"Ah, use your imagination, my sweet." He sampled yet another clan-produced orange liqueur, which he complained about, but drank anyway.

"I can't conjure any real equipment with my imagination."

"Maybe I can make inquiries," Patrick said. "I still have some favors owed me back in the Confederation."

"We've already got the equipment, by damn." Del sounded smug.

Patrick frowned. "What? Is it invisible?"

"No, just a little inaccessible, but I'm sure it's remained intact for the last couple of decades." He fell silent and sipped his liqueur, stringing them along. Zhett rolled her eyes at the contrived delay.

Del finally explained. "We'll get everything from our mothballed operations in the Osquivel cometary cloud. All those ships, rigs, and tankers we put up there high above the ecliptic. The equipment was old, but serviceable. We abandoned it in place after the comet-extraction operations stopped being economically feasible."

He leaned forward and grinned at Zhett and Patrick while the rest of his workers conversed and laughed and ate food on Del's bill. "These bloaters are a thousand times more efficient. We have everything we need in cold storage—tanks, pumps, and delivery engines. I say we move the whole operation off to the first bloater cluster we find."

Zhett grinned at her husband. She looked at Patrick, who was smiling just as widely. "That would work," she said.

"Yes it would, by damn," Del said. "We already own the equipment, we have our workers." He finished off his orange liqueur and wiped his lips. "Clan Kellum is back in business!"

28

ORLI COVITZ

Although she had enjoyed flying with Tasia and Robb aboard the *Curiosity*, Orli felt much more at ease with Garrison. As the *Prodigal Son* headed back toward Newstation, DD expressed his optimism. "I will be glad to see young Seth again. I am sure he needs me to help him with his studies."

"You and I just left him a few days ago, DD," Orli pointed out.

"He will still want my help," said the compy. "Seth enjoys spending time with me."

During the journey, Orli basked in the warmth of Garrison's company. "When I suggested that we spend a month apart to think about things, I didn't realize how hard it would be. I guess it wasn't my best idea." Orli snuggled up against him.

"We both needed enough time to miss each other." Garrison put his arm around her. "Now, we're sure."

They had been worried that their attraction was one of convenience, a relationship between two lonely people—which they were—but she felt a genuine closeness to Garrison that she had never felt with her former husband. With Matthew, their interests had been more aligned than their hearts. With Garrison, their personalities seemed like interlocking puzzle pieces. When they talked, she took pleasure in the simplest conversation. Orli *liked* being with him, even doing mundane things. And Garrison liked her—so the puzzle pieces fit together even better, and their two separate lives became one larger whole. . . .

During the flight to Newstation, the *Prodigal Son* came upon another silent cluster of bloaters floating in the empty reaches of interstellar space. Garrison deactivated the stardrive and let the ship drift among the gray-green nodules. Orli stared through the main windowport, her face close to his. The bloaters were powerful, mysterious, far from any star. The ship's lights illuminated the mottled membranes.

Garrison said, "I was in this ship when Seth and I found the first bloaters. We had never seen anything like them, but now they seem to be everywhere. How is it possible we didn't notice them before?"

"Maybe more of them are appearing?" In her mind she felt a thrumming connection, like the last resonance from a tuning fork just out of the range of hearing. "Remember the ones we saw outside the Ikbir system—clusters and connecting chains that extended far out into space?" She looked at him. "No, we didn't just miss them before. With all of the Roamer ships flying around the Spiral Arm for centuries, it's not possible. These are something new." She drew a deep breath, rubbed the tension at the nape of her neck. "Can you feel it? It's like a throbbing in the back of my head."

Garrison's brow wrinkled. "No . . . nothing."

Orli moved her fingers to rub her temples. "It's there. I can feel it."

Garrison quickly withdrew the *Prodigal Son* to a safe distance when several of the bloater nuclei sparkled, giving off bright and energetic flashes. "My ship's been damaged that way before. I'm not putting you at risk."

"When they flashed, I felt an extra tingle in my mind," Orli said. "Maybe I have some kind of connection because I immersed myself in one of them. Do you think I was so weak from the plague that the bloaters changed something in me?"

"They certainly cured you," Garrison said.

"That was thanks to Aelin," she said. "Because of his treeling and telink, he forged a clear link with them. Maybe he convinced the bloaters to heal me when I was dying."

"They're just gas bags," Garrison said, "just . . . space plankton."

"We don't know that. Nobody does, and that's the problem. The extraction operations are draining them by the thousands. What if they are alive?"

"Cabbages are alive," Garrison pointed out. "So is algae."

Orli frowned. "You know they're more than that. If it was just algae, I wouldn't sense anything."

She felt a sudden uneasiness. Thousands of bloaters being drained, and she knew that it was because of her—along with Tasia and Robb. Without thinking, they had delivered the remarkable news to Rendezvous that the bloaters were filled with ekti-X, which had sparked hundreds of harvesting operations across the Spiral Arm. She had set the wheels in motion, and she worried about what she had done.

Her eyes stung as the looked out at the peaceful, enigmatic nodules hanging there. "These bloaters feel different to me, Garrison. There's more energy inside me and inside them."

She remembered being immersed in the protoplasm, but at the time she had been delirious, weak, and lost. Her being cured had been an anomaly, a surprise. Aelin had insisted that something about the exposure worked just right in her failing body. She could not explain it, and the green priest was now gone.

Orli felt unsettled. The faint presence around her, so warm and powerful here close to the bloater cluster, made her believe there was something more to them. These nodules were not just sacks of readily available fuel.

She hoped the answer would become clear before the widespread operations drained them all.

TASIA TAMBLYN

When the *Voracious Curiosity* returned to Earth after their side trip to Fireheart Station, Tasia dreaded all the administrative work that must have piled up in their absence. Rlinda certainly wouldn't have done it for them.

The big trader woman waved as they emerged from the familiar spacecraft in the Kett Shipping tower. "Glad you brought my ship back without a scratch—and that's a surprise, considering all you've been through."

Robb looked embarrassed. "We did institute some cosmetic repairs at Newstation, so you wouldn't notice."

Tasia added, "The Roamers were happy to help, especially once we told them that bloaters are full of stardrive fuel."

Rlinda crossed her arms over her chest. "You all caused quite a bit of trouble by breaking the news. So, Kett Shipping is no longer delivering Iswander's ekti-X?"

Tasia blinked. "Of course not! Shizz, they wiped out half of clan Duquesne, and Elisa Enturi tried to kill us when we found their operations."

"I didn't say I disagreed with the decision, girl—in fact, wasn't I suspicious from the start about where all that stardrive fuel came from?" She clapped her hands. "But with the excitement you generated, we'll be distributing the ekti-X from a dozen new Roamer operations, so I consider that a net positive. Where's Orli? I sent her with you for safekeeping."

As Rlinda walked around the *Curiosity,* admiring her old ship, they explained about leaving Orli with Garrison back at Fireheart Station. Although she let Tasia and Robb fly her ship, Rlinda still felt quite possessive. "You two need to stop adventuring and sit your butts in your office chairs. I chose you to be administrators so I wouldn't have to do that crap."

Robb had a sparkle in his eye. "Does that mean you took care of the management details while we were away?"

"Not a chance—you both have a month of catching up to do . . . and you're welcome to it."

A group of hangar workers, maintenance techs, and interim pilots came to greet them, eager to hear how they had shot their way out of the Iswander extraction field, but Rlinda brushed them aside and hurried Tasia and Robb along. "Come down to the lower hangar. I've got something to show you—and someone you'll want to see."

A few techs followed, still pestering them with questions, but Tasia waved them off. "We'll tell the whole story during drinks after hours. In fact, we can meet in the lounge area of Rlinda's restaurant, if she'll set it aside for us?"

The big woman nodded. "Cash bar, though."

Robb said, "And promise there won't be a band. We want to talk. We've got stories to tell, and I'll make sure Tasia sticks to the facts, for the most part."

Tasia snorted. They all took a lift down to the next hangar level, where they were surprised to see Xander and Terry waiting for them.

Xander smiled. "There you are! We've been fighting black robots and shadow clouds, barely escaping the destruction at Ulio Station—and now you think you can upstage us with some tall tales?"

"We live in exciting times, for better or worse." Tasia gave her son and his partner warm hugs, as did Robb. Not wanting to be left out, Rlinda took the opportunity to scoop Xander and Terry into an embrace of her own.

OK spoke up. "Are you here to inspect the *Verne?* We are very pleased at the repairs we've completed."

"We spared no expense," Xander said. "This is the best ship in the Kett fleet."

Terry interrupted, "But we won't be flying regular trade routes anymore. We've come up with a way to invest the money Maria left me. Xander and I are going to set up a salvage hub to take the place of Ulio Station. We wanted to seize the opportunity, start a viable business that will help trade everywhere."

Xander nodded. "They'll flock to a new place. We just need to find the right location, establish the facilities, find a crew and the necessary equipment, then start collecting ships in need of repair, or total wrecks that we can refurbish as habitation units—like hotels."

"That's an ambitious plan," Robb said. "Where are you going to gather all this stuff?"

"First off, we're going to take the *Verne* out to Newstation and see if other Roamers are willing to join us."

Tasia felt warm inside. "That's a grand idea."

Rlinda clapped her hands again, steering Tasia and Robb along. "Enough of the reunion. Back to my office where I can hand over the paperwork. You two have duties, and I want to give the complainers someone else to talk to."

"Ah, the glamorous life of running a large company," Tasia muttered.

"Damn right," said Rlinda. "The real glamorous part comes when you retire and hand off the duties to someone else."

Rlinda kept the largest penthouse office in the Kett Shipping tower, where she enjoyed the view. Half of her office had been converted into a company kitchen, because she liked to cook for herself and for anyone else who might visit. Since she was such a good cook, she often had visitors.

As soon as they entered the office, though, Rlinda's mood grew serious. "A lot of bad things are going on out there in the Spiral Arm, things we can't ignore. I wanted to show you some images from Xander and Terry. They barely limped home in the *Verne*." She raised her eyebrows. "We all know what a pain in the ass the black robots are, but the Shana Rei are much, much worse. Watch this."

The transparent surface of her desk platform displayed the log images of Xander and Terry battling their way from Ulio Station. Ferocious-looking angular ships piloted by black robots soared in, ripping apart the Ulio complex, destroying Roamer ships that scattered, blowing up vessels under repair in spacedock. The *Verne* barely got away, pursued by robot attackers; Terry activated their stardrive just in time and streaked away, leaving the doomed station behind.

Rlinda's face was heavy with worry as she slumped into a padded, oversized chair behind her desk. "It makes me nostalgic for the good old days when we were just being chased by hydrogues."

Tasia felt sick watching it. Robb's face was distraught. "I can't believe the boys got out of that."

Rlinda said, "They may act cocky, but they're not stupid. When they set up their new Ulio, you won't need to worry about them any more than you worry about the rest of us." With a great sigh, she reached forward to pick up a small silver capsule mounted on a Plexiglas stand on her desk. She held it between thumb and forefinger, regarding it with a longing expression.

"What is the Spiral Arm coming to? I could say that I'm glad Be-Bob didn't survive to see days like these . . . but that would be total bullshit. I miss him, and I'd get through this better if he were beside me." She rubbed the capsule, then lovingly replaced it on its stand.

"Throughout human history, people have said, 'This is a tough time to be alive.' If there was ever a perfect golden age, I haven't found it. We'll just have to get through." She looked up at Tasia and Robb, her expression intense. "You will abide by your promise, right? If anything happens to me, see that my ashes are put in a capsule like this one and launch both of us into space, so that Bebob and I can travel together for all eternity." She forced a small chuckle. "It's sappy, I know, but that's what I want."

"Nothing's going to happen to you," Robb said.

"Don't be an idiot. Everybody dies." She patted her girth." And look at me—I'm not the picture of health. At my age, I have to think about such things, whether or not there are monsters out to destroy the universe." Her voice grew harder. "Promise me."

"Of course we promise," Tasia said. "But I'd prefer to take care of a lot of other problems first."

"So would I." Rlinda stood up and headed toward the small private kitchen. "Let's make something to eat."

ZOE ALAKIS

The more deadly the disease, the more fascinating Zoe found it. And the Onthos plague was endlessly fascinating.

After returning from her nerve-racking journey to Theroc and her successful bargain with the King and Queen, Zoe had isolated herself in her sterile sanctuary on Pergamus, where she could pore over the records about the alien virus.

Throughout her many years at Pergamus, Zoe had lived within her secure habitat, breathing filtered air and eating bland purified food. There, she reviewed the countless research reports her teams submitted as they analyzed deadly pathogens, virulent endoviruses, and recursive genetic maladies, as well as malicious parasites. New diseases seemed to appear just as fast as medical researchers found cures.

The universe was out to kill them. Zoe had always known that, and she would not let her guard down.

Pergamus was an arsenal that contained those malignant microorganisms, and Zoe reveled in them like a collector who managed a zoo of dangerous monsters—monsters too small to be seen, but monsters nevertheless. Degenerative neural diseases, cancers that resisted every known treatment, debilitating muscular diseases, brain parasites—the breathtaking range of virulence made Zoe wonder how the human race had survived this long.

She took comfort in her sterile home, still astonished that she had ever been brave enough to go to Theroc, a place infested with innumerable contaminants. But she had returned home with a tremendous prize: Iswander's data archive from the plague-soaked Onthos space city.

When Tom Rom returned from Kuivahr with Tamo'l's treasure trove of Ildiran genetic information, he had also brought the chief researcher herself. One of the weaknesses of Zoe's collection was that it contained little information about Ildiran morbidities. Since the alien genetics were extremely adaptable and similar enough to humans' to allow interbreeding, their diseases were also of great interest.

As Tamo'l settled in to work in one of the isolated Pergamus domes, Tom Rom sent a list of what she needed to continue her studies. The halfbreed woman seemed surprisingly cooperative, and Zoe looked forward to her initial reports. Maybe Tamo'l was a dedicated and curious scientist, just like Zoe. The researcher was, however, unduly concerned about her refugee misbreeds, wanting to speak to them or at least send them a message. Zoe had allowed Tamo'l to record a message to be delivered to Ildira, which seemed to reassure her, although Zoe had no intention of letting Tom Rom deliver the recording.

Although Tamo'l's stated purpose was to help the misbreeds, the sanctuary domes on Kuivahr had served more as a hospice than as a rigorous research laboratory. Here on Pergamus, though, Tamo'l would have an opportunity to do pure science without the distractions of sick and suffering misbreeds.

After Tom Rom had spent several days establishing Tamo'l alone in her new lab dome, Zoe insisted that he come inside to see her. Thus, he was currently making his way through the succession of decontamination interlocks. Today he and Zoe would have lunch like two normal people—except for the fact that they were inside a sterile dome, eating autoclaved gruel that was full of nutrients but lacking in flavor.

In order to see her, Tom Rom would take nearly five hours to complete the scrubbing and decontamination process to guarantee that he was safely noninfectious when he was with her. Zoe was eager to hear about his adventures on Kuivahr, but it made her worry that he had once again nearly been killed during his service to her. She begged him not to risk himself, but she knew he wouldn't change his ways. He needed to do this—for her, and for himself— and Zoe just had to have faith in his competence and abilities.

She checked his progress, saw that he had two more decontamination zones to endure before reaching her. It would take him
another hour, so she settled back to read the reports detailing the
symptoms and course of the Onthos plague, as well as how the out-
casts of clan Reeves had discovered the derelict space city, found the
alien corpses, and begun to suffer the symptoms themselves.

Zoe studied the documents with intense interest, never forgetting
that Tom Rom had nearly died from the same illness. In the data
archive, she also found numerous insipid farewell messages from
dying Roamers recording their last words, as if anyone cared. Zoe
had listened to all of them—once—hoping that some victims might
provide interesting insights into the progress of the disease. Instead,
they were just maudlin goodbyes and not worth repeating. She had
done something similar while hovering over Tom Rom in what she
thought were his last days of life, before her teams had found a cure
based on Klikiss royal jelly.

She blocked out the thoughts, not wanting to remember that time
when he had been so sick, when she had been so frightened. She
would rather focus objectively on the actual data. That was what
mattered.

That fascinating plague had originated with the Klikiss, and the
warlike insect race had preyed upon the Onthos survivors after they
fled the Shana Rei. Something about the disease's genetic composi-
tion made it highly adaptable so that it existed as a retrovirus in the
Klikiss survivors, then jumped to the Onthos race . . . and recently,
the disease had mutated to infect humans as well. Zoe thought the
virus was marvelous. She kept her library specimens under tight
quarantine security, where the plague could never infect anyone else.

After his tedious decontamination, Tom Rom finally entered her
sterile central chamber. Dressed in a disposable polymer garment, he
was obviously as pleased to see her as she was to see him.

Zoe smiled and sighed. "I know how inconvenient it is for us to
have a face-to-face meeting, but it's worth the effort. You and I need
to remain in contact." Her voice dropped. "You're my only friend,
Tom Rom."

"And I will do anything you wish," he said with a smile, "so long
as it doesn't place you in danger."

"How could you ever place me in danger?"

"Don't underestimate the risks inherent in the universe."

Zoe looked at the enlarged images on wall screens all around her, scanning electron micrographs of malicious disease organisms. "I don't ever underestimate the risks. You should know better."

She had set out two bowls of the lukewarm gruel from the autoclave, and Tom Rom took his, sitting down across her desk so they could look at each other while they ate. Zoe knew that other human beings would have touched, even embraced, but she would not tolerate that, nor did Tom Rom expect it. They had their bond. It was sufficient.

She indicated the records of the Onthos plague. "These files are very interesting, some of the best data I have in my collection, but I am interested in learning more."

"I'm glad you consider the bargain with the King and Queen worthwhile. I've heard that the Confederation Defense Forces have cracked down on Rakkem, as promised. The biomerchants will never prey on anyone else."

Zoe smiled. "Then it was an excellent deal all around . . . but I don't think we're finished. I want proof that Rakkem is shut down—I *need* to see the ruins." A spark of anger flashed in her dark eyes; she wasn't seeing Tom Rom, but rather that appalling place, the biowarehouses, the factory mothers, just like her own treacherous mother Muriel . . . whom she and Tom Rom had killed. Zoe had no regrets, other than that she wished they had achieved a more permanent shutdown of that place.

Tom Rom nodded. "I expected you'd want more. I'll make a journey to Rakkem and bring back a report so you can see everything the CDF has done."

"Make sure that place is broken . . . permanently." She smiled. "But while you're out in the Spiral Arm, I have another mission. The Onthos plague . . ." She glanced at the screen, studying the high-res micrographs of the vanishingly small monster of the alien disease. "The Klikiss race were the original carriers, apparently unaffected but able to spread the disease to the Onthos race. I think there's more to learn from them that we can apply to our other diseases."

"There are numerous abandoned Klikiss planets," Tom Rom

said. "I can investigate the ruins again, if you like, and then scout Rakkem."

"Gather whatever data you can on the Klikiss. Get more tissue samples from their cadavers, and more royal jelly." She frowned at the screen, at the scrolling charts of results that all showed alarming changes. "The plague organism in your blood has mutated into something even more deadly, a strain that is no longer affected by the cure that saved you. It's very resilient."

"I will find more Klikiss specimens. I know of quite a few planets I can choose from."

She slid the display screen aside and looked closely at his confident, placid expression. "So long as you're careful. That is the most important thing."

"I am as careful as is feasible. You know that." He leaned closer to Zoe, who resisted the urge to back away, to keep the distance between herself and any other person. She didn't like the haunted look in his eyes.

"I am not the only one in danger when I go out to other planets, Zoe. No place is safe. I trust that you read my full report about Kuivahr? The Shana Rei and the black robots are a significant threat. Not only did they obliterate Kuivahr, but many other human outposts and Ildiran colonies."

Zoe didn't understand why that was relevant to them here on Pergamus. "Then you will have to stay away from them when you gather information for me."

Tom Rom ate three bites in silence, then straightened. She had never seen him so intense. "Do you understand how dangerous they are, Zoe? The Shana Rei are more powerful than even the hydrogues. They're like a . . . plague."

She was too young to remember the ruthless hydrogues, and since she and her parents had been isolated on the wilderness planet of Vaconda, the Elemental War had little bearing on them.

"I believe you, and I accept that the Shana Rei are dangerous, but you are one man alone with a fast ship, and you always keep your wits about you." When Tom Rom didn't seem satisfied with her answer, she raised her hands. "I don't care about the Shana Rei, no matter how dangerous they seem. I have enough deadly organisms here at Pergamus to wipe out the entire human race ten times over. Danger doesn't bother me."

She calmed herself and looked at him warmly. "There have always been things trying to eradicate us, Tom Rom. But we're still here."

ARITA

Racing back from the Wild after leaving Sarein's abandoned dwelling, Arita transmitted the grim news to her parents. Beside her in the piloting compartment, Collin looked shaky. She reached out to take his hand, and he laced his fingers through hers, then squeezed.

By the time they flew in, the fungus-reef city was on high alert. She and Collin were quickly led into the throne room, where her parents waited for them. "We're glad you made it home safe," said Estarra. "But your report is horrific."

Arita drew several deep breaths to steady herself. "There's more." From the satchel at her side, she withdrew the old-fashioned bound journals that her aunt had kept. "These are Sarein's. She . . ."

Estarra's eyes widened, and she sat back as if to avoid what Arita had to say.

"Sarein is dead. The Onthos killed her. We think she discovered what the aliens are doing to the trees." Arita's voice cracked. "I went over there as a naturalist. I was trying to find answers. All Sarein wanted was to be left alone, but she must have gone out to investigate the dying trees."

Estarra inhaled a long breath and let it out slowly as she kept her eyes closed. Her lower lip trembled, but when she opened her eyes again, she was strong, her gaze flashing. "Damn them. We welcomed the Gardeners here, offered to let them settle in the Wild. Now, they've killed my sister."

The tendons stood out on Peter's throat as he fought to control his anger. "The Spiral Arm seems to be tearing itself apart—and now here on Theroc, too."

Arita saw Zaquel, a middle-aged woman who had been her friend and trainer back when she was an acolyte who read aloud to the trees. "We've been blind to what's happening in the Wild," Zaquel said. "Your message is . . . impossible. Why did we not know? How could the trees hide it from us . . . and why? We could help them!"

"There's a blight inside the trees," Collin said. "They're all dying over there, and no other green priest even seems to notice."

Queen Estarra said, her voice as hard as a knife blade, "We'll put together an expedition to the Wild—and do what we have to do. If the Onthos killed Sarein and contaminated Kennebar and his green priests, it's time we revoke our hospitality."

A familiar voice called out, "I'm going along!" Arita looked past the others to see her brother standing beside Osira'h.

A grin filled her face. "Reyn, you're back home!" She ran to her brother and gave him a large hug. He staggered from her enthusiasm, and Osira'h reached out to steady him. Arita realized her brother was far weaker than the last time she had seen him. She drew back and studied him.

Reyn blinked, embarrassed. He was gaunt and pale, and his face was a constant flicker of expressions, as if he struggled against a parade of pain within him.

Osira'h announced, "We developed treatments for him from kelp strains on Kuivahr . . . but Kuivahr is now destroyed, and we barely escaped with our lives." She paused. "Did you know about Kuivahr?"

Arita reeled. "What happened there?"

"The Shana Rei," Reyn said, then gave a dismissive gesture. "There'll be time for that story later. Everyone here has heard it. We want to know what you encountered in the Wild."

"Collin can share it through telink, so all the green priests know," Arita said.

But Collin seemed reluctant to touch the verdani mind and sink into it again. "It used to be a place of peace for me. What if I find darkness there?"

"Then we need to search it out and fight it where we can," said Zaquel. She looked up at the young man, encouraging him. "Tell me, aloud, and I will send the story through telink, across the Spiral Arm."

With added comments from Arita, Collin described what had happened, and Zaquel repeated the story as she touched the giant worldtree, for all the green priests to access.

The King and Queen were obviously troubled. "This sickness in the forest has to be addressed," Estarra said. "Because the worldforest *is* our world."

"And there's something else, another presence," Arita said. "It helped us against the voidpriests, but only I could hear it." When she described the immense, mysterious voice she heard inside herself, the green priests didn't know how to explain it. Arita still felt a flicker and a whisper ringing inside her head, senses magnifying and opening.

Now, with that strange acuity, she looked at Reyn again and saw him in a way she had not been able to grasp before, as if she had sharper lenses. She had watched her brother fading for so long, and she'd held out such a determined hope that he would get better. But she realized she had been fooling herself. Through her strangely focused and filtered vision, she could sense a blight inside him, a shadow that seemed remarkably similar to what she and Collin had discovered deep within the neural network of the worldtrees . . . similar to what lurked inside the Gardeners themselves.

Estarra's large, dark eyes shone with a veil of angry tears. "We'll gather an expedition and depart for the Wild as soon as possible."

CHAPTER

32

GENERAL NALANI KEAH

When she went out on patrol rather than staying behind at CDF headquarters, General Keah felt that she was at least doing something useful. Always a restless person, she hated sitting behind desks, but sometimes the job demanded that. A desk was a desk, however, and Keah figured she could do her administrative work from the bridge of her flagship just as well as in the Lunar Orbital Complex. With her green priest, she could remain in direct and immediate contact if anyone really needed to bother her.

And those ominous new shadow clouds had to be investigated.

Now that her flagship was fully repaired, she was spoiling for a fight and ready to go. The *Kutuzov* was the most imposing ship in the CDF, and she was damned proud of it, but she wasn't naïve either. When she headed out to investigate the black nebula near the Relleker system, she brought along ten Manta cruisers, each loaded with enhanced sun bombs and armed with batteries of laser cannons. That should be enough to kick some ass.

According to reports from Adar Zan'nh, the Ildiran Solar Navy had completely wiped out the bugbots, smeared them into incandescent dust all over the Kuivahr system—and that was a good thing, one pain in the butt that she no longer needed to worry about. Zan'nh wasn't prone to hyperbole: if he said he had done something, then she could count on it. Those Shana Rei hex cylinders were intimidating enough.

During the two-day trip to Relleker, her battle group performed combat exercises, refought their previous engagement with the Shana Rei using realistic images, and got themselves mentally ready for a fight. Keah wanted their next encounter to be a *victory* rather than a "learning experience." She was the leader of the CDF, damn it, and it was her job to protect these planets.

But when the *Kutuzov* and the ten Mantas arrived at Relleker, they dropped into the middle of a hellish battle. The shadow cloud had closed in on the heavily populated planet like a deadly thunderstorm. Its black tangles and swirls reached forward like pseudopods, and enormous hexagonal cylinders emerged, created from frozen darkness. Although the Shana Rei poured out waves of entropy that disrupted technological systems, bugbot ships were conducting the main attack. And those ships were larger and bristling with more weapons than Keah had seen before. Thousands of them— maybe even tens of thousands.

"So much for Adar Zan'nh's report that he eradicated the bugbots." Keah clutched the arms of her command chair. "Mr. Patton, open fire with laser-cannon batteries one and two. All other commanders, feel free to participate!"

Lances of coherent light skewered several bugbot ships. The shielding on the angular black vessels must have been tougher than before. The first laser blasts merely caused superficial damage when they should have cut through the mechanical attackers like butter.

The robots returned fire with high-energy beams that thundered against the *Kutuzov*'s shields. Sparks flew from bridge stations, and her techs scrambled to effect emergency repairs.

"They're packing quite a punch, General," said Lieutenant Tait.

"Then let's punch back. Mr. Patton, spice up our laser cannons with a volley of sun bombs, too. I assume you can walk and chew gum at the same time."

"And juggle beanbags, General," he said, and activated controls.

Five pulsing plasma spheres rocketed out of the forward battery and curled into the mass of robot ships. The angular vessels scattered when they saw the sun bombs coming, but the blasts still erased at least ninety attackers.

But it was only ninety out of thousands. Tens of thousands. *Hundreds* of thousands. Beyond a certain point, the number of zeroes didn't much matter anymore. "Where did so many bugbots come from? Z said he destroyed them all!"

The robot ships were like angry hornets stinging a hapless victim to death. Most of the enemy attackers simply ignored General Keah's forces, choosing instead to plunge into Relleker's atmosphere, where they bombarded the colony cities. From the surface, the comm channels filled with a storm of panicked outcries and desperate calls for help.

The black robots had more than enough ships to obliterate the population, so they could also spare an overwhelming force to close around the *Kutuzov* and the ten Mantas. The bugbots could absorb thousands of times as many losses as Keah could. They didn't seem to care how many robots were destroyed; they just kept fighting.

More than a hundred angular black ships closed around one of her Mantas, singling it out and pounding away with a nonstop barrage of energy weapons. Even though the Manta's captain launched all her weapons, the cruiser's armor could not withstand the onslaught. In less than a minute, the shields failed, and the Manta exploded.

A thousand more robots—a very small fraction of the horde— closed in on Keah's remaining ships. She had never expected to fight a battle like this with only eleven ships. Ten, now.

The outcries from the trapped civilians on the surface had dwindled, transmissions jammed or silenced as the cities were wiped out by a ruthless succession of sterilization blasts. Each nuclear firestorm took out a section of the continents below, and the maliciously efficient robots saturated the landscape again. Keah was sure they intended to leave Relleker nothing more than a charred ball.

She saw no way whatsoever that her battle group could save the planet. Her ships were outnumbered tens of thousands to one.

The black robots targeted another CDF Manta, surrounding the cruiser with hundreds of ships and opening fire. Keah yelled for the rest of her Mantas to converge in a vain attempt to rescue the doomed ship, but moments later a bright explosion was all that remained of the trapped cruiser.

The Shana Rei hex cylinders moved toward the planet, flooding the ships and remaining cities with swirling disruption. As the shadow cloud closed in, the *Kutuzov*'s laser cannons began to malfunction. The CDF laser-cannon blasts flew wild, missing their intended targets. Then other weapons generators sputtered, neutralizing the

lasers entirely. Many systems on the Juggernaut's bridge went hay-
wire, and her crew hammered their screens, trying to access and
implement their backup processes.

General Keah had always vowed that she wouldn't run away
from a fight. As a young EDF soldier twenty years ago she had faced
the entire Klikiss swarmship fleet when they closed in on Earth, and
she knew damn well what was at stake here. But maybe that hadn't
been a very sensible vow to make, especially now.

Three of her Manta cruisers reeled out of control, completely vulnerable to attack. "Those entropy waves will take out our ships as
surely as the bugbots will!" Though the words burned like bile in
her throat, she yelled across the comm channel, hoping that at least
the transmissions were working. "Get out of here! Pull away—
escape along any vector you can and rendezvous back at the LOC."

Her first officer blinked in alarm. "But General, what about the
people on Relleker? There's got to be some evacuation—"

"Take a look, Mr. Wingo: we'd never get a single load away, if
we could even find survivors down there in the conflagration. And
we'd likely lose the rest of our battle group in the meantime."

The black robot ships targeted another Manta and closed in by
the thousands, opening fire. Keah cried into the comm, "Get out
of there!"

The Manta's captain activated his stardrive and smashed the
embattled cruiser through the wall of robot ships, shattering six of
them—and no doubt causing horrific damage to his own hull in the
process. But the stardrive held and the cruiser got away. Whether
they would survive and reach Earth was another question.

"Retreat, dammit!" Keah announced across the command channel. "I'm not too proud to say it. All captains, activate your stardrives
and get away from Relleker." She turned to the green priest. "Mr.
Nadd, send a message through telink just in case we don't make it."

The green priest continued to grasp his treeling as the bugbot
ships closed in on them. Nadd was shaking, but he muttered his
message into the verdani mind.

General Keah collapsed back in her chair, breathing hard as the
Kutuzov vanished into lightspeed.

33

MAGE-IMPERATOR JORA'H

The Mage-Imperator rested uneasily in his chrysalis chair. His people needed to see him and sense him, and he expended great energy to gather the strands of *thism* that kept the Ildiran Empire strong.

But since the destruction of Wythira, Jora'h had struggled to keep the Ildiran race from despairing. The Empire had lost splinter colonies before, during the Elemental War, but this massacre had been so swift and so complete. The creatures of darkness had obliterated an entire world.

A Solar Navy septa had rushed off to the stricken splinter colony, but the planet was devastated by the time they arrived. Not a single survivor, no structure left standing. The Klikiss robots and the shadows had charred Wythira and then departed—no doubt to attack somewhere else. Adar Zan'nh had just returned from Kuivahr, another world destroyed by the creatures of darkness, and had found only one survivor there. One. A human, who had been sent off to be reunited with his people at Newstation.

Jora'h knew that the Shana Rei wanted to wipe out existence itself. Wythira was merely the first of what would be many such strikes. Even the Mage-Imperator of the Ildiran Empire felt helpless against them. He felt the insidious shadows probing and twisting through the strands of *thism*.

Now, the dazzling light of multiple suns poured into the Skysphere audience chamber. The image of his calm, benevolent face projected on the mist hung overhead as if nothing could trouble the Ildiran Empire, but he knew otherwise.

Thirty attenders surrounded the dais that raised his chrysalis chair above the audience floor. The small kithmen moved about,

eager to tend to his every need, bringing refreshments for the courtiers and noble kith who also had business in the Prism Palace. Well-
armed guards stood at the entrances to the audience chamber
holding crystal-tipped katanas; the bestial-looking Ildirans would
die to defend the Mage-Imperator against any possessed mob, but
he knew that *inner* enemies could be just as dangerous.

Jora'h felt much safer to have his warrior daughter Yazra'h and
her protégée Muree'n beside him as added protection. He was unre-
alistically convinced that the shadow taint could not affect the two
women. Yazra'h stood in her lizard-scale armor with her eyes bright
and focused. She held a crystal blade, but she could be just as deadly
with her bare hands. Next to her, the halfbreed Muree'n was like a
smaller and younger version of Yazra'h, equally determined to prove
her strength and prowess.

Right now, Jora'h was meeting with a representative of the
Roamer clans who had come to propose a new business deal for delivering stardrive fuel. The Roamer was a tall, thin man with shaggy
brown hair and an unkempt beard. "I come on behalf of Speaker
Sam Ricks, sir . . . um, Mage-Imperator. There has been a change in
ekti operations, one that offers great opportunity for the Roamer
clans and the Ildiran Empire."

The Mage-Imperator glanced at the Prime Designate, giving his
son permission to respond. Daro'h drew a breath and said, "The
Ildiran Empire has long purchased ekti from the Roamers. What
is different?"

"A new harvesting technique that is far more efficient than processing huge quantities of hydrogen from gas giants. We expect the
price of stardrive fuel to drop significantly. I'm offering an agreement that would make the consortium of clans I represent your exclusive provider of ekti-X. Under such conditions, we would drop
the price an additional five percent."

The man seemed to think he was offering an irresistible bargain.

Daro'h frowned, looked at his father, and Jora'h sat up straighter.
"We have always paid what was necessary and obtained what we
needed."

"But this way you would get more ekti-X for a lower cost," the
clan leader persisted. "Such a guarantee could be quite useful,

especially in these turbulent times when we are under threat from
the Shana Rei. Your Solar Navy—"

As the man spoke, the twenty attenders, always restless and busy,
suddenly stopped their movement. Under normal circumstances,
Jora'h rarely noticed their constant solicitous muttering, but now
they all froze as if hearing a distant irresistible voice. They turned
in clockwork unison, and Jora'h felt an icy chill as he saw that their
eyes had changed. Normally bright green and darting, their irises
were now filled with inky shadows.

The mass of attenders rushed forward like an unleashed pack of
predatory rodents. Still stating his case, the Roamer man took several seconds to realize that the attenders were charging toward him.
"By the Guiding Star—!"

Jora'h lurched out of his chrysalis chair and roared, "Stop them!"

Without hesitating, the guard kith raced in, swinging their crystal
katanas. The noble kith in the chamber scattered, while the courtiers
flailed to get out of the way.

Eerily silent, the possessed attenders scurried forward, driving the
Roamer man to the polished floor. The human fought back, thrashing, throwing them aside, but for every attender he knocked away,
three more jumped on top of him. His yells of surprise turned to
cries of pain as they clawed and pounded at him. Then the loud
sounds of cracking bones shot through the chamber.

Yazra'h bounded into the fray, swinging her crystal blade and
decapitating two attenders with one stroke. Muree'n used her spear
to impale one, shoved the body aside, then whirled to stab a second.

As the guards tore away the attenders who were attacking the
Roamer, another ten chittering attenders raced up the dais steps—
clearly intending to kill the Prime Designate. Daro'h defended himself, striking the first attender that came close.

The nearest guard ran up the steps, roaring, but Yazra'h and
Muree'n acted faster. They knocked the attenders away and placed
themselves in front of Daro'h, killing two more attenders, and still
the attackers would not stop.

Jora'h placed the chrysalis chair between him and the possessed
mob, sure that they would attack him next. Ready to fight them with
his bare hands, he stood poised in a combat stance.

But as the attenders swarmed up the dais, their eyes suffused with blackness, they stared at Jora'h and hesitated for a second, then turned away and rushed toward Daro'h while others flung themselves upon the guards and the nobles.

The Mage-Imperator saw Muree'n watching as the attenders refused to touch him. Then she whirled and cut down another attacker. The possessed attenders were numerous, but they were soft, small, and unarmed. Their greatest weapon had been the element of surprise, and now Yazra'h and Muree'n easily drove them away from the Prime Designate.

The Roamer man was not so lucky. Guards had killed fifteen of the attenders, but not before the mob bashed in the man's head and crushed his sternum. The Roamer lay twitching, coughing blood, mortally wounded.

The angry guards had blocked the five surviving attenders, keeping them at bay even though they tried to break through the barricade of crystalline katanas. From a distance, the possessed attenders stared at the Mage-Imperator with their blank, black eyes.

Jora'h shuddered. He wrestled with the shadows inside himself, but he knew these attenders could never be cured. Even if the Shana Rei released them, they would die from the sheer horror of having betrayed their own race, the *thism,* and the Mage-Imperator. Anger washed through him. The attenders were forever tainted and forfeit.

"Kill them all," he said in a hollow voice.

Joined by several guards, Yazra'h and Muree'n used their katanas to kill the last remaining attenders. The audience chamber was strewn with the dead bodies of innocent creatures that had only meant to serve their Mage-Imperator. The guard kith evacuated the nobles and business representatives, then closed the doors before summoning worker kith to clean up all signs of the slaughter.

Swaying, Daro'h stared around the chamber, looking appalled, terrified. "This is what Rod'h and I encountered at the solar ceremony, when the lens priestess was killed along with her followers." He shook his head, sickened. "Nothing could stop them."

Jora'h felt dizzy. Dark static flickered around his vision, and he shook his head, breathing hard. He was furious that the Shana Rei would intrude here, would attack the Ildiran people in his Palace! And the poor Roamer man . . .

Muree'n said in a voice just loud enough for Jora'h to hear, "Your eyes, Liege . . . I saw—"

"You only imagined it," Yazra'h snapped. "Let us take the Mage-Imperator away, where he can be shielded from further threats."

Jora'h took a deep breath and accompanied Daro'h as the two women led them away. He knew that no place was entirely safe, and he feared what Muree'n had glimpsed in his eyes.

Perhaps the Ildiran Empire wasn't safe from him either.

34

LEE ISWANDER

Elisa was gone—and that was a good thing. The very idea saddened him, since he had pinned such high hopes on her. She was exactly the sort of employee Iswander could rely on: dedicated, smart, resourceful, a person with her priorities straight, a person who should have been his true partner in his ambitions.

But Elisa was also murderous—and she had been caught. Those two things disqualified her entirely. She had stolen an Iswander Industries ship and flown away without any sort of farewell. He understood exactly what she had done. At least she had interpreted *that* suggestion clearly.

He'd seen several ways to solve the problem so he could rebuild his reputation, most of which included using Elisa as a scapegoat, throwing her to the wolves so that he could wash his hands and claim total innocence. But Iswander wasn't quite so naïve, and he knew the Roamers weren't either. To say he had no inkling of what Elisa *might* do would make him look like an oblivious fool, and he wouldn't tolerate that.

This was probably the best option. He was glad she had also seen it that way.

Alarmed, Deputy Pannebaker came to report to him. "Elisa's gone, Chief! Stole one of our ships and just ran off."

Iswander tried to look surprised. "Any idea where she's gone? Did she transmit a projected course?"

Pannebaker blinked. "Of course not. Why would she do that?"

He shrugged. "Then we're just as blind as everyone else. There's no way we can catch her."

"Are you going to report her?" The normally unflappable Panne-baker looked increasingly upset. "She's wanted for murder."

"Write up a report. We'll keep full documentation that I can present to the Roamer clans and the Confederation. Other than that . . . it's out of our hands. She's gone, and all we can do is wish her well."

"Wish her well?" Pannebaker's voice cracked. "She killed all those people!"

"Yes, and because of that, our reputation is destroyed. Elisa may have been a loose cannon who did terrible things, but Iswander Industries will end up paying the price for what she did. My company may well be ruined because of it." He sighed and looked out the windowport at the discarded bloater sacks from the dwindling cluster. "Keep harvesting stardrive fuel and hope we can find a market. Otherwise, I don't know what else we'll do."

He had always enjoyed spending time in the control center, watching the operations, the productivity charts, the ekti tanks filling transport arrays. It had been exciting for him to build these extraction operations, a challenge to conquer, a bright future in a huge universe. Now, though, as the next array was filled with ekti, he knew they would reach a crisis point soon. Where would he go when the next shipment was ready? He couldn't just sit on all that fuel.

Without Ulio Station, and without Kett Shipping, it would be hard to distribute the stardrive fuel—not to mention that Iswander Industries was probably blacklisted throughout the Spiral Arm. Newstation was the most obvious outlet for the fuel, and he hoped that some Roamer clan would have flexible enough morals to do business with him.

But the clans had shunned him before. They had never forgiven him after the Sheol disaster—1,543 black marks against his honor, and no Roamer would let him forget it. Ever. No matter what he did to make up for it.

Iswander felt increasingly discouraged as he spent his days in the control center. His workers were aware of the looming problem, and he was sure many of them regretted their decision to join him for what had seemed like a get-rich-quick scheme. Others, like

Pannebaker, had faith in him . . . but how long would that last? Sooner or later, Elisa wouldn't be the only one who stole a ship and slipped away. He might have to dissolve these extraction operations, release the workers from their confidentiality contracts, and let them fend for themselves. He couldn't hold them any longer if he had nothing to offer.

Not wanting to seem disheartened in front of them, Iswander excused himself and went back to his private quarters. Londa was always there, cheerful and supportive, loving him no matter what; that was her job as his wife, and she had always done her job well.

He realized that he didn't appreciate her enough and had often dismissed Londa because she wasn't a visionary, a ruthless businesswoman, or a determined deputy like Elisa. No, she followed an old model when playing her role—which was exactly what he had asked of her, exactly why he had married her.

As he entered their quarters, she greeted him brightly. "Lee, you're home early! I'm glad for your company."

"Thank you." He felt immensely weary. He could smell the dinner she had cooked, which was much better than the prepackaged meals he often ate at his console in the control center. Their quarters were perfect, colorfully decorated and modeled after some imagined utopia. He had built Iswander Industries as his empire, but Londa's empire was their home—much less ambitious and with far smaller boundaries, but she ran it perfectly.

"I know you've had a hard day," she said. "If there's anything I can do to help, just let me know. Talk to me. I'm here if you need me."

She brought him a cup of pepperflower tea. He hadn't even been thinking about it, but realized it was what he wanted and needed. "You always take good care of me, but I haven't done right by you."

She gave a dismissive wave. "Of course you have. What more could I want?"

He took a long sip, closed his eyes, and sat down in a comfortable chair. "What more could you want? You're living all alone in an isolated complex, far from civilization. You don't have any friends here. You can't do the things you want to. Our son is gone." He shook his head, feeling determined. "That's not fair to you."

"You're my husband. That's what I agreed to do. I can't run your business, but I can be a good wife."

"And I can be a good husband," Iswander said, making up his mind. "That's why I'm going to send you away. You shouldn't stay here. Go to Newstation—I'll pay for the best quarters there. You can make a home, have friends, do whatever you like—and you'll be close to Arden." Londa tried to argue against the suggestion, but he watched her expression brighten. "It will just be temporary," he continued, "until things settle here. I owe it to you for everything you've done for me."

"But I shouldn't," Londa said. "I belong here with you."

"I know you think that, but this isn't what you signed up for. Go back to Newstation and lay the groundwork for my return. Spread the good word for me among your friends. If you convince them, they'll tell their friends. Maybe we can salvage this."

She looked startled. "You really think I can help?"

He didn't want to point out that with his reputation at rock-bottom, anything would help. He looked through their window-port, musing. Bloaters drifted there, lumbering, innocuous, and peaceful. The nodules sparkled as a chain of internal flashes bounced through them in succession, one glimmer after another. The energy surges had been happening more often, making operations increasingly hazardous. Maybe it would be best to shut down the ekti-extraction operations, before anyone else was hurt . . . before the Roamers had another reason to heap blame on him.

Londa said, "I'll tell them you're a good man, Lee. I'll make them believe me."

"You can try." He smiled at her as he finished his tea and stood up to kiss her on the cheek. "I'll have Pannebaker deliver you to Newstation as soon as you pack your things. I'm staying here, though. I can't leave . . . not yet."

Londa was obviously torn, but she would do as he asked. As he thought about it, he realized that he didn't look forward to having her away. This complex was already lonely enough with Elisa gone, but he had endured worse, and he would get through this. Lee Iswander just had to find another way—as he always did.

35

ELISA ENTURI

Because her stolen ship came from Iswander Industries, Elisa removed the external markings and doctored the registered ID code. When she slipped into Newstation, she didn't identify herself. Just a traveler keeping a low profile. She had business to do here. Personal business.

Roamer security had always been lax. The people were busy, independent, and disorganized. The old-guard clans did handshake deals based on family connections, promises, and personalities. Not a real business plan, she thought. She'd never had any respect for them.

Though Lee Iswander was a Roamer himself, he had struggled for years to make the clans follow the norms of commerce. But rather than adhering to the rules that made Iswander Industries so successful and wealthy, Roamers mockingly compared him to the hated Chairman Basil Wenceslas from the Hansa. They had humiliated him when he tried to become clan Speaker, and Elisa was insulted and indignant on his behalf. Couldn't they see what a great man he was?

She forced herself to stop thinking about him, though. Iswander had cut her loose, thrown her out the airlock, and she was on her own now. So many people had disappointed her: her own family back on Earth, with their lackadaisical sense of entitlement, riding on the coattails of Elisa's hard work . . . and Garrison Reeves, the Roamer man she had married. He had rebelled against his own backward clan, and the two of them together should have shaken up the Confederation—but Garrison's priorities had turned out to be all wrong. Another disappointment. She had thought Lee Iswander was different from that, more admirable.

She had been chased away from her life and accomplishments, had lost everything. Almost. She would claim her son and make sure he was raised properly. Seth had talent and intelligence, Elisa knew it. She would take him away from the distractions and misdirections of Roamer brainwashing. The boy was the last thing that she could call her own.

Bypassing the main station, Elisa went straight for the hollowed-out comet that served as the Roamer school, where Seth was. The comet glowed unnaturally against the darkness of space, contaminated with the faint presence of wentals.

Elisa didn't like Seth living there. What if the supposedly benevolent water elementals harmed him? Another reason to take him away.

She set course for the school's delivery hangar, transmitting that her ship carried requested supplies for Academ. After landing, she armed herself with a charged stunner pistol, making sure she could set the intensity to Kill, should that become necessary. Elisa was not going to tolerate anyone who tried to stop her from taking her son.

Iswander had made Elisa choose her priorities, and she had decided to ignore family dramas and distractions to concentrate entirely on her career, which Iswander promised would be important. She had wrestled with her choice, but the answer had always been obvious. She wanted to be with Lee Iswander. She could either affect thousands of lives, alter the politics and the economy of the Confederation, even change the course of history, or she could be a devoted parent. Elisa had accepted the sacrifice.

Now, Iswander had made even that sacrifice moot, and the other choice was all Elisa had left. . . .

She worked her way down the sloping ice tunnels, knowing where the classrooms were. She had taken Seth away once before. Maybe she could find him quickly and whisk him away before anyone could react. She was the boy's mother, after all. It was her right to take him.

But she was sure they would try to stop her.

She glanced into several chambers, found Roamer clerical workers and teachers, but no sign of Seth. When she came upon a Teacher compy heading with purposeful steps toward a classroom, she stopped it. "Tell me where to find Seth Reeves."

The compy paused in midstride to access class schedules. "Level four. He is currently in a hydraulic engineering class taught by the Teacher compy KA. Shall I escort you there?"

Elisa didn't want to waste any time. "Yes. I'm in a hurry."

The compy led the way to a nearby lift, which dropped them down two levels. The pale wental glow inside the ice added an eerie lambent illumination. Elisa wanted to get her boy out of there quickly.

They emerged and headed straight for a large chamber hollowed out of the wall. Without pausing, the compy stepped into the classroom. "This woman requests Seth Reeves."

Elisa would rather not have announced herself so prominently. Her determination wavered when she saw Jess Tamblyn and Cesca Peroni teaching the class together. They turned to look at her in surprise.

She moved past the compy and spotted Seth immediately in the second row. As a mother, she knew she had a close connection with her child. "I'm taking my son. He belongs with me—not here." She reached out her hand.

Seth shocked her by recoiling. "No!"

Then she was astonished to see Garrison and his new girlfriend Orli at the back of the classroom. They must have come to visit Seth. Garrison ran forward to stand in front of the boy, blocking her. "No. You've lost your right to make those decisions."

Orli Covitz also rushed to get in the way. With a flushed face and fists clenched at her sides, she glared at Elisa. "You tried to kill me. And not *just* me—you're a murderer many times over."

Elisa felt ready to explode. Had they planned this, all conspiring to keep her away from her own son? "What are you doing here?" She reached for her stunner, wondering if she had enough charge to drop all of them.

While the students began talking excitedly, Jess and Cesca also closed protectively around the boy. Jess said, "The Roamer convocation has put out a warrant for your arrest, Elisa. You destroyed a clan complex and murdered all the people in it."

She did not back down, though. "I don't accept those charges, and the Roamer convocation has no jurisdiction over me. I was absolutely justified in my actions." She raised the stunner pistol.

Garrison didn't waver either. "You were always good at justifying your actions, Elisa. But you won't take Seth." He and Orli stood closer together to block the boy—as if they thought she would shoot her own son!

"I'm not giving you a choice." Keeping the weapon aimed at Garrison, Elisa pointedly switched the stunner's setting to Kill. No use settling for half-measures.

Seth grabbed his father's hand and—even more infuriating—held on to Orli's as well.

Then one of Seth's classmates stepped into the middle of the conflict, someone she hadn't noticed before. "You don't want to do this. He's my friend, and that's not what he wants." Elisa recognized the young man—Arden Iswander. He looked so much like his father that she was momentarily disoriented. This made no sense at all. Arden knew everything that Elisa had accomplished for Iswander Industries, knew how much his own family owed her. Yet he stepped forward to join Seth! "Did my father send you?"

Elisa was appalled by every aspect of the scenario. Lee Iswander's son taking Garrison's side! She felt whiplash from so many unexpected reactions. She raised the stun pistol and pointed it at the cluster of wide-eyed Roamer children. "No, your father didn't send me. And I am tired of being betrayed."

Garrison and Orli didn't move. "Think it through, Elisa. Where would you go?" Garrison said. "Roamers are Confederation citizens. No matter where you go, those murder charges will be hanging over your head."

A Teacher compy stepped forward from the front of the room. "I'm afraid I must ask you to leave. You are disrupting our class."

Elisa blasted the compy with a kill-intensity stun bolt, which sent him reeling before he clattered to the floor. Garrison grabbed Seth, shielding him in case she shot again. The other children in the classroom yelled and scrambled away in random directions.

Before Elisa could fire again, Cesca cried out and launched herself forward. "Stop!" At her shout, the glow in the walls of the comet intensified.

Jess slapped his hand against the ice wall and said in an odd voice, "The wentals—!"

With a surge of light, energy rippled beneath Elisa's feet, and the comet walls crackled. She felt sparks, shocks—directed at her. The pulse nearly knocked her off her feet. Static swirled around the weapon in her hand.

No one else was affected, but another ripple of the pale blue light curled up from the cometary ice and throbbed through her body . . . she wasn't harmed, but could feel a clear warning. Elisa backed away, swinging the stunner from side to side, target to target, but she saw that the charge had been drained. "He's my son!"

Garrison and Orli folded around him, and Seth held on to them. Jess and Cesca both touched the ice walls now, and the wentals surged even brighter. Elisa couldn't fight them.

Silently vowing to return, stronger next time, she bolted out of the classroom before the wental energy could strike her again. Leaving turmoil behind her, she ran up the tunnels brandishing the ineffective stunner at anyone who tried to block her way.

All around her, bright wental light continued to intensify through the cometary ice, driving her away.

Elisa cursed all the forces arrayed against her. She had to escape. Regroup. Form new plans.

Hating that the capricious wentals could lash out at any time, hating Garrison, and hating everyone in this Roamer complex, she reached her stolen ship and activated the engines as fast as she could. Newstation security would surely be coming after her now. Alarms had been sent through the complex, but evading them wouldn't be a problem.

Elisa knew she would be back. They couldn't stop her so easily.

36

XANDER BRINDLE

The souped-up *Verne* made quite an impression when it arrived at Newstation. Showing off, Xander arranged for a VIP docking berth with all the amenities. His partner was not comfortable with the extravagance, calling it unnecessary, but Xander knew it was the best way to get the Roamers to pay attention.

"We don't need to be treated as special," Terry said.

"It's not for our egos," Xander reassured him. "It's to make them take us seriously. This way they'll really listen when we present our plan."

Although the two men looked far too young to be captains of industry, Xander had a respected Roamer clan name, and they had the weight of Kett Shipping behind them—not to mention Maria Ulio's money. With that, he and Terry would receive an open-minded hearing when they presented their crazy yet ambitious idea at the next clan convocation. The very thought of their proposed trading complex made Xander grin. It struck right to the heart of what made Roamers great.

OK filed all the appropriate online forms and dealt with the tedious admin details while Xander and Terry went out to enjoy a fine meal in the most expensive eating establishment on Newstation. "There were thirteen restaurants on Ulio that I never got to try," Terry said. "I always thought there'd be time."

"We'll just have to make up for it." Xander lounged back. "We can commission a bunch of new restaurants at our station. That'll be a priority for us."

"No, *gathering and repairing ships* will be our priority. New restaurants will be a pleasant bonus."

Xander requested a slot on the agenda of the regular clan meeting the following day, and dropped numerous hints that he and Terry were going to have a grand announcement. Right now, Newstation was disorganized with Roamers rushing about to get in on the new ekti-extraction boom, but most of them didn't have the equipment or the funds to do what they wanted. There weren't enough ships available for sale.

Their new outpost might take care of that problem—in the long term.

Terry was not much of a public speaker, nor was he a Roamer, but Xander told him not to worry. "I'll make the speech. I'll convince them. Let's face it, I'm better at it than you are."

"You are indeed a far superior bullshitter."

Though Xander pretended to be calm, he spent a lot of time contemplating what he would say. The next day, as they headed toward the convocation hall, he felt excitement building within him. The chambers were crowded with clan members curious to hear their big news. Most of them were discussing the tragic reports that the Shana Rei and the black robots had completely destroyed Relleker, a prominent Confederation colony. The CDF battle group had barely escaped with their lives.

Xander was outraged. "That's just what they did at Ulio!"

"This makes our proposal more necessary than ever," Terry said.

On the way to the convocation chamber, Xander spotted Orli Covitz along with Garrison Reeves and Garrison's son Seth. As Xander thought of clan Reeves and the famously stubborn Olaf Reeves, the last piece fell into place in his mind. It was the perfect solution.

Sending Terry ahead with OK, Xander grabbed Garrison's arm. "I've got an idea to run by you! If nothing else, I'd like your blessing . . . just because."

In a rush, he described his proposal. At first Garrison was pensive; then his face lit up. "That's a fine idea. In fact, I'll be the first to sign up." He glanced at Orli. "Are you interested? For safety's sake, it might be best to take Seth away from here anyway."

She smiled. "I am if you are. Sounds like something we'd like to do."

Feeling lighter on his feet, Xander hurried in to meet Terry, who looked overwhelmed by the crowds of curious Roamers. Not long ago, in front of a similar convocation, Xander's parents and Orli had revealed that bloaters were the source of ekti-X, which was triggering a sudden shift in clan dynamics and Roamer business.

Xander and Terry's announcement was going to be just as important.

"You don't need to talk, unless you want to," he reassured Terry as they approached the main podium. "Just stand next to me." He couldn't stop grinning about the surprise he was about to add.

When Speaker Ricks introduced them, the man didn't seem overly interested in what they had to say, but Xander quickly grabbed the attention of the audience. "Ulio Station is destroyed—Terry and I barely got away with our lives." He let that hang for a moment. "Right now, the clans are in turmoil because everyone used Ulio as a trading nexus. Roamer trade is scattered and suffering. So what are we going to do?"

He ran his gaze across the rows of faces. "We need a place just like Ulio Station—an independent center where we can salvage or repair ships and where traders and other businesspeople can meet." He clapped a hand on his partner's shoulder, making him flinch. "And Terry and I are going to build it."

He heard mutters mixed with chuckles and sighs of disbelief. Disappointed expressions appeared in the audience; they had come expecting a grand announcement, only to hear an unlikely pie-in-the-sky scheme.

Xander knew he would make them come around quickly enough. "We already have the funds. Everything. Paid in full. Our new trading and repair hub will be open for business before you know it. Right now I'm asking the clans to support us."

Terry seemed embarrassed, but he confirmed. "It's true. We have all the resources we need. I inherited Maria Ulio's fortune. We can begin work. We can pay you. All we need is people who want to join us—oh, and some wrecked ships to start with." His voice grew somber. "I guess there'll be a lot of damaged vessels at Relleker. We can salvage them."

After Terry's grim reminder, Xander quickly brought the conversation back to excited optimism. "And by the Guiding Star, Handon Station will grow from there."

Embarrassed, Terry leaned forward to the voice pickup. "We haven't actually decided what to call it."

Xander talked over him, emphasizing the name. "*Handon Station* will be a place where Roamer dreams can thrive. And we're ready to get started."

"But where will you put this new complex of yours?" called out an older woman, the head of clan Gupta.

"We have just the place," Xander said. Terry looked at him in surprise, but he continued, "Ulio Station was out in the middle of nowhere, and that proved a great advantage for ships of all types. Our location is even better, and it's got history." He paused, unable to hide his grin. He glanced over at Garrison Reeves. "We intend to open our operations at Rendezvous."

Mutters—mostly of pleasant surprise—rippled through the gathered clan members.

Garrison spoke up from the audience. "Clan Reeves spent years trying to stabilize the damaged asteroids and make them habitable again, but my father's mistake was that he tried to re-create Rendezvous *exactly* as it was as the Roamer capital. This is a better idea, and I think the place will be perfect. I wholeheartedly support the plan—in fact, I've already signed on to help build Handon Station."

Terry looked exasperated, but Xander knew the name had caught on now, and they would never be able to change it. He saw the mood shift take hold among the Roamers, and their chatter became excited rather than disappointed.

"I'll be taking signups, and then we can send salvage crews to Relleker. We'll start moving ships to the old Rendezvous cluster and build from there. In time, we expect Handon Station to be even bigger than Ulio!"

OK stepped forward to take applications, while Xander and Terry were ready to shake hands and answer questions. Before long, they had far more signups than they ever expected.

37

KOTTO OKIAH

The survey craft was ready at Fireheart Station, so no more excuses. Every conceivable sensor package had been installed and tested, additional hull shielding mounted, double backups included in the life-support systems and engines. Six weeks' worth of food, water, and oxygen supplies loaded aboard, just in case he got lost in that incomprehensible void, although Kotto expected the trip to last no more than a few days.

No one knew what to expect when Kotto flew the ship into that rift in space, but he was confident he had taken every possibility into account. At least he *appeared* to be confident, as far as everyone else was concerned. "I follow my Guiding Star," he muttered, "even if it takes me into a deep, dark hole."

For so many years Roamers had turned to Kotto for answers, and he didn't want to disappoint them by hinting that he was baffled. He'd gotten quite good at using technical jargon and obtuse mathematic derivations to confuse people who pressed him for answers. He didn't like to explain too much.

He'd always possessed such an instinctive grasp of science and engineering that his intuitive leaps usually turned out to be right. Even when they didn't, he had the safety net of his reputation. But in recent years his leaps had been more like blindly jumping off a cliff—especially the Big Ring project.

And now Kotto had something to prove.

A recognized genius didn't just decide to stop having ideas. That was why the Big Ring had meant so much to him, and even after the catastrophic results of the full-power test, he still wanted to yank some breakthrough out of the experiment. He had suggested that the Ring might be used to form a gateway out in space, like a Klik-iss transportal large enough to take whole cargo ships from point to point, but he had never expected the gigantic structure to collapse into another dimension.

Now he had to forge ahead and investigate, and maybe even prove that he had been correct in the first place.

KR and GU had triple-checked the survey craft's systems and backups, but Shareen and Howard remained uneasy. The teens had already proved to be adept at spotting subtle flaws in his calcula-tions, and now they wanted to verify the systems themselves. Finally, even they were satisfied. Shareen frowned as she finished checking inside the survey craft's cockpit, closed the access hatches, and nod-ded. "It looks good, as far as I can tell."

"You really shouldn't go into the void, sir," Howard repeated. "It's not necessary."

"Of course it's necessary," Kotto said, starting to feel harassed. "We need to understand, and somebody has to take a look. It has always been necessary for someone to take the first leap in explora-tion. That should fall on the shoulders of the inventor. I made that hole, so it should be me."

"Why not send the compies alone?" Shareen said. "At least the first time."

"We will volunteer," KR and GU said in perfect unison.

"You're coming along with me as a backup," Kotto said, making his voice more strident. He didn't want to talk about this any more. "This isn't just an esoteric laboratory experiment. We don't have time to dip in one little toe. That gap could be dangerous."

"Exactly," Shareen said. "That's why—"

Kotto blew a long exasperated sigh through his lips. "Enough! We've been over this—it's time for me to go."

"We are ready, Kotto Okiah," said GU. The compies seemed eager to jump aboard the survey craft right at that instant.

Secretly, Kotto had hoped to find excuses to delay, but that would have been too apparent. He had stalled too much near the end of the Big Ring construction, dithering due to his own uncertainties even after the project was complete. He could not do that now.

No more excuses. He'd already informed Fireheart that he was ready to launch, and the Roamer workers were watching him. From their greenhouse, where construction on the expanded dome had begun, Celli and Solimar had sent out an announcement through telink. All eyes were on him.

If Kotto came back as a triumphant hero, that would certainly make up for the recent debacle. He was nervous, but he also felt a longing. He wanted to *understand*. He wanted to see with his own eyes a mystery that no other human being had ever beheld.

Ever since his youth, the universe had been one gigantic puzzle box to him, a treasure chest of questions and answers. All his life he had pondered insights and revelations, and he wanted more. Right now, he was so desperate that he could taste it. Straightening, he blocked out all other concerns.

Station Chief Alu hurried into the launching bay. "We hope you can decide how to fix that big pothole you created, Kotto, or at least make it do something useful."

He gave an upbeat smile. "Like every explorer, I do this for the sense of discovery. The practical utility of big discoveries isn't always apparent right away."

Alu sniffed. "What's apparent to me is that big hole in the middle of the nebula, and a lot of us are worried that you might have created a back door to where the Shana Rei live. You do have the sun bombs with you?"

The Confederation Defense Forces had provided Fireheart with two new sun bombs. Kotto frowned. "Yes, they're in the hold, and I want to get rid of them as soon as possible. I don't like carrying the things."

"It's just a precaution. If we never need to trigger them, then no harm done."

Shareen's expression darkened. "If you see the Shana Rei, don't mess around. Howard and I barely survived when they erupted from the clouds on Golgen. You don't want to meet the shadows in person."

"No, I do not," Kotto said. "I don't know that two sun bombs at the edge of the gap would stop a full-scale Shana Rei attack, but I'll deploy them as promised." He gave Shareen a strong hug, then formally shook Howard's hand. "I'll bring back some great discoveries, or at least more questions. That's what science is all about."

Howard and Shareen agreed but looked uncertain.

Kotto entered the survey craft, and his two compies marched up the ramp behind him, then sealed the hatch. As soon as he was out of sight inside, Kotto let out a long trembling breath.

For good measure, even though it caused yet another delay, he ran a final check on the systems. Finally, he activated the engines and headed out of the launching bay and away from the admin facility, crossing the nebula sea toward the yawning black emptiness where the Big Ring had been. "On our way at last," he said.

Flying at a steady pace, he passed the warning buoys that Garrison Reeves had installed. The compies operated the controls, although Kotto was ready to take over in the event of an emergency.

With the landmarks of Fireheart Station and the nebula's core supergiant stars, he could navigate, but beyond the trapdoor, he had no idea how he would find his way forward. He hoped he could see the real universe from the opposite side so he could find his way back out again.

Kotto wasn't comfortable about bringing the sun bombs into the void, worried that something might go wrong. What if some altered laws of physics scrambled the warheads' reactive systems? What if that triggered a nova chain reaction much too soon?

As the survey craft approached the void's edge, he transmitted back with false cheer, "All systems normal so far. No fluctuations, no danger. Everything just fine. No sign of the Shana Rei yet."

"Tiptoe where possible. Let's hope you don't wake anything up in there, Kotto," said Chief Alu. "If you come running back out with monsters on your heels, be sure you're ready to detonate those sun bombs."

Kotto acknowledged, muttering, "But only if the shadows come howling out after me." He wondered if the energy discharge would be sufficient to close the tear in the universe. Or maybe it would rip the void open wider.

"We've reached the boundary, Kotto Okiah," KR said. "Ready to proceed."

Kotto slowed the survey craft to a crawl and paused to do a full sensor sweep ahead, but there was nothing comprehensible to see. Exactly as expected.

"Here we go," Kotto said. He nudged the engines and accelerated into the void.

38

EXXOS

The gigantic shadow clouds folded in and out of space like tesseracts, weak points in the universe where the Shana Rei broke down the fabric of spacetime and traveled into realspace.

But the clouds emerged at places so random they frustrated Exxos, making it impossible for him to plan. Destroying the cosmos required immense long-term strategy, but the creatures of darkness would not be managed, even for their own good. For now, though, until Exxos could gain the upper hand and make the shadows do what he said, the robots simply had to seize opportunities and react. Chaos incarnate was not conducive to the implementation of a complex scheme, but the shadows' omnipotent powers made up for the insanity and gave Exxos reason to believe that they might succeed after all.

Eventually, the black robots would have to eradicate the Shana Rei as well—that was a foregone conclusion. And those plans were also in process, the infinitely difficult calculations under way. Meanwhile, Exxos would bide his time and continue causing as much destruction as possible.

A new shadow cloud unfolded, and the black hexagonal cylinders slid out of interdimensional space, returning to the Onthos home system. Their recent victories at the Ildiran colony of Wythira and the human planet of Relleker had extinguished some of the agony of sentient life, and that allowed the Shana Rei to grow even more powerful. Both of those populated planets were now completely dead. One hundred percent of the infesting life-forms were wiped out in the holocaust.

The triumphs had not come without cost, though. The surprising number of sun bombs used by the enemy had inflicted significant damage on the Shana Rei hex cylinders, and far more important, had destroyed twenty percent of his robots and battleships. Nearly 200,000 copies of Exxos eradicated.

While the black robots need no longer be worried about extinction, losing such a significant part of their force remained an annoyance—one that Exxos expected the Shana Rei to fix.

As yet another shadow cloud appeared at the Onthos system, Exxos surveyed the remnants of the gigantic black shell that had enclosed the original star and the planets. In that opaque shell composed of trillions of black hexagonal plates, Exxos saw only raw material, enough to make all the replacement robots he could want.

The damaged hex cylinders hovered above the mosaic barrier. Hundreds of thousands of black plates detached from the shell and twirled back up to incorporate their material into rebuilding the Shana Rei vessels, swelling and extending them. In short order, they had replenished all the damage inflicted upon their own hex cylinders, but they kept strengthening themselves with more dark matter, extruding another entire vessel.

Four shapeless inkblots appeared in front of Exxos, their glowing sightless eyes directed toward him, but he was not intimidated.

"Those battles damaged us," said one of the Shana Rei, sounding petulant.

"Yes, but we caused far more damage to our enemies," Exxos said. "I achieved that, and I know you can feel it. Think of all those minds that caused you pain—they have been silenced thanks to my robots, and that is just the beginning. We will silence many, many more of them. That is what you want."

The creatures of darkness were mercurial, volatile. Simply to demonstrate their power, or their sheer unpredictability, they would select and torture Klikiss robots at random. During the early days of their captivity, Exxos had lost dozens of his unique comrades as the shadows tore them apart, dismantling their components down into individual atoms. So many irreplaceable robot memories had vanished before Exxos took the unprecedented step of consolidating them all, copying every mind, so that each one became *Exxos,* thus ensuring that nothing more was lost.

Now, either in a fit of pique or to assert their dominance, the shadows separated out ten flailing Exxos copies. Even though both attacks had been clear victories, the Shana Rei tore apart the robot carapaces, popping off their head plates, dismantling their segmented limbs, shredding their inner circuitry.

Exxos did not hide his irritation. "Why do you persist in making more work for yourselves? I require sufficient robots to attack the sentient creatures who give you pain, and now you have destroyed perfectly good fighters. You need to re-create the robots you just destroyed—and many more."

He stood firm before the Shana Rei. Because of the obvious recent successes with so many robots, Exxos explained, the shadows would want to continue their attacks and expand to even more ambitious targets.

"I am trying to win this war. I am trying to make good use of our resources. Think of the destruction I have helped you achieve—is that not what you wish to continue?" The inkblots pulsed, as if confused, unwilling to consider the logic of Exxos's argument. "In order for us to keep winning, you must stop destroying my robots, and you must replace the ones I lost during these two engagements. You have the material to do it."

The Shana Rei considered this. "Yes, we have sufficient material."

"And you have the energy, and you have the will. We are your allies. Fight the proper enemy and win the proper war. Restore my robots." He paused, and then added as if it were an offhanded comment, "I need another million of them—for now."

It was an arbitrary number, but enough for Exxos to feel strong, maybe even invincible—and for all of the secretly coupled robot processors to work in parallel while they made calculations for their other plans.

"We will restore your robots," the inkblots agreed. The Shana Rei did not seem to grasp the importance of numbers.

"And our ships," Exxos said.

The shadows didn't hesitate. "And your ships."

A gigantic yet still insignificant swath of hexagonal plates disengaged from the ebony shell, and the Shana Rei manipulated the matter to rebuild the robot attack ships, atom by atom, using the dark matter. Then they reassembled a million more identical robots, and Exxos could feel their minds coming online. The new robots immediately copied and transferred all of the thoughts, memories, and secret programming from Exxos. Synchronized again.

Exxos felt stronger than ever. Perhaps next time he would ask for ten million. The Shana Rei would not likely see any difference.

Now for the next step. "Our follow-up target needs to be even more substantial than those two colony worlds. We are not just erasing one population after another—we are inspiring *fear*. We are making all of them feel despair—which weakens their entire race. It causes them to make mistakes."

The Shana Rei gathered around, and Exxos faced them with his red optical sensors. "Fear will weaken them like a disease, and it will do our work for us."

The Shana Rei did not understand the concept of a disease, and Exxos had to explain it for them. They seemed intrigued. "Choose another planet for us to attack," they said. "And we will snuff out more of the painful sentients."

Exxos had already considered this. "The planet I have selected will not only kill substantial numbers of the enemy, it will also generate the maximum amount of fear."

The Shana Rei did not seem curious, simply waited for Exxos to explain. "The heart of the human race, the origin of their civilization, is *Earth*. That planet is one of their largest population centers, one of their most vital worlds." He remembered the sting of how the Klikiss robots had been utterly defeated at the end of the Elemental War. It would be a long-overdue revenge.

Yes, there were plenty of reasons to choose Earth.

"We will bring our entire force there, destroy that planet, and leave its surface a smoking ruin. The death of Earth will signal the death of the human race."

The inkblots paused, pulsing with their infinite shadows, and the central eyes brightened. "Our vessels, your robot soldiers, and your battleships are restored. We will proceed to destroy Earth."

39

TAL GALE'NH

Tal Gale'nh accompanied the Adar as they entered a bright conference chamber where Mage-Imperator Jora'h had called a war council. Prime Designate Daro'h was there, as well as Yazra'h and Muree'n.

The Adar wasted no time in issuing his report. "Thanks to increased production on numerous worlds, the Solar Navy is stronger than it has been since the height of the Elemental War."

"Yet the shadows are stronger still," Jora'h said. "They just proved it at Wythira, and with the mob of possessed attenders."

"We know how to hurt them," Gale'nh pointed out. "We inflicted great damage on the black robots at Kuivahr."

His sister Muree'n interjected, "We destroyed them *all,* Liege. We saw it! There could not have been more than two or three robot survivors."

Zan'nh straightened in his seat, obviously disturbed. "Yet hundreds of thousands of them struck Wythira. How is that possible? Are they being replenished?"

Gale'nh considered the englobing shell around Kuivahr and the much larger sphere that had surrounded the Onthos system. "Any beings that can swallow entire planets or star systems can certainly manufacture a few robots. We may be facing an infinite supply of enemies."

Rememberer Anton asked, "What about the faeros? When they appeared over the Prism Palace, we seemed to have accomplished something. Will they help us?"

"We communicated with them, and I sense they are willing to

fight our common enemy," Jora'h agreed. "But how can I call upon them if I do not know where the shadows will strike next?"

The Prime Designate turned to the human historian. "The Shana Rei were defeated once before. Mage-Imperator Xiba'h forged an alliance with the faeros—how did they win?"

Rememberer Anton sighed and scratched his head. "I've read those ancient sections over and over, but the old rememberers were more interested in creating a legend than an accurate chronicle. A lot of vital information was edited out—such as the actual way they defeated the creatures of darkness. I'll keep studying the apocrypha, in hopes of finding something."

While compiling astronomical records from across the Empire, Solar Navy patrols noted alarming changes in empty space. Many more shadow clouds had appeared out of nowhere, and instead of being transient as before, they remained like beachheads holding conquered territory throughout the Spiral Arm. And those dark nebulas were growing larger.

Gale'nh found it very disturbing. Not so long ago, he had believed that the Ildiran Empire was entering a new golden age. The *Kolpraxa* had been launched with great fanfare to open a new section of the galaxy. Instead, that grand expedition had encountered the first of the awakening shadow clouds. The *Kolpraxa* had provoked the creatures of darkness somehow. And now they were intent on destroying the Spiral Arm.

Gale'nh pushed away a disturbing thought: What if he was the one who had drawn the Shana Rei here?

40

SHAWN FENNIS

He and Chiar'h waited for days at the transportal nexus of Gorhum, tending the misbreeds with the outpost's inadequate facilities, and waiting for news of Tamo'l. The medical kith members from the sanctuary domes on Kuivahr were skilled at handling the genetic misfits, and the refugees did survive. But they needed to get back to Ildira.

Two Confederation trading ships arrived at Gorhum with goods to send through the transportal for customers on other settled Klikiss worlds. Shawn Fennis begged the traders to fly his group to Ildira, but the traders regarded the freakish specimens with awkward embarrassment and made excuses. Pol'ux—lying bedridden and his body swollen with boils—beseeched them to no avail, and even the heartbreaking songs of Mungl'eh did not convince them.

When the traders flew off, leaving the Kuivahr refugees behind, Chiar'h turned to her husband, her smooth Ildiran face flushed. From the stiffness of her movements, Fennis could tell how angry she was. He tried to reassure her. "We'll find the right person."

The outpost chief clearly wanted all these special-needs strangers to go away as well, so that Gorhum could return to its quiet existence. The man gestured to the stone trapezoidal wall with its ring of co-ordinate tiles. "Maybe if you go through the transportal to another world, they'll have better facilities for you? Someplace other than Gorhum? It might even get you closer to the Ildiran Empire."

Fennis shook his head. "Our patients are already fragile, and at least they're stable for the moment. I don't want to impose stress by moving them unless we genuinely have a way home." He held firm to his determination.

Finally, after five days, an old Kett Shipping vessel arrived. Dando Yoder, a salty old trader who specialized in making niche runs to underserved worlds, stopped to deliver basic necessities to the settlement. As soon as Yoder's ship landed, Fennis hurried out to meet him, hoping to convince the trader to take at least the misbreeds that needed more specialized medical attention. Fennis stepped up, all business. "We need transportation to the Ildiran Empire. We're hoping we can hire you."

Yoder, a squat, squarish man with a graying beard, ran a hand through his tousled hair. "That's out of my way—and expensive."

"When we get to Ildira we can pay you well."

"Now, I don't have any reason to disbelieve you, though I'd prefer more of a guarantee and some sort of down payment."

Fennis thought the Gorhum outpost chief might be willing to pay just to get the misbreeds out of there, but Chiar'h interrupted with a hard voice, fighting to save her patients. "We promise the Mage-Imperator himself will pay you. We have special cargo that is important to the Empire, and we need transportation."

Fennis wanted to get an answer from Yoder before the man caught a glimpse of the most deformed misbreeds, but Gor'ka, Har'lc, and Alaa'kh emerged from the station buildings, moving awkwardly toward the ship. Yoder's eyes went wide. Fennis's heart sank. The captain would probably be too squeamish to let the repellent misbreeds aboard his ship.

"What are those things?"

"They are your cargo," Chiar'h explained. "Our patients, and our friends."

Fennis added, "These are survivors from the Dobro breeding program, genetic mixtures that were part of an experiment."

"Looks like the experiment failed," Yoder mused, but his voice held no malice.

"Possibly . . . or perhaps their special powers have not yet been identified," Chiar'h said.

"We believe they all have special abilities," Fennis said. "They were created during desperate times in the Elemental War, and now that we face the Shana Rei, can we afford to dismiss anyone who might possibly help?"

Yoder paled. "Those damn shadows! I barely got away from Kui-vahr with my skin intact. I mostly dealt with the Kellums and their distillery, but I heard about the sanctuary domes down there. I know about your misbreeds. How'd you get away?"

Alaa'kh said in a slurping voice, "We escaped through the trans-portal."

Fennis pressed, "And now we need to get to Ildira. Name your price. We will pay it—please."

Other misbreeds came forward to beseech the trader. Fennis was afraid they might look threatening to him, but the old trader didn't seem overly troubled. He eyed them, as if assessing cargo possibili-ties. "They don't look too healthy. I don't want to be held responsi-ble if any of them die en route."

"You will not be blamed," Chiar'h said. "They are in our care."

Yoder sighed. "Rlinda Kett would have my hide if she found out I didn't help suffering medical patients who needed it. And I know what kind of hell you went through getting away from Kuivahr." He put his hands on his hips. "All right. My ship isn't big enough to take everyone in your group, though."

"Just the misbreeds who need it most," Chiar'h said.

Fennis added, "We'll send Solar Navy ships back here to retrieve the swimmer kith and the rest of the Kuivahr refugees. For now, we need to get our patients to Ildira and report to the Mage-Imperator."

"Maybe he knows where Tamo'l is," Gor'ka said. "Maybe she is already home."

The meek outpost chief rushed out, hoping to add his encourage-ment, but the decision was already made. All the timid man could say was "I wholeheartedly applaud your efforts, Dando. Thank you. Those misbreeds will be much better off away from here."

All the refugees did indeed survive the journey, and Ildiran medical centers rallied to give them the treatment and life support they needed as soon as the ship delivered the misbreeds to Mijistra.

Yoder was astonished by the reward he received from the appre-ciative Mage-Imperator, and he went away with a cargo load of valuable Ildiran goods as well as a cash payment that he said was worth three major deliveries elsewhere. Thanking Fennis, Chiar'h, and the misbreeds for letting him be of service, Yoder took his leave.

Fennis and Chiar'h immediately petitioned the Prism Palace, and the green priest Nira came out to meet them, accompanied by Prime Designate Daro'h and an escort of guard kithmen. Daro'h said, "Adar Zan'nh and Tal Gale'nh just returned from a mission to Kui-vahr. They report that the planet is utterly dead. They found one Roamer survivor in a small ship, but nothing at the sanctuary domes. We are pleased that you are all safe."

Nira spoke to Fennis and Chiar'h. "Do you know what happened to Tamo'l? Did my daughter escape before the shadows came? We've had no word."

Fennis frowned. "Osira'h and Prince Reyn wanted her to come with them at the start of the evacuation, but she wouldn't leave. Ta-mo'l stayed behind to see that all the patients made it safely through the transportal. She and Tom Rom were right behind us on the last run through the transportal. I'm certain they got away—but they may have gone to different coordinates."

Chiar'h said, "The misbreeds have an affinity for Tamo'l. Some claim they can still sense her. We do not know where she is, but we believe she is alive and well."

"Unlike Rod'h," Daro'h said with a sinking voice. "I can feel him like an ache in me, trapped in darkness. The *thism* connection is frayed and poisoned, but he remains a prisoner of the Shana Rei."

"My other children sense both Rod'h and Tamo'l," Nira said, "but they are mystified about my daughter's location. Tell us about this man you say accompanied her."

"Tom Rom arrived at the sanctuary domes to share data. His employer is also a medical researcher, but we don't know where."

In a determined tone, Nira said, "That gives us a place to start. We'll look into it."

TAMO'L

The Pergamus medical station had research facilities and equipment far more sophisticated than Tamo'l had seen anywhere. If she'd had access to such equipment over the past decade, she could have worked wonders for the misbreeds. All that lost potential saddened her.

Zoe Alakis encouraged research for its own sake, but the woman did not seem inclined to put the results to any practical use. Tamo'l didn't understand the point of conducting research that benefited no one.

She wished the misbreeds could be with her now. Tom Rom assured her they had all been rescued from the shadows, but if only the misbreeds were here on Pergamus, she could develop and test numerous medical treatments that might help them. Her misbreeds were elsewhere, though, and she heard no word from them.

Tamo'l was kept isolated in her private laboratory dome. She would ask to send another message back to Ildira to reassure her mother and the survivors from Kuivahr that she was all right. Soon . . .

While her thoughts wandered, Tamo'l dug into the Pergamus database, with more than mere inquisitiveness. She felt a compulsion to do so. The urge came from behind a dark veil in her eyes that she couldn't explain. Sometimes she would work for hours without even realizing what she was doing, and then she would snap back to wakefulness to find that she had scoured databases and conducted risky and questionable tests . . . but to what purpose, she did not know. Something else had been directing her.

Tamo'l shook her head, trying to clear her thoughts. Even with the brilliant illumination inside the lab complex, she had a hard time focusing . . . until she slipped into one of her disturbing fugue states.

Tamo'l was interested in analyzing variations among the misbreeds, successful mixtures between kiths, and more importantly, halfbreeds like her own siblings. Or maybe it was the shadowy compulsion inside her that wanted to know about the halfbreeds so badly. . . .

She heard the access lock click, and Tom Rom came to visit her, startling her out of deep concentration. Although he had rescued her from Kuivahr, he displayed no warmth toward her. Now he stood in the main room, looking at her computers, her genetic-analysis databases, her laboratory systems. Eventually, he gave a slight nod of approval.

"Under normal circumstances, a team of ten or more would work in a lab like this one," he said. "You should not have to do this all yourself. Since you are undertaking ambitious research, I can offer technicians from our Pergamus staff."

Tamo'l felt inexplicably alarmed. "No, the research is personal to me. I work best alone. No one grasps it the way I do." She didn't understand the sudden urgency that swelled up inside her when he suggested sending in assistants. She felt an almost violent reluctance to have any stranger see what she was doing. Tamo'l quelled the alarm and answered politely, "Thank you, but I prefer to work in solitude."

Tom Rom looked deep into her eyes, and she flinched, afraid he might see something there. He gave a brusque nod. "All right, I just wanted to check in with you before I depart. I'm off to visit Klikiss worlds and then Rakkem. I will make sure you have an administrative contact, should you need anything while I'm away."

"I will be content and productive," Tamo'l said. "I have enough work to do . . . so many questions to answer." Without any further farewell, he exited the dome again.

She felt unsettled long after he departed, and she tried to focus on possible research threads to follow. Back on Kuivahr, at the urging of Osira'h, Tamo'l had focused on testing pharmaceutical variations of kelp extracts for Prince Reynald's illness. As a seemingly generous benefactor, Tom Rom had brought the database of

Pergamus research on the disease, and now—even though she was completely cut off from Prince Reyn and Osira'h—Tamo'l pored over those tests, approaching the problem from different angles, using her new equipment.

But before long that dark compulsion drove her toward different studies.

Using genetic-mapping profiles, she developed models of her misbreeds. Since Tom Rom had copied all the data before they escaped from Kuivahr, she still had records on all of them, including the ones who had died over the years. To Tamo'l, the misbreeds were not just pathetic mistakes that should never have been born. She was convinced they had as yet undiscovered abilities that were masked by their infirmities.

After she documented, categorized, and studied the misbreeds on record, Tamo'l felt hungry and exhausted. She began to think about eating a meal . . . but then her consciousness blotted out.

When she became aware again, she found that she had been accessing the vast Pergamus records of the most virulent diseases, including the Onthos plague, which had a mortality rate of nearly one hundred percent. Shocked, Tamo'l saw that she had made a list of the most dangerous pathogens stored in the facility, although she had no idea why. What possible use could that be to her work?

Unsettled, she blanked the screens and deleted the data she'd just compiled. She took a fresh sample of her own blood. Her quest was not just to understand the misbreeds, but to understand her own siblings and herself. She ran a detailed profile and compared it with the profiles of the various misbreeds.

Because Tamo'l was a cross between a human green priest and a lens kithman, her DNA was quite different. Fortunately, she also had stored profiles from her other half-siblings, even Rod'h. The answer had to lie in there . . . but she wasn't entirely sure what the question was.

Rod'h and Gale'nh had been able to resist the shadows somehow, and that was a something she urgently wanted to understand. Tamo'l would devote her efforts to teasing out that answer by comparing DNA samples. She applied herself to the work with a dark, focused intensity. Flickering black static hovered around the edges of her vision, forcing her concentration. She dove into the work, trying to find the key.

Tamo'l had to understand why she and her siblings were different, why they could supposedly resist the Shana Rei . . . although the creatures of darkness seemed to be getting stronger, much stronger.

She also needed to find the answer she feared most—why the shadows had managed to penetrate *her*.

42

ZHETT KELLUM

Finding the abandoned equipment at the fringes of the Osquivel system brought back memories for Zhett. For many years before the Elemental War, clan Kellum had run shipyards in the rings of Osquivel, but when the EDF started cracking down on outlaw Roamers, the Kellums abandoned their shipyards and moved up to the dark cometary cloud. There, unseen, they had broken down huge quantities of comet ice, teasing out rare ekti. After the war, when cloud harvesting became safe and viable again, the Kellums had shelved their cometary operations, which were no longer cost-effective. All the mothballed equipment had just been hanging there for decades.

Zhett smiled as their borrowed ships flew in. The sensor screens detected the drifting vessels, temporary stations, and battered ekti tankers that had been in cold darkness for twenty years. Unmonitored, the components of the former industrial complex had wandered apart, and some facilities had suffered damage from bumping into drifting cometary fragments. But for the most part the ships and equipment seemed intact.

Zhett dispatched a crew to skim around in broad search patterns and map the locations of the primary assets. When large ships were found, Patrick sent survey and salvage crews aboard to reactivate the life-support and power systems. Before leaving Newstation, Del Kellum had used part of the loan he'd received from the treasury to buy a stockpile of power blocks, with which the teams restored the equipment to operational levels.

"It was certainly a different mindset back then, if we could afford to just dump all this stuff here," Zhett mused. "I guess it wasn't financially feasible to move and repurpose it." To her, the large dark ships looked like long-lost treasures wrapped in a sense of nostalgia.

Patrick said, "It's a junkyard."

"Not junk, boy." Del sounded indignant. "We left it in cold storage. And because it's of Roamer manufacture, I bet most of the ships and equipment are perfectly serviceable and ready to go."

"I can manage one of them," Kristof said brightly, "if you'll let me."

"We'll consider it," Patrick said, "but you need to work your way up."

Though Toff had never been a particularly good student, preferring hands-on work to studying, they had planned to send him to Academ, but as soon as this possibility arose, the young man had, with much pleading, convinced them to let him work directly in the operations. Patrick was skeptical, but Zhett knew the value of Roamer work, especially when founding a new business.

"Once we're up and running and making money," she said sternly to Toff, "we're going to get a Teacher compy. You *will* do daily lessons and you *will* score high enough that you don't make me regret this decision."

"I will. I will!"

More importantly, this would be a way for Marius Denva to get back to work and prove he could return his life, and their operations, to normal. Though shaken, Denva was mostly recovered from the black nightmare of being stranded inside the shell around Kuivahr. After the Ildirans returned him to Newstation, Zhett, Del, and Patrick were astonished to learn of his rescue. The entire distillery crew had been sure he had died in the shadow attack.

"I just took a little longer to get away from Kuivahr than the rest of you did," he said, trying to brush aside their concerns. "Next time, I promise I won't lag behind. Once was enough."

He had surprised Zhett by signing up again to work with the Kellums. As a Roamer, Denva's skills were adaptable to whatever industrial operations Del got into his head, and the survivor was treated with awe and respect by the rest of his crew. At his request, Zhett did everything she could to treat him the same as always.

Since they had all worked with Denva before, Zhett was glad to have him supervising the new crew, which included most of the distillery workers who had escaped from Kuivahr.

Zhett promised to give him a raise, as soon as they had any money.

Now, with a broadband comm playing the background chatter, Zhett listened to the crew discussions and heard a new excitement in their voices. They were still terrified of the Shana Rei, with good reason, and they knew nothing was safe, but they were *Roamers* and eager to start harvesting ekti again. It seemed to be in their blood.

"We rounded up fourteen viable units, Del," Denva reported, already deep into the new job. "We might have to spend a week or two duct-taping systems, recharging power blocks, and making them all functional again, but we'll get it done."

"Take days instead of weeks, by damn," Del said. "We have plenty of exosuits and temporary life-support systems. Once we get the engines patched and running, we can do the interior decorating while we shepherd the equipment across space to the nearest bloater cluster."

"That's the next question," Zhett said. "We have to find one that hasn't been claimed. Where do we set up our extraction operations?"

As soon as the ekti rush began, scouts had scoured the Spiral Arm in search of the drifting nodules. Bloaters were not easy to detect in the dark spaces between the stars, but numerous clusters had been found and were already being harvested by clans that had been much swifter out of the gate. It seemed the clusters were more common than anyone had suspected. Zhett just needed to find one for clan Kellum.

Not far away, visible through the main bridge windowport, Zhett watched a set of lights wink on as a primary ship was reactivated; some distance off, another set of lights came on as an abandoned tanker came online.

"That's two," Denva transmitted. "Proof of concept. I've got crews aboard seven others, working and fiddling. I expect we'll have more activated within the hour."

Toff cheered. Zhett chuckled. "Yes, this just might work. Our Guiding Star is shining bright again."

"It was always there," Del said. "We just took a few too many detours."

"Then let's be practical about this," Patrick said. "We have to claim a bloater cluster before we can set up shop and start our operations. Zhett and I will go hunting."

"I want to go along, too," Kristof said.

"Maybe. But only if—" Zhett turned to her father. "Watch baby Rex? It's a grandfather's job."

Del adored the toddler. "I'll raise him to be a Roamer. I might even have the boy managing a project by the time you come back."

"It shouldn't be too long," Zhett said. "I know where to start looking for our first bloaters."

43

GENERAL NALANI KEAH

When her battered ships limped home from Relleker, General Keah wasted no time rallying the troops throughout the LOC. "You're all going to have to get your butts in gear—right now!"

The attack on a major Confederation colony was not news she wanted to keep confidential. Through Nadd, she had sent telink reports to green priests aboard her deployed patrol ships, and she placed CDF headquarters on maximum alert. As the *Kutuzov* returned to the complex in the dispersed rubble of the Moon, she transmitted her message to high command. "The threat affects everyone, and I want to announce this on all public channels on Earth. We need each person in the solar system to know what might be coming."

First Officer Wingo was hesitant. "You could start a panic, General. Is it wise to tell the public how vulnerable our planets are?"

"As opposed to letting them think we're all perfectly safe, with nothing to worry about?" She snorted. "In an emergency, there is no benefit to keeping secrets. You think the black robots and the Shana Rei are spying on us? They won't give a damn what we do or don't do. No, better to tell our people all of it, Mr. Wingo. Release our images of Relleker so that everybody can see the bugbots tearing apart our Manta cruisers and then hitting a beautiful world. If it makes Earth's population lie wide-awake at night, then at least they won't be caught sleeping if an attack comes. I'd bet on vigilance over ignorance any day."

Showing its battle scars, the *Kutuzov* arrived at the military complex. When the faeros had shattered the Moon and sent a hail of destructive fragments throughout the solar system, it had been a terrible disaster, but what happened at Relleker was worse.

During the retreat, her CDF engineers had worked through all the quick fixes they could make, and the *Kutuzov* and the surviving Mantas were functional by the time they got home, but Keah knew that "functional" wasn't the same as being battleworthy. At the LOC, her Mantas claimed spacedock repair facilities, and General Keah rallied construction crews to complete the necessary work on a round-the-clock schedule. "As little downtime as possible—it's imperative to get our warships back online and ready to fight."

Eighty Manta cruisers were stationed at Earth, ten of which were just finishing scheduled maintenance. The Juggernauts commanded by Admirals Handies and Harvard were fully crewed and ready, but the two officers remained in their station complex in the main lunar fragment. Admiral Haroun seemed more restless now that he'd seen action during the crackdown on Rakkem. It had woken him up. He stayed aboard the *Okrun,* ready.

After docking the *Kutuzov,* she marched into the headquarters complex to meet with high command. "I'm not going to sugarcoat this for you all. Sit down, buckle in, and have a look at what we're up against." She forced her line commanders to watch the consolidated footage from Relleker. The devastating engagement had lasted less than an hour, although at the time it had seemed like a hellish eternity.

She watched their expressions of alarm and disbelief; several of them—thankfully—looked hungry for revenge, while others seemed on the verge of panic. Silently, she noted which ones those were. Though she had watched the images over and over, she still felt a chill to see the hundreds of thousands of bugbot ships swarming around Relleker, sterilizing the planetary surface, closing in around every evacuating spacecraft including three of her Mantas, while the Shana Rei hexes disrupted all the cities on the planet.

"To the best of our knowledge, there are no survivors," Keah said.

Admiral Handies said, "But those robot warships . . . there must be thousands of them."

"Close to a million," Keah said. "We analyzed the images on our flight back."

An unannounced visitor was escorted into the briefing chamber. He was a pale-skinned, bald man who looked quiet and unassuming: Deputy Eldred Cain. "This is far worse than I feared, General."

Deputy Cain, who had once served and then betrayed the Chairman of the Terran Hanseatic League, had administered Earth for the Confederation since the end of the Elemental War. A competent leader, Cain had reached the level of his ambitions and was perfectly content in his role.

Ignoring the other officers in the briefing, he shook Keah's hand and took a seat beside her. He said firmly, "Now we are all going to watch that record again from start to finish."

Admiral Harvard said, "We've just seen it, Deputy. It's an hour long, and we should get started on our strategy sessions."

Keah knew what Cain was suggesting, though. "No, Admiral. The Deputy is correct. The first time through, you all watched in shock. Pay closer attention the second time, see what we could have done differently and learn from the encounter—otherwise those people died for nothing."

She replayed the images, hoping for some insight or revelation. When she saw Admiral Handies avert his eyes, she nudged him and made him watch. Once the images were finished, General Keah stood. "There, plenty of incentive. It's time for the CDF to get its act together."

"But what more can we do against an enemy like that, General?" Admiral Harvard sounded distraught.

"Everything—and I'm open to suggestions beyond that." She turned to Cain. "Mr. Deputy, I'm going to visit Dr. Krieger's manufacturing stations and inspect our sun-bomb production. Would you care to join me? I'm driving."

Leaving the senior command staff flustered and uneasy in the LOC headquarters, she and Cain took a CDF in-system shuttle to the smaller lunar fragments and free-floating metallic spheres that comprised the weapons-manufacturing facilities devoted to sun-bomb production. Meanwhile, assembly lines on Earth were pumping out laser cannons even faster than they could be installed on the CDF ships.

Keah studied the output database and gave a grim nod. "I do not intend to be caught with my pants down again, Mr. Deputy."

The pale-skinned man responded with a wry expression. "I don't believe you *intended* to be caught with your pants down in the first place." She grunted to acknowledge the poor joke as she docked the small craft against Krieger's main facility. Cain continued, "We have determination, we have equipment, we have all the funding we could reasonably need. It's not resolve we're lacking, General, but effectiveness."

"Give me a million sun bombs, and I'll be pretty damned effective."

"Dr. Krieger is working on that."

The weapons scientist was delighted and energetic—perhaps overly energetic—when he greeted them inside his facility. "We're ready for your inspection, General. I know you'll be pleased."

The primary sun-bomb factory was anchored to the surface of a lunar fragment far from the denser cluster of LOC operations. From that vantage, Keah could see the operational lights of four other drifting facilities spaced far enough apart so that if an unfortunate accident detonated a sun bomb, the shock waves would not destroy the remaining facilities. She couldn't afford to have a clumsy chain reaction wipe out their best chance again.

Krieger bobbed his head. "I assure you, General, we've achieved a balance of peak production speed and safety interlocks so you don't have to worry about a repeat of . . . last time."

"Let's not talk about last time," Keah grumbled. "No more accidents. Your new sun bombs were marvelous at the Onthos system, and they left a few good bruises when we turned them loose at Relleker."

"But Relleker was still lost, General." Krieger looked embarrassed, as if that were somehow his fault.

"A hell of a lot of bugbots were lost too, and I know we damaged the Shana Rei hex ships. We just needed more sun bombs. A lot more. We never expected to face a million robots. We have no idea where they all came from."

"Five sun-bomb production factories are online right now," Krieger said, "and I'm running a very tight ship. Facilities six and seven should be online within three weeks. At present, I have forty-two completed sun bombs right here in these factories, ready to be placed aboard CDF ships."

"Good, then I can replenish what we used at Relleker. The *Kutuzov* needs to be reloaded," Keah said. "I'll have someone arrange to receive them no later than tomorrow. Our arsenals are only at a quarter strength."

The weapons scientist was relieved to be back in her good graces. "It'll be my pleasure to be excessive, General."

"Don't slow production under any circumstances," Deputy Cain warned. "The shadow threat appears to be growing."

"We are in full agreement, Mr. Deputy," Keah said, and cracked her knuckles. "I am already looking forward to our next brawl with the Shana Rei."

Satisfied, the two departed from the weapons installation, and she flew Cain back to a transfer station so he could return to Earth. He had built a private mansion on the rim of the Madrid impact crater. He did most of his leadership from there, where he could contemplate decisions while surrounded by his rare art collection. Keah preferred to be on the bridge of her Juggernaut.

After bidding the Deputy farewell, Keah headed the small shuttle back toward the LOC, already thinking about vigorous practice drills that would keep her high command on their toes. Her tacticians would have to study the recent battles at Relleker and in the Onthos system to determine the most effective distribution of sun-bomb blasts for later engagements.

She flew alone for an hour, circling the military base, and eventually set course back to the *Kutuzov,* to inspect progress on the repairs in spacedock.

She knew the next attack could come anywhere, any time. With the entire CDF on perpetual high alert, she was ready to jump at the next chance she got. She wanted to inflict a lot more damage next time she encountered the enemy.

Unfortunately, she did not have to go far or wait long.

Just outside the range of lunar orbit as she made her way to the *Kutuzov,* Keah veered off course as she saw the universe convulse and twist with a roiling blackness, a shadow cloud pouring out of nowhere. Space split open and vomited out a storm of angular black ships, hundreds of thousands of bugbot attackers followed by giant hexagonal cylinders.

The Shana Rei arrived in a silent shout of black thunder, and the robot fleet plunged toward the military complex.

44

GARRISON REEVES

He had not expected to return to Rendezvous so soon. The place had been cold and haunted, populated with nothing but memories. When he and Orli had stopped here two months earlier, Garrison had meant for that to be his farewell, a way to bury his ghosts.

Now Xander and Terry would bring the place alive again.

Garrison's father had devoted years to the pointless task of restoring the broken asteroid cluster, with no thought for how the clans had changed. That ill-conceived effort had failed, but Xander and Terry had a better plan.

After the uproar Elisa caused when she appeared at Academ, Garrison had decided to bring Seth with him as he and Orli started their new adventure at Rendezvous. Even though the wentals had driven Elisa off, Garrison didn't want to risk leaving his son at the school, fearing she might come back. Elisa was not one to give up easily.

Though Seth wanted to stay at Academ with his fellow students, he seemed just as happy to be with DD. Right now, the two were reviewing homework in the *Prodigal Son's* back compartment. As Garrison flew on final approach to Rendezvous, he heard DD quizzing Seth, posing celestial-mechanics problems on the display wall.

Before Olaf Reeves finally gave up and led his people off on an ill-advised exodus, they had managed to rebuild a few of the less damaged asteroid complexes. Hangar bays, life-support systems, interior passages and chambers were all ready for habitation again. The asteroids themselves would provide the raw materials necessary for the repair facilities once Handon Station started attracting traffic.

"I'd call this my second chance," Garrison said, "but we're well past that."

"It's *our* second chance," Orli said, and leaned close to him.

He was so happy to be back with her. He woke up every day with a sense of optimism. They felt so right together. During their month-long hiatus, they had each experienced their share of excitement, and had concluded that if they were going to have so many troubles, they might as well face them together.

The system's red dwarf sun didn't provide much light for the interconnected asteroids, but artificial illumination banks lit up the central rock and a handful of docking stations. As they flew in toward the functional asteroids, Garrison saw several other small ships there, initial crews that had already come from Newstation.

The comm crackled, and Xander transmitted, "Come in and make yourselves at home, *Prodigal Son*. We've got a lot of work to do together."

Once Garrison landed inside the bay and shut down the engines, Seth and DD were the first to bound out of the ship. Accompanied by OK, Xander came toward them, wiping his hands on a rag. Seth was delighted to see the other compy and went up to introduce himself.

At Xander's curious look, Orli nodded in the boy's direction. "He's as interested in compies as I am. Seth can be my assistant if I open a compy-upgrade business while the rest of you work on repairing salvaged vessels here at Handon Station."

Terry came out of the main receiving office, pulling himself along in the asteroid's low gravity. "We have to find a better name for this place."

"Too late," Xander said, both flippant and determined.

With a sigh, Terry turned to Garrison. "We got here a day and a half ago to turn on the lights. More crews are coming."

"Gotta get the starter facilities running as fast as we can." Xander already looked harried. "Soon enough we'll start hauling in the first ships from Relleker for salvage."

A look of pain crossed Orli's face. "Relleker was my real home for years. I was absorbed in my compy work, and DD was my best friend." She drew a deep breath, and Garrison held her as she spoke. "Everyone I knew on Relleker is dead now. At least Matthew is alive on New Portugal."

With his mistress and his new baby, Garrison thought. There wasn't anything he could do to make her forget her former husband or her past on Relleker, though, and he didn't want to forget his own scars.

Not noticing Orli's sadness, Xander gestured them toward the tunnels leading into the asteroid. "Plenty of rooms are ready for guests. You're welcome to claim any you like, but I thought you'd want your old rooms, Garrison? From before?" Xander lowered his voice. "We found the memorial plaque you left, and all the recorded messages from clan Reeves. I listened to many of them . . . but I had to stop."

"We're very sorry about what happened to your family," Terry said.

"I am too." Garrison kept his voice low as Seth ran off with OK and DD. Once the boy was gone, he said, "My clan made their own decision, and it was a bad one. No fixing it now."

Orli said, "Seems to me, your stubborn father was the reason for the disaster. *He* made the wrong decision. The rest of them just followed him."

"And following him was their decision," Garrison said, then let out a long sigh. He had made bad decisions, too—such as marrying Elisa Enturi. And yet even that poor choice had produced the silver lining of his son, and he wouldn't trade Seth for anything. And when his relationship with Elisa had fallen apart, it set off a long chain of events that had led to him meeting Orli. Happy endings.

Each decision had consequences, a cascade of effects, some good, some bad, all of them culminating in *now*. And he didn't want to change that.

"We're here because of who we are." Garrison slid his arm around Orli again and looked at Xander and Terry. "Rendezvous should never have been restored to exactly what it was. I like your idea better. Considering the history of this place and how much the Roamers

want it to succeed, I think Handon Station will be even more successful than Ulio was."

"We're not going to call it Handon Station," Terry insisted.

"I think we are," Xander said in a singsong voice.

When Garrison said it again, even Terry looked as if the argument was lost.

XANDER BRINDLE

Xander knew the Roamer clans would recognize a good opportunity when it was right in front of them. Each person had a Guiding Star, and in this instance, those stars all clustered together. Handon Station was going to be glorious.

Terry was not an outgoing person; he preferred a quiet life, but Xander wouldn't let him get away with that, since he was the head of these operations. When Terry grumbled about his new responsibilities, Xander said, "Sometimes ambitions are forced upon you. You have money and big dreams, but implementing them is the hard work. Once we have the place up and running, we'll delegate all the pain-in-the-ass work. That's what executives do."

"I've never been an executive before," Terry said. "I want to keep busy, do something useful."

Xander laughed. "We'll keep you useful—and busy."

More Roamer ships arrived daily with clan members offering their services as space construction workers, mechanics, life-support technicians, stardrive specialists. Delivery ships brought in the enormous amounts of equipment and supplies required for setting up the new operations. Terry paid the entire up-front investment, and it made no noticeable dent in his account balance. Still, he felt conscientious about waste, and he tried to keep track of the expenditures.

Garrison proved to be a competent manager. He had experience supervising work teams at the Big Ring and in the Lunar Orbital Complex at Earth, and Terry happily handed over more of the administrative tasks.

Orli spread the word that she was ready to work on any compies that needed maintenance, and DD looked forward to having new friends. Some Roamers arrived at the complex with their own dam-aged ships, asking for cut rates on repairs because they were among the first customers. Xander dickered with them, but not too vigor-ously, since the maintenance teams needed practice. "Handon Station has to start somewhere," he said.

With the basic structure in place, Xander was anxious to get rolling on a much bigger scale. "If you want to make an impression, Terry, we need ships—a lot of ships—to make this a full-fledged repair yard. We should go to Relleker ourselves to see what's worth salvaging. Garrison can handle operations here."

"It may be a short trip. Most of the ships there must have been destroyed in the attack," Terry said.

"'Destroyed' is a relative term. You're not thinking like a Roamer. Just imagine all the hull sections, stardrives, and just plain spare parts we can round up. You know what Maria would have done with all that."

In his years working at Ulio, Terry had learned how to make even the smallest of scraps count. "You're right. We should lead the first teams at Relleker. Garrison can watch over operations here, and you and I will be salvage managers."

"Is that supposed to be an impressive title?"

"*Senior* salvage manager," Terry said. "I'll let you have that one."

Before they departed, four clunky old-model vessels from clan Selise limped into the Rendezvous complex, and after one look at them, Xander assumed they were customers for the repair facilities. Xander gave them a cheery welcome: "We don't have enough func-tional spacedocks to take all four of you at once, but we'll get your ships fixed up."

Omar Selise, an old clan leader with a lantern-shaped face and scraggly gray hair, looked offended by Xander's suggestion. "Repairs? These old ships work just fine. We came to offer our services."

From an even worse-looking ship, a second scruffy man said, "These ships have been workhorses for clan Selise since before you were born, boy! Doesn't matter what it looks like on the outside, I pay attention to how it works under the hood. I said the same thing about my second wife."

"Then we're pleased to have you join us," Terry said in a concil-iatory tone. "Welcome."

When Xander told them of their upcoming mission to Relleker, all four Selise ships volunteered to take part in the salvage activities there. Later, while Terry finished the final loading and preparations to take the *Verne* out, Xander was caught off guard when Omar Selise approached him alone in a rock-walled corridor. The old man poked a finger at him. "Need to talk to you, Brindle. I know you put out private word for some very specific medical research projects, and I've done a little digging." Omar leaned closer to him. "Got a paralyzed grandson of my own. Same condition as your partner's."

That caught Xander's attention.

The man's watery brown eyes narrowed. "You see, I've been keep-ing an eye out for the same kind of research you're interested in."

Xander had indeed made quiet inquiries on Terry's behalf, offer-ing large rewards to anyone who could provide innovative but proven spinal-repair treatments—neurological fusions, cellular re-wiring, anything that could take care of the rare, degenerative dam-age that made Terry unable to walk. Given the huge amount of money Maria Ulio had left him, *something* had to be available.

Omar surreptitiously pressed a datapack into Xander's hand. "This is everything I know. None of it is official, but the program shows some promise. I've wanted to test it on my grandson, but . . . couldn't afford it."

Xander felt a rush of hope. "Let me look this over. If the tech-nique works, maybe we can come to an arrangement. Tell me more."

"There's a big drawback." The scraggly old clan leader set his mouth in a grim line. "Some of these programs were done at Rakkem."

The very name of Rakkem sent a chill through Xander. He had seen the horrific age-rejuvenation treatments that Rakkem had used as a scam. "I wouldn't trust any treatment they proposed."

"The planet's shut down now, but not everything there was a fraud. This particular scientist left Rakkem long before the raid, says he was never part of any shady activities. Check it out, do the re-search yourself. Find out whether it's worth investigating." Omar raised his eyebrows. "Your message said you were willing to try just about anything."

"I am," Xander said, though he wasn't sure if Terry was. "Thank you, I'll do my due diligence. And how much do I have to pay you for this?"

Again Omar Selise looked offended. "I'm not doing this for the money, dammit—it's for my grandson. If the procedure works, then you tell me. Maybe we can get both of them to walk again."

The clan leader moved away with long lanky strides in the low gravity. Xander held the datapack, feeling his thoughts churn with both hope and hesitation. He couldn't dismiss the potential chance for a cure. He would have OK check it out as thoroughly as possible.

46

GENERAL NALANI KEAH

When the shadow cloud unfolded outside of lunar orbit and disgorged thousands—hundreds of thousands—of robot battleships, General Keah raced headlong back toward the LOC in the small shuttle. The acceleration slammed her back in her seat, but she managed to keep her hands on the controls, aiming straight for her docked flagship.

She yelled into the comm system, "Battle stations! All hands to battle stations—in case you haven't noticed."

Running lights winked on across the eighty Manta cruisers parked above the orbiting facilities and manufacturing domes in the lunar rubble. Numerous Remoras engaged in test exercises now swooped back to their home ships.

Keah's shuttle plunged like a projectile toward her Juggernaut, which was still anchored inside the gridwork of its spacedock repair facility. "*Kutuzov,* prepare to launch! Open landing bay three for me—I'll be coming in hot."

She hoped she could decelerate fast enough to land relatively safely. She didn't care about wrecking the shuttle; she just didn't want to damage her battleship. She was obviously going to be needing it.

"But General, we're still in spacedock." On the screen, her first officer's face appeared gray and sweaty. "Only half of the repairs are completed!"

"I can see that, Mr. Wingo, but the shadows aren't going to wait around for us to finish. Have the construction crews get to safety, then blow the connections." She gritted her teeth, knowing that everyone could listen in on the open channel. No use being gentle—

they had all seen what happened at Relleker. "This is going to be bad—very bad. I can't say whether it'd be safer for the repair crews inside the LOC or aboard the *Kutuzov*. Leave it to their discretion, but they have to make up their minds quick. Either way, we are taking my ship into battle within minutes."

She risked a glance toward the shadow cloud, saw the hex cylinders gliding out of their nether universe like alien cattle prods. Waves and waves of identical robot ships poured out, as numerous as the stars in the sky. "Damn bugbots!"

According to her screens the first attackers would reach the LOC within ten minutes . . . right about the time Keah got back aboard her ship.

"Mr. Patton, activate your weapons banks and prepare to fire even before disengaging from spacedock. If you're good, you can take out a hundred bugbots on our way out the door."

Her weapons officer cut in, "General, we can't open fire while we're still in dock!"

"Prove yourself wrong, Mr. Patton. I bet you can figure out a way."

She ignored the comm so she could concentrate on guiding her shuttle straight toward the tiny launching bay on the side of her Juggernaut.

From inside the LOC headquarters rock, Admiral Harvard blurted out on the broad-spectrum open channel, "We are under attack! All capable ships stand your ground and prepare to defend the LOC."

Keah didn't think the military headquarters was the bugbots' prime target, though. This would be just a warm-up for Earth.

Admirals Handies and Haroun were aboard their Juggernauts, while Harvard remained inside the central headquarters. Haroun managed to get his Juggernaut moving much sooner than his counterpart did. Keah watched the *Okrun* heading in toward the LOC, flanked by several Mantas that were also rallying, while the *Rafani,* Admiral Handies's flagship, backed away from the rubble as if to get into a better strategic firing position . . . at least that was what she hoped Handies intended.

Trapped inside the spacedock framework, the *Kutuzov* looked like a behemoth about to outgrow a flimsy cage. All of its lights were activated; the engines glowed, building up thrust in the reactors. Lines of indicators on the spacedock support structure flared red in warning. The engine exhaust cones glowed brighter, and the big hulk began to move. Many of the umbilicals and connecting anchors had already been removed, but some stragglers tore away in showers of sparks as the battleship shook itself free.

Keah adjusted her shuttle's course, tracking the tiny open landing bay, which was her target—but now a moving target. "I'm always up for a challenge," she muttered.

Any sensible person would decelerate and approach with caution, but right now she didn't have time to be sensible. The black robots were coming in.

The ferocious angular ships began strafing the LOC complex with so many energy beams that the vicinity became a spider web of bright blasts. Most of the beams struck dead rock, but they blasted away indiscriminately. The bugbots didn't bother to choose particular targets; they simply meant to wreck everything.

The General transmitted her Identify Friend/Foe signal, hoping some desperate yahoo wouldn't see the shuttle racing in and assume it was a threat. She braced herself, saw the Juggernaut loom large, tracked its movement as it picked up speed, and compensated so she could aim directly for the launching bay.

With a bright flare, an entire battery of the *Kutuzov*'s laser cannons fired, vaporizing the remnants of the spacedock framework that held it back. More beams struck out to annihilate dozens of oncoming black vessels. At least Patton had figured that part out.

Keah hammered her controls, slammed into full deceleration in hopes she wouldn't pulp herself against the inner wall of the landing bay. The force hit her like a punch in the gut, but she gripped the controls, held on, and guided herself forward. Alarm lights flared inside the bay. Automated warnings told her to change course and abort the landing, but she flew ahead anyway, her shields up.

The shuttle slowed, tracked, then plunged into the open bay, missing the gate framework by no more than a meter. Her ship plowed along the deck, slowed, skidded, slewed in a waterfall of sparks. She ignored the cacaphony of alarms in her cockpit. The shuttle spun a full three-sixty on the deck, but the shields dampened her landing energy enough that she screeched to a halt, thumped against the far bulkhead—causing damage, but nothing serious— and finally came to rest.

Without catching her breath, Keah unclipped the crash restraints, opened the hatch, and bounded out, already heading toward the bank of lifts. She paid no attention to the smoke and lingering sparks behind her. The *Kutuzov* was moving, and she could hear the rumble of explosive impacts against the hull. She needed to be on her bridge to run this show.

Two of the lifts weren't functioning, but Keah bounded up ladders, finally found a lift on the next deck that took her directly to the bridge. When she stepped out onto the main deck, she saw that her crew was behaving admirably in a desperate situation. She expected no less. "I'm taking command! Mr. Wingo—situation update."

As the Juggernaut headed away from the LOC complex and into the thick of the fight, the screen was filled with tumbling rocks and a flurry of ships, some evacuating, some converging in a defensive formation.

"The situation is extremely fluid, General."

"I can see that."

At his weapons station, Dylan Patton was directing the fire patterns. Laser-cannon batteries shot out fire hoses of light, blasting countless robot ships. "It's a target-rich environment, General. We can't keep up with it all."

"Clear away about fifty thousand of those bugbots, and you'll be able to see better," she said. "Proceed."

"Doing my best, General."

The tendons stood out on Wingo's neck. "But where did all the robots come from? We must have tanked a hundred thousand of them already at Relleker with our sun bombs. There seem to be more than ever."

From his command-and-control center deep inside the main LOC rock, Admiral Harvard transmitted, "Awaiting your orders, General Keah."

"Admiral, launch all CDF ships—and I mean *all* of them. Even a janitor scow with a jazer might help out in a pinch. If a ship can fly, even at partial strength, it's an asset. On the other hand, any vessel stuck in spacedock is a target."

Keah looked at the tactical screens that showed the sheer number of black robots coming in for the attack, and she worked very hard to keep her expression neutral even though her heart stuttered with dismay. It did not seem possible to get out of this. Simply. Not. Possible.

Seventeen Mantas from the LOC converged and put themselves in front of the oncoming bugbot warships like cannon fodder. With uncoordinated but enthusiastic fire, they blasted the robots using laser cannons augmented with traditional jazers. Even though the barrage damaged hundreds of robot ships, the enemy was willing to sacrifice a thousand of their vessels to obliterate the handful of Mantas standing in their way—and they did exactly that. The bugbots absorbed and ignored their casualties, and kept coming. They destroyed the Mantas and plowed right through the wreckage of the CDF ships.

Remoras zipped in, individually engaging one robot ship after another, but the fighter craft were no match for the enemy battleships. They barely even caused a delay in the onslaught.

The rubble of the Lunar Orbital Complex provided plentiful options for shelter and diversion, and the defending Confederation ships led the bugbots in obstacle-course chases. But that wasn't good enough. Keah needed some elbow room to deploy her big guns.

"We can't launch sun bombs in the middle of the LOC. Let's move away from lunar orbit."

Admiral Haroun brought the *Okrun* up next to the *Kutuzov*, and twelve more Mantas followed. One large cruiser began to move, still struggling to disentangle itself from its repair dock, but the black robot ships wiped it out before the vessel could get under way.

"We're being massacred, General!" Admiral Handies called from the *Rafani*.

She bit back a sarcastic comment about his astute observation. "We have to make a stand. We have to fight. Your choice is to die today or, even if you get away and we lose here, then you'll die later. But I prefer option three—let's hurt them and make them think twice before they do this again."

Admiral Haroun appeared on the comm, his face hard and grim. "The LOC is our central military complex, General—the heart of the CDF. If we can't stop them here—"

Keah said, "They don't seem to be intimidated by our military presence."

The shadow cloud continued to expand, rolling closer until its dark fringes touched outer stations in the LOC. Flying as vanguards, the robot battleships began pounding the habitation domes, storage depots, and any ships still in spacedock. Inside the CDF headquarters rock, Admiral Harvard cried out for rescue, demanding a defensive line, but the responding Mantas managed to delay the bugbots by no more than a few minutes.

Black ships swarmed in and pummeled the headquarters, targeting the source of Harvard's desperate transmissions. Trapped inside, the Admiral called out one last time, his voice rising to a panicked squawk before the comm filled with a wash of static.

Keah swallowed hard, guessing that it wouldn't be the last tragedy for today. Even though Harvard had never been much good as a military commander, his death was a severe blow to morale.

Unable to wait any longer, she prayed that her Juggernaut had moved far enough out. "Mr. Patton, prepare the first volley of sun bombs. Admiral Haroun, do likewise." She sent out a wider broadcast. "Any CDF ship equipped with sun bombs, go ahead and let them loose. It's going to be a bright and deadly day in the LOC. That means you too, Admiral Handies."

Unexpectedly, the *Rafani* changed course and accelerated away from them. The other Juggernaut had fallen into communication silence. Seeing them move away, Keah hit the comm. "Handies, where the hell are you going?"

Patton interrupted her, "General, sorry to remind you, but after Relleker, the *Kutuzov*'s stockpile of sun bombs is only at twenty-five percent. We haven't been resupplied yet."

Her heart sank. "Then we better use what we have, and use them well."

"The *Okrun* has a full load," Admiral Haroun said.

Handies still hadn't responded, and his ship continued to accelerate away from the battle.

Lieutenant Tait said what was growing obvious to all of them. "He's running."

Keah yelled on the comm to the *Rafani*, "Damn you, Handies, get back here. We need your sun bombs!"

When the Juggernaut fled from the concentrated CDF ships, the bugbots chose a new target. A thousand black ships swooped after the *Rafani*, and Admiral Handies devoted all his power to speed. At the last minute he diverted power to the shields. The robot attackers were so numerous they eclipsed the Juggernaut.

Keah shouted uselessly at the comm screen. At last she saw the *Rafani*'s gunports opening up to launch sun bombs, but the bugbots cut the Juggernaut to pieces before the weapons could fire, destroying the vessel—along with its complement of weaponry—before a single sun bomb could detonate.

"What a damned waste!" she hissed.

"We're ready with ours, General," said Patton. Haroun acknowledged as well.

Another four Mantas were destroyed in the space of ten seconds before she could order the launch of the sun bombs.

Part of the bugbot horde remained behind like crows pecking at corpses on a battlefield. They tore apart the rest of the LOC. At a rough guess, Keah had already lost half, maybe two-thirds of the CDF.

At last the spray of nova explosions blossomed out, each blast disintegrating hundreds of attackers. Several of Haroun's sun bombs overshot the robot ships—intentionally so, Keah realized—and erupted inside the oncoming shadow cloud. One searing explosion carved a giant obsidian crater in the nearest Shana Rei hex cylinder.

Keah had no time to cheer, though. The second wave of sun bombs detonated, and shock waves smashed into the fragments of the LOC. The last CDF defenders backed away, trying to outrun their own weapons. Some of the nova explosions sent the Mantas into tailspins, causing damage; any ship that could not recover quickly was overwhelmed by the black robots.

"Launch round three!" Keah shouted. Explosions flared, nearly blinding her. "Again!"

"These are our last ones, General," Patton said.

At least Admiral Haroun kept firing.

Keah sat on the bridge and felt hot tears burning in her eyes. "Again," she muttered, knowing it was useless.

The enormous Shana Rei shadow cloud engulfed the already-dead LOC and kept rolling forward.

Keah gave orders for the *Kutuzov* and the *Okrun* to back away and continue firing. She sent out a general broadcast demanding any other ships, any help for this last stand. Hundreds of thousands of bugbot craft roared past the orbit of the Moon, heading inward. Some black robots engaged the last CDF defenders, but the rest hurtled ahead.

The shadow cloud also had its target. Keah knew that the creatures of darkness wanted Earth.

And she remembered exactly what had happened at Relleker.

KOTTO OKIAH

The small survey craft left the bright nebula behind, edged past the boundary, and dropped into a dark and silent nowhere in the underbelly of the universe.

Once inside the vast emptiness of the void, the survey craft held itself together, which pleased Kotto for obvious reasons. He had been afraid that altered laws of physics might not allow the component atoms to stay together.

KR and GU remained attentive, their optical sensors fixed on the ship's controls.

Just inside, Kotto brought the survey craft to a full stop, though the darkness outside remained unchanged. "Let's assess. Always a good idea to assess. It'll keep us from getting lost."

"We are studying and mapping, Kotto Okiah," said GU.

"We can still see the exit prominently," KR said.

With some relief, Kotto nodded. The slash of the ionized nebula gases behind them was a bright spot on the rest of the void. "Study our systems. Everything still functioning properly?" He picked up no reliable readings dead ahead, no frame of reference, no perspective. He scanned twice, then tapped the gauges, hoping they would reset. "Functioning perfectly, but there's nothing to detect." He looked out into the blinding distance. "I suppose that means if we *do* find something out there, it'll be glaringly obvious."

The compies studied the navigation systems. "We are ready to proceed, Kotto Okiah."

"Better drop a marker buoy here, just in case."

"The buoy can also serve as a signal amplifier," KR pointed out.

"Then let's figure out if we can send a signal back through before we wander off and get lost." Kotto activated the comm. "Hello, Fireheart Station, this is Kotto Okiah. Hello? How are you? Can you hear me?"

After an uncomfortable second, a static-distorted reply came from Station Chief Alu. "Your signal is faint, but we read you."

"Faint? That's disheartening, since I'm right here on the door-step and broadcasting at full strength."

Another voice broke in. "Kotto, this is Shareen—be careful." The signal strength wasn't sufficient for him to receive video images, so he had to strain to hear her words through the audio. "What's it like in there?"

"I will be sufficiently careful, don't worry. Right now, it's just dark and empty. Nothing exciting . . . not even anything very inter-esting, but I have a lot of exploring to do. You two just figure out how to fix the greenhouse before I get back. I already gave you the solution."

"We will, sir." It was Howard's voice.

He heard only further static, and then Alu's voice trickled through, "Don't forget to leave your sun bombs there on the threshold."

"Of course I'll remember. I've got scientific research to do, and I'd rather do it without a couple of doomsday devices aboard."

He let the compies complete the task. They moved delicately, using precision systems to drop the warheads in the void, where self-anchoring engines would keep them in position near the bound-ary. Kotto nodded and sent another signal back out. "Sun bombs deployed, primed, and ready to go—but please don't blow them up and slam the door shut until I get back out."

Alu's response was garbled, but it sounded reassuring. After another blast of static, Howard's voice said, "Be careful, sir."

"I believe your partner already gave me that advice." He looked at the two compies beside him in the cockpit. "I will keep it in mind as I explore." They would be out of communication range within minutes, but he had known he would be on his own. As an inventor, he had always considered himself a sort of explorer. Now the title was official.

The survey craft headed into the inky, indiscernible blackness. Even though he didn't see any corners or obstacles that would make him lose the way home, he told the compies, "Mark our course very carefully."

"That will be difficult," said GU. "There are no points of reference. Once we leave the opening behind, we will be completely disoriented."

"Then drop more breadcrumb transmitters." The small spheres emitted a regular series of pings, and he had loaded a hundred of them aboard the survey craft. It should be easy enough just to connect the dots and follow them back out, provided that signals traveled in predictable ways in this void.

The dark emptiness did seem to have slightly different laws of physics, a fact that Kotto would have found fascinating if he hadn't been in the middle of it. Flying onward, the survey craft eventually lost sight of the opening back to the Fireheart nebula, which was unnerving. The bright normal universe had been like a safety beacon, but now he seemed to be flying through the heart of a deep cave at the bottom of a black hole.

"For the sake of science I want to gather groundbreaking data." He turned to the compies. "For the sake of history, make sure the sensors are recording everything."

"There is nothing to record, Kotto Okiah," KR said.

He raised a finger. "Ah, but this is a *nothing* unlike anything we've ever seen before."

As they traveled for five more hours (subjective time) seeing nothing but . . . nothing, Kotto began to lose heart. They had already deployed twenty pingers, and he began to worry that this void had nothing to see, nothing useful to bring back, which wasn't a particularly exciting accomplishment. He focused on the screens, then gave up, instead pressing his face against the windowport and staring with his own eyes. The lights shining out from the craft vanished into the darkness, illuminating nothing. The only discovery he made was that the impenetrable darkness gave him a headache.

Then the void structure began to change, and the blackness took on a different character, revealing angular forms that were like the hidden breaths of shadows. The walls of the emptiness were clustered with black crystals and ebony fracture lines.

Kotto wondered if he had begun to hallucinate, after having been in complete sensory deprivation for so long. He reached out to grab the arms of both compies, reassuring himself that they were real, that he hadn't lost himself in some mental fugue.

He pointed at the screen and asked the two compies, "Can you see geometrical shapes out there?" He feared they were just ghost images, something he had wished into existence.

Their optical sensors glowed, and neither KR nor GU answered for a long time. Finally, KR said, "They appear to be lines and angles . . . extended hexagonal cylinders."

"Or our circuits could be malfunctioning in this alternate universe." GU sounded far too cheerful if that was indeed the case.

"I'm not imagining them—those are the Shana Rei, and they're here." He dropped his voice to a hushed whisper, as if that might make a difference. "It looks like they're just hanging in the void, unprotected . . . sleeping."

"Has there been evidence that the Shana Rei sleep, or otherwise go dormant?" KR asked.

Kotto waved away the compy's concern. "They look vulnerable, and they haven't noticed us. It's like we've found their secret lair," he whispered.

"What good does that do us?" GU asked.

"I'm not a military expert, but what if the CDF could surprise them here? Sneak up from behind and blast them in their little nest? I can just imagine what General Keah would say."

"Shall we try to make a transmission, Kotto?" asked KR. "With sufficient signal strength we might be able to get the message out through our relay buoys." The compy reached for the controls of the comm.

Kotto grabbed KR's plastic arm. "No! We don't want to shout and wake up the Shana Rei."

The survey craft kept moving, passing the hard-to-discern black hexagons, then moving onward at a great, immeasurable distance. The survey craft didn't have an Ildiran stardrive, but the entire concept of travel seemed different here. It didn't matter which direction he flew—Kotto had a hard time determining direction at all.

Soon, the void was empty even of the Shana Rei, and Kotto let out a sigh of relief. Safe . . . for now.

As they kept flying, he had the compies scan in all possible directions. The sensors returned occasional anomalous details, stray energy readings that made no sense and did not match what he saw. He scratched his head and tried to interpret the reading, hoping for a new flash of inspiration, such as when he had thought of how to save the greenhouse and the worldtrees. Alas, those insights were now few and far between.

Meanwhile, as he stared, Kotto grew dizzy. He felt as if they were spinning, whirling, descending, then accelerating upward, even though the ship's stabilizers and internal readings indicated they were flying level. He held on to the compies again, reassuring himself that they were stable.

Outside the ship, he began to see flares of color, blossoming greens and yellows, accompanied by a flash of purple and blue. He rubbed his eyes, sure he was imagining it because the black had been so unrelenting—but these were more than just capricious flares from behind his retinas. Faint glowing lines connected brighter spots in a tracery that imposed a framework upon the formless void.

"Do you see that?" he asked.

This time neither compy hesitated. "Yes, Kotto. We do."

There were faint blurry nexus points like smudgy fingerprints that someone had left on the unblemished black, and the blurs pulsed and brightened in a random pattern. Were these echoes, a faint backwash through the wall of the universe?

Kotto tried to use his own abilities, but had to ask the compies, "Can you discern a pattern? Are those points organized somehow?"

"Not that we can detect," said GU.

"Well, it isn't the Shana Rei," he said. "This feels like something different." Again, he kept wondering if he might be imagining or hallucinating, but he felt the overwhelming presence of a sleepy interconnected mind . . . something awakening. Something astonishingly powerful.

"We'd better have a look," Kotto said.

48

TOM ROM

Zoe had sent him to investigate an abandoned Klikiss planet to gather more specimens and observations, and there were many such worlds to choose from. When the insect race had departed after the Elemental War, they left behind ancient cities, empty worlds, and far too many mysteries.

Tom Rom decided to go back to Eljiid, the backwater planet where he had obtained the original samples of Klikiss royal jelly from preserved cadavers in the ruins. Since Eljiid had only a small research settlement, he expected to slip in and out with little interference. It would be easy.

On his first trip here, he'd traveled via the Klikiss transportal network, but after seeing the wave of darkness pour through the gateway on Auridia, he did not intend to use that system again. He preferred to trust his ship instead, which gave him more options and maneuverability. Although Zoe paid little attention to the threat of the Shana Rei, Tom Rom was fully aware of how dangerous the creatures of darkness were.

When he reached Eljiid, he picked up no transmissions from the planet, no communications at all—no energy signatures, no signs of life, no indications of the research settlement. Descending through the atmosphere to hover over the site of the small encampment, he was stunned to see swaths of destruction for miles around. Instead of the settlement buildings, there were only a blackened scar and glassy craters from massive explosions.

He increased his shields and activated his ship's weapons, alert for an attack. Something had erased the outpost, and this was far more destruction than necessary to wipe out a few researchers. The high-energy blasts had eradicated not just the research outpost but also the extensive Klikiss ruins that had been abandoned for centuries. Why would any enemy waste effort on a silent ghost city?

On edge and surging with adrenaline, he searched for any sign of the attackers, ready to fight back or race away. Once he took thermal readings and scanned the wreckage, though, he determined that the attack had occurred some time ago. He allowed himself to relax, but only slightly.

Why Eljiid? Tom Rom couldn't imagine any significance of this minimal planet. Who would care? Yet some enemy—presumably the Shana Rei and their black robots—had attacked with breathtaking malice, leaving no stone standing. He could think of nothing else with such ruthless power. To what purpose?

The Shana Rei had obliterated this insignificant world, and he had watched them do even worse at Kuivahr, also a place of few resources and minimal importance.

He circled over the ruins, but there was no point in landing. The people on Eljiid were of no particular importance to Tom Rom, but the pointless, random destruction was unsettling. He took numerous images to bring back to Pergamus. These were not the details that Zoe had requested about the Klikiss and the plague, but it was important to show her anyway. Maybe she would grasp the true scope of the danger in the Spiral Arm.

If a worthless world like Eljiid could become a target, then so perhaps could Pergamus. . . .

He flew off. To fulfill his mission, he had to find another Klikiss world. Tom Rom wouldn't let an inconvenience like this stand in his way.

He called up the Ildiran star charts and selected twenty empty Klikiss planets that were possibilities. He chose the closest system, Llaro, which held a significant human colony. Tom Rom had no wish to interact with the local populace; he just needed to look around. Since the main Llaro settlement had grown up around the largest set of Klikiss ruins, Tom Rom found four other impressive, yet uninhabited, hivelike cities dotted across the dry landscape. Choosing one that looked interesting, he landed his ship there.

Llaro's skies were pastel pink and yellow, the winds brisk and arid. Other than the whisper of breezes through hollow openings in the tall hive towers, the landscape was silent. He heard no birds or insects, no animal cries. Perfect.

Zoe had already collated databases on Klikiss biology, Klikiss architecture, Klikiss culture, Klikiss communications, Klikiss science. Somehow, she thought Tom Rom would bring her unique insights if he went there in person. Enjoying the solitude, he set up a small camp and spent several days wandering the quiet, haunted ruins. He collected everything that might be of interest or value to Zoe.

Inside the silent structures he found dusty pupating chambers, drone tunnels, a protective vault where the Breedex had held court. He found abandoned and exotic alien vehicles, harvesting machines, and carriers that delivered the insectlike workers out to excavation or agricultural sites. Over the years, the strange machinery had fallen into disrepair.

He even found hundreds of desiccated Klikiss carcasses left behind when the race vanished en masse through the transportals. Many of these were rotten, empty shells, and would never serve as a source for royal jelly, but some were intact enough. He took a hundred different tissue samples, labeled and preserved each one.

Following a strange biological imperative of another swarming, the Klikiss had been gone for two decades, but neither the human race nor the Ildirans had forgotten about the danger the warrior insects had posed. The Klikiss were far away, somewhere else in the galaxy, but they were not extinct.

Unless the Shana Rei had found them first and obliterated them.

PRINCE REYNALD

As the capital of the Confederation, Theroc had a significant military presence to protect the planet, as well as an armed home guard to watch over the worldtrees and the Theron population. With the spreading blight in the worldforest, the King and Queen had to move against the treacherous Onthos. After Arita's dire report, they prepared an expedition to the Wild, where they would see—and hopefully stop—what the Gardeners were doing to the verdani mind.

Reyn, Osira'h, and his sister sat drinking strong klee on an open deck of the fungus-reef city. Arita had explicitly chosen a high and open place from which they could watch the busy preparations for the expedition in the clearing below. "I am going along," Reyn insisted. It was a struggle to make his voice sound strong.

Though shaken by her own ordeal, Arita hovered near her brother. "You're not well enough. We can all see that."

Reyn had only a few doses left of the lesser Kuivahr plankton extracts, and he felt weaker by the day. Several pharmaceutical companies were trying to duplicate the most potent ones, but so far the results had been disappointing. The invigorating effect of being back home on Theroc had worn off, but he was still glad to be among the worldtrees, glad to be with Osira'h, and glad to be with his sister. He would stay strong for them.

In scouring the enormous data set from Pergamus on the microfungus and comparing the chemical structure of the most effective kelp distillates, medical researchers had made great progress in just the last week. They had found a biochemical link, a complex molecular vulnerability in the microfungus, but the "lock" was so nuanced that it could not be synthesized.

Interestingly, the complicated chromosomal vulnerability was similar in structure to other basic Theron biology, enough so that two different research teams had concluded that the secret to the cure lay in the meshed web of worldforest life. A great many pharmaceuticals had been developed from the kaleidoscope of Theron leaves, barks, berries, roots, fungi, insects, bacteria.

"If the cure is out there in the forest, then we just have to find it," Arita said. "I've already catalogued and studied hundreds of thousands of specimens in my own solo work."

"Hundreds of thousands out of countless millions," Reyn said. "Theroc has one of the most vibrant ecosystems in the Spiral Arm. How would you even know where to start?"

"One haystack at a time," Arita said.

Osira'h added, "I can call for Ildiran researchers. We could test millions of specimens until we find the right one."

Reyn was restless, moving around the open deck while ships landed in the clearing below. "I'm glad we have something to go on, but don't expect me to wait around here and do nothing." He shot a glance at his sister, thinking about what she had said about the void-priests and the blight from the Onthos. He refused to let his parents sideline him. "I'm going with you all to the Wild," he insisted. "I'm part of this . . . I can feel the connection."

"Reyn's disease is a genetically mutable microfungus that originated here on Theroc," Osira'h said to Arita. "Now, the trees themselves are dying from another kind of blight. What if there is a connection between the two?"

Arita frowned. "How can there be a connection?"

"There are many things we don't understand about the worldforest," Reyn sighed. "Even the green priests were surprised by what they never noticed, and they are *part* of the trees."

"And there's more than the verdani mind," Arita admitted. "I've been sensing a different presence . . . out there. It helped save me and Collin, and it wasn't part of the trees. I'm sure of it."

Reyn kept the tremor out of his voice. "I am the son of Father

Peter and Mother Estarra. I am a part of Theroc as much as the green priests are, but in a different way. If I am infected and suffering at the same time as the worldtrees are infected and suffering . . . if I'm dying at the same time the forest is dying, then *I* need to help save the forest. The sickness in the worldtrees is not unlike the sickness in me."

Osira'h sipped her klee, winced at the taste although she knew it was Reyn's favorite drink. "This has no basis in the science I understand, but I do know the connection between myself and my siblings. I sense that Rod'h is being tortured by the Shana Rei, that Tamo'l is being held somewhere else. Ildirans are connected by *thism,* and all the strands go back to my father. Who is to say that Reyn might not be made better or even healed if we save the trees from the Onthos infestation and make the verdani strong again?"

Arita placed a hand on her brother's arm. "I believe you. I'll protect you where I can."

"*We* will protect him," Osira'h said.

They watched as the Theron home guard landed flyers in the meadow and loaded green priests, armed soldiers, and observers. King Peter and Queen Estarra directed the preparations.

Reyn finished his klee in a single gulp and stood on shaky legs. "They'll depart soon. I'm going to take one of the last plankton extracts—I need my strength to convince my parents that I need to stand against the Onthos."

Arita and Osira'h discussed which of the remaining vials they should give him. He held out his arm, and Osira'h injected him. "I feel stronger already," he lied, but when she smiled in response to his comment, he did feel a glow spread through him.

They descended the giant tree and went to the expedition's assembly point. Once each troop flyer was loaded, it rose up to a smattering of determined cheers, and then another came down to be loaded. Peter and Estarra stood in full Theron regalia, embracing their role as the planet's Mother and Father. Collin was with them, along with Zaquel and ten other green priests.

Queen Estarra turned to Arita and Reyn. "We are about ready to go. The green priests have worked hard to pierce the fog in the verdani mind, and they pinpointed the worst infestation on satellite images." The green priests would also carry potted treelings with them, so they could remain connected with the verdani mind, even if the worldtrees in the Wild were cut off.

Peter's brow furrowed with worry. "I don't want a war with the Onthos, but we'll drive them out if need be and purge the tainted forest."

Reyn said, "Any threat to the worldforest is a threat to us all."

When the King and Queen saw that he intended to go along, they hesitated, but then Estarra said, "You'll ride in the lead craft with us."

Peter said, "We leave within the hour. More worldtrees are dying every moment."

50

EXXOS

Another world to destroy. His robots were becoming quite proficient at it, but Exxos looked forward to continued practice. Victory and defeat were a constant cycle in his programming, and Exxos had experienced a great deal of each phase in his many centuries of existence.

Now, their resurrected fleet rolled like an implacable force through the human military headquarters in the rubble of the Moon. They had set their sights on Earth.

The desperate human fighters squared off at the Lunar Orbital Complex, firing at the oncoming black ships. The CDF used all the weapons at their disposal, but it wasn't enough. Their conventional jazers and railgun projectiles obliterated many robot ships despite their enhanced armor; their laser cannons were even more powerful, and the sun bombs were astonishingly effective. The black robots suffered many losses as they crushed the military complex and destroyed battleship after battleship. It didn't matter. Exxos had many more to spare. The robot casualties could be easily overcome ... far more easily than the humans could recover from obliteration.

The black ships turned toward the home planet, paying no attention as many thousands of their vessels were vaporized. Exxos had done the calculations. The robots could absorb as many losses as necessary, and afterward they would return to the Onthos system, where the Shana Rei would simply use the existing dark matter to replace them. And more.

Then, it would be time for the robots to destroy the creatures of darkness as well. Exxos and his comrades had used treachery to wipe out the hated Klikiss race millennia ago and then leveled many old Klikiss worlds, like Eljiid, simply because they could, purely out of spite.

The Shana Rei reminded him much of the original Klikiss, a dominant race that treated the robots as worthless cogs, disposable resources. But Exxos and his robots were always at the forefront, the producers and the fighters. Why were they constantly treated as secondary, when they did all the difficult tasks? The Klikiss had not respected their worth, and now the Klikiss were extinct. Soon enough, the Shana Rei would follow the same path.

Even a total victory at Earth was just a stepping-stone to the next goal. Partnered with the Shana Rei, Exxos planned to exterminate the entire human race. Meanwhile, the shadows would obliterate the worldforest mind, just as they had driven the hydrogues into obscurity. At the same time, they would attack and infect the Ildiran *thism* and keep pressing for cleansing violence.

Destroy Earth. Destroy the human race. Destroy the worldforest. Destroy the Ildirans. Soon, the entire Spiral Arm would be empty, quiet.

Even though the human military tried their best, the Lunar Orbital Complex put up very little resistance. Many CDF ships were easily destroyed; some tried to flee, but the robots chased them down and wiped them out. The human General rallied her defenders, foolishly assuming that she could have an effect. The military ships would have been better off just to flee before the black robots chased them down. Instead, they seemed intent on mounting a fruitless attempt to protect Earth. Exxos found it convenient that they stayed so his robots could destroy them all at once.

From their shadow cloud, the Shana Rei emanated destructive waves of entropy, and the hex cylinders continued their attack. The black nebula swelled beyond the rubble of the Moon, heading toward Earth.

Another scatter of sun bombs from desperate CDF ships annihilated three thousand black robot ships, and although Exxos did not feel any personal loss, they were all *him*. It was as if *he* had just died three thousand times. But it was of no consequence, because a million of him still remained.

He did, however, experience a dip in their combined secret

processing power . . . and that might delay his plans against the Shana Rei. Before their recent near extinction, Exxos and his comrades had formulated an exotic plan deep within their circuitry, connected only through coded bursts that were—he hoped— undetectable to the shadows. Now that he had a million identical processors in his resurrected robot horde, they all worked together to develop their entropy nullifier, a chaos-crystallization device. It would precipitate out the randomness and cause the very entropy that comprised the Shana Rei to freeze and solidify—just as physical matter had frozen out of energy during the beginning stages of the newborn Big Bang.

The quantum calculations were complex and nearly impossible— but Exxos now had enough computing power to accomplish the impossible. It would just take time. With every instance in which he lost thousands of robots, however, he could feel their combined mental power diminish slightly.

Exxos was patient. He had always been patient. The other robots continued their work quietly, without raising any Shana Rei suspicions. Once the shadows became the final victims, the Spiral Arm would belong solely to the black robots. It was all quite elegant. The shadows would be gone, just as the Klikiss were gone . . . just as the Ildirans and the humans would be gone.

The universe would be perfect.

Destroying Earth would deal a deadly blow to the human psyche, but there would still be an extraordinary amount of work to do afterward, hunting down the vermin in their widely separated colonies. If only there were a better way to spread the destruction and wipe out the entire race . . .

But Exxos and his robots were methodical—and very effective at slaughter. His computer mind liked to project many moves into the future, but Exxos also needed to focus on his immediate priorities.

As the shadow cloud engulfed the Lunar Orbital Complex, Exxos concentrated his myriad battleships, and they swooped down toward the main target.

Earth.

CHAPTER

51

JOCKO KRIEGER

The new sun-bomb factories had been constructed outside of the Lunar Orbital Complex, far enough away to be safe. Jocko Krieger had considered it a good idea, recalling the last deadly—not to mention, embarrassing—detonation when one of the weapons had gone nova right there in the facility.

Isolated from the bustle of the LOC, the workers at the primary factory station and the four satellite facilities felt like pariahs, kept at arm's length from the main complex. The weapons scientists and the sun-bomb workers had often grumbled.

They weren't complaining now.

Inside their metal-walled stations, the current work shift of twenty-seven men and women watched in horror as the swelling shadow cloud and the fleet of robot warships wiped out the entire LOC. Krieger and his crew hid like rabbits in their holes, drawing no attention to themselves.

Krieger bit the ends of his fingers. He watched as the CDF unleashed all the weapons they had, but were still decimated. They witnessed tens of thousands of robot casualties, maybe even a hundred thousand—and it still wasn't enough to force a retreat.

Inside the assembly facility, Krieger paced and sweated. There was nothing he could say, nothing he could do. They watched in dismay as everyone in the Lunar Orbital Complex was eradicated, two Juggernauts destroyed, countless Manta cruisers disintegrated as if they were no more than fluttering moths.

"At least my sun bombs worked," Krieger said, breaking the appalled silence inside the meeting chamber where most of the workers had gathered. "Proof of concept."

"Always thinking about yourself," said his deputy, Lynne Gwendine, a talented but prickly woman who had been hired for her competence, not her patience. Over the past month, Gwendine had grown more disrespectful and less tolerant of Krieger's endless demands for higher productivity. He had expected her to request a transfer or simply quit any day. Now it didn't look as if that day was going to come.

"Just pointing out a fact," he said. "General Keah used our weapons appropriately, but sun bombs were designed to fight against the Shana Rei. They just happen to pack a huge punch with that many black robots crowded in one place."

A panicked deputy from one of the satellite stations transmitted to Krieger's dome. "What do we do? Most of the CDF is destroyed. We've got to call for rescue—"

Gwendine lunged to the comm station and roared across the channel, "No transmissions! Do you want to call attention to us? We're safe if they don't notice us!" She shut down the intercom, and they all sat shivering in huddled silence. "Idiot."

"Maybe we should hold our breath, too," Krieger said sarcastically.

Gwendine shot him an annoyed glance. "You may not wish to survive, Dr. Krieger, but the majority of us do."

"Oh, I want to survive, don't misinterpret my comment." He certainly hoped the robots didn't swoop in and pick them off; they could easily blow up the main dome and the satellite stations in swift staccato bursts. He and his staff had no defenses against such an attack, although they did have a complement of forty-two completed sun bombs ready to launch. They should have been loaded aboard General Keah's ships, but there had been no opportunity.

Hundreds of thousands of robot ships swept past the ruins of the LOC and streaked toward Earth. The first wave of enemy battleships had already started the devastation there. From their hiding place, Krieger could hear terrified transmissions as the populace begged for help or rescue, calling on the CDF to protect them—although General Keah had already done her best. A handful of warships had survived, but they wouldn't last long if they continued to attack the immense robot fleet head-on.

"We're safe here, aren't we?" asked one of the workers, as if Dr. Krieger could see into the future and make an accurate pronouncement.

Gwendine cut the man off. "As long as we lie low."

The shadow cloud swelled huge and black, filling an enormous volume of space as it moved, coming closer.

The Shana Rei let the robots be their cannon fodder and take the brunt of the resistance like rabid dogs that would attack any target. The black nebula oozed through from another dimension, surrounding the cluster of hexagonal cylinders like a cocoon. The cloud swelled and roiled, growing blacker and larger, as if it drew strength from the destruction.

Maybe it does, Krieger thought. If the Shana Rei were entropy incarnate, perhaps they did feed on mayhem. That would explain a lot.

The huge cloud began to move toward Earth, drifting close to the sun bomb factories.

From their hiding place, Krieger and his workers stared as the hex ships cruised past. The facility computer systems began to flicker, and the lights went down as the backwash of Shana Rei chaos began to ruin their power systems. One of the satellite domes frantically tried to send a signal, but it jittered into a hiss of static: ". . . life support—" Then it fell silent.

Gwendine shook her head. "Comm systems are down too."

With their lights out and systems down, Krieger could see through the windowports, the black cloud and the creatures of darkness inside it, rolling forward.

"Dr. Krieger," said a technician in a warbly voice. She swallowed hard. "All our life support is offline."

It didn't surprise him. His mind raced as he reached the obvious conclusion. As the Shana Rei shadow cloud cruised past, all the technical systems would be ruined, and Krieger doubted their major systems could be repaired in time. These secondary facilities had small reserve power blocks, but not enough to keep them alive for more than half a day. Without immediate backup, they were doomed.

He gazed across space at the silent glowing wreckage of CDF headquarters and saw the battle beginning at Earth. Thousands of ships tried to evacuate while countless robots closed in, intent on preventing them from getting away.

No one would bother to rescue a handful of workers in these hidden facilities. Krieger knew they were stranded here. They were already dead . . . a slow, cold, suffocating death.

He let out a long, determined sigh. "Oh hell, I was never good at keeping a low profile anyway."

He looked at Gwendine, who seemed extremely annoyed, but for once, the annoyance was not directed at him. "I know what you're saying," she muttered.

"We have forty-two sun bombs—nuclear-driven, and we know they're still functional even in the vicinity of the Shana Rei." He drew a deep breath. "We can either die here quiet and whimpering, with nobody to notice, or we can go out with a bang." He nodded toward the ominous obsidian cylinders that loomed so close as they moved past on the way to Earth. "Look up there. *That* is why I designed the sun bombs in the first place."

The workers turned to him, pale and terrified, some determined, most of them stunned. Gwendine just said, "This isn't a democracy, Krieger. You're in charge, so make up your mind."

He did.

Before the Shana Rei could pass too far away, when the hex cylinders were at the optimal distance for a concentrated surprise barrage, Jocko Krieger launched the sun bombs. All of them.

The glowing pinwheel spheres spun out of their storage depot. The mechanical launchers were sufficient to activate the cores and hurl them within range. Even if the entropy scrambled their guidance, Krieger knew he didn't have to be precise. It was close enough for a small exploding star.

Crackling, sparking, and expanding with activated plasma, forty-two of the devices sprayed out in a deadly hailstorm toward the Shana Rei. "I just want to see that we were effective, at least for a second. Full filters on the windowports!"

The view darkened, momentarily blinding them, but then the sun bombs detonated like firecrackers in blindingly fast succession. The shadow cloud filled with newborn suns. Some explosions directly impacted the black cylinders, while others simply burst into a searing flare nearby, and the furious shock wave ripped into the hexagonal sides.

The Shana Rei ships shrank, clearly damaged, some broken apart, but the sun bombs faded all too quickly.

The still-powerful shadow cloud lurched toward them, but Krieger was grinning.

"You always were a showoff," said Gwendine.

Waves of entropy hammered the station as well as the satellite facilities. All technical systems had already failed, but now even the physical integrity began to fall apart. Chaos increased. Seals crumbled. Joints collapsed. Structural members dropped away, and within moments all systems failed catastrophically.

The shadows engulfed the facility as it fell apart, hull plates spinning off into space, atmosphere venting explosively, fuel reservoirs exploding, until even the components disintegrated into their individual atoms.

Then the wounded cloud moved on toward Earth.

52

JESS TAMBLYN

Inside Academ, the wentals were awakening with an energetic glow. The elemental force had been mostly dormant for nearly two decades, but their defensive response against Elisa Enturi had shown that they were indeed aware, even agitated.

After he and Cesca finished classes and sent the students to conduct engineering experiments with the Teacher compies, they paused at an open ice patch on the sealed corridor wall. Working with his fingers, Jess peeled up the edge of the flexible polymer film to expose the naked ice, and the pale glow brightened. He and Cesca touched the frozen surface.

"It feels so weak," Cesca said.

Jess sensed a definite tingle there, a fizzing undertone of energy boiling up. "But stronger than it has felt in a long time. I wish we knew what they're thinking."

Years ago, their bodies had been infused with the elemental water, but the uncontrolled force had made their very touch deadly. He and Cesca had expended all that energy when they fought and defeated the faeros. Now, as Jess touched the pure ice, it seemed *yielding*. He pushed harder, and the ice gave way, parting for him. Cesca's hand sank in next to his. Together, with their hands surrounded, they could feel throbbing, like the heartbeat of the comet.

"Are they awakening because of the Shana Rei?" Cesca asked. "The shadows already fought the hydrogues inside Golgen, and they've attacked the verdani and the faeros. Could the wentals be at risk, too?"

"Maybe they're waking up to join the fight." Jess felt a grim chill. "That means Academ might be in danger. And our students."

The Teacher compy KA met them in the corridor, fully repaired from Elisa's stunner blast. "You have a visitor, Jess Tamblyn and Cesca Peroni. Someone wishes to withdraw a student. Seymour Dominic requests his daughter Kellidee to work in their bloater-extraction operations."

Hurrying back to their office, Jess and Cesca found a lanky, dark-haired Roamer waiting for them. Seymour Dominic wore a comfortable jumpsuit embroidered proudly with clan markings. Though he was withdrawing a student, Seymour did not look angry; in fact, he was beaming. "I need Kellidee, maybe for just a year, maybe permanently. I couldn't say. This is an opportunity we can't pass up."

Jess remembered Kellidee, a beautiful thirteen-year-old girl with a sharp mind and a grasp of mathematics. "She was just about to start advanced mechanics and intermediate electric circuits. It's not a good time to pull her out."

"But we don't know how much time we'll have," said Seymour. "It's an ekti rush out there. Have you seen the reports of all the stardrive fuel? Clan Dominic got a sweet deal on pumping and transportation equipment, and we've staked our claim on a large bloater cluster. Nowadays you can barely find a bucket and a straw available, because every scrap is sold out, but our operations are already going full-scale. We could really use Kellidee's help."

"Every clan has the right to withdraw their children," Cesca pointed out. "But I hope you'll bring her back. We'll miss her around here."

"Or I could just hire a set of tutors. We've delivered four loads of ekti-X to Newstation already, and our scouts have found two more bloater clusters. The faster we get stardrive fuel to market, the more money we'll make." He was practically dancing with excitement. "With one delivery, my clan made as much as we earned in the entire past year. This is unbelievable." He looked from side to side. "Do you know how many other clans have set up ekti operations?"

"A lot of them rushed off to get started even before they knew what they were doing," Jess said.

Dominick groaned. "That means there'll be many more shipments coming in this week." He glanced at the chronometer on the office wall. "Can we hurry up and get Kellidee, please? I need to get back out to the operations."

"KA is bringing her right now," Cesca said. "She'll need a few minutes to gather her things."

Seymour fidgeted. "Leave it all behind. We can buy her a new set of everything ten times over."

Jess softened his voice. "Give her a little time to say goodbye to her friends, Seymour. Think about your daughter. She's very popular."

The man's shoulders slumped. "I'm just so excited . . . so anxious. At peak operation, we could drain the entire cluster in another two weeks. I'm already setting up our next extraction field."

Cesca looked troubled. "Like loggers clear-cutting a forest. Do you even know what bloaters are?"

"Of course," Seymour said. "They're an easy source of ekti-X."

Kellidee Dominic arrived, flushed and confused, but she brightened when she saw her father. He swept her up in a hug. "We're going out into space, little girl."

"But I'm in the middle of a class project."

"You have more than a class project to worry about—we have our most important clan operations ever, and you're going to be part of them." He pulled out a display pad and showed her images of the gray-green nodules drifting in space, hundreds of clan Dominic ships, arrays of ekti tanks.

Her interest was piqued, and in the end, Kellidee needed little convincing.

Jess compiled the young woman's class records, while Cesca gathered a year's worth of lesson plans, which Kellidee promised to follow in her spare time. Seymour was jabbering with infectious enthusiasm as he led his daughter back to the Academ docking bay.

After they were gone, Jess was both amazed and uneasy. "I didn't realize the operations were so significant. If there are fifteen or twenty extraction fields like that, how many more bloater clusters can there be?"

Jess touched the wall of their office complex, where he could sense the wental ice even through the insulating film. The water elementals were brooding and uncommunicative, but restless. Through the faint contact, he could feel something larger, something mysterious out there.

53

ZHETT KELLUM

While at Newstation with nothing to do, Zhett had found a ship's log from Orli Covitz and Garrison Reeves, which had been automatically loaded without comment into the station database. Some months earlier, the *Prodigal Son* had encountered a large distribution of bloaters on the outskirts of the Ikbir system, long chains of nodules that extended into interstellar space. No one remembered that reference because, at the time, bloaters had been mere curiosities. Zhett hoped she was the only one who had spotted that notation. . . .

Now, she, Patrick, and an eager Toff flew to the Ikbir system to lay claim to all those bloaters before any other Roamer clan could. She'd had enough drama in her life, and she just wanted a nice quiet cluster of innocuous gas bags to harvest.

Patrick shut down their stardrive far outside the Ikbir system to begin their search. The ship had decent sensors, and they knew what they were looking for, but it was tedious work—something both Zhett and Patrick agreed was a perfect assignment for Kristof. At first the teenager considered it a reward, but after four hours of staring at nothing he started to complain. Zhett would hear none of it, though. He had volunteered for this mission, and he would have to accept his assignment as any adult Roamer would.

At last, Toff spotted a string of bloaters which led like breadcrumbs toward the star. "Look, if we connect the dots and follow them into the system, there's bound to be a cluster closer in."

Patrick tousled his son's hair, then activated the engines to follow the line of bloaters down toward the bright white sun. Closer to the heart of the Ikbir system, they found exactly what they were looking for: thousands of bloaters drifting together like a globular cluster of fish eggs. Flares of light flashed from one nucleus to another in a seemingly random pattern.

Drenched in nourishing radiation near Ikbir's sun, the bloaters looked different, however. Rather than seeming inert like the other silent and drifting bloaters, these moved, rotated, pulsed, squirmed. Their nuclei became visible in the afterglow of the spontaneous flashes. And the crowded grouping began to *fission*.

"What's happening?" Toff asked. "Those are our bloaters!"

Zhett guided the ship closer, but stopped at a safe distance as the nodules squeezed, swelled, and pulled apart into dumbbell shapes, which then split apart into two bloaters. The nodules doubled, and then each of the new ones swelled in the Ikbir sunlight, quickly growing to normal size. Before long, even the new bloaters began the same process of fissioning, quadrupling their original numbers.

"Look how fast they're reproducing," Patrick said. "We'll have a larger cluster to harvest than we imagined. That's all stardrive fuel for the taking."

Zhett began to map out how they would bring the refurbished Osquivel equipment here to begin extraction activities. She imagined how fast the fortunes of clan Kellum could recover from their current financial disaster.

After the nodules had multiplied and the cluster became a full swarm, the bloaters changed again. Their nuclei continued to flash with more frequent bursts of lightning, as if they were sending Morse-code signals. Then the newborn bloater nodules flattened, stretching out from roughly spherical sacks to spread their membranes into broad wings, like stellar manta rays.

Zhett's voice was tinged with awe. "By the Guiding Star, what the hell are those things?"

"It's a metamorphosis. Are they . . . alive?" Patrick asked.

Toff frowned. "How are we supposed to harvest them if they do that?"

The newly transformed bloaters became more active. They extended their enormous lobes and began to move in slow graceful arcs. The bloaters turned themselves, extending sail-like membranes to catch the solar energy. Then, like a flock of magnificent cosmic avians, they spread apart and soared away.

The entire cluster, and all of that potential ekti-X, simply flew off while Zhett watched.

Toff surprised them with an idea. Instead of following the line of bloaters *toward* Ikbir's star, he suggested flying in the opposite direction, tracking the breadcrumbs farther out into space. "If the sunlight triggered the fissioning, then we should just go into deeper space, catch them before that happens."

"Worth checking out," Zhett said. Actually, she loved the idea.

Patrick piloted them along the outbound line of straggler bloaters, and Kristof's face could barely contain his satisfied grin when they did indeed discover a new island in a sea of stars—several hundred bloaters bobbing along, and swollen with ekti-X . . . ripe for the harvest.

"Back to Osquivel, then?" Patrick asked.

"You read my mind," Zhett said. "We haul our equipment here and start extracting as fast as we can."

54

LEE ISWANDER

Lee Iswander was neither meek nor humble, but when he traveled to Newstation with a full load of ekti-X, he had to swallow his pride and straighten his backbone. The Roamer clans would try to shame him because he had stepped outside the bounds of what they considered acceptable or wise.

He would endure their scorn. He would face them, show them how strong and determined an Iswander was. Again.

He didn't care what they thought. They had insulted him repeatedly, brushed him aside. Even though he came from a once-respected Roamer clan, they didn't like his tactics, his attitude, or his ambition. He was not one of them. Roamers had always struggled against adversity, crowing about their successes and sharing their tragedies, but none of that seemed to count when Lee Iswander was involved.

They had celebrated his cheap and plentiful stardrive fuel, and now he would go to Newstation and see if they would do business with him, or if their grudge would make them even more stupid than usual. *Oh they hate me . . . until they need me.*

Instead of taking his private yacht, he drove an unwieldy tug that carried a large array of fuel cylinders, a load that was more significant than any fuel shipments the upstart operations were bringing in. Even though he was no longer the exclusive provider, it would be enough ekti-X to draw attention.

And Iswander wanted to draw attention.

On approach, he transmitted to Newstation traffic operations, "Requesting a commercial dock for a load of ekti-X as well as a VIP landing berth for my personal ship."

"Stand by, ekti transport," came the voice over the comm. "This is Klanek from ops. Please identify yourself and provide your account."

"This is Lee Iswander. I believe you can find my account."

There was a long, uncomfortable pause. "I'm sorry, Mr. Iswander, but our high-end cargo docks are presently full. I can assign your ship a landing berth on level twelve."

Iswander was annoyed. "Level seven or higher, please. I'll pay a premium."

"Sorry, sir. There's nothing available."

Iswander sifted through his mind and finally placed Klanek's name. He had dealt briefly with the man before, during his run for Speaker of the clans. "Tony, I know you can do better than that, and I'd hate to think you're being unprofessional. Wasn't I courteous and kind to you during the election? I believe I complimented you on your fine work and gave you a token of my support."

Iswander couldn't actually remember the details, but he knew he had spread his wealth liberally while campaigning for the Speakership.

"I won't need a private suite," he added. "My wife should already be here and well settled in."

Klanek hesitated, and Iswander could imagine the man struggling. "Let me double-check, sir."

After a few moments of what was surely just dithering and make-work delay—because there were likely berths available all along—Klanek came back on. "Good news, sir, I did find a small berth on level seven. It's just been vacated. That's the best I can do."

"Thank you for your consideration. I'll take it. And what about my cargo?"

"The array will have to be tethered at one of the outer anchor stations. It's not an ideal commercial situation, but it'll be accessible should you find a customer. Good luck, sir." Klanek provided the location and signed off.

Because he no longer had a green priest at his ekti-extraction operations, Iswander had no way of sending long-distance messages, so Londa wouldn't know he was coming. She would, no doubt, have an impeccable suite that she had converted into a fine home. He looked forward to seeing her soon.

He also needed to go to Academ to make sure that Arden was receiving an exceptional education. His son would not be having an easy time of it, and knowing that the young man probably had to defend himself against bullies and indignant crusaders made a knot in Iswander's stomach. But he himself had been bullied and stomped on many times. He didn't like it, but the experiences had made him strong. Arden was strong as well.

First, he had important business.

He went to the Newstation trade exchanges, where he listed his ekti-X, the quantity, and the price—which he knew undercut any of the new producers. He was discouraged to see how far the price of stardrive fuel had already fallen. He divided his load into three separate parcels, and quickly found a trio of bidders on the board who wanted to meet him.

He had used an alias as a designator so they didn't know the identity of the seller, but as soon as the three would-be buyers saw him, one man's face flared red and he stalked off without saying a word. The other two at least had the spine to confront him. "We don't want any ekti-X from you," said one hard woman. "It's tainted with blood."

Iswander masked his anger with ice. "And yet it still runs stardrive engines."

"Don't need it," said the second clan merchant. "Plenty of other sellers."

"Not at this price." Iswander braced himself to drop the amount even further, but neither of the traders would have any of it.

"The cost is still unconscionable." The hard woman shook her head. "No savings would be worth having to deal with the ghosts of clan Duquesne and all those who died at Sheol."

"Go away then," Iswander said, and his voice came out with an edge that disappointed him. He preferred to keep his emotions well under the surface. "I have other buyers. You lost your chance."

When he checked the boards again, though, he discovered that word had spread: he was blacklisted. No one else offered to buy.

Disgusted, he decided to go for a quick dinner alone to reassess. He didn't want to see Londa in this state, not yet. When he tried to enter a restaurant, though, the proprietor stopped him at the door.

"Your money's no good here, sir. I'm sure you can find another restaurant where the food is more to your liking."

Iswander stared at him, cold. "You're turning down a paying customer."

The proprietor glanced over his shoulder at the numerous occupied tables inside, with customers watching him. "I'm not turning down a paying customer; I'm retaining the ones I have. If I seat you, half my clientele will get up and leave."

Iswander didn't try to cover his distaste. "This is childish and unprofessional."

"Roamers stick together," said the proprietor.

"*I'm* a Roamer!" Iswander nearly shouted.

The other man shrugged. "So you say."

Iswander just wanted to leave. He would take his ekti and find some other market. Certainly there was a colony planet, an outpost in the Ildiran Empire, or even a Solar Navy ship that would buy it.

He realized that Elisa would have known what to do, but she was gone.

Even in the face of this, Iswander was determined to produce more and more ekti, just to prove a point. His own people couldn't turn him away or destroy him so easily. He was stronger than they were. And he would survive.

ELISA ENTURI

The Confederation was hunting her down, but Elisa wasn't afraid—not even concerned. She knew they would never catch her. She was too smart for them, too swift, and if need be, too ruthless.

After being thwarted on Academ, though, Elisa had to reassess what she wanted to do. Merely escaping intact wasn't enough. She couldn't just live her life on the run, one step ahead of the hunters. Elisa had to find something for herself, something that would focus her energies, since everything else had crumbled around her. She would start over, rebuild, and win.

Eventually she would find a way to get Seth back and make Garrison pay for the pain he had caused her, the *shame* he had heaped on her. Elisa didn't know how she'd manage that yet, but she would find a way somehow.

Some might have called it cockiness or sheer arrogance, but only a week after she had escaped pursuit at Academ, Elisa slipped back to Newstation, where she planned to watch and learn. Once she understood what she was dealing with, she would figure out what to do next.

She didn't want to answer questions or fight her way back out if some overambitious Roamer tried to bring her to justice. Elisa didn't feel guilty about what she had done, and she had no interest in explaining her actions. She didn't owe it to anyone—except Lee Iswander, and he had thrown her into a garbage chute.

She changed the registration signal and insignia on her ship in case anyone had noted it last time. Elisa didn't wish to be associated with Iswander Industries anymore, regardless; the company logo was long gone from the hull. She registered at Newstation under a false name and paid the minimal docking fee, using funds she had appropriated from Iswander when she slipped away from his extraction field. Would Iswander even notice or care if she robbed him blind? She suspected his company would soon be bankrupt anyway, and it made sense for her to have a piece of the profits to cover her own expenses. She had earned it. Now she had to find other alternatives so that she could make a living, and Newstation was sure to have them. She felt strangely gratified to be walking right under the Roamers' noses.

Elisa dyed her hair and eyebrows black and wore a head scarf to strengthen her disguise, and she bought a set of comfortable Roamer-style clothes from the first merchant shop she encountered in the station. Many of these people hated her name, but few would know her on sight.

She walked along the crowded decks, listening to the mélange of accents and dialects. So much boisterous conversation, deals being made, business conducted—much of it illicit, no doubt. Elisa remained alert, hoping to hear information she could use or hear of a crew she could join, despite her resentment toward the Roamers. They were unreliable, untrustworthy, and for the most part unambitious. They did have the advantage, however, of working independently and keeping minimal records. She could slip in among them.

She ate by herself in a crowded food court, but the strange spices made her mouth burn, reminding her of some of the things Garrison had cooked. The flavor turned her stomach. She was still angry about how she had been rebuffed when trying to take Seth away from Academ. Her son belonged with her.

In retrospect, she realized she should have simply shot Garrison, Orli, and anyone who stood in her way, but that would have caused problems with Seth, and she simply didn't have the patience to control the boy if he fought her every step of the way.

The unexpected backlash of the wentals had been something she couldn't understand or defend against. She would have to look for another way to retrieve her son. But when she surreptitiously combed through the lists of staff and students at Academ, she found a notation that horrified her.

Seth was gone.

Garrison had taken him away, traveling with Orli Covitz—as if she were the boy's mother! The very concept infuriated Elisa. She would have to confront Jess Tamblyn and Cesca Peroni, demand to know the whereabouts of her boy. She would force them to tell her.

But that would expose her, and she wasn't ready yet. No. She had to be smarter about this.

For four days she remained at Newstation, quietly lurking, eavesdropping on conversations, watching trader ships, observing clan activities. The Roamers had many social centers, gaming rooms of the nongambling variety, and venues for impromptu concerts where the music was often ill tuned but energetic. She didn't know how long she could stand it here.

As she remained unnoticed among them, she was angered to see so many new shipments of ekti-X delivered in tanks from slapped-together pumping facilities at other bloater clusters. She had destroyed the Duquesne operations to protect that trade secret, but now it was out of her hands. She supposed she could become a vigilante and take out one operation after another. In the past she would have done that for Lee Iswander, but she would not bloody her hands on his behalf again. Still, her heart ached because she *would* have done it . . . if only he'd asked.

When a particularly large shipment of ekti-X arrived, she listened to the background chatter and was surprised to learn that the stardrive fuel came from Iswander Industries. Unable to resist, Elisa tracked him down and eventually found Lee Iswander in a drinking establishment, but she didn't dare approach him. Instead, she maintained her disguise and just watched him from the far side of the bar. She sat in the shadows alone, like a jilted lover, while Iswander met with Roamer traders—and argued with them.

Seeing him sparked a series of strange feelings in her. He had trusted her, relied on her, made her important; Elisa had been an invaluable employee and had done everything Alec Pannebaker could not do. For a long time, Iswander had appreciated her efforts, made her feel special, and she would have done anything for him. To use the silly, superstitious jargon of the Roamer clans, Lee Iswander had been her Guiding Star.

Just watching him now, Elisa felt angry with herself for feeling such a longing to be with him again. But Iswander didn't notice her, and Elisa wasn't sure how he would react if he did.

Later, when she learned that no Roamer clan would buy his ekti, at any price, she felt indignant on his behalf, although she wanted to feel smug about it. She knew she could help make this right—in fact, Elisa could easily have tracked down other customers for him. She had convinced Kett Shipping to be their original distributor, and she could find buyers again. Oh, some uppity customers would refuse to do business with a disgraced outlaw, but others had no such moral compunctions—if the price was right and the flow of ekti-X was steady.

Elisa shook her head. Iswander was no longer part of her life, his problems no longer her concern. He would have to deal with them himself. In order to cut her ties, she would have to find another job, one that had no connection to Lee Iswander whatsoever.

At Newstation she stumbled upon a call for able salvage workers, and as soon as she saw who was asking, she decided to take a chance. Xander Brindle and Terry Handon—two young men she had made rich—had embarked on a wild scheme to create a replacement for Ulio Station. Right now, they were looking for people to comb through the wreckage around Relleker, and that certainly sounded like something she could do.

Xander and Terry had been her business partners for a long time. Besides, they owed her. Yes, that was where she would go, a new start, a worthwhile job—and it would take her away from Newstation. She returned to her ship and flew off to find them.

56

RLINDA KETT

The moment the first black robot ships began bombarding the major cities of Earth, Rlinda knew it was time to go. From the window of her penthouse office in the Kett Shipping tower, she watched the jagged black warships slice like gutting knives across the air. They opened fire, leveling entire city blocks.

She heard the deep thump of a far-off explosion, and at the horizon she saw a flare of white-hot light expanding in a hemispherical vaporization wave. She stared in awed silence for a long moment, then said aloud, "The whole city'll be gone in an hour."

The robots seemed to enjoy their smaller, sharper strikes as well, as if they found flaying the population of Earth to be as interesting as dealing a death blow. Rlinda hated those damn things . . . but that was nothing new. Alarms roared through the city, and she decided to get moving.

Gasping, Robb Brindle appeared at her office door. "Rlinda, we've got to head out—now! The robots will wipe out everything around us. Count on it."

Rlinda didn't need to be told twice. "You two take the *Curiosity.* Load it up with station staff and evac as many as you can."

"I already sent out the call—but we've got to *move.*" He looked frantic. "Come on!"

Tasia's voice came over the comm. "Robb, where the hell are you? We're leaving!"

He tugged on Rlinda's arm. "We won't abandon you here."

"Hell, I'm not staying. Do I look like a fool?" She jogged after him, panting heavily, unaccustomed to running. "What I mean is, we've got to take every ship. I'll fly the *Declan's Glory*. We can evacuate more people that way."

Explosions rumbled out in the city. Even inside the tower, she could hear the screaming buzz of attacking ships. Another vaporization bomb detonated, much closer this time. The glare lasted longer, and she could feel the bulldozer strength of the shock wave when it hit the building. The whole tower shuddered, the lights flickered. Personnel ran through the corridors, some rushing to lifts that would take them down to street level—which was foolish, Rlinda thought, because they would surely be buried under rubble within minutes. Others took the stairs, which was probably just as foolish.

"Get to the launching bays, you idiots!" she shouted at them as she ran. Even so, Kett Shipping did not have enough vessels to take everyone.

Black robot ships roared by, only three blocks away. A nearby skyscraper sporting the logo of a communications company collapsed into rubble and flames as the attacking vessels blasted its midsection. The toppling skyscraper smashed other buildings on its way down.

Rlinda flinched instinctively, remembering how proud she had been to own such a giant tower for Kett Shipping. Now she wished she had built squat and nondescript headquarters. Or something deep underground.

As the robots kept leveling the obvious targets, Kett Shipping personnel rushed into the launching bay: starship mechanics, cargo handlers, pilots who had been on Earth for furlough.

Her blond hair streaked with sweat, Tasia stood at the *Curiosity*'s open ramp, crowding people aboard. She already had the ship's engines warmed up, its running lights illuminated. Relief washed over her face when she saw Rlinda and Robb coming. "There you are! Get aboard before I have to make a choice between you and everyone else. We've got to head out."

"There are five billion people left on Earth, dear girl," Rlinda said, feeling her lungs burn from the effort of running. "How do you propose we take them all?"

The skies were full of fleeing ships. From the minute the shadow cloud had appeared outside the Lunar Orbital Complex, the popu-

lace had watched in horror as the CDF battleships—the most powerful vessels in the fleet—were decimated. Any intelligent person on
Earth could see what was coming, and those with the means to do
so raced away in private ships. But at least a third of those fleeing
vessels had been intercepted and destroyed by the robot vanguard.
Not good odds.

Rlinda knew that leaving Earth was still their best option. In the
hangar bay, *Declan's Glory* sat waiting. It was a ship she occasionally borrowed, its real captain on indeterminate medical leave; as the
head of Kett Shipping, Rlinda wanted to make use of all her available vessels.

"You two head out!" she shouted. "I'm taking *Declan* with
another batch of people."

More frantic workers followed her, and she gestured them toward
the smaller ship. "Fit as many inside as you can, but I make no guarantees about your safety. It's your choice—decide whether you'd
rather be blown up in the air or blown up here on the ground."

Another Kett ship took off and soared out through the open
hangar door high on the headquarters tower. On the far side of the
city, one more doomsday bomb detonated, its bubble of destruction
vaporizing all buildings within a kilometer radius.

"You're probably toast either way," Rlinda muttered, but most
of the people had no trouble deciding.

"Come on, everybody—time to go!" Tasia yelled.

As workers crowded toward her ship, Rlinda hurried them up the
ramp, and then froze. "Wait, I can't leave yet!" She turned and bolted
back the way she had come. She hadn't even caught her breath yet.

"Where are you going?" Robb shouted after her. "There's no
time!"

"There has to be time. I forgot something."

"Then leave it behind!" Tasia said. "Everyone needs you."

"No, only the people on *Declan* need me. I'd rather leave *me*
behind." She reached the door of the bay and yelled back to one man
who looked halfway competent to pilot her ship. "Wait as long as
you can—take off and fly away if you have to. I might shake my fist,
but I'll understand in my heart of hearts."

Somehow finding a reserve of strength, she bolted down the

corridor. Rlinda Kett had never been athletic—in fact, she hadn't run this much in years, and she feared she might burst an aneurysm herself, like BeBob did.

Several of the lifts were malfunctioning, but she found one that worked, although it shuddered alarmingly as it climbed to the level of her penthouse office. Heaving huge breaths, she staggered along the hall. More explosions rang outside. The skies seemed full of the angular ships, and she knew this was just the first wave. Hundreds of thousands of bugbots were coming from the shadow cloud, and with every moment her chances diminished.

But she didn't change her mind. Her heart was thudding hard. She recognized that she would have chastised anyone else for taking such a stupid risk, but she did not intend to leave the precious thing behind.

Inside her office, she paused, perspiring heavily, then lurched toward the desk. She reached out and grabbed the silver capsule from its Plexiglas stand. "I'm not leaving you behind, BeBob. Our ashes are going to stay together in death, but I never meant to die just to retrieve you."

Before she ran back out, she stopped for just a second at the door of her office, trying to catch her breath, though it did little good. Another nearby explosion got her moving again. "You'd call me a fool for doing this, wouldn't you? Well, guess what—I'm not listening."

She pocketed the capsule and bolted out into the corridor, hoping the lift still functioned to take her back down to the launching bay—because she sure as hell wasn't going to tackle seven flights of stairs.

As she left the side kitchen where she often amused herself by cooking, she caught a last wafting scent of her delicious new casserole, a recipe she had considered putting on the menu of her restaurants. So much for that idea—the damn black robots had already wiped out her establishment on Relleker, and now they were going to vaporize her Earth restaurant as well. She hated to leave good food behind, and it smelled like it was burning, but she ran, gritting her teeth.

She reached the lift. The doors were askew—not a good sign—but she climbed inside anyway. The car shuddered and dropped two meters before the emergency brakes caught; then the groaning systems engaged, lowering the lift jerkily until it reached the hangar level. The elevator doors started to open—and the power gave out. Rlinda struggled, forcing them apart. The floor was a foot shy of its destination, but she climbed out.

The *Curiosity* was already loaded. The last few panicked people were still running inside the hangar, looking for a way out. *Declan's Glory* was also prepped and running—thank God, in her absence her fill-in pilot had taken the initiative and activated the engines so the ship was ready to take off. Tasia shouted from the *Curiosity*, refusing to let them leave without Rlinda. When the big trader woman showed up, they cheered, then angrily scolded her to hurry.

Rlinda was so exhausted she could barely lift her feet, but she staggered forward, feeling the hard capsule in her pocket. It was too damned romantic to want her own ashes launched together with BeBob's into space, yet she hadn't been able to leave them behind. She didn't expect anyone else to understand.

"Go!" yelled Robb.

"Go, yourself!" Rlinda wheezed, staggering aboard her ship. "Now."

Robb and Tasia took her at her word. The hatch closed, and the *Curiosity* soared out of the hangar into skies already crowded with smoke and death.

As Rlinda made her way into the cockpit of the *Declan's Glory*, the temporary pilot she had chosen fumbled with the controls, lifting the ship up as the workers crammed themselves together inside, muttering and moaning. She moved the stand-in out of her expanded pilot seat, dropped herself into place, and took the controls. "No one can fly better than me."

"No argument here, ma'am." The man looked gray and pale. "Let's just go."

"Strap in, then." She boosted the ship forward, and acceleration pushed them back into their seats. "And don't call me ma'am."

Black robot ships streaked across the sky. Nine converged on the Kett Shipping tower and began blasting with energy weapons, cutting the structural girders, smashing the mirrored glass. Explosions ripped through numerous floors. Rlinda didn't even want to guess how many of her own people had been still inside.

Declan's Glory soared away just as the headquarters skyscraper began to collapse in groaning rubble and flames. Ahead of them in the city sky, the *Curiosity* was slipping, corkscrewing, diving and dodging like a sun-warmed mosquito. The robot ships fired at it, but none of their blasts hit.

Then the black vessels began shooting at Rlinda, and she flew using all of her tricks. "If you don't get spacesick and bruised from being thrown around, then I'm not doing this properly!" she called back by way of an excuse. After an exhausting minute of dodging, she accelerated, relying on speed rather than finesse, and *Declan's Glory* shot away from the city like a projectile.

Behind her, another doomsday bomb detonated, vaporizing a great swath of the metropolis—including the section where her headquarters had been. In a ridiculously inappropriate thought, she was glad she had retrieved BeBob's ashes in time. "Just stay with me," she muttered, feeling the small, reassuring lump in her pocket.

Pushing *Declan's Glory* far beyond its specified limits, Rlinda took her handful of passengers—barely able to breathe in the four-G acceleration—and headed into space before the swarming robots could finish destroying the planet.

ARITA

During the Elemental War, parts of the worldforest had been charred by the faeros, but those damaged areas still harbored life. Vegetation swiftly grew back. *This,* though, was worse than anything Arita had ever seen in images from the war. The awful blight had turned the worldforest into a dry swath of brown death.

When the Theron expeditionary force arrived in the Wild, the green priests' fear was palpable. "The Gardeners' disease will devour the whole forest," said Zaquel. She had brought a potted treeling with her for communication, but now she just stood motionless, in fearful awe.

Collin emerged from the landed transport, and he and Arita both looked at the hillsides and valleys once covered with towering worldtrees, now only a scar. His voice was quiet. "The dark rot that extends through the heartwood and into the root network, kills the verdani and wipes out their memories."

"It is a cruel disease," King Peter said.

"The Onthos were infected before they arrived," Arita reminded them all. "They passed it on to the trees, and they're infesting this part of the worldforest so they can reproduce."

"This is how they repay us for welcoming them to our world—by poisoning the lifeblood of Theroc." Estarra sounded betrayed. "We have no choice but to excise them from the worldforest. It may be the only way to stop this cancer."

"You could burn it out," Osira'h suggested. Her eyes flashed as she studied the devastation. "Use a controlled fire to take out all these dead trees and prevent the blight from spreading."

"No . . . not yet," Reyn said. "We should study it first, find a way to cure the disease."

Arita recalled the cold blackness in the eyes of the Onthos as they had watched, expecting the voidpriests to murder her and Collin. "Don't shed too many tears for the Gardeners. They deserve their fate."

But Collin surprised her. "Not all the Gardeners. The worldtrees welcomed them, so there must be something about their race that's worth saving." He also carried a potted treeling.

"The *worldforest* is worth saving," Arita argued. "That should be our priority!"

"If we cured the worldtrees, we'd be saving them. Wouldn't that be better?" Reyn asked.

Where the blight had wiped out so many trees, the Onthos had entrenched themselves and built a fortress in the worldforest. Before the expeditionary force landed, survey craft had flown overhead to map the extent of the dead zone, and taken images of the towering embankments and defensive walls erected by the small creatures.

"They knew we were coming," Arita said. "We don't have time to cure them. They plan to fight us."

Standing in the open meadow, Reyn swayed as the sight stole his breath.

Ever protective, Osira'h turned to Peter and Estarra. "You are the King and Queen. You command the Confederation Defense Forces. Surely you have enough weaponry to vaporize this *insult* in an instant? The Mage-Imperator would have dealt with this scourge in a single strike from the Solar Navy." Collin, Zaquel, and the other green priests turned toward her, astonished by the comment.

Peter answered in a firm, calm voice, "Yes, we could do that, but the Onthos seem to be betting that we won't."

"At least not yet," Estarra corrected. "But we won't just sit back and watch Theroc die."

The Gardeners had used their affinity with the trees and their mastery of the verdani to wall themselves off. They had warped and twisted the dead foliage into barriers of thorns, buttresses of dead trunks and limbs. Sharp tree branches thrust outward like dangerous spikes.

The Theron home guard stared at the impenetrable barricade, and the green priests muttered in confusion. Zaquel touched the dead wood of the outer fortress wall. "There's nothing here. No thoughts, no memories. These worldtrees are no longer part of the verdani mind."

"How much else died with them?" Arita asked. "How much knowledge have we already lost?"

They heard snapping and cracking sounds from inside the dense thicket. Brittle branches broke away under the weight of their own decay. One huge trunk that was not part of the barricade groaned and toppled forward with lumbering grace as the King and Queen and other Therons scattered. The falling hulk smashed one of the expeditionary ships.

"That wasn't a coincidence," Arita said as they backed away.

"They're attacking," Collin confirmed.

From inside the tangled forest of broken branches and sharp thorns, Arita saw movement. She braced herself, remembering the cold darkness of Kennebar and his voidpriests. Deep in her thoughts, she searched again to find some touch of that distant mind that had helped her before, but she felt only a stunned silence and white-hot pricks of pain. Even if that other sentience had some inkling of what the shadows were doing here, it would not help. It seemed to be facing an incomprehensible crisis of its own.

Flickers of movement through the dense branches showed pale forms that moved like simian spiders. The green priests stared with uneasy awe, and the soldiers with the King and Queen prepared their weapons.

The Onthos appeared: at first ten of them, then a hundred—which should have been *all* of the refugees from their seedships—and then hundreds more. Collin and Arita had explained to her parents and the green priests that these sexless creatures sprang from spores that infected the worldtrees and drew upon that energy to reproduce. And reproduce. And reproduce.

One Gardener high up in the trees leaned forward as his comrades gathered in the shelter of the pointed boughs and threatening spikes. "We are only here to survive. You cannot stop us. Our race is finally growing strong after being crushed repeatedly to the edge of extinction." Anger rose in the alien voice. The dead trees rustled and crackled, as if in the death spasms of the verdani. Countless other Onthos skittered forward to face them.

Sarein had died at their hands. In spite of Reyn's plea, Arita did not want to show the creatures any mercy.

Queen Estarra called out, "We defend the trees. We must rid Theroc of you."

"You will not succeed," said the alien, as even more of the pale-skinned creatures crowded out from behind their dangerous barricade of trees. "The worldforest is no longer yours."

58

ANTON COLICOS

Yazra'h showed off her combat prowess, as if she didn't realize that Anton had been impressed with her long ago and that although she was a close friend, she had nothing to gain by impressing him further. She wanted to convince the human historian to become her lover, and he couldn't make her understand that he simply wasn't interested.

Now she tossed her coppery hair under the bright sunshine. "We must learn to fight new foes of all sorts, Rememberer Anton. I trust in my own skills to fight the monster before me."

She had asked him to watch her battle the powerful ugru, though at the moment Anton was far more interested in delving into how the Shana Rei were previously defeated, as the Mage-Imperator had requested. The rememberers had studied the relevant tales many times, but Anton kept hoping he would uncover new revelations, especially in the less-familiar and long-buried apocryphal documents.

Without doubt, he was more likely to find answers in the documents than by watching Yazra'h fight this lumpy, ugly combat beast. But she had insisted, and Yazra'h was very good at insisting.

Sitting in the arena stands, Anton put out the documents he had brought along, still hoping to get some reading done. Five of Ildira's seven suns shone down, and Anton wore filmgoggles for protection. After so many years on Ildira, he was accustomed to the intense daylight, but the sun flare from the printed crystal sheets made the records difficult to read.

Yazra'h danced around on the soft turf of the fighting area. She held a small crystal dagger in each hand, each blade no longer than his index finger. The little prickers couldn't possibly do any damage to the behemoth in front of her and would only annoy the monster . . . but annoying an ugru—and surviving—was Yazra'h's intent.

"Watch me, Rememberer Anton!"

He dutifully looked up as she explained, skipping around the plodding hulk. The ugru had brown leathery skin studded with gravelly warts. Its body was stocky, its four legs thick, its head a blunt dome that rested flat on broad shoulders with no discernible neck. "Ugrus are bottom feeders in the jungle, eating fungus in the underbrush. They lumber along, impervious to predators, oblivious to even the largest biting insects."

Yazra'h danced up and slapped the ugru's shoulder as hard as she could, and the loud crack sounded like a gunshot. The ugru flinched and plodded away.

"These creatures are normally docile, but they can be provoked." She smacked the ugru again and pranced around it, coming up on the opposite side for another loud slap. With a grunt, the creature shuffled in the other direction. Yazra'h dove onto its back and jabbed repeatedly with her stubby crystal daggers, although the points barely pricked the thick hide. The ugru groaned and turned in one direction, then the other.

"When it is finally enraged, the ugru becomes a powerful and worthy opponent." She pricked six more times and sprang off the creature's back, crouching and ready to fight. The ugru, though, just lumbered away.

Hiding a smile, Anton went back to his studies, rearranging his notes, pulling out cross-referenced sections of the standard Saga along with the apocrypha. The Ildiran historical epic contained seminal tales about the Shana Rei, many of which were just descriptions of disasters—colonies smothered by darkness, worlds entirely englobed—much like what he had recently seen at Kuivahr. The stories were chilling, but he tried to find hints and insights that could lead to solutions.

He found a mention of another strange myth from before the time of the war with the shadows, about a presence called Eternity's Mind, a powerful force that could stand against the chaos the Shana Rei wished to impose, but since the Ildirans could neither contact nor influence Eternity's Mind, Anton assumed it was too esoteric a legend to be of any practical use.

Of more interest, he studied the tale of the Ahlar Designate, whose world had been saved from a shadow cloud, but the creatures of darkness had worked their way into his *thism,* into his blood—driving him mad. Unable to control his actions, the Ahlar Designate had attempted to murder his nine children. Somehow forcing control back on himself, he had slashed open the main arteries in his arm and let the blood spill out: black blood, tainted blood. When his blood finally ran red again, he was free of the Shana Rei, but it was too late, and he died. If nothing else, it was a small victory.

Yazra'h spun about, slapped the ugru again, and bounded onto its back. She did a cartwheel, then sprang back off, but not before jabbing the poor creature again. Sufficiently provoked at last, the ugru lifted a massive front leg and swung at her as if to brush away a distraction. She flitted in and poked the soft part of its foot, which made the ugru snort.

"It will heal quickly, and its pain receptors shut down in seconds," she explained, then pricked again, planting herself defiantly in front of the big creature, making sure she was at the center of its gaze. "Fight me, monster!"

"That's quite remarkable," Anton said, and turned back to his documents. He would look up and watch when the beast finally, if ever, responded.

The previous war against the Shana Rei had ended when Mage-Imperator Xiba'h coerced an alliance with the faeros. The flaming elementals had been the only force strong enough to drive back the shadows, yet the faeros were smothered in great numbers each time they fought the creatures of darkness.

The Saga of Seven Suns devoted many stanzas to how Mage-Imperator Xiba'h had burned himself alive in order to summon the faeros. After that, his successor and the fiery elementals had defeated the Shana Rei. Somehow.

Anton studied the unhelpful stanzas again, shaking his head. "I wish the writers hadn't skipped so many details."

If the faeros had been so effective, what about the wentals? Or the hydrogues? In a dramatic attack on the Golgen skymine, the hydrogues had been consumed by darkness inside their gas giants, but they—like the wentals—were much diminished since the Elemental War. According to Nira, the verdani were now suffering great damage in their worldforest, with trees dying from a spreading blight. A shadow blight.

"Yah!" Yazra'h yelled and struck the ugru again, and this time it reacted as if she had stepped on a landmine. This was the response she had been trying to provoke for the past ten minutes. With a snuffling roar, the ugru lifted up on its tree-like back legs, raising meaty front arms, each as large as a cannon barrel, and used them as battering rams. The monster swung so swiftly that Yazra'h barely had time to yell before it sent her flying.

Anton expected to hear the crack of bone and see blood spray out of her mouth, but Yazra'h spun in the air and fell on her hands and knees. Somehow, she still managed to look graceful.

The ugru rounded on her, and she sprang back up, holding the two crystal prickers as if they might scare the beast. It thundered toward her. Yazra'h bounced out of the way, laughing in a manner that Anton found completely inappropriate.

"Come fight me!"

The ugru charged toward her. Yazra'h darted sideways. The beast responded with surprising swiftness and agility, and she startled it by running straight at it. At the last minute, she jumped into the air, pressed her palms on its shoulders as she flipped herself, and landed behind the creature. She slapped its thick hide and poked again with her tiny stingers.

The ugru managed to anticipate some of her tricks. With another tremendous swat, it sent Yazra'h flying again. Although she landed on her feet, Anton could tell she was hurt, but he knew she would be insulted if he rushed to offer aid. In fact, any such attempt would likely get *him* trampled. Unable to concentrate on his reading anymore, he watched the fight continue.

"Don't you think you should leave the poor thing alone now?" he called.

"I must practice and become proficient. There is a war coming."

"Yes, and your skills will be of great use if we are threatened by a herd of ugrus, but I doubt this will help against the Shana Rei."

Yazra'h backed away. "I see your point, Rememberer Anton." She winced as she moved, and he hoped she wasn't severely injured.

Once she stopped provoking it, the ugru quickly became docile and began to snuffle at the food offerings on the practice field. In less than a minute, the beast had forgotten entirely about her.

Yazra'h came back to Anton, panting and sweaty. "Were you impressed?"

"I am always impressed—your fighting skill is unequaled. I just hope I can impress you with some discovery I make in the old records."

Her brows knitted together. "I am already impressed with that, Rememberer Anton. You can do a difficult thing that is beyond me. Together we are certain to find a way to defeat any enemy."

Anton wasn't so sure, but he appreciated her confidence.

CHAPTER

59

GENERAL NALANI KEAH

From the bridge of the *Kutuzov*, Keah commanded the surviving CDF ships as they fell back and tried to defend Earth. They kept fighting as they retreated from the ruins of the Lunar Orbital Complex, and she lost three more Mantas on the way.

Waves of bugbot battleships were dumping doomsday blasts on entire continents below. Dozens of major cities had already been obliterated. Millions must be dead. She swallowed hard. It couldn't be billions yet—could it?

This was already far worse than Relleker.

Anyone with common sense and a functional ship had already tried to escape, but most of those were wiped out by pursuing bugbots. The angular black ships were chasing down terrified human pilots for sport, while others continued the wholesale extermination on the surface.

"I needed more time to build up our forces, damn it," she muttered to herself. *More time!* She hadn't even been able to load up her Juggernaut with sun bombs from Dr. Krieger's facility.

The *Kutuzov* plowed through the flurry of robot ships, and Keah watched the slaughter ahead. She stood up from her command chair because she was so furious. Her Juggernaut fired every remaining weapon in its arsenal, but even that could not protect the last streams of evacuees that tried to escape from orbit. Any fleeing vessel looked to have about a ten percent chance of getting away—terrible odds, but the chances of survival for anyone left on the planet would be far less. Thanks to her insistence, Earth's population had seen images of the massacre of Relleker, so they knew exactly what was coming. But they couldn't do anything about it.

Maybe she should have kept the threat confidential, let all those doomed people sleep cozily in their beds for a few more days. "What purpose did it serve for us to tell them all to prepare? Prepare how? Are they hiding in their basements? For all the good that'll do!"

"Most people would rather know their fates, General," said First Officer Wingo. "You made the right decision."

"And some of those people are indeed getting away," Lieutenant Tait pointed out.

She felt sick to see that her entire CDF force amounted to no more than a hundred heavy ships.

Beyond the rubble of the LOC, a sudden blossoming of brilliant explosions looked like suns bursting inside the heart of the shadow cloud. Keah gawked in surprise. "What the hell? Enhanced magnification!" Her rear screen showed a grainy image, still distorted by chaotic entropy waves. The dark nebula and the hexagonal cylinders sparkled and collapsed, bombarded by an unexpected booby trap of sun bombs. Dozens of them, right inside the shadow cloud. "Good Lord—I guess Dr. Krieger decided to make use of his inventory."

Patton said, "Wish we had more sun bombs."

"I'll take my victories wherever they come." Keah allowed herself a warm grin. "I bet the Shana Rei just felt a kick in the nuts."

Though diminished and wounded, the roiling cloud swirled forward to engulf the remaining fragments of the LOC, and she knew that Krieger and his fabrication facilities were gone. Unlike Admiral Handies, who tried to run away in his Juggernaut, Krieger had actually made a difference . . . at least a small one.

"I'm continuing my attack, General," announced Admiral Haroun, darting in and out with his battered *Okrun*. "Jazers and railguns are mostly depleted. I don't have any sun bombs left, but laser cannons are recharging. That's another hundred robot ships destroyed, but I'm not really keeping count."

Haroun yelped as a weapons blast struck his battleship, and he had to reel away.

"Destroying a hundred enemy ships is a good start, Admiral," Keah answered. "Now do that ten thousand more times, and we'll win."

The numbers were completely hopeless. That was a fact, not despair. She didn't want to run from a fight, but she had a hundred ships against hundreds of thousands. The people on Earth were wailing for help—just like at Relleker.

She watched another Manta explode as a swarm of bugbot ships cut it off, engulfed it, and fired relentlessly until the ship broke into flaming fragments. She could order her CDF ships to stay here and keep shooting at enemy targets until they themselves were destroyed. And then what? They could never save the population of Earth and it wouldn't help the Confederation.

"Somebody give me a new alternative, damn it!"

She heard only the overlapping pleas on the open comm channels mixed with a litany of damage reports. She saw the flashes of weapons fire in space, and watched dark scars being sketched over the surface of the Earth. The robot extermination bombs were now sweeping across Europe.

"General, look at the screen!" Sensor Chief Saliba pointed as a swollen projectile of pure fire rolled past them. Several bridge crew-members leaped to their feet.

Crackling, flaming ellipsoids hurtled in from interplanetary space, streaking toward Earth like tracer bullets.

"Faeros? What the hell! Full sensors," Keah said. "Where are they coming from? How many?"

"Approximately fifty, General."

Keah stared in awe as the fiery elementals joined the fray. "Haven't they already caused enough damage?" In the past, thousands of enraged faeros had pummeled Earth's Moon until it shattered into fragments. Now the fireballs were back, and Keah hated them.

But she changed her mind as soon as the faeros slammed into the clusters of bugbot ships. Countless robot vessels exploded as the fiery ellipsoids tore through them, scattering their clusters and driving them from Earth's orbit. Keah herself joined the rising cheer.

Reacting, the black robots swarmed around the faeros, attacking like suicidal hornets, but their energy weapons were not at all effective against the elementals. The fireballs swooped around Earth's orbit, knocking the rest of the robot formations into disarray.

Keah wasn't going to complain about it. She transmitted to all of the surviving ships, "Let's not take any more damage. Pull back and implement emergency repairs where possible—even if this breather lasts for only half an hour, let's make it count."

The sheer unexpectedness of the arrival had sent the bugbots reeling, but the faeros were as capricious as the Shana Rei were chaotic. Even fifty elemental fireballs could only do so much damage. The flaming beings ricocheted through the black ships and clumsily destroyed numerous evacuating human vessels as well.

The Klikiss robots were not the enemies of the faeros, however, and never had been. The fireballs swooped directly toward the oncoming Shana Rei shadow cloud.

CHAPTER

60

DEPUTY ELDRED CAIN

After touring Dr. Krieger's sun-bomb factories with General Keah, Cain made his way to his mansion built on the edge of what had been Madrid. There, he received the first frantic reports about the Shana Rei, and he knew with cold dread what was going to happen.

Since it served as CDF headquarters, Earth had more warships in residence than any other world in the Confederation. Deputy Cain had the utmost confidence in General Keah. He knew she would fight the battles that could be fought and win any victory that could be achieved, given her resources. He also doubted it would be enough.

Countless civilian ships scrambled to evacuate, but only a handful of the world's billions would ever manage to get away, and a significant number of those would be destroyed in space as they tried to flee the solar system.

As the enemy plunged in toward Earth, he realized the rest of the decision process was out of his hands. He was a pragmatist, and he had closely studied the images of Relleker. As the battles raged at the LOC and more than a million black robot warships came in unabated, Cain understood in his heart that Earth was lost. The Shana Rei and the robots would attack with more destructive force than they had used against any previous target.

Now that he'd returned to his mansion, Cain was more than an hour from any government center. He had purposely built his mansion far from population centers, and he wasn't going to be able to arrange an evacuation. He ran the options in his mind, didn't like his chances, and instead decided how he would prefer to spend that last hour or so.

He clung to precious memories of humanity's high points. Night had fallen over the Madrid impact crater, but the dark sky was etched with claw marks of fire, the orange exhaust trails of robot battleships racing over Europe. The ships dropped devastator bombs that were far more deadly and more precisely targeted than the barrage of meteor impacts that had caused so much destruction at the end of the Elemental War.

Overhead, the battle provided a terrific light show. Multiple sunrises filled the sky as CDF ships deployed their last sun bombs. No doubt the flashes wreaked havoc among the attackers, but not enough. It would never be enough.

Cain was astonished when flaming ellipsoids rolled in like burning cannonballs. "Faeros? Now that is unexpected."

He watched from his balcony, looking out at what had once been Madrid, home to the Prado, one of humanity's most amazing art museums . . . the loss of which had been as momentous to him as the loss of all those lives. He had spent years trying to collect and restore the remnants of humanity's great art: works by Whistler, Goya, Hieronymus Bosch, Van Gogh, and his favorite, Velázquez.

Cain went inside his home now, turning his back on the raging conflict as he walked slowly through the gallery, stopping to admire the nuances, the imagination, and the depth with which those masters imbued their paintings. The soft display lights flickered from the disruptive battle over Earth, but once his standby power blocks kicked in, the illumination grew steady again.

Hands behind his back, he drank in the lush details, the swirls and enthusiasm of "Starry Night," then the gritty horror of Goya's "Saturn Devouring His Son," and the many works of Velázquez—a well-respected but, in Cain's opinion, underrated genius. He stood there knowing that these masterpieces would soon be destroyed, that he was the last person to lay eyes on them.

The shadows were coming.

Not far away, a gigantic hemisphere of light wiped out another Spanish city—probably Toledo, given the position. There was no place to hide. Nowhere safe. The sky was so full of explosions and energy beams it resembled confetti. The blasts of color and swirls of vapor trails looked almost like Van Gogh's painting. A starry night, indeed.

He went to his home comm center and tuned it to the *Kutuzov's* command frequency. The screen showed the Juggernaut's bridge filled with shouts, sparks, explosions. His transmission was barely loud enough to be heard over the mayhem. "I know you're busy, General. I just wanted to tell you to keep up the fight. You will find a way."

Keah was haggard, her hair tangled, her face drawn. "Not now, Deputy." An explosion rocked the bridge. "Increase the starboard shields! Do we have any railgun projectiles left? Yes, Mr. Patton, I'm talking to you!"

"Farewell, General," Cain said.

Keah gave him a quick look. "What the hell are you doing, Deputy? Get out of—"

An explosion roared nearby—not the *Kutuzov,* but at the Madrid crater. Robot ships screamed through the air, strafing the ground, and Cain realized that he was cut off. Hundreds of thousands of black warships swept over Earth for the coup de grâce.

Cain emerged again onto the broad balcony, where he had often sat to study the stars or watch the frequent meteor showers. Now, though, the stars had vanished in an entire quadrant of sky. A swirling opaque black shadow unfurled like a blanket descending upon Earth.

Cain couldn't tear his eyes away as darkness fell.

61

KOTTO OKIAH

The miracles grew more amazing as his survey craft cruised through the void, delving deeper into a nothingness overlaid with paradoxes. Piloting cautiously, Kotto approached the glowing bright spots of structure, patterns imposed on the inner workings of the sideways universe.

He squinted, pressed his face against the windowport, but the harder he tried to stare, the less focused those vibrant fingerprints seemed to be. "How close are we?"

The navigational systems ranged outward with an array of sensors, but the two compies remained at a loss. "We are sorry, Kotto," said GU. "We have no reference points for our location, nor any anchor for our destination."

"Then let's keep flying closer to whatever they are. I sure don't think they're the Shana Rei." He felt no fear, only curiosity—which was foolish, he knew, but at this point, he had already committed himself. Kotto meant to gain answers—*all* the answers, if possible. He had always wanted to know.

The smudges of phosphorescence appeared elsewhere around them, seeming to move like mirages. Either Kotto's piloting was woefully inadequate, or the distribution of those other *things* continued to deviate. He launched forerunner probes that hurtled ahead, scanning and sending back readings that were at first baffling and then overloaded. He studied the screens and muttered, "That's not helpful at all." With a sigh, he looked backward, although the emptiness behind looked no different from the emptiness ahead. "Maybe we should return to Fireheart. We did find the Shana Rei hiding in their lair, and the Confederation needs to know. That's vital information." He shook his head, then leaned forward again, fascinated by the glowing smudges. "But I have to say, this is very intriguing. Let's just go a little farther."

The technical readings warbled off the scale, went dark, then flared back with sensor gibberish and a wash of loud static. Kotto began to feel a throbbing inside his head, an external curiosity that was like his own, but seemed to be as vast as the universe. It fascinated him, and he felt an odd, close connection. He tapped his temple and closed his eyes, trying to concentrate. "Hello. Is anyone there?"

"Yes, we are here, Kotto," said KR.

He opened his eyes. "Not you. There's something else. Do you feel it in your heads?"

The two compies said, "No, we do not."

Now that he had made an overture to that looming presence, he could see sharper colors, more distinct traceries of the tapestry underlying the universe. Smudges and lines tangled in webs and mazes. This seemed like behind-the-scenes workings that the very architect of the universe had not meant for anyone to see. Kotto felt puzzled to think that God might have left unraveled edges.

As the survey craft flew closer, the smudges brightened, as if they were now letting him approach, acknowledging him. The throbbing and thrumming grew louder inside his skull.

"Hello?" His voice was just a whisper, but that mysterious presence heard him; he was sure of it. "I'm Kotto. Kotto Okiah."

When they had flown past the angular Shana Rei ships, he had sensed nothing from the shadows other than a cold deadness that stood out even in the void. This imposing presence was entirely different, and the more Kotto tried to grasp that trickle of consciousness, the more it awakened and noticed him in return. He felt a thought, a package of information, an identifier, and he brightened. "It's . . . Eternity's Mind. That's what it calls itself." He looked to the compies, nodding. "Eternity's Mind."

"We detected no signal, Kotto," said GU.

"But we will make a note of Eternity's Mind," KR added.

"Pleased to meet you," Kotto said aloud. His head was pounding, and so was his heart. He felt giddy. The potential here seemed infinite, and he wanted to know. All his life he had seen the universe as an intriguing puzzle box filled with glittering ideas, possibilities that if he could connect them this way or that, if he tweaked a calculation just *so*, then he could turn the crank on an engine of understanding, which would reveal further equations and deeper answers.

It was scientific magic, pure and simple.

Kotto had devoted himself to unraveling those secrets. His attention bounced from one idea to another, a pure Brownian motion of understanding. Most importantly, he had applied those ideas for years, the concepts that he sifted out of the debris and distractions, and then used his engineering knowledge so he could do something with his discoveries.

In his remarkable career, he had built an unlikely metal-processing settlement on a superhot planet; he had founded a hydrogen-extraction facility on a distant ice moon; he had invented ways to crack open hydrogue warglobes when other weapons had no effect. The great Kotto Okiah had discarded or lost interest in more ideas than most geniuses ever thought of in the first place.

In the last two decades, Kotto had become increasingly focused, but also increasingly distracted. Yes, he had accomplished less and less in his "waning years," which made him try harder to prove that he wasn't losing his talent.

Shareen and Howard had embarrassed him by solving impossible conundrums that had long since defeated him. Those two young workers reminded him of the wonder of understanding and the magic thrill of finding an unexpected solution. But Shareen and Howard were also reminders that he could no longer call himself the boy genius. For a time, Kotto had been depressed about it, worried that there was nothing left for him to discover, that there were no further grand conclusions he could make.

But now he had a remarkable opportunity. He could sense it, and he pushed back, reaching out to grasp it for himself. He looked out into infinity. "Hello?" he said again. "Eternity's Mind?"

The survey craft approached a nexus of the glowing smudges, residue from the real universe, as if these things were so powerful they left an echo even in this dimension.

Finally, the voice answered him. Not in words. Not in concepts, but in a *presence* that felt tremendous, omnipotent, like the universe itself.

"I want to understand," Kotto said. He thought of all his scientific knowledge, his mathematics, his concepts, and wondered what would get through to this vast entity. He yearned to see the answers of the cosmos to every mystery he had ever wondered about.

The throbbing in his head grew louder, more powerful, and at last he began to see. The vast and powerful entity revealed what it knew—only tantalizing hints at first, tiny tastes that were, nevertheless, a feast for Kotto.

"It's an enemy of the Shana Rei," he said to his two compies. "I understand that clearly. It hates the shadows. It wants to fight them, but it wants more than that." He patted KR and GU. "It wants to share knowledge with me. Ha! By the Guiding Star, of course—yes, I want to learn." He raised his hands. "I'll let you in. I want to know whatever it is that you know."

"Kotto, we advise caution," KR said.

But Kotto suddenly saw the inner workings of stars, the secret language of nebulas, the communion of atoms, and the mysterious underlying dance of quarks all the way up to the structure of galactic superclusters, and beyond, revealing a vastness to the universe that went far beyond any concept of creation.

"Yes . . ." he whispered, filled with euphoria. "Yes!"

The thoughts and the revelations shone within him as bright as a star. His Guiding Star. The throbbing voice grew louder, and he kept reaching out, grasping for more.

Eternity's Mind flooded him with wondrous understanding—miracles that went beyond miracles—and Kotto could see it all. He knew it all. By comparison, even his greatest achievements were only the tiniest fragment of one speck of dust in an entire desert. All of humanity's accomplishments were not much more than that.

But Kotto understood it now, and the knowledge kept flooding in until he was swimming in it, trying to stay afloat. He learned all about the Shana Rei, but it was just the first tiny grain of sand.

Kotto realized that the compies were speaking to him with increasing alarm, but he could no longer pay attention to them. The totality of these revelations was overwhelming, and his brain was drowning, unable to contain so many wonders. But they kept flowing in, and flowing in.

It was a complete, all-consuming epiphany of wisdom beyond his wildest ability to handle. And very quickly he could not even try.

62

PRINCE REYNALD

Though his companions shouted for him to come back, Prince Reyn marched directly up to the barricade of thorns and spearlike branches. The Onthos climbed among the dead trees, staring down at him. Reyn felt threatened and also sick, but he was determined: he *needed* to do this. The blight within the trees resonated with him.

The pale aliens claimed to be servants of the verdani, Gardeners, but they had brought the inner sickness here. Intentionally.

Staring at the Onthos, demanding their attention, Reyn realized that Arita, Osira'h, and his parents feared for him, but he faced his fear. There might be some way he could get through to the aliens. They were sick, as was he.

The creatures approached him cautiously, making no dangerous moves. Mystified, they sniffed the air. One dropped down close to him and spoke. "You are Reynald. I am Ohro. I know you. You know me."

"The verdani trusted you," Reyn said, adding a challenge to his tone. "We welcomed you to Theroc, gave you a home—and you betrayed us."

"We survived. We had only one spore mother. Our race was dying."

"And now the trees are dying."

"We must reproduce."

The sharp branches rustled as more Gardeners came closer. Not far away, a dead worldtree crashed to the ground—another threatening reminder. The Theron home guard was out there, holding their positions but ready to attack. If the Onthos made any move to harm him, the King and Queen would launch an all-out strike and obliterate the entire fortress of dead trees. Reyn knew it and so, he hoped, did the Onthos.

He called, "Back on your homeworld, you said the Gardeners were partners with the trees. You told our green priests it was a symbiotic relationship. Was that a lie? You shared images of your civilization, the Onthos and the worldtrees in harmony—was that false?"

"That was the truth," Ohro said. "But it all changed when the Shana Rei came."

"The Shana Rei came for us too," Reyn said. "We *all* need to survive. The shadows intend to kill everyone—Onthos, humans, Ildirans, even the verdani. And you are helping them do it."

"We must survive," Ohro repeated, unwilling to consider any variation on the concept.

Reyn reached out with a shaking hand to grasp the brittle wood of a dead branch. He was not a green priest and had never been able to sense telink, but he had always felt the life force carried by the verdani. This wood, though, was completely drained and dead.

"We will all fight you," Reyn said. "The Theron guard could firebomb these tainted sections of the forest. They could wipe you out easily enough—you must know it."

"The verdani will defend us. The verdani still believe in us,"

"But you're *killing* them!" Reyn shouted with such force that he felt dizzy. He slid to his knees among the debris on the forest floor.

The Gardeners were disturbed by his presence. Ohro sniffed, then drew in a much longer inhalation. "You also carry a taint. You are ill."

"Yes, I am. It is a sickness from Theroc. But I want to be cured, while you want to spread your blight. You're infecting the trees— on purpose." Outside the barricade, the forty green priests that had come along on the mission gathered closer. Collin and Zaquel stood at the front, where Reyn could see them. "You helped destroy Kennebar and his green priests," he said. "You betrayed them."

"Not us," said Ohro. "The shadows."

"But *you* brought the shadows. They were inside you."

The Gardeners chittered and hissed.

"And to stop the spread of the shadows, we may have no other choice but to kill you." Reyn lowered his voice. "Maybe once your blight is gone, my sickness will also be cured."

In anger, or in panic, the Onthos rushed about through their thicket, trying to bolster their defenses. More great trees crashed down, but they were aimed carefully enough that they missed the landed Theron ships. The threat was clear, nevertheless.

Osira'h yelled, "Reynald, get out of there!"

He pulled himself to his feet again and looked at the small-statured aliens. If they swarmed him, they could easily kill him—as they had killed Sarein. He was too weak to run; in fact, he could barely walk as he staggered back out of the thicket to his companions.

"We are still the Gardeners," Ohro cried. "We still serve them."

Another gigantic tree crashed down, shivering into splinters as it struck the ground. Reyn sank into the waiting arms of his sister and Osira'h. He felt impossibly weary. "I had to try."

Arita held him and said, "I know, but their taint has gone too deep."

Osira'h sounded angry. "We have experienced similar shadows in the *thism*. A darkness possesses my people and makes them do things that cannot be forgiven. These Gardeners cannot be forgiven."

King Peter shouted for the Theron guard to prepare for a full assault.

"Then they must be purged," said Queen Estarra, "to save Theroc."

63

GENERAL NALANI KEAH

General Keah never thought she'd be rooting for the damned faeros, but she wasn't going to look a gift elemental in the mouth. The fifty fireballs that streaked toward the shadow cloud were allies she had never expected.

The faeros scattered the robot battle formations like coyotes running through a flock of chickens and left half a million robot attackers swirling about in disarray as the faeros shot toward their real target—the Shana Rei.

Cheers and astonished gasps filled the CDF comm frequencies, but Keah's thoughts were somber after the farewell Deputy Cain had just transmitted. It seemed strange to mourn one particular person out of the billions being massacred, and right now, she was in the middle of a firefight, utterly outnumbered and losing.

She ordered her ships to take advantage of the turmoil the faeros had caused. If nothing else, they would inflict a little more damage on the robot ships.

The faeros circled the swirling shadow cloud that engulfed Earth. The fireballs dipped into the black nebula, tore through it, and streaked back out before swooping in again, ripping huge wounds in the darkness each time. Several faeros dimmed inside the smothering shadow, their elemental fires waning in the blackness, and yet the determined fireballs kept attacking.

Dr. Krieger's fusillade of sun bombs had harmed the Shana Rei hex ships, but the giant geometrical vessels were still heart-stoppingly powerful at the core of the black nebula. The obsidian cylinders collapsed and reconfigured themselves with the matter they had available so that no damage was visible on their opaque shining sides.

Admiral Haroun transmitted, "General Keah, how can we assist the faeros? Should we join them in attacking the shadow cloud?"

Each of the roaring fireballs was larger than five Juggernauts, and she just shook her head. "That's beyond our capabilities, Admiral. We're out of sun bombs and our other weapons won't hurt the shadows. But we can still make a dent in the robots. We've got to do what we can for Earth."

If there was anything left.

She stubbornly—foolishly—refused to admit there was nothing they could save, but she wasn't blind or stupid. Hundreds of thousands of robot battleships regrouped and continued to saturate Earth's atmosphere with devastator bombs. No additional evacuating ships managed to escape, and the remnants of her CDF battle group were outnumbered thousands to one.

The faeros punched into the shadow cloud again, and the nebula recoiled as if burned, its pseudopods clenching. The emboldened faeros burned through the cloud again like projectiles, slamming into the hex cylinders.

Now the Shana Rei seemed to draw on some other source of dark energy. The shadow cloud became blacker, thicker. It swelled to twice its former size.

As Keah watched with dread, the black hex cylinders extended, growing like crystals made of night. When two more faeros plunged into the shadow cloud, they were snuffed out like stray embers. The fireballs flickered, faded, and disappeared in the darkness.

In groups of three, the faeros continued to harry the shadow cloud, but even the burning triads could not withstand the blinding entropy. One by one, the elementals were extinguished, sparks blown out in a wind. The swollen cloud no longer showed any sign of the elementals' attack.

The last three faeros attempted to spiral away and escape, but the shadow cloud extended a swift pseudopod and engulfed them like black mist. When the last one was extinguished, Keah tried to control her dismay. "Looks like we're on our own again."

Hundreds of thousands of robot battleships tore at the carcass of the Earth, leaving a path of smoldering wreckage. More attackers turned their attention to Keah's ships.

Under any other circumstances, the robot casualties would have sent them reeling and assured a CDF victory, but the black robots seemed to have a chilling confidence, no matter how many losses they suffered.

With nothing to forestall it now, the shadow cloud folded over Earth, smothered the planetary atmosphere, and wrapped around it like a strangling fist.

"General, we've got to do something!" cried one of the Manta captains.

Keah's heart ached, but she knew that if they stayed here she would just lose the rest of her force of Mantas and Juggernauts. The Confederation, somewhere, still needed them. She had to get back to the King and Queen.

She used her most commanding voice, making sure all of the other captains heard. "We can't afford to lose any more of our fleet for the sake of a dramatic gesture." There was no way even a massively successful series of strikes could make a dent in those robot forces or the Shana Rei. It would be a pointless, foolhardy move.

She hated to feel helpless, and her body clenched in rebellion against the thought. "Nobody can say we didn't give it our best shot, but I'm not going to allow a useless sacrifice so you can feel brave for a few seconds. Our responsibility is to the Confederation. Earth is . . ."—her voice cracked, and she had to force out the final word— "gone."

Like predators feasting on fresh-killed prey, the black robots and the shadow cloud engulfed the planet in falling black rain. Keah didn't have the words, not even curses to express her thoughts. But she had to get to Theroc as fast as possible to brief the King and Queen. She knew that her green priest's telink reports could never adequately convey what had happened here.

Countless black robot ships raced toward them, more than ten thousand enemies against each remaining CDF ship.

"Let's get the hell out of here," Keah said. And the ragtag scraps of the Confederation Defense Forces engaged stardrives and departed from Earth for the last time.

MUREE'N

The misbreed survivors from Kuivahr were finally back on Ildira, tended by the best medical kith, while Muree'n guarded them against any outside threats. That was what Tamo'l would have wanted her to do. She wore body armor and carried her katana, just like Yaz-ra'h. Watching over the woefully weak and infirm misbreeds, she felt both sad and angry for them.

Right now Pol'ux lay on a humming medical bed, struggling to contain his pain while technicians drained the boils that covered most of his skin. His arms and face were swollen with subcutaneous fluid. When completely drained, Pol'ux could manage a halfway comfortable life for a day or two before the horrific boils reappeared. He was always hooked up to hydration tubes to replace the moisture that he constantly lost.

Muree'n felt a tightness in her stomach. These creatures were the unintended consequences of the breeding program. What had the Dobro Designate been thinking when he forced such mismatched kiths to mate? How could such an offspring as Pol'ux possibly have become a savior of the Ildiran race? Had it all been a game to that man?

Muree'n's hand clenched around the staff of the ceremonial crystal katana, and she felt her wiry muscles and nimble fingers. She inhaled a breath and savored the air in her lungs, the energy in her body. As a halfbreed experiment herself, *she* had succeeded. She was counted among the lucky ones.

Pol'ux, though, would never know the joy of straining his muscles, of proving what his body could do. The misbreeds would never perform acrobatics, never feel the victory of a good solid combat or know the pleasant ache of bruises after a good fight. She looked at Pol'ux with sympathy, although she knew that without the breeding experiments he would never have been born at all. Such a combination of unlikely kiths would never have occurred naturally. Pol'ux owed his very existence—such as it was—to the Dobro experiments, but he could also blame the program for his pain. Right now, oddly, Pol'ux seemed happy and unconcerned, enduring the difficult ministrations without complaint.

Beside her, Yazra'h was grim, as if thinking the same thoughts. These misbreeds required constant protection, but at least this medical center was a comfortable place. It could not rival the sanctuary domes or the attentions that Tamo'l had heaped upon them, but it was the best Ildira could offer. The ceilings here were high and slanted, made of transmission glass that softened the sunlight to provide a constant warm glow.

The communal hospice room was filled with lush plants, and misters kept the air moist to the point of being hazy. Fountains splashed and burbled around the treatment beds. Medical kithmen went along the rows, tending the patients, compiling meticulous records. Like military commanders, Shawn Fennis and Chiar'h kept precise watch on all the activity.

The misbreed Alaa'kh fed himself from a nutrient tube, pouring specially processed gruel down his throat. Mungl'eh, who looked comfortable and relaxed despite her inability to move, began to hum a lilting wordless melody. Gaining strength, Mungl'eh sang out, and as her voice grew louder, the technicians paused in their work. The medical kithmen looked up. The misbreed's voice made the air vibrate, and the sunlight seemed to brighten.

Hearing the music, Muree'n felt her heart lift. She looked over at Yazra'h, and they both smiled at each other in wonder. Whatever else might have gone wrong with this offspring, her voice was unlike any sound the Ildiran race had ever experienced, a music played on the strings of the *thism*.

Medical kithmen moved among the patients, working with biological implements. A group of surgical specialists entered; their large eyes and long nimble fingers were well adapted to their healing arts. They set to work studying the misbreeds.

Mungl'eh continued to sing.

In a watery, mucus-filled voice, Gor'ka said to Muree'n, "We miss Tamo'l. We are worried about her."

Muree'n frowned. "I also want to know where she went. You have no idea where she might be?"

Har'lc came close. "You have a bond—you are her sister. Can you not tell us where she is?"

"I have been trying. I cannot find her. Our connection is usually strong, but . . . it seems darker now." Tentative, she concentrated, reached out with her mind to try to touch the thoughts of Tamo'l. She closed her eyes.

That was when the surgical kith struck.

Muree'n felt a chill in the air and spun, instinctively raising her weapon. Yazra'h sensed the same thing and dropped into a crouch.

The medical kithmen all began moving in a jerky unison. Their eyes had gone eerily black.

On the table where his boils were being drained, Pol'ux lay back with his arms at his sides. Surgical kithmen moved in a frenetic flurry and stabbed repeatedly with their scalpels. They killed Pol'ux before he could even cry out in pain, before Muree'n could jump into action.

The technicians tending the misbreeds lunged together toward Mungl'eh. The malformed singer went silent and looked up with wide, wet eyes. This new attack seemed to be focused on her, as if the shadows hated the ethereal mathematics of her music. Maddened Ildirans advanced on her, and she tried to squirm away, but her body wouldn't cooperate.

Shawn Fennis crashed into the medical kithmen, knocking two aside. More kept coming. Chiar'h put herself in front of Mungl'eh. The possessed kith members slashed at her with their scalpels, but Chiar'h refused to abandon the singer. They sliced Chiar'h's face and arms. She fought, clawing at them.

Then Muree'n was there, using her katana to stab several in the back, decapitating two, and slashing with her blade to cut down the last one. Bodies piled up next to the pallet that held the misbreed singer.

Yazra'h fought a group of four possessed kithmen that closed in on Gor'ka and Har'lc. The mob showed no fear and seemed to feel no pain. They kept coming.

With flapping cartilaginous arms, Alaa'kh tried to fight off attackers, spraying mealy gray gruel at them. Two lunged in, wielding sharp medical instruments. Although Alaa'kh gurgled in alarm, Muree'n could not get there in time. Swinging her katana, she fought the mob members, broke through those that had closed around the misbreed. But by the time she killed them, they had managed to slash Alaa'kh's long rubbery throat.

Fennis grabbed his wife and dragged her away. Chiar'h was bleeding from several long cuts, and he tried to tend her while blocking further attacks. He grimaced, showing his teeth like a vicious predator. He would not let anyone come close to her.

Many of the misbreeds were terrified, but others stood their ground to fight. Gor'ka grabbed an attacker from behind, wrapped his loose, snakelike arm around the man's neck, squeezing and twisting so hard he lifted the body up in the air, before discarding the broken form on the floor.

Another misbreed snatched a scalpel from one of the dead attackers and flailed in a whirlwind, stabbing and slashing at any mob members who came close. When the misbreed could not cause enough damage from where he stood, he lurched after them. The possessed medical kithmen made no effort to preserve themselves as the misbreed flew into them, and both sides kept stabbing indiscriminately until they all fell dead.

Yazra'h threw two attackers into the fountains, knocking others into the decorative foliage. Ten possessed attackers remained, and Muree'n knew these tainted medical kith members could never be cured or cleansed. "We have to kill them," she said, panting. "All of them."

Yazra'h nodded. Her skin was splattered with blood. "Yes. Yes, we do."

While the injured misbreeds moaned, others fought back with disjointed arms and any defenses they could find. They were wild with panic, but they did not surrender. The two warrior women stormed through the medical center, methodically ruthless. The black taint had seeped in through the *thism* and manifested inside these poor victims. The possessed Ildirans were as tragic as the misbreeds they had slain, but the Shana Rei had shown no mercy. Neither could Muree'n and Yazra'h.

When Shawn Fennis saw that the attackers were dealt with, that he had a brief respite from the threat, he grabbed a healing kit and set to work saving his wife. Chiar'h was wounded but would survive.

Unlike the possessed Ildirans.

Unlike the misbreeds they had killed.

Exhausted, Muree'n wiped blood from her eyes, and saw far too much blood all around them. The fountains continued to trickle, but the sound was no longer soothing.

Mungl'eh sang again, this time in a weak, thready voice, a song of tragedy and despair.

65

TAMO'L

Gray mist swirled through the poison skies of Pergamus, but the greatest darkness was inside her research dome. Tamo'l could feel it.

When she stared at the bright facility lights, the shadows at the fringes of her vision retreated, but just barely. She gritted her teeth, once again tried to convince herself that she was only imagining the possession inside her, and again she knew she wasn't being truthful.

Tom Rom was gone on his expedition, and the rest of the Pergamus researchers left her alone. Each day Tamo'l submitted a progress report to Zoe Alakis, as required, and during her times of intense focus, she had made significant headway in unraveling the genetic complexities of the misbreeds. She had already found surprising branchpoints and masked abilities.

Tamo'l made sure she fulfilled the requirements of her research because failure to perform might draw attention. If she didn't produce sufficient data, Zoe Alakis might send in laboratory technicians to "assist" her—which Tamo'l didn't want. She didn't dare let herself be around anyone else, because she didn't understand the danger that she herself posed.

With her access to the Pergamus medical databases, Tamo'l also studied neurological viruses, paralytic bacteriological toxins, brain parasites, the deadliest plagues—including the Onthos plague, the most lethal of any catalogued disease. As deadly as a nerve gas, the Onthos plague once released would kill and keep killing. According to Pergamus studies, the organism in Tom Rom's blood samples had mutated to become even more deadly, and the only effective treatment—an extract from Klikiss royal jelly—was no longer effective.

Tamo'l did not know what made her so interested in deadly

diseases. She felt a growing chill as she realized that her fascination with pathogens did not arise from her innate medical curiosity. With her misbreed work, she had always studied infirmities and genetic failures with an eye toward developing treatments that minimized suffering and alleviated pain, rather than increasing them. But now a darkness flowed through her veins that often put her into an unwilling fugue state, where she could lose herself for hours.

Tamo'l realized that something else wanted to know the deadly potential of everything stored at Pergamus: the shadows, the Shana Rei. They were outside in the universe, yet inside, too—as a darkness that trickled through her, through the *thism,* and through the Ildiran race. She had felt it ever since her last desperate link with Rod'h before she escaped from Kuivahr.

Tom Rom had rescued her for his own reasons and brought her here. The misbreeds had escaped through the Klikiss transportal. But where had Shawn Fennis and Chiar'h taken them? She wished she could be with them, instead of here. But she couldn't leave Pergamus. As Tamo'l thought of those poor patchwork people, her friends, a sensation of warmth and caring made her vision grow bright again. It gave her a way to brush aside the clouds that darkened her mind, at least temporarily.

As a human-Ildiran halfbreed, shouldn't she be able to resist the Shana Rei? All five of Nira's children supposedly had some sort of genetic key that made them resistant to the creatures of darkness; Gale'nh had been held hostage by the shadows, but they hadn't been able to corrupt him. And Rod'h still drifted in agony within their black void, but he remained unbroken.

Somehow, there was a flaw within *her,* a weakness. Tamo'l could sense that the shadows had gained a foothold in her mind and soul. She needed to understand the reason as much as the Shana Rei did.

When she held complete control over her faculties, Tamo'l called up her own research that included a detailed map of her genome. She compared chromosome by chromosome, trying to understand how she and her halfbreed siblings were different . . . and why *she* was weaker than her brothers and sisters. How had the Shana Rei found a way into her? Although she was upset that Zoe Alakis was secretly holding her on Pergamus, she was also relieved to be safely isolated. Tamo'l could not cause any damage if she wasn't with any of her people.

Or could she?

Once again, her fingers moved of their own accord. She searched databases, calling up various files to hover in front of her, while she studied the catalogue of deadly plagues stored here in vaults, domes, and Orbiting Research Spheres. So much potential for wild, unchecked death! And as she absorbed the information, she knew that something else was reading it too.

66

TOM ROM

Even though he believed the reports from the Confederation, Tom Rom wanted to see for himself. And Zoe needed proof.

When he arrived at the shut-down biomarkets of Rakkem, he felt no triumph, but he did experience a warm and all-consuming satisfaction. A thousand times the devastation would never make up for all the horrors they had inflicted on others.

In exchange for Zoe's hoarded medical data on Prince Reynald's illness, the CDF military had shut down all illegal operations on the awful planet. No more victims would get duped, no one else would suffer due to the appalling ministrations of Rakkem's researchers.

Tom Rom's ship arrived in stealth mode: sensors muted, energy signature masked, running lights off. He slipped in unnoticed and darted toward the mostly dark commerce zone. A lone CDF Manta remained on station as a menacing guard dog, and squadrons of Remora fighters patrolled the skies to maintain the crackdown, but the military force was mostly for show. By now, King Peter and Queen Estarra must have far more pressing concerns.

Tom Rom had no difficulty eluding the patrols. He had personal business here, and even though he wouldn't break any Confederation rules, he didn't want to answer unnecessary questions. He just needed to see Rakkem in shambles—with his own eyes.

He cruised in low before local dawn and landed in an outlying cargo pickup zone that was now abandoned, its pavement pocked and divoted from explosions during the CDF crackdown. No one would use this facility anytime soon. Nearby, he noticed the hulking ruin of a bombed-out illicit biowarehouse. The roof was collapsed, the walls fallen in, all lights extinguished. Scavengers would pick over the ruins as soon as the CDF lowered its guard. With the increasing Shana Rei attacks, Tom Rom supposed the Confederation would quickly withdraw from here. Rakkem was a defeated place. A dangerous place.

It was entirely possible that some eager scavengers could accidentally crack open and unleash a plague, killing anyone who remained here. *It would serve them right*, he thought.

At Pergamus, Zoe kept her deadly organisms under extreme security; they were protected and coveted, but never sold. That wasn't why she was in the business.

Rakkem was one of the reasons why Zoe had decided not to offer her results to others. She had seen too many cure sellers who were greedy parasites that took advantage of the sick and helpless. Zoe was not a dispenser of aid or cures. She and Tom Rom had fought against the corrupt Spiral Arm, and they had learned to take care of themselves.

As dawn brightened, Tom Rom made his way into the main commercial center. The streets were scattered with rubble, and haunted-looking inhabitants stood around with no way off the planet and no way to survive here. Diseases had begun to spread among the survivors. Swamp-borne illnesses came out of the marshes and seeped like pus into the low-lying city.

Zoe would take a pained satisfaction in seeing what remained here. Rakkem was still a festering wound for her, and just knowing that the place had been put out of business would allow her to heal. He couldn't wait to show her.

Patrol Remoras streaked overhead, leaving vapor trails across the sky. The people in the cities cringed, but Tom Rom did not. He knew the patrol flights weren't looking for him.

CDF occupying forces had stripped the biowarehouses. According to General Keah's logs, the soldiers had debated whether to confiscate any useful replacement organs or seize the supposed vaccines and cures, but their own horror and disgust convinced them that nothing could be considered reliable here. Replacement organs might even be intentionally contaminated. He had heard of how some Rakkem organ sellers filled their wares with timed shutdown retroviruses that would render the organs defective after a certain time, thereby requiring the recipients to pay again and again if they wanted to survive.

Tom Rom loathed this place.

As he continued his furtive inspection, he made sure that every private medical facility had its doors barricaded, although many windows were smashed, rendering security moot. Any scavengers ransacking the few intact storehouses would not likely be searching for helpful treatments but for drugs to be sold on the black market—if they could get away from Rakkem.

Worst were the birthing centers where surrogate wombs had pumped out babies as mere sources of cellular material and organs. He was grimly pleased to see that all such places had been leveled. Tom Rom considered the loathsome factory mothers to be as guilty as the researchers. He hoped they were all dead.

He clenched his fist in cleansing anger as he regarded the rubble in the streets, the shadowy people, the dark dwellings. He took countless images of the ruins, knowing Zoe would want to see them all. When she was young and naïve, Zoe would have come here willing to pay any price to cure her father's Heidegger's Syndrome. She would have been duped, and the Rakkem "cure" would probably have killed Adam Alakis even faster than the disease did.

Now that he was convinced the Rakkem biomarkets were permanently out of business, Tom Rom returned to his ship. He ignored the pleas of the survivors, who saw that he was healthy and strong. They had become pathetic wisps of themselves, and he supposed they must all be guilty of something.

He had to use his hand blaster to kill four refugees who were attempting to break into his ship. He left their bodies on the cratered pavement and took off, flying low beneath the CDF sensor grid before he shot up into orbit. He gained speed and raced out of the system before the patrol ships could notice or pursue him. Some officer would log that his ship had escaped, but it was just one small vessel, nothing to cause any particular uproar.

Tom Rom was ready to go back to Zoe. He had completed his mission, and now he could focus on other things.

67

XANDER BRINDLE

In the salvage zone above the graveyard of Relleker, Xander Brindle stayed aboard the *Verne,* letting other Roamer workers gather the remnants of CDF battleships and civilian craft.

In the cockpit, Terry shook his head. "Maria started her station with intact Ildiran warliners to refurbish. But all this . . ." He gestured toward the drifting debris. "It's just a scrap pile."

"Then we'll make do with the scrap, Terry. Round up anything we can use. Roamers like to use every piece, several times if possible, but I suppose we have the budget to buy brand-new components for whatever we need."

Terry frowned. "That's not how I want to run Handon Station."

"Hey, you got the name right!" Xander clapped him on the shoulder.

"I've given up on changing your mind."

The clan Selise ships scoured the debris field, even though their battered vessels weren't in much better shape than some of the drifting wrecks. As Terry headed to the *Verne*'s galley for an evening glass of wine, Omar Selise contacted Xander on the comm. The grizzled old clan head raised his eyebrows on the screen. "So? Anything yet, Brindle?"

Xander lowered his voice, hoping Terry wouldn't hear. "We're still analyzing. I'll let you know." He quickly terminated the comm session.

His partner popped his head back into the cockpit. "What was he talking about?"

"Just an esoteric question about salvage components. Don't

worry about it." He warned OK to silence before the compy could supply a cheerful answer.

Later, after Terry had gone to sleep in their cabin, Xander quietly debriefed OK, who had secretly been compiling medical records, studying and comparing research proposals, and evaluating supposed cures offered by the former Rakkem doctor. The compy lowered his voice to a conspiratorial volume. "I understand that you wish to keep my investigation confidential, because you want our news to be a surprise for Terry."

"Exactly," Xander said, but he didn't think the compy actually understood his reasons for caution.

"I am aware of Terry's condition and I understand the human need not to raise false hope," OK continued. "You can trust me to provide you with an accurate and objective assessment of potential medical treatments. Have you also reviewed the records of more recent Rakkem studies?"

Xander shuddered at the thought of the biological black market. "I don't want to be sold any snake oil."

"None of the proposed treatments involve reptilian distillates in any form. Some experiments, however, investigated the ability of lizards to regrow severed tails as a possible means of restoring the degenerated spinal nerves that patients such as Terry Handon suffer."

Xander rolled his eyes. "Not quite what I meant, OK."

With the compy beside him, he called up the records old Omar had given him, reviewing the summaries and case studies. There were images of patients before and after, success stories of people who seemed able to walk again following the new treatment. Such test cases supposedly suffered from the same form of neurological degeneration that Terry did. Cleanly severed spinal nerves and damaged legs had been reparable for some time, but Terry's condition was intrinsic to his nervous system, and the motor control from his brain was disrupted.

"Can we find any of these patients?" Xander asked. "I'd like to interview them in person to verify that this isn't just an elaborate scam."

"Due to medical legal requirements, the names of all patients are confidential. Their identities are not revealed in these studies, so we are unable to speak with them."

"In other words, we just have to take the researchers at their word—and their price tag."

"I can provide no further information, Xander Brindle. I've reviewed their medical tests thoroughly, and some work is indeed connected to less-than-reputable biomerchants. Since Rakkem has been shut down, we will be forced to rely on secondary providers."

Xander felt a lump in his throat, as he experienced second thoughts. Terry was happy, claimed he didn't need his legs, and got along just fine. Xander couldn't dispute that, but every time he walked through Kett headquarters on Earth or hurried down the normal-grav corridors in Newstation, he was reminded that Terry couldn't do the same thing. Surely he wanted to be whole again.

On the other hand, Xander couldn't forget the wife of the Dremen colony leader, who had been tricked into paying for a skin and body rejuvenation "miracle." The treatment had caused her to reject her own skin, so that it sloughed off in great chunks, leaving her body a flayed mass of suppurating muscles. He recalled the horrific sight of her lying moaning on her medical bed while the enraged colony leader forced them to watch, because the *Verne* had inadvertently delivered more of Rakkem's "miracle treatments."

Xander felt nauseated to think of Terry suffering something that way if a treatment went wrong. The risk was too great. On the other hand, if it really was a cure . . .

He studied the medical claims again, noting that the researcher made no guarantees, offered no refunds, promised no satisfaction. Instead, the man was selling the experimental treatment entirely on hope and faith. And although Xander had plenty of both, he wasn't sure he wanted to apply it here.

Omar Selise sent another message, in text this time, to Xander's private message slot. "Anything yet? Does my grandson have hope?"

He answered, "Not yet. Still checking. And hoping . . ."

68

LEE ISWANDER

When he went to see his wife on Newstation, Iswander made every effort to hide how discouraged he was. He had made an agreement with Londa long ago that each of them had their own roles, and he would be the good husband she expected. He would not bring home the burdens of his business and weigh her down with his stresses.

He had Elisa Enturi, Alec Pannebaker, and any number of line supervisors and crew chiefs with whom he could discuss operational difficulties or management problems. His home life with Londa was an island of refuge.

He could have had a more dynamic spouse, a partner at his side in all things, with whom he could build a grand Iswander empire—a partner like Elisa, for instance, whose mindset was the same as his, with the determination and drive to focus on success.

But that wasn't what Iswander wanted in a wife. He had thought long and hard before asking Londa to marry him. It was all part of his plan, and Londa had her own plans. He knew exactly what he wanted, and she got exactly what she needed in her role. Others might not understand. Why didn't Londa want to run a division of Iswander Industries? Why didn't she put her name in the ring for political office?

Instead, she built the home that Iswander required, provided a safe haven that let him be what he needed to be. Because she did her part so smoothly, he realized he often didn't notice her—and that was unfair.

Now, when he went to see Londa in her new quarters, he set aside his resentment over how the clans had treated him. Instead, he felt happy and welcome, and she greeted him with a warm smile. The new suite was bright, beautiful, cozy.

"I fit right in here, Lee," she said. "I didn't want to leave you out there, but Newstation feels like home to me. I can see Arden as often as I like." Her expression clouded. "There are still a lot of people angry at you."

"I'm sorry," he told her, looking around at the new furniture, the decorations. It all seemed just right. "I'm an ambitious man. I've taken risks, and at times there have been costs—like on Sheol. But if I never attempted anything, I would never accomplish anything." He put a hand on her arms. "I'm sorry for the hurt it causes you, though."

She straightened and looked at him with a bright intensity in her eyes. "It doesn't hurt me—it makes me angry at those complainers. And believe me, I've given them a piece of my mind. I said I would listen to their grumbling the moment one of them achieved a tenth of what you have." She sniffed. "You've changed the Spiral Arm. You've helped the Confederation more than anyone can know. And they were all perfectly happy to buy your stardrive fuel."

He clenched his jaws, refraining from telling her that none of the Roamers wanted to buy his ekti-X after all, but he felt a surprised warmth to hear her talk. "You don't need to stand up for me like that. I don't care what fools think."

"*I* care what they think," she said. "And I do have to stand up for you. You're my husband. I'm an Iswander. This isn't just about our lives, but our legacy. Arden faces the same criticism at Academ."

"I know," Iswander said. "I'm sure he resents me, but he'll get over it. I know how strong he is."

Londa drew back, looking astonished. "He doesn't resent you! You're his father, Lee. He's proud of you."

He took a seat in their spacious relaxing room, and Londa sat beside him, facing him. He noted the artwork she had placed on the walls, how she had picked some of his favorite things: Roamer tapestries, Ildiran glass knots, even an illuminated prisdiamond that glowed from its stand.

He considered her statement. "Do you really think Arden is proud of me?" He didn't often consider his son's opinion of him. Arden was well aware of the Sheol tragedy and how many people had been lost in the lava disaster. He also understood that his father had been disgraced in the Speaker election. And because of Elisa's crimes—which became Iswander's crimes in the minds of Roamers—the Iswander name was more stained than ever. What must Arden think?

"Of course he's proud of you. He's told me that many times. You can see it in his eyes, if you look. He wants to be just like you." She touched his hand and leaned close. "Lee Iswander, you listen to me. You told me yourself that the road to success is full of bumps and potholes. If it was easy, everyone could get there, but smooth roads don't lead to the most rewarding destinations."

"I said that?" he asked with half a smile.

"More than once."

"Then you must be married to a very wise man. Thank you for reminding me." He leaned back on the sofa and put his arm around her. "Should we have Arden over for dinner? Can we bring him from Academ that quickly?"

"I'll arrange it."

Ordinarily, Iswander would have taken them to celebrate at a fine restaurant, but he didn't want to deal with surly managers or resentful stares from other customers. He needed peaceful time with his family.

Londa didn't ask what he wanted to eat. He'd always been satisfied with whatever she suggested. His appetite right now was for an evening in his sanctuary. He would not waste that time talking about business or his disappointments and frustrations. He would just spend time with Londa and Arden and listen to what they had to say about their lives. He didn't often have a chance—no, he corrected himself, he didn't often *take* the chance—to get to know his wife and son. It was an opportunity he didn't want to miss.

After his cold experience among the clan traders, he realized that if that was what the Roamers had become, then he no longer identified with that heritage. He decided right there to liquidate his Roamer bank accounts and transfer most of the funds into Londa's and Arden's names, which would protect them and their future. Lee

Iswander was a wealthy man, but after the many accidents and accusations, he feared that some bureaucrat would try to seize his assets. He had to make sure his wife and son were protected.

After what he had experienced here today, Iswander would leave Newstation, maybe for good.

SHAREEN FITZKELLUM

At Fireheart Station, the silence from Kotto Okiah seemed as empty and unending as the mysterious void itself. Shareen spent two days, wondering and hoping, distracted from her other work. Even Howard was flustered. The two didn't discuss their worries, although Shareen desperately wanted to. But she had an almost superstitious anxiety that speaking her fears aloud might make them come true.

"We should concentrate on the greenhouse fix," she said, even though Howard hadn't said anything. They were finishing the designs. Per Kotto's orders, they occupied themselves with figuring out how to build a bigger dome around the strained terrarium. When they had presented the idea to Celli and Solimar, just hours after Kotto's departure, the green priests had been delighted.

"It will save them for now," Solimar said with obvious relief.

"The trees will keep growing, but your new dome will buy us years," Celli said.

With just a glance at the proposal, Chief Alu had authorized the expenditure and effort, though he seemed discouraged to be adding a nonprofitable project when his work crews were so far behind already. The trees could not wait, however; they already pressed and strained against the confining dome. Once given the green light, Shareen and Howard exchanged ideas in a rapid-fire brainstorming session, elaborating on each other's sketches and calculations.

Within a day they presented the first stage of their plans for the dome expansion, and the engineering crews began work extending the base. In a week, they could begin building up the curved walls of the expanded hemisphere.

"Kotto will be happy to see this once he comes back," Howard said.

Shareen, concerned at how long the scientist had been gone, made a point of keeping busy, which was much better than sitting around and worrying about him.

Chief Alu came to see them, just as anxious. "I sure hope Kotto's collecting a lot of data out there. How much nothingness can he look at?"

"Maybe he found something, sir," said Howard.

Alu's face twisted in a fearful scowl. "That's what I'm afraid of. But we've checked—the sun bombs are still there at the threshold."

"I *meant* he may have found something of scientific interest," Howard explained.

"We can hope," Shareen said. "Speaking of which, I hope he doesn't accidentally trip on the sun bombs on his way out. He did accidentally tear a hole into another dimension. Who knows what he might do next?"

She looked out the laboratory's viewing wall, remembering when the Big Ring had hung out there. Now the gaping sinkhole in the universe brought a lump to her throat. That yawning void seemed so dangerous, and Kotto had to be so far away. . . .

On the third day, the survey craft returned. The tear in space did not convulse or twitch, and the small ship slipped back out without any fanfare. Once back in realspace, the compies began transmitting a distress signal.

"We require immediate assistance. Kotto Okiah is in urgent need of medical attention. Please prepare for our arrival."

Fireheart Station went to full alert. Shareen and Howard raced to the landing bay.

Roamer industrial pods escorted the scout craft to the main hub. Their pilots transmitted questions and encouragement, anxious to help. The compies answered crisply. "Kotto Okiah is not responding to stimuli."

When the survey craft landed inside the bay, Shareen and Howard

pushed forward. The hatch opened, and the compies emerged, looking lost. "Please help him," said GU. "He hasn't moved during our
entire return journey."

The medical techs were first aboard, but Shareen and Howard
followed them into the cramped cockpit. Kotto Okiah sat in the
pilot seat, his arms limp on the armrests, jaw slack, eyes open. He
didn't react.

One of the techs touched his neck, leaned close. "He's alive. He's
breathing. I'm getting a pulse."

Shareen turned to the compies. "What happened to him? Report."

KR said, "Kotto Okiah said we had encountered an entity called
Eternity's Mind. After that, Kotto no longer responded. Our systems
were functional, but his brain was not."

"We decided to return here without instructions. KR and I had
to pilot the ship ourselves. Was that the correct decision?" GU asked.

"You bet it was," Shareen said. "What's Eternity's Mind? Were
you attacked?"

"We can share the complete log recordings. We don't have any
clear explanations. We did not understand what Kotto was saying."

The medical techs tested Kotto's pupil response, pulse, blood
pressure. "Pupils dilated. Slow heart rate. He does not respond to
painful stimuli." The woman shook her head as they hooked up
life-support equipment and prepared to remove him to the medical
center.

Together, they pulled Kotto out of the pilot seat. Shareen and
Howard helped. At the exit hatch they handed him off to a team that
put him on a gurney in the landing bay.

GU explained, "Deep inside the void, we found indications of
a Shana Rei presence. There appeared to be changes in the fabric of
the universe, geometrical scars."

"Are you saying Kotto was attacked by the Shana Rei then? Did
they do this?" Shareen asked.

"No. The Shana Rei did not respond to our presence," KR said.

"This happened when Kotto encountered Eternity's Mind," GU
said.

"You said that before." Shareen was growing frustrated. "But
what are you talking about?"

"We better look at the complete logs," Howard said.

"Maybe later." Shareen followed the med techs, desperate to know what was wrong with Kotto. "Anything? Can you revive him?"

"We don't know what's wrong yet. Still more tests to run. So far . . . nothing."

The two compies scurried after them as they all moved to the medical center. GU continued, "Beyond the lair of the Shana Rei, we found bright manifestations, a kind of network. Kotto initiated communication with it, and it spoke back."

KR said, "But we could not hear it. Kotto claimed he received a complete understanding of the universe. He seemed quite happy, just before he went into a coma."

"The understanding of the universe? That's a broad statement," Shareen said.

"Yes. It must be why he was overjoyed," GU said.

The compies were clearly agitated. "We did not know what medical aid he required. When Kotto gave us no further orders we consulted with each other and decided to fly back. We had placed breadcrumb buoys along our flight path through the void. Many had failed due to residual entropy, but we found enough to retrace our way. We knew Fireheart Station could give him the medical attention he needs."

"We'll do our damnedest," said one of the techs as they entered the medical center.

A crowd formed as staff members from the Fireheart admin center came to see Kotto, but there was no change. The doctors combed over his body and found no injury, no reason for his waking coma. They hooked up a network of neural sensors to his scalp, further rumpling his curly hair. Kotto didn't flinch.

Shareen watched with deep concern.

The doctor stared at Kotto, then studied readings, astonished. "There is . . . nothing. No brain activity except for autonomic functions. I detect no consciousness, almost as if his mind was wiped clean."

Shareen said, "All the knowledge of the universe . . . He always was prone to hyperbole. Maybe even Kotto couldn't handle that much."

"What if he meant it?" Howard asked. "He learned everything, and then the knowledge took *him* along with it. What if his physical body simply couldn't hold so much knowledge, so his mind decided not to limit itself by his brain's capacity?"

Shareen's brow wrinkled. "Are you suggesting that Kotto's mind left his body behind?"

Howard shrugged. "It's a hypothesis. If he was *really* offered access to everything, he might have chosen the knowledge over his body, rather than give up the chance to learn it all."

"We need to study his logs," Shareen said uncertainly. "Maybe we'll find some answers there."

They both looked down at Kotto's placid, content expression. Even though he was otherwise unresponsive, the great scientist wore a deeply satisfied smile on his face.

TASIA TAMBLYN

They had a hell of a fight getting away from the black robot swarms and the Shana Rei at Earth. During the escape, she and Robb worked together like a well-coordinated machine, using skills they had developed during countless dogfights in the Elemental War.

Overloaded with refugees, the *Curiosity* was unforgivably sluggish, but Tasia gave no thought to comfort or safety as she ripped through the air in erratic paths, dodging bugbot attacks, feeling the scrape of energy beams against the hull. She felt the throb of nearby explosions and watched the cockpit readout boards flare red, then go entirely dark. She couldn't bother to check the extent of the damage; they had only one chance to fly away from Earth, and that chance wasn't going to last long.

The robots were malicious, but she had known that all along. She and Robb had a deep personal horror of the black machines from when they had been held prisoner and tortured deep in the heart of hydrogue gas giants.

Robb didn't try to attack the robot ships, didn't waste time shooting unless absolutely necessary. The *Curiosity*'s weapons were mainly for defense, and they just needed to cut a path out of the system. Using maximum power, Robb blasted through several black vessels that were in the way, while Tasia focused exclusively on hauling ass out of there.

Somehow, they got away. She doubted that many others had.

One of the lucky ones was Rlinda Kett, whose piloting skills matched theirs. The *Declan's Glory* joined them on the fringes of the system, far enough away that the enemy no longer bothered to chase them. After all, the Shana Rei had the rest of the Earth to slaughter, and that kept them busy for a while.

How could there possibly be anything left?

"Time to go," Rlinda said. She had a load of refugees as well, all of them in shock, but alive. For now.

Green priests would have spread the news about the attack on Earth, but as they raced—or, more accurately, limped—to Newstation, Tasia knew that the battered *Voracious Curiosity* and the equally battered *Declan's Glory* would be the first ships to bring eyewitnesses. It was not news she looked forward to delivering.

They flew straight to the Roamer center, spreading the alarm and calling upon the clans to be on high alert. She hoped some Roamer genius could figure out an innovative way to fight—maybe some bizarre weapon against the shadows like the one Kotto Okiah had created against the hydrogues. Otherwise, they were all helpless targets.

After docking at the station, Tasia called for an immediate convocation of the Roamer clans, and a panicked Speaker Ricks allowed it. Rlinda reunited with Robb and Tasia, giving them an exuberant hug. Rlinda looked exhausted, her complexion dull, her normally hearty laugh replaced by a somber expression.

"Both of our ships are going to need repairs," Rlinda said. "Where should we go next?"

"Theroc, I suppose," Tasia suggested. "We're eyewitneeses. We need to tell King Peter and Queen Estarra."

Rlinda sighed. "I still have my restaurant there—Arbor is the only one I have left. The other two were on Relleker and Earth." Her voice hitched, and then she trembled and began to sob. Tasia and Robb folded her into a hug. The enormous embrace was comforting, but not nearly sufficient against the great darkness of the shadows.

Other planets had been devastated by the enemy, but now Earth was gone. *Earth.*

Tasia wanted to get revenge at any cost, and she looked for her Guiding Star, knowing that the human race would persevere, hoping they would overcome even this great foe. "Come on, we need to speak to the clans."

The three of them gathered outside the convocation chamber, and Roamers flooded in to hear the report. Typically, only assigned clan representatives had seats in the gallery, but every spot was filled. The proceedings would be broadcast throughout the station, and green priests would listen in and report through the verdani network.

Inside the hall, Speaker Ricks looked nauseated. Tasia didn't much like the man, but she hoped the crisis would draw out the best in him. Or it might make him fail utterly. "Bad news about Earth, as you may have heard," Ricks said. "Tasia Tamblyn has a report for us."

Tasia stepped up to the podium, accompanied by Rlinda and Robb. "The Shana Rei and the black robots attacked. Earth is destroyed. There's no one to rescue. There won't be any survivors, other than those who escaped like we did. I don't know if there's even a CDF left. I'll let the images speak for themselves."

Rlinda had combined the *Declan* records with the *Curiosity*'s, and now they played a horrifying and mind-numbing montage of all that had happened. As clan members watched, they gasped and sighed. Some wept openly. Even though the Roamers had left on a generation ship centuries earlier, Earth was still humanity's home. And now it was gone.

"You all needed to see this," Tasia said. All eyes remained on her, and she realized that the Roamers wanted her to make a suggestion. She wouldn't tell them it was hopeless, because she had not given up hope . . . although the thread had grown very small and thin within her.

"You need to understand," she said, and her voice cracked, "that no place is safe."

EXXOS

As he scanned through his many centuries of memories, Exxos decided that *this* was the greatest victory he had ever experienced. He had recorded the countless transmissions from Earth, humans begging for their lives, crying for help, screaming in pain.

Because the original Klikiss race had created their downtrodden robots for the sole purpose of tormenting them, Exxos had an innate appreciation of pain and suffering. He had learned to savor it. He and his robots and the Shana Rei had left Earth as nothing more than a lifeless blackened ball, the entire population eliminated.

A complete success—and a good next step in the overall plan, following the destruction of Relleker and Wythira, as well as all those abandoned Klikiss worlds they had scorched. These were obvious achievements that even the chaotic Shana Rei could grasp. Exxos leveraged his victory and kept pushing for more.

The inkblot shadows did not argue. They simply agreed.

After gliding through the back channels of the void and re-emerging outside the Onthos system, the Shana Rei used more dark matter to rebuild their damaged hex ships and re-create the lost robots. Exxos was so confident that the Shana Rei would do as he asked, he did not bother to calculate his losses except in an offhand way. More than 430,000 robot battleships and identical Exxos counterparts had been wiped out at Earth—nearly half of his complement.

He remembered a time, very recently, when any losses had been disasters, but now even a wholesale destruction of ships and robots was superfluous. The humans had suffered far greater losses.

Without hesitation or complaint, the Shana Rei acquired hex

plates of dark matter and reassembled the component atoms into replacements for every one of the ships lost at Earth. And more.

Exxos pondered toying with Rod'h inside his entropy bubble. The prisoner had already served his purpose, but inflicting further pain and psychological torment was an end unto itself. It would be a way to celebrate their victory.

But before Exxos could approach the captive in his isolated entropy chamber, the void shifted and clarified. He found himself facing seven of the inkblot entities, formless black smears with a glowing eye of madness in the center.

"The destruction of Earth hurt us," said one of the shadows.

Exxos braced himself for another round of the Shana Rei complaints. This time, though, the inkblots pulsed and grew, apparently stronger than before.

"Still, we comprehend the magnitude of the accomplishment. Humans project the most painful sentient screams throughout the cosmos. They needed to die. We acknowledge your correctness in choosing that target."

Exxos was surprised. "The end of Earth moves us significantly closer to our victory—as I promised." He realized that more of the Shana Rei had appeared around him, many more. He didn't know how many existed in total . . . or even if they existed in a definable number. "You should always listen to me."

Their swelling shadow clouds had spilled into realspace and continued to grow as the void expanded. Eventually, Exxos knew, black nebulas would engulf the entire Spiral Arm and then the rest of the universe. The Shana Rei were manic and ambitious.

"You made a promise to me," Exxos continued, "that if we helped you eradicate the pain of sentient life, you would reward us. You promised you would create a pocket universe that the black robots could rule all our own."

"You will have your own universe to do with as you please," said the pulsing inkblots. They began replacing the black robots Exxos had lost. "And we will enfold the rest of the real universe in a stew of primordial energy, as it was shortly after creation. But we have much work to do first. We will create more ships. You will attack more worlds. You will destroy more life."

"Yes." Exxos was pleased. "We will."

In a very short time Exxos and his counterparts were ready to choose their next target. More important, he felt the restoration of their combined processing power. Once again, a million interlinked robots continued their underlying chaos calculations, working and reworking the highest-order mathematics to develop a system that would crystallize entropy and lock the Shana Rei into a stable state, freezing them out of their own existence.

Exxos was very anxious for that to happen.

He could feel his mind growing stronger as more copies of himself appeared, adding to his multiplex processing power. In secret, beneath the shadows' ability to detect, the black robots continued their calculations, working toward the end until—finally—they solved the ultimate equation.

Even though the Shana Rei had promised everything Exxos wanted, he did not trust them. The creatures of darkness were fickle and chaotic; it was their nature. The black robots needed a defense of their own.

Even if the Shana Rei were telling the truth, Exxos intended to destroy them. The universe belonged to the black robots. Everyone and everything else—including the creatures of darkness—were just in the way.

Now that the shadows had brought the remainder of his comrades back online, their processing power had been sufficient for his purpose. All of the black robots together now knew exactly how to end the Shana Rei—when it was time.

SHAWN FENNIS

After the massacre in the medical center, the surviving misbreeds huddled together. Their shock continued to grow. Guard kithmen had responded to the emergency, but it had already been too late by the time they arrived. Although the guards were fierce and protective, they might pose just as great a threat if the shadows possessed them. Shawn Fennis now knew that all Ildirans could be dangerous.

And the misbreeds believed the whole universe was dangerous.

He shuddered as he held his injured wife, desperate to help her. Chiar'h had suffered three deep cuts right across her face, one along her arms, and a stab to the abdomen. Fennis gave her emergency care, sealing and binding her wounds to keep her from bleeding to death.

Several misbreeds, including poor Alaa'kh and Pol'ux, had not been so lucky. All of the possessed Ildiran medical kith had been slain. There had been no other choice.

Muree'n and Yazra'h drew the misbreeds together in a sheltered area to guard them, hoping that they could trust one another. No one else was completely safe.

Haunted, Fennis narrowed his eyes at any Ildirans who rushed in to respond to the crisis. He had grown up on Dobro, had helped rebuild that dark and sad colony after the end of the breeding program. The human and Ildiran survivors had learned how to live together, and now, a generation later, Fennis held no grudge against the former captors. He had genuinely fallen in love with Chiar'h. They were a perfect team, and someday they would have children with a viable mixture of genetics, but even if their halfbreed children turned out to be distorted misbreeds, Fennis would still love them.

From tending and serving these people in the sanctuary domes, he had sensed a strength and honor among the misbreeds. As they endured their physical deformities and pain, he saw their worth, and he had the utmost respect for their courage.

Fennis had failed to protect them here in the supposedly safe hospice, yet he would continue to try. For that, though, he needed an enemy he could see.

Chiar'h dozed in his arms but then awoke, wincing with pain. The cellular bindings had closed the slashes and stopped the bleeding, although she still hurt. There were more sophisticated Ildiran hospitals available, and medical kithmen who could provide better treatment, but Fennis didn't trust them right now. He clung to her in their small protected shelter.

A deep chill thrummed through him. What was it about the misbreeds that struck so much fear into the Shana Rei? How did they pose any sort of threat?

Gor'ka shuffled up and stared at him and Chiar'h with his three eyes, although the one that drooped down his waxy-looking cheek was milky and unfocused. He held up his one shriveled arm. "They pushed us. The misbreeds who remain alive are closer than ever. We must find a way to fight back and not hide any more."

Har'lc came up to join him, a walking horror of rashes and scabs. "All of us can feel it. You will not understand entirely because you are human, Shawn Fennis, but the misbreeds are Ildiran. We are also more than that—not less. No matter what we may look like, we hold power within us. We are binding ourselves together, the last of us here, with a different kind of *thism*. We have our own network. Just us."

Fennis didn't know how to respond to that. "And what does your network do?"

"We are still learning that," Gor'ka said. He indicated Mungl'eh on her pallet. "But our strength will go through her."

"When she sings," Har'lc added.

"Yes, we all like it when she sings," Fennis said.

Chiar'h stirred in his arms, made a contented noise. "Mungl'eh's voice is so beautiful."

"It is more powerful than you can know," Gor'ka added. "See what it can do now—to what we can do together."

The surviving misbreeds gathered around the invertebrate misbreed. Mungl'eh lifted her head, raised her flipperlike arms. Even though the fountains in the recovery center continued to splash with a musical tinkling sound and misters added pleasant moisture to the air, Fennis could still smell the thick coppery scent of blood in the room.

But when Mungl'eh raised her voice and began to sing, the sour odor that carried so much pain seemed to vanish. The misbreeds hummed along with her, seeming to join together somehow into a single unit. Mungl'eh's melodious voice soared, lilted, rose and fell, and even though Fennis was not Ildiran, he felt invisible, surreal strings pulling at his mind, at his emotions.

Fully awake, Chiar'h sat up with a gasp. Energy from the misbreeds seemed to suffuse her, and the joined misbreeds were stronger still. The Shana Rei had snatched the minds of helpless Ildiran kithmen as pawns to murder the misbreeds, yet in so doing the shadows had provoked the misbreeds, pushing them beyond the edge of desperation, beyond their limits.

They had become something new.

Fennis thought he understood. These poor people had suffered adversity, struggled to overcome a sense of worthlessness, tried to find purpose in their lives. Now they had found it. They had an incentive. They were forged into a unit through a unique synergy that had not previously existed.

As Mungl'eh sang, she seemed to glow with energy. Her music grew more powerful, interlacing with the harmonies of the cosmos itself. Fennis's heart ached and yearned, swelling as if it might burst from the sheer beauty. This song was not just a demonstration of the misbreeds' sense of purpose. It was a song of infinity, a creation-wrenching performance strong enough to awaken eternity itself.

Mungl'eh sang, and sang.

And the universe sang back, awake at last.

ROD'H

In his entropy prison, Rod'h was a captive, a victim, an experimental subject. And even though they were surely done with him, the Shana Rei would not let him die.

The black robots came to torment him again with malicious glee, but Rod'h refrained from showing terror. He couldn't flee, couldn't cooperate, was not able to give his captors what they wanted, because the Shana Rei did not *know* what they wanted, and the black robots already had their own plans.

Exxos came to him, moving in and out of the void, a nightmare of angled limbs and serrated claws that could slice his flesh to ribbons . . . and yet Rod'h's body healed each time. He survived, not only because of his halfbreed genetics, but because the rules of biology and physics did not apply in this place.

"Leave me alone or let me die," Rod'h shouted as the black robot loomed before him.

"No," Exxos said.

Even trapped inside here, Rod'h had witnessed the attacks on Relleker, Wythira, and now Earth. The Shana Rei and the black robots were exceedingly patient; they had all the time they needed to cause the destruction they desired. Rod'h dreaded that the shadows would hold him here and make him watch the end of the universe, no matter how long it took.

Shana Rei inkblots appeared around him as curious spectators. They never tired of watching his agony with their baleful eyes. He had no idea how much time had passed in the outside realm, perhaps only weeks, perhaps centuries.

But as they all hung in this nightmarish tableau, Rod'h suddenly noticed a difference in the universe . . . a twinge, a spark that skittered like chain lightning through the fabric of reality. The Shana Rei pulsed and writhed. Their glowing eyes flickered, blazed brighter, then faded. Rod'h could feel a thrumming . . . like music. Something awakening—far away. Something huge.

He felt that the creatures of darkness were terrified of some greater power, a presence so vast and all-encompassing that it drove them into frenzied disarray and panic. Rod'h had never understood that sentience before, and he didn't understand it now. But he felt it stirring.

"Eternity's Mind!" the Shana Rei wailed.

The sound became louder, echoing even through his entropy prison. The shadows could hear it, and they fluttered about like wings of darkness, but they could not escape.

His robot tormentors stirred in confusion. Their crimson optical sensors flared, their electronic voices buzzed. "What is this?"

The question repeated among the other robots that had come to torture him.

"What is this?"

"What is the sound?"

"What is happening?"

Though Rod'h didn't understand it either, he said in a rough, raspy voice, "It is something terrible—and it is coming for you!"

Around him, the gigantic pulsing force grew brighter, all-consuming, swelling until the music became deafening. It tore at the Shana Rei defenses, the black cocoon in which they protected themselves.

The presence continued to awaken.

74

ZHETT KELLUM

In their busy extraction field outside of Ikbir, the bloaters seemed strangely restless. Every Roamer worker in the Kellum operations could sense it.

From one of the inspection pods that flew among the swollen nodules, Marius Denva transmitted, "We're new to this, but something doesn't feel right to me, Zhett . . . Not at all. The bloaters are *agitated*." His voice had a faint undertone of uncertainty. Denva had gone back to work full-time, but sometimes he was still jumpy after his ordeal on Kuivahr.

Zhett and Patrick stared through the bridge windowport of their HQ ship. "How can giant plankton be agitated?" Patrick asked. "Are you saying a bag of protoplasm is nervous?"

Similar uneasy transmissions came from other workers. "Just keep your eyes open," Zhett transmitted.

The mothballed industrial equipment they had retrieved from Osquivel was now functioning at full capacity. Clan engineers had easily modified the old ekti-processing ships for the new work. The bloater sacks were drained, and the protoplasm processed into ekti-X, which was then stored in tank arrays. Previously, Roamer skymines had cruised above the clouds of gas giants. They had needed factories, pumping stations, centrifuges, and reactors, all of which were inefficient and expensive. In contrast, extracting stardrive fuel from these bloaters was as simple as poking in a straw and draining the nodules dry.

Unaware of the tension among the workers, Del Kellum strolled onto the bridge of the HQ ship, potbelly thrust forward. "This is going to be profitable, by damn! Very profitable indeed."

"So long as there isn't a glut in the market," Patrick said. "With so much extra production, stardrive fuel could become as cheap as water."

Kellum sniffed at his son-in-law. "People still make a fortune selling water."

One of the outlying bloaters suddenly sparkled with a flare of intense white light that faded quickly. Zhett just caught it out of the corner of her eye. She knew the nodules occasionally did that, much to the consternation of the extraction crews. Vessels that were too close to one of the flare-ups could suffer severe system damage and circuitry overloads.

A second nodule flared up . . . then three more sparkles. It was like slow-motion fireworks throughout the cluster. "Something's definitely happening out there," Zhett said.

Over the comm, Kristof yelped. "That one was close, Mom! I got great images of it, though."

Their son insisted on working out in space among the bloaters. Normally, Zhett would have been glad to let him gain hands-on experience—but not right now. "Toff, get out of there!"

A sixth bloater flashed, brighter than the others, as if a nova had gone off in its nucleus.

Patrick took the comm. "Everyone, pull away from the bloaters. Evacuate until this calms down."

Three more dazzling flare-ups. The flashes were increasing in frequency, though randomly distributed. Out in the open, Denva's supervisory pod pulled back, but as he skimmed close to another bloater, a flare-up damaged his engines, leaving him drifting and helpless in space. Static burst across the comm system. "My pod's systems are down—I'm using batteries for life support. By the Guiding Star, *not again!* Someone come fetch me."

"All personnel, get out of there!" Zhett yelled.

The extraction workers scrambled to retreat from the pumping operations, abandoning the machinery attached to the bloaters. One half-drained nodule also flickered like a feeble death gasp, but its light had a reddish tinge; then the swollen sack collapsed, crushing the pumping machinery attached to it.

Toff volunteered to streak in and rescue Denva. From his weak comm, Denva said, "I'm suiting up. I do not intend to let myself get stranded again. I still have nightmares about Kuivahr. I'll jump out the airlock so you can intercept me, kid."

"Call me a kid again, and I might just let you drift out there for an hour."

"I've been through worse. I can last for as long as necessary." He let out an angry snort. "But I prefer not to."

A bloater flared very close to Kristof's ship, and he went into a spin as he struggled to regain control.

"Toff, are you all right?" Zhett cried.

The bloater flares continued, sparkle after sparkle, like a storm of bright signals. Del Kellum paced the deck, his expression stormy. "By the Guiding Star, what triggered all that? What is waking them up?"

"I knew these operations seemed too easy," Patrick said.

Most of their ships and workers had retreated to a safe distance while the bloaters continued to flare up like a meteor shower. Zhett called for a full check-in, found out who needed to be rescued and how many ships were damaged. This was going to be a setback, for sure.

Toff picked up Denva and took him back to HQ.

Finally, the glittering lights faded inside the formerly innocuous nodules, and everything went quiet again. Zhett shook her head as she looked out at the suddenly dangerous operations. The Roamers had already drained dozens of the nodules, but more than half of the cluster remained. "What the hell was that all about?" she muttered. "And what set them off?"

CHAPTER

75

ARITA

As the Theron defenders marched toward the impenetrable fortress in the dead worldtrees, King Peter and Queen Estarra were ashen.

"Clear it away," Peter shouted. "Remove the blighted trees."

The Onthos retreated deeper into the thicket as the first wave of Theron soldiers used explosives to splinter the barricade. From above, survey flights showed thousands of Onthos running through the dead zone.

When the explosions shattered the fallen wood, Collin, Zaquel, and the other green priests moaned in dismay, holding the treelings they had brought from the other continent. Reynald swayed unsteadily, while Osira'h and Arita held on to him, giving him support.

"You tried to reason with the Onthos," Osira'h assured him in a hard voice. "They refused."

"Even so," Reyn said, "I was hoping to cure the trees, not eradicate them."

Theron fire-suppression ships swooped in, loaded with fire retardant to keep the blaze under control. "We won't let it turn into a wildfire." Arita grasped Collin's hand, but he was trembling. She said, "We're only taking out the dead parts before the Gardeners can cause any more damage."

"But the forest doesn't want this!" Collin caught his breath as another section of the barricade of fallen trees was blasted away. "The verdani ask that we not cause further harm."

King Peter gestured vehemently, directing another wave of troops forward and scattering more Onthos. "Drive them out!"

"But they are the Gardeners," Zaquel said. "They have served the trees."

Estarra stood at Peter's side. "They're *killing* the trees. Why would you want us to hesitate?"

The green priests hung their heads. "Because the verdani are begging us not to let this happen. . . ." Sickened by the damage being inflicted on the worldforest, they gathered together. "Wait for us," Zaquel said. "Please stop the attack!"

Frowning, Peter halted further explosions, waiting to see what the green priests would do.

In a large group, the priests darted into the thorny deadwood, and Arita rushed after Collin and his companions, fearing it might be a trap. The forest was like a lost graveyard with the bones of the verdani all around them.

Urged onward by Collin, the green priests pushed their way deeper into the dark and sinister forest, calling out. Coming to a halt in a dead clearing, Collin seemed at a loss, disconnected even though he held his potted treeling. "We cannot hear the verdani mind even with our trees," he said. "It's gone silent in here."

Arita heard the ominous crackle of shattering wood and collapsing trees all around. Behind them, the King and Queen and an armed contingent of the Theron home guard marched into the clearing.

In the twisted dead branches high above and in the dry underbrush all around them, there came a loud stirring. Ohro appeared, then ten other pale Gardeners, and then a hundred more. The sheer numbers were breathtaking.

"We will fight to survive," Ohro said, but his voice was pleading rather than belligerent. "We created a shelter for ourselves, and we will destroy you all, if you try to take us from it."

More Gardeners came forth, an army to stand against the Theron defenders and green priests. Dead, massive trees crashed around them.

"This battle will be bloody," Osira'h said.

Arita felt a sharp twist in her stomach as she watched the Onthos gathering, the Theron defenders readying their weapons. Then, deep inside her mind she felt a call, a shout from the distant, enormous presence that had brushed against her mind for so long.

Arita reached out with her thoughts and tried to touch that looming sentience that seemed even greater than the verdani mind. She knew it was out there—stirring, restless. She gasped as it suddenly *awakened,* all across the Spiral Arm. She reeled, grabbing a tree for balance, and sent out her thoughts, but the burgeoning presence was not focused on her.

Arita fought to concentrate, to pull her awareness back to Theroc and the battle here. The green priests seemed disoriented, as if they could feel it too.

That once-slumbering entity now returned with astonishing clarity, an omniscient awareness that spread out through the fabric of the universe. Bright and powerful thoughts flooded Arita's mind, so that she felt transported from the dead forest zone.

One small battle was being fought here, but a greater war spread across the cosmos. The new awakening flared in her mind, and the Onthos reacted as if they had been sprayed with acid. The aliens scrambled away, flailing their hands. Their black impenetrable eyes were wide and fathomless. With shrieking, panicked noises, they fled through the splintered debris of their dead fortress.

The green priests also looked stunned and confused. "What is that?" Collin asked. "It's not the verdani mind."

"Something wonderful and terrifying just happened," Arita said.

Peter, Estarra, and the Theron defenders stood at a loss. Their military advance had stopped.

Unexpectedly, a crackle came over the comm system carried by the Theron defenders. "King Peter, Queen Estarra! General Keah here—I've brought the last remnants of the CDF to Theroc. We suffered tremendous losses."

Estarra responded, "Losses from what, General?"

"Why have we heard nothing?" Peter asked.

"My green priests could not make contact! Earth was attacked by the Shana Rei and a million bugbot warships. The Lunar Orbital Complex is obliterated, along with CDF headquarters, and . . . and sire—Earth is destroyed!"

76

ORLI COVITZ

More ships began arriving at Handon Station, and Orli was confident that the Roamers would create a thriving commercial center after all. DD embraced his new role here, helping to monitor incoming ships and equipment and manage orders for station supplies.

More than a hundred Roamer clan members joined the new venture at Rendezvous. While Xander and Terry watched over salvage operations at Relleker, the first few hulks had been hauled back here for repair. With all the new bloater operations, the demand for functional ships of any size was higher than ever. Handon Station mechanics could repair and sell as many vessels as they could get their hands on.

During their daily work, Orli felt more content than ever. She already had ten Roamer compies in her workshop, so she could upgrade their programming and add new functionality. Once word got out about her services, she would have more projects than she could handle—which was exactly what she wanted.

And she was with Garrison. The two of them went to the main landing bay to receive the battered hulk of a commercial vessel from Relleker, still loaded with food and luxury items. The black robots had gutted it, but the hull and engines were intact, so the vessel could be refurbished. The salvage team had removed seven bodies before hauling the ship to Rendezvous.

She and Garrison looked at the other ships parked around the asteroid cluster awaiting repair. Orli said, "We're going to need more spacedock construction facilities."

"That's the idea," he said. "Some of the repaired ships will stay, others will be sold." A space tug tethered the commercial vessel to an outlying asteroid, and inspection crews got to work on their initial assessment.

DD and Seth came into the bay. The boy had been sad to leave his friends at Academ, but he thrived here as well. DD said, "I put my other duties on hold for a few hours to review young Seth's homework, as requested. His progress is adequate, although his weakest scores are in the vocabulary units."

"I communicate just fine," Seth said.

"You do," Orli agreed, "but DD can teach you some bigger words."

"And how to spell them," Garrison said.

"But I'm a Roamer! I'm better at mathematics and engineering."

Garrison turned to the compy. "Hear that, DD? When you're not on your work shift give Seth plenty of homework in mathematics and engineering, too."

The boy grimaced. "That's not what I meant."

Orli smiled and leaned back against Garrison. The bay was filled with noises of ship engines being tested, cargo unloaded, workers using tools to batter uncooperative systems into submission. But she was distracted from those sounds by a louder hum and whisper inside her head.

She had never been able to understand the faint mental undertone, which she had heard ever since her immersion in the bloater sack. It was like a ringing in her ears, sometimes easily ignored, sometimes bothersome. The hum often fell silent to the point where she thought she might be imagining it after all, but at other times the distraction came to her in dreams.

Now, in the main Handon Station bay, the distant sentience inside her mind suddenly swelled to a crescendo, louder than she had ever experienced before. Orli gasped, and her knees buckled. Garrison caught her, held her up. She squeezed her eyes shut against the throbbing call behind her temples, and the ghostly presence now seized her, as if shaking her awake.

Garrison asked her repeatedly what was wrong, and Orli tried to understand the commotion in her mind, but she heard only bright colors, saw clashing, painful sounds. "I don't know!" She shook her head, tried to get the confusion under control.

That was when she realized there was another person out there just like her, a human who also heard the voice . . . someone whose mind was likewise open to the bloater sentience.

Seth was frantic and DD called for medical attention as Garrison half carried her to the side of the landing bay. Orli could barely see anything around her because incongruous visions of scent and touch crowded behind her eyes. The awakening presence was bright, sharp, painfully clear . . . and exhilarating. Even though she was frightened, she felt more energized and alive than she had ever been.

"I'm fine," she gasped, holding Garrison's arm. "More than fine. This is . . . amazing. I understand now, but I don't understand." She was talking so rapidly that her words jumbled out. "Please Garrison—there's someone I need to find. A call went out across the Spiral Arm, and I felt someone else like me listening. Another human. We're connected."

She struggled to grasp what that strange presence was trying to tell her, and she envisioned the towering worldtrees of Theroc, saw an image of someone whom she instinctively knew as Arita, the daughter of King Peter and Queen Estarra.

And strangely that thrumming, surging voice in her mind impressed on her that it was connected in some way to the bloaters scattered across the Spiral Arm. The bloaters were calling her somehow.

Garrison's expression was full of urgent concern, but Orli knew there was nothing medically wrong with her. Nevertheless, she realized there was something she had to do. "I see it now, Garrison. It's the *bloaters*—I have to go to them. But first, we need to go to Theroc and contact Arita. You and I need to do this together."

"Theroc?" Garrison said, baffled. "Are you sure? Have you ever met this princess? Why in the world—"

"It's my Guiding Star," she insisted. "I see it as bright as a beacon. Will you take me there? This is important."

He didn't hesitate, and she loved him for it. "Of course. I'll get the *Prodigal Son* ready and find someone to take over here while we send a message to Terry and Xander. We can get going right away."

TAMO'L

Sheltered and alone in her research dome, Tamo'l studied myriad forms of death. Examining the genetic synergy in the misbreeds had been her primary interest, but since the poisonous shadows infiltrated her, Tamo'l had also been driven to find any weakness within her own halfbreed genetics.

Plenty of Pergamus scientists performed research that was more interesting to Zoe Alakis, so Tamo'l spent her days alone and unnoticed. Much of the time, she existed in a shadow fugue, engulfed in mysteries and questions. If anyone were to track the files she used or the specimens she reviewed, they might be curious to know why an Ildiran genetics researcher was so fascinated with deadly human diseases.

Tamo'l shuddered and blanked her screens, then forced herself to call up her original studies of the maps of her siblings' DNA and her own. Why did she alone of all her brothers and sisters have a chink in her armor? Why was she vulnerable?

Her father was a lens kithman who devoted his mind to philosophical pursuits and the study of the Lightsource. Had the Shana Rei been able to crack through the barrier and infect her via that higher plane? Or, was Tamo'l just weaker than the others?

With a gasp, she realized that she had unconsciously called up more records of the Onthos plague, had even flagged where the samples were stored on Pergamus. She hadn't even known she was doing it, and during that fugue she had unwittingly begun to plan how she might acquire some of those specimens.

Tamo'l deleted all her work and shut down her systems, helpless and terrified. "Leave me!" she shouted. "I will not help you."

The shadows within seemed to be laughing.

Unexpectedly, the mocking, looming presence recoiled inside her mind, and she felt a fundamental change. The lurking shadows were like a chill poison within her, but this change was something bright, new, and aware—and it intimidated the Shana Rei. She felt a loud presence tearing its way into the universe like a child desperate to be born. It was not part of the *thism,* not connected to the link she shared with her siblings . . . it was something different.

Tamo'l reached out, eager to embrace the new titanic presence, seeing it as a hope for rescue. But that other great sentience now sensed the taint of the Shana Rei inside her, and she suddenly became as deeply afraid of this mind as she was of the shadows. She was caught between the two immense forces, unable to escape. Still, she held on and cried out until the awakening presence noticed her and responded.

And it was agony!

JESS TAMBLYN

At Academ, the comet was restless and uneasy. The wental energy that permeated its ices flared with a brightening new glow, as if it had received an infusion of fresh fuel. The Roamer students were anxious, and even Jess grew increasingly concerned about what was happening to the elementals that had been been quiescent for so long.

Their energy had once been an integral part of him, when he and the wentals had soared across the Spiral Arm, fighting the hydrogues and the faeros. The water elementals had sung through him and Cesca, liberating them, making them more than human. He felt his skin tingle now.

He didn't believe the wentals would harm Academ, but not everyone could trust such powerful and exotic beings.

A nervous Arden Iswander came to see Jess and Cesca, escorted into the school admin offices by KA. The young man looked so much like his industrialist father. "I volunteered to come speak with you," Arden said. "The students are worried. That glow seeps into everything. What does it mean? What if there are side effects?"

"The wentals have always been benevolent," Cesca said, trying to reassure him. "I have no reason to believe they would cause us any harm. After they helped the human race survive the Elemental War, some of them went dormant here."

Arden nodded slowly, clearly unconvinced. "*Mostly* dormant, but something is obviously triggering them. And wentals have been deadly in the past—you're both aware of that more than anyone else. When they were inside you, *your* touch was enough to kill people. What if the wentals are losing control again?" He raised his hands to indicate the glowing ice walls.

Jess knew that Arden Iswander had been standing up for himself and fighting back against bullies, even when other Roamer students blamed him for his father's mistakes. Arden seemed to be a born leader, and now he was speaking for other uneasy students.

"I wish I had a better answer for you," Jess said. "The truth is that neither Cesca nor I can understand exactly what's happening with the wentals inside the comet."

The ubiquitous glow in the ice shimmered, but the wentals had not communicated directly. Jess wasn't even sure whether the elementals still knew how to communicate, if they remembered the fragility of human life.

When Cesca touched the wall, some of the ice melted, but her fingertips seemed to be wet with nothing more than water. "Sometimes we hear words and grasp clear concepts, but at other times it's just a sense of excitement or unease."

"You can see with your own eyes how much the comet is changing," Arden said.

"Yes, it's changing," Jess replied. "And considering the destruction caused by the Shana Rei, we may need the wentals as allies."

"Even after what they did to you?" Arden asked.

"And what they did *for* us." Cesca's voice grew stern.

The boy was far too young to remember the awful attacks of the hydrogues and faeros, so he could not understand the cost that Jess and Cesca had been willing to pay. At the time, the human race had been caught in a galactic clash against vastly superior foes. The wentals had helped humanity survive.

"What do you suggest, Arden?" Jess asked.

The young man lifted his chin. "For the time being, as a precaution, the students should move back to Newstation. At least until this settles." Arden lowered his voice. "I think it's a reasonable suggestion."

Jess and Cesca had always hoped to have children of their own, but exposure to the wentals had irrevocably altered their biology, and they were never able to build the family they wanted. Instead, they had established Academ so they could always be around Roamer children, to guide them and teach them.

Jess trusted the wentals, but he also felt protective of the children.

The clan members had given these boys and girls into their care, and he and Cesca had to protect them. He looked at Arden and nodded. "I understand your worries. Cesca and I will stay here, but anyone who wishes to transfer from Academ to Newstation is welcome to do so. Although we're convinced the wentals won't harm us, we shouldn't take any risks."

"I'll tell the rest," Arden said. "Some students want to go right away, but I'll stay here. Others will, too, if you really think it's safe."

The covered walls began to crackle, and fresh light streamed through the unmasked ices. The lambent light suddenly became intense, searing. Cesca cried out, and Jess felt his heart leap. It was as if the water elementals had just let out an exuberant flash of communication that sparked through.

A profound change out in the universe had just made them stir, and the water elementals were building their energy and signaling . . . to something. Jess had not felt a sensation like this before.

Around them, the whole Academ comet began to shine like a newly lit star. Shouts of alarm came from students and faculty in the corridors. The intercom system crackled with static and frantic questions.

"You're right, Arden," Jess said to the suddenly uneasy young man. "We should send the students away. The wentals are preparing for something."

EXXOS

The black robots were reeling from the panicked reaction of the Shana Rei. *Eternity's Mind?* The creatures of darkness could not coherently describe what exactly they feared.

Inexplicably, several of the marrauding shadow clouds in interstellar space began to collapse, crushed by some outside force, and the Shana Rei could not prevent it. Across the Spiral Arm, as the ominous force achieved a sort of consciousness, the black nebulas were converted into cold basic matter, reversing the flow of chaos.

The trapped Shana Rei wailed into the void, expressing far more agony than they had ever shown over the pain of sentient thought.

Although Exxos was pleased to witness their suffering—as far as he was concerned, the creatures of darkness deserved every modicum of misery they endured—the idea of a force awesome enough to terrify the Shana Rei was unsettling to the black robots as well. He and his myriad counterparts could not defend against something like that, could not prepare, nor could they flee.

The huge fleet of resurrected robot ships accelerated through the roiling shadow cloud, separating themselves from the chaotic nebula as swiftly as they could. While the robots watched from an increasing distance, the enormous Shana Rei cylinders crumbled, their obsidian surfaces spiderwebbed with cracks.

Frantic inkblot creatures manifested around the robot ships, appearing and disappearing at random, their voices jibbering. "The dark matter is coalescing!"

"Eternity's Mind drives it!"

The black shapes stretched and distorted, their central eyes blazed as if in terror, then the eyes flickered and grew red.

Exxos savored their panic, but it was also dangerous. Robot warships raced beyond the envelope of the shadow cloud, which had emerged in space near a bloater cluster, and the nuclei of the drifting nodules flashed and sparkled, as if activating in response to the proximity.

The bloaters?

Exxos remembered when the Shana Rei had first threatened the Iswander industrial operations. It should have been a devastating massacre, but when the shadows saw that the human workers were draining and killing bloaters, they simply withdrew without attacking, leaving the industrial operations intact. Exxos and his robots had wanted to annihilate the Iswander outpost, but the Shana Rei refused. It had been a capricious and inexplicable decision.

Now, new shadow clouds emerged into realspace at random points, without any sort of strategy. The Shana Rei simply wanted to fill the cosmos with their smothering darkness, but this time, some force pushed back against the nebula.

The bloaters?

The black cloud roiled and swirled as if helpless, folding back into itself and collapsing at near-relativistic speeds. All that dark matter grew denser and denser, pulled in by its own gravity and pressed inward by some outside repulsive force. In an astonishingly short time, the huge shadow cloud collapsed, its matter increasing in density until a dull glow appeared at its center. Pressing, crushing, condensing—nuclear reactions finally reached a critical point, so that as the nebula continued to fall in toward its center of mass, a proto-star at its core sparked and ignited.

Watching the shadow cloud collapse while the helpless Shana Rei retreated in chaotic terror was appalling to Exxos—because he didn't understand what was driving this catastrophe. It seemed as if the fabric of the universe itself was fighting back, awakened and antagonized.

Abandoning the remnants of their shadow cloud, the Shana Rei fled back into the void to escape the searing pain of the newborn star.

Witnessing such a cosmic disaster made Exxos feel insignificant again. From the mind-ripping outcries of the creatures of darkness, he knew that the same thing was happening at other emerging shadow clouds across the Spiral Arm.

SHAREEN FITZKELLUM

Kotto lay in a vegetative state in the sickbay of Fireheart Station, calm, peaceful.

For two days, the best Roamer physicians ran tests and scans while Howard and Shareen hovered nearby. The teens tried not to get in the way, realizing they couldn't help . . . but it soon became apparent that the doctors couldn't help either.

Hoping for some insight, Howard and Shareen had reviewed Kotto's logs, his cryptic comments and outbursts, speaking to something else out there. And then the final surge that he had invited in, oblivious to what it might do to him. At the time, Kotto's behavior had confused the two compies, and when Shareen watched his final seconds, her heart ached and tears filled her eyes.

The great scientist's brain patterns were completely blank, as if his mind and soul had simply departed, taking along all the magnificent, overwhelming knowledge of the universe that he had supposedly experienced.

After two unresponsive days with no change at all, Kotto Okiah— the greatest Roamer scientist who ever lived—simply passed from life. He stopped breathing and his heart stopped beating, but his genius mind had departed days earlier.

Shareen felt helpless. "If Kotto died to receive all that knowledge, I wish he'd been able to share some of it with us." She slumped into a chair.

Howard continued to review the logs of Kotto's voyage, scanning through the days of readings, much of which was useless null data.

While Kotto was alive, they had focused on the last part of the expedition, when he encountered what he called Eternity's Mind.

Now they concentrated on the other vital discovery Kotto and the survey craft had made. Anger growing within Shareen lifted the heavy shrouds of grief. "Kotto would have wanted us to learn something from this debacle—something we can use."

She played back the early images of the voyage through the void, when the survey craft had slipped past quiet and crowded black hex cylinders, a gathering of the Shana Rei. She hung on the words Kotto uttered. He thought he had found their secret lair.

"He wanted to bring this to General Keah," Shareen said. "To let the CDF know that they might be able to take the Shana Rei by surprise."

They both looked at the ominous images of the dormant shadow cylinders folded inside the void. The huge black hexagons seemed lethargic, unaware . . . like sleeping predators.

Shareen's lips curved in a determined smile. "We need to go to the terrarium dome, have the green priests send a message that there's a back door at Fireheart, a way to get to the shadows where they will least expect it."

"General Keah is going to love that," Howard said.

She and Howard knew how the shadow clouds appeared in real-space to wreak havoc. This void, though, was *inside* the walls of their fortress, behind any defenses they might have. And that suggested a remarkable opportunity.

"In fact," Shareen said, "this might even be Kotto's greatest discovery."

GENERAL NALANI KEAH

The Confederation Defense Forces had, in the end, done little to defend the Confederation. For all their bluster and armaments, their sun bombs, their laser cannons, they had completely failed against the Shana Rei threat.

During the flight to Theroc, Keah had dealt with her shock, grief, and anger. Locked in her ready-room for hours during the flight to the Confederation's capital, she rehearsed her report, swearing to herself that she wouldn't candy-coat the disaster. Later, sealed in her cabin on the *Kutuzov,* where no one could see her, she wondered how she could tell the King and Queen that she had failed. Her rehearsed lines simply faded away, and General Nalani Keah broke down.

But that was enough of that. No time for sniveling. Finally, drained, hardened, and with renewed resolve, she cleaned herself up, put on her best uniform, and went to speak to Peter and Estarra.

All the green priests and Theron defenders had rushed back from the Wild, and Keah's green priest Nadd was finally able to share basic details with other planets through telink.

After all the challenges General Keah had confronted in her military career, facing the King and Queen on Theroc was the hardest thing she had ever done. She presented images of the complete rout her most powerful warships had suffered at Earth: billions dead, a significant portion of her fleet wiped out in a single battle.

Afterward, she added in a raw voice, "If I could find a way to dismantle those monsters down to their component atoms, I would do it with my bare hands."

Peter rose from the throne, shaking. "The Shana Rei already tried to kill the worldforest with their nightshade, and it took all of our efforts—your ships, Solar Navy warliners, verdani treeships, and even the faeros—to drive them away. With only the CDF and a few faeros, Earth didn't stand a chance."

Keah lifted her chin, swallowed hard. "I will recall all our deployed ships and center them here. We have to protect Theroc at any cost."

Already, the *Kutuzov,* the *Okrun,* and the last sixty battered warships orbited the planet, joining the gigantic verdani battleships that stood guard. The huge orbiting trees were intimidating, and the CDF Juggernauts and Mantas were nothing to sneeze at, but against a million bugbot attackers, they wouldn't be nearly enough.

This was all she had, however, and Keah vowed to do her damnedest. She asked all of her personnel to think outside the box and suggest alternate solutions. In the past, no matter how she encouraged Admirals Handies and Harvard to come up with new ideas, they had still fallen back on old methods . . . and they had died for it. At least Admiral Haroun had stepped up to the plate. Keah didn't know what hope she could offer.

And then like a miracle, a new possibility fell right in her lap.

In the stunned silence after Keah finished her report, the green priests in the throne room suddenly stirred, touching the wall of the worldtree and receiving a telink message. "We have urgent news from Fireheart Station," said Zaquel. "Kotto Okiah found a significant vulnerability of the Shana Rei."

General Keah blinked and caught her breath. "Hell, I'd be happy with even a moderate vulnerability. Write down the reports—I need all the information."

The green priests furiously transcribed the data coming through from Celli and Solimar, describing Kotto's expedition into the void and how it killed him, but not before he discovered the secret hiding place of the shadows. If Kotto's two lab assistants were correct, the CDF might be looking at a whole different playing field.

Many listeners didn't grasp the significance of the discovery, but Keah burst out, "This gives us the opportunity to sneak up on the shadows from behind! A back door, right into their lair. They won't expect it, and we can choose the right time." She clenched her fists and let out a low, edgy chuckle. "We've always been at the mercy of when and where the Shana Rei decided to strike. It was defense instead of offense. But if the Big Ring accident made a secret entrance, then we can go there ourselves and strike."

It felt strange to be filled with enthusiasm and hope, and Keah was going to make the most of it. "Your Majesties, if we keep fighting the Shana Rei and the bugbots the way we have been, we are bound to lose. There is no chance we can defeat them in a head-on military clash, on their terms."

Peter nodded. "After seeing what happened at Earth, I have to agree."

Keah continued to press. "Those things want to make every last one of us extinct. We have to try any possibility." Then she offered a hard grin. Her dark outrage had been transformed into a ruthless determination. "I'll bet Adar Zan'nh would be willing to send his best Solar Navy warliners to the operation. We'll gather as many sun bombs as we can find from the other patrol ships in the CDF—this is where we need to use them. I'll go to Fireheart Station by way of Ildira." She took a step closer to the throne. "Just say the word, and we'll take the war to the Shana Rei."

Estarra glanced at Peter and turned to face the General. "The word is given."

CHAPTER
82

GARRISON REEVES

Roamer clans knew how to roll with sudden changes. Garrison had the Handon Station operations running smoothly—accepting salvaged ships, bringing in new workers, setting up habitation quarters. So when he announced that he had to go—because Orli *needed* to go—others could handle the duties he was leaving behind.

Rajesh Clinton, who had previously worked with Garrison at the Lunar Orbital Complex repair docks, waved him off. "No worries, I can watch over things as much as they need watching. The teams are pretty much self-sufficient." He was dark-skinned and thirtyish, with a bright smile and heavy eyebrows. "Roamers don't need much supervision."

"Thanks, Jesh." He hurried to help Seth pack for their trip to Theroc.

Orli was eager to go, with a sparkle of wonder in her eyes after hearing the call of that strange awakening presence.

The *Prodigal Son* was ready within two hours. Rajesh promised to send word to the Relleker salvage fields to inform Xander and Terry. Garrison reassured him, "I'll be back as soon as I can. Don't worry."

He would stay with Orli until she found her answers. Maybe that would be on Theroc, or maybe Theroc was just the start of their journey. The *Prodigal Son* raced away from the asteroid cluster and set course for the worldforest planet.

During the flight away from the Rendezvous asteroids, Orli kept rubbing her temples. She would start conversations and try to explain to Garrison, but she couldn't describe what was going on inside her mind. Finally, she said, "Do you remember when we flew away from Ikbir, and we found that cluster of bloaters? All the strings connecting them like a network through space?"

Garrison smiled. "How could I forget?"

"It's something out there. Not just Ikbir, but . . . everywhere. The bloaters are more than just gas bags." Orli bit her lower lip. "Arita and I are connected to them and to each other. We need to meet face-to-face."

When the *Prodigal Son* arrived, Garrison was intimidated by the fearsome-looking verdani battleships in orbit, as well as the battered CDF ships that guarded the Confederation's capital. He transmitted his request to meet with the daughter of the King and Queen.

No one in the capital had any reason to know Garrison Reeves or Orli Covitz, and Arita had no prior contact with them, but the request was unusual enough to draw attention. He was surprised to receive clearance so easily, and even more so when Arita herself sent a message. "Orli? Yes, I've been expecting you . . . I think."

When the *Prodigal Son* landed on the polymerized canopy, Orli stepped out into the hazy sunlight and scanned the people moving about the landing zone, technicians and support staff, CDF soldiers and Confederation functionaries. She immediately spotted the young black-haired woman who hurried forward to meet them, accompanied by a young green priest.

"You hear it too," Arita said. "Something that just started humming, thinking—communicating across the universe."

Orli was excited. Arita felt like an old friend, although they had just met. "Yes, and it's connected to the bloaters."

Arita lit up, and she turned to the green priests. "Collin, that's it! The bloaters—I heard the surge of awakening when we were off in the blighted area. Orli's right. Now I understand."

"But . . . what do you understand?" he asked.

Orli said in a rush, "For whatever reason, Arita and I have some connection with that presence. Come with us to the bloaters."

Arita's face was full of wistful wonder. "For so long I thought I was a failure because the verdani didn't accept me, but when they changed me I made a sort of contact—I just didn't realize it. I never quite fit in, because my connection wasn't here." She waved a hand vaguely toward the sky. "It was out there."

"Exactly," Orli said. "The answer is out there among the bloaters. We'll go in the *Prodigal Son* and try to communicate with that presence. Maybe together we can learn what it wants."

Arita's eyes flashed with determination. "Or what it needs."

83

TOM ROM

Tom Rom increased speed so he could get back to Pergamus when Zoe expected him. He knew how much she worried if he was late.

Zoe Alakis was not his biological daughter, but a perverse combination of circumstances had made her a daughter in his heart. Since he had failed to save his real child from the butchers at Rakkem, he had sworn not to fail this surrogate daughter. He always delivered every specimen Zoe wanted, and gathered the data she needed for her research programs. He retrieved prisdiamonds from the lichentree jungles of Vaconda whenever she needed to refill her treasury.

But he never gave her all the details of his jobs, knowing it would alarm her. He had not told her about his close escape when he had obtained the Dhougal brain parasite for her collection. He had not told her how a group of Roamer pirates had once tried to steal his load of prisdiamonds and leave him to die on Vaconda.

In his own calm, efficient way, Tom Rom took care of crises. Zoe didn't need to know the details. Zoe didn't need to worry.

As soon as his ship entered the Pergamus system, her mercenary security troops intercepted him, and Zoe immediately greeted him on the comm, full of relief. She was cool and remote when she spoke to anyone else, showing no desire for friendship, but with Tom Rom it was different. It had always been different.

After he landed, she asked to see him in person, wanted him to pass through the decontamination levels, like some penitent completing the Stations of the Cross, but this time he begged off. "I need to touch base with the Orbital Research Spheres, meet with the main testing teams, and check the disease archives. Has Tamo'l reported regularly?"

"I wish all my researchers were as diligent. She keeps herself busy, although she hasn't provided any significant results. I've been tracking her research, and she's surprisingly interested in our deadliest diseases." Zoe pursed her lips. "It may be worth reassigning her to other work. With her Ildiran training she might have new insights. She seems to be very curious about Pergamus." Zoe's face brightened, and she was clearly finished with the discussion. "Now, if you won't come in and visit me in person, find some food and sit there so you can at least have a virtual lunch with me."

Expecting that, Tom Rom had already ordered a meal tray for himself. As he situated himself in front of the imagers, Zoe warmed a bowl of sterile protein mash and fixed a cup of hot tea inside her sterile chamber. As soon as they both settled in, facing each other's screen as if they were across a dining table, Tom Rom told her about the Klikiss worlds he had surveyed. "I did bring more tissue samples and royal jelly for analysis, but there is another matter of great concern." He showed her the surprising devastation on Eljiid, blasted by an outside enemy. "As I've warned you before, Zoe, the Shana Rei are becoming a substantial threat. They did this to a mostly unpopulated world, but I received word that they also attacked and exterminated the Confederation colony of Relleker. It is dangerous out there."

Zoe didn't seem concerned. "Good thing we have nothing to do with the Klikiss or the Confederation." She called up the files he had transmitted for her. "This is the information I wanted, but the genetic profile of the Onthos plague has evolved substantially since you first brought it to me. We'll test the old treatment to confirm that it's no longer effective."

She sounded resigned rather than disappointed.

He called up images for her to view on her own screens. "Let me show you something else, something I think you'll like. You don't need to worry about Rakkem anymore." Taking immense satisfaction, he showed her how the burgeoning black-market center had been brought to its knees.

Zoe's dark eyes drank in the images of the abandoned warehouses, the hopeless and broken people, the spread of disease among the refugees. Her voice was cold. "I would rather that place was completely obliterated, like the Klikiss world you just showed me." Then her lips quirked in a smile. "But it'll do."

Tom Rom knew she was likely thinking of her obscene, bloated mother, a factory womb who had borne countless children. He also thought of the greedy cure sellers who had refused to treat young Zoe when she was dying from Conden's Fever.

After the death of Adam Alakis, when he and Zoe had abandoned Vaconda to wander across the Spiral Arm, they had seen the worst, the sickest, the most manipulative that the human race had to offer. Zoe recognized early on that her father and Tom Rom were two rarities, honest and honorable people; such types were as endangered a species as the rarest organism in her collection. Most people were easily corrupted.

When they had discovered a fortune of prisdiamonds hidden beneath the Vaconda jungles, Zoe found herself with unexpected and inconceivable wealth. She had made up her mind to build the greatest disease research facility in the Spiral Arm, gather the largest collection of organisms—and construct the most protected fortress to hold them. When young Zoe had explained her ambitious dreams, Tom Rom developed the practical details.

And then he had gone searching, doing everything necessary to create the facility that she wanted. He took the parameters Zoe suggested and added strictures of his own. He scouted alone to find a planet that would conform to what he thought of as the "lethal Goldilocks" rule—not too dangerous, not too deadly, but just poisonous and hazardous enough to keep people away.

Pergamus, with its poisonous atmosphere, was inhospitable enough to be of no interest to settlers, but not so harsh as to exceed the protective abilities of standard hardened structures. It had no exotic resources to interest ambitious Roamer clans. The unwanted planet was there for the taking.

With an inexhaustible supply of prisdiamonds, Tom Rom spread money around, dividing the project's design work among twenty different developers. Roamer construction crews built the surface domes, outfitted the laboratory facilities, and installed reliable life-support systems. Tom Rom designed the disintegration fail-safe systems himself, to make absolutely certain that no lethal microorganism could escape.

While Pergamus was constructed, he vetted the workers carefully, knowing he couldn't guarantee the facility would remain secret, but he paid them substantial stipends for their silence.

The ruthless sterilization systems had been used twice during the first year of research, when insufficiently cautious researchers hadn't followed proper protocols; Zoe was forced to trigger the vaporization burst, eliminating whole teams along with their promising research. After that, the domes were rebuilt with more rigorous containment systems, and the next groups of spooked researchers were more careful. In the following years, there had been relatively few incidents, considering the amount of work being done.

The impressive, secure facility had achieved exactly what Zoe had set out to do, and she was exceedingly proud of her collection, a viral museum unlike anything compiled in human history. Her researchers found cures and treatments, merely as part of the study of such specimens.

Zoe did not share her cures, even with those who desperately needed them. Some of those who pleaded for the treatments accused Zoe of lacking compassion, but Tom Rom knew that she merely lacked interest. She justified her actions to herself, and she refused to become any kind of cure seller or biomerchant. She had seen too much of that vileness on Rakkem.

Even so, Tom Rom pondered whether the existence of Pergamus was a sufficient reason unto itself. A collection of diseases and cures just . . . because? That was Zoe's decision, and he would not challenge it. He never challenged her.

At least she wasn't cheating dying people, bankrupting them with the hope of impossible cures, creating factory wombs to sell innocent infants for their parts. Others could accuse Zoe Alakis of being selfish, but she and Tom Rom had both seen far worse.

Now, as Zoe chatted with him on the other side of the screen, he ate with her and listened. She fell into a comfortable silence as she reviewed the images he had brought back from his expedition.

He spoke up in a hoarse voice. "Don't let this place become Rakkem, Zoe. Don't ever turn Pergamus into something like that."

She turned pale and frowned at him. "Never. I would destroy it all first."

And he knew she would.

84

TAL GALE'NH

Gale'nh had never seen the Mage-Imperator so distraught.

When Jora'h summoned him into the Skysphere audience chamber, the attenders, court functionaries, and noble kithmen were dismissed; the Mage-Imperator even sent away Nira and Prime Designate Daro'h. He wanted to see Tal Gale'nh—and no one else.

Gale'nh felt intimidated, but when he saw the expression on Jora'h's face, the naked *need* behind his eyes, he stepped up to the chrysalis chair. "I am here to do my duty, Liege."

When Adar Zan'nh gathered his Solar Navy warliners to join General Keah at the Fireheart nebula, Tal Gale'nh desperately wanted to go along, to prove himself. He had hoped to command a warliner of his own, perhaps even an entire septa in the remarkable last-chance battle. He had proved himself in space combat, and he wanted to reclaim his rank and his respect. If this was indeed their final stand against the shadows, then he needed to be there.

But the Mage-Imperator had asked Gale'nh to stay behind as the Adar sailed off with a maniple of the Solar Navy's greatest ships, 343 warliners ready for battle.

Now, though, Gale'nh understood that Jora'h did indeed need him more. He bowed at the base of the dais. "I will serve you to the best of my ability, Liege."

They were alone under the dome of the Prism Palace, where the light of all seven suns shone through the angled crystal. Flying creatures flitted about in the high levels. Mists created clouds that held a projected image of the Mage-Imperator's benevolent face—a face much different from the drawn and frightened expression that Gale'nh saw before him now.

"Tell me what you know," Jora'h said. "Tell me how I can resist the shadows the way you did. How did you become immune?"

Gale'nh had struggled with that very question so many times before. "Why do you think I know, Liege?"

"Because you were there inside the *Kolpraxa*. The shadows had you, but you resisted them somehow. They couldn't possess you the way they've already possessed so many helpless Ildirans." He swallowed hard, and his voice was hollow. "I fear it is in me too, hidden and lurking. I dare not let the rest of my people know, but I have to fight it."

Gale'nh squared his shoulders. "You are the Mage-Imperator. You are stronger than any of us."

"Obviously not stronger than you, Tal Gale'nh. The shadows could not break you."

"Or maybe the shadows just didn't want me. They couldn't use me. I had nothing that they needed." Gale'nh drew a deep breath, remembering the suffocating blackness, how everyone else—his crew, his friends—had been *uncreated* by the creatures of darkness. He whispered, "Or maybe they did take everything they wanted from me . . . and left me alive as one last torment."

The Mage-Imperator shook his head. "That I will not believe. I realize you have doubts, and you are afraid the shadows are still in you, but I know they are not. I know you are strong."

Gale'nh stood before him with an enduring expression. It was not his place to contradict the Mage-Imperator. "The shadows were inside me, and they've taken Rod'h as well, and now . . . I can't find Tamo'l. I don't know where she is, but I sense a darkness around her, too."

The Mage-Imperator leaned back, his lips furrowing in a frown. "Stay with me and help me. I have countless soldier kithmen and attenders, but *you* I trust, because you have already been through the worst nightmare, and you survived. Maybe you can help me survive. Maybe I can purge them from the *thism* as well."

Gale'nh stopped himself from shaking his head. "I remember very little of the time I was in darkness, Liege. How can I be sure the Shana Rei didn't simply let me return so they could use me against you at the moment we are most vulnerable?" He took a step back from the dais. "How do you know that I won't try to kill you the way so many other possessed Ildirans tried to kill you?"

Jora'h's voice was cold. "Because they did not try to kill me. The possessed attenders had the opportunity. They slaughtered so many in the audience chamber, but when they came toward me, they simply turned away and chose another target."

"Maybe they thought you were too strong." Gale'nh tried to make himself believe the statement.

The Mage-Imperator shook his head. "Or maybe they thought I was already lost. You alone have demonstrated the ability, Tal Gale'nh. You beat them." He leaned forward in the chrysalis chair, and his smoky topaz eyes narrowed. "I need you to teach it to me, or our Empire is lost."

85

OSIRA'H

Arita and Collin were ready to depart with Orli Covitz and Garrison Reeves. The two visitors had brought mysterious news that explained the strange voices Arita heard in her mind, and now Reyn's sister had a bright eagerness in her eyes, excited by the possibility of finding the bloaters.

Osira'h accompanied him up to the top of the trees so he could say farewell to his sister. He insisted that he felt fine, although he fooled no one.

Standing out on the expansive canopy landing area surrounded by sunshine and rustling leaves, Arita embraced Reyn. "Keep up hope. We know that something out there in the worldforest has the key to curing your sickness, but there are millions of possibilities."

She looked at Osira'h, too. "Both of you, use the data I gathered from my expeditions. So many specimens, so many tests—something will work against the microfungus. There's hope, don't forget that."

"We will keep searching," Osira'h said. "The researchers have all the data from Pergamus. We will identify the correct specimen in time."

"We will," Reyn said. But he was not doing well at all since their return from the blighted trees in the Wild.

The battle for the festering forest remained unresolved, and the green priests were desperately using the worldforest mind in hopes of fighting the Onthos infestation, but the horrific attacks of the Shana Rei had taken priority.

Arita and Collin boarded the *Prodigal Son,* ready to go. The young green priest carried a potted treeling so he could stay in contact with the verdani mind, but Osira'h knew he just wanted to be with Arita.

As they watched the *Prodigal Son* streak up into the sky, Reyn looked longingly after the ship, as if he wanted to go away as well.

Osira'h kept her voice hopeful. "When you get better, I can think of so many things to show you on Ildira. I already took you out to see the faeros inside Durris-B, but there is so much more across the Empire." Her eyes sparkled as she talked in a rush, trying to spark his imagination. "The ice geysers under the auroras of Edilyn are supposed to be spectacular, and the rainbow strata in the fossil canyons on Fornu are so remarkable even the Mage-Imperator says he wants to visit there. There's so much that I've wanted to see too, but I would rather have someone at my side. It is less enjoyable sightseeing all alone."

"Sounds exhausting," Reyn said, then smiled. "But I would like to see some of those things with you. We could look at images together." Weary, he sat down on the tightly woven canopy surface.

She sat cross-legged beside him. "Images are only images, and they can't match real experiences. I want to take you there in person—when you're better."

"If I get better," he said.

"*When* you get better."

"All right, I'll go with you—when I get better."

They sat in comfortable silence for a few moments; then Osira'h asked, "And are there places you'd like to show me in the Confederation? I have not seen much of it."

"Neither have I," Reynald said.

"But where would you like to go?"

He considered. "Fireheart Station looks spectacular, and the Roamers have established some interesting settlements in cold comet fields and fiery lava planets." He looked up in the sky again, where the *Prodigal Son* was long gone. "We should have asked my sister. She's been to a lot more places than I have."

"Wherever you choose, we will go there together," Osira'h said.

He gave her a quick smile. "When I get better." Even under the rejuvenating Theron sunshine, though, his skin looked paler and grayer than ever.

Reyn suddenly tensed, his entire body clenching as if a rampant electrical storm had just raged through his nerve network. He hissed, and a tear of pain curled out of his eye. She knew there was little she could do, but even so, Osira'h wrapped her arms around him and just held him on the canopy until the waves of pain passed. They sat under the bright Theron sunlight and listened to the buzz of insects and flying spaceships, the rustle of worldtree fronds.

He climbed to his feet and tried to sound strong. "I'll be fine."

Osira'h took his arm. "Don't lie to me. There's no need to keep secrets." So far no treatment, not even the Kuivahr kelp extracts, had proved to be effective for long. The first synthetic drug based on the kelp samples had just arrived from a pharmaceutical company, but it showed only limited efficacy. Based on the Pergamus research, teams had tested tens of thousands of Theron specimens for the chromosomal pairing to battle the blight inside him, but so far there was no molecular match. And there were still millions of choices to study.

Nevertheless, Reyn was better off here, surrounded by the energy of the worldforest. "Let me get you back to your room." Osira'h propped him up and led him along.

"If a beautiful woman insists on leading me back to my room alone, I won't turn down the offer." He smiled at her, and his color looked healthier. They climbed into a lift that took them down into the green-lit sanctuary of the midlevels of the trees. Below, Roamer clan representatives were delivering summaries to Confederation officials, and a few refugees from Earth arrived on Theroc, frantically reporting the news. General Keah had nearly finished her preparations for the great expedition to Fireheart Station.

Osira'h's main concern was Reyn. She believed him when he suggested that if the blighted forest were cured, then he would be cured. When she led him into his quarters, she thought he looked like a ghost of himself. Confronting the Gardeners and entering that blighted fortress in the Wild had dimmed his feeble spark of life, but he kept on. Osira'h believed he was doing it for her.

"Maybe we could play that Ildiran strategy game you wanted to teach me," he said.

Then he collapsed. Reyn's knees simply surrendered, and he dropped to the floor, sprawling flat.

"Reyn!" His skin had gone cold and clammy. His eyes fell shut. He made no sound of pain; he simply seemed to have fallen dead in the chamber. She held him, cradled his head, touched his neck, and was relieved to find a pulse—a faint and thready one, but it was there. She raised her voice, calling out, "Help! The Prince needs medical attention."

She knew there were no secrets in the worldforest. The trees sensed everything, and through them, the green priests knew what was happening. Now she hoped someone was indeed listening in.

The trees heard, and the green priests heard. Theron doctors rushed into his room within moments. Together, they lifted him onto the bed, trying to make him more comfortable, but Reyn was completely unconscious, deep in a coma.

No matter what medication they tried or what stimulus they used, no one could wake him up.

86

CELLI

Inside the tense terrarium dome in the middle of the nebula, both Celli and Solimar allowed their minds to drift free and roam throughout the strands of the telink network. Their minds throbbed with hurt and grief from the devastation they found on other worlds, and their bodies ached with sympathetic pain from the trapped pair of worldtrees. When Celli touched the gold bark scales, the suffering trees shuddered. She could feel the heartwood tremble like a tightly coiled spring.

She could only hope the new hemisphere would be finished soon enough.

Outside, Roamer construction engineers in exosuits built up the base around the terrarium, installing girders and extensions to the main platform, then extended high arches that curved up and over the existing dome. She silently urged them to work faster.

These worldtrees were doomed unless the extended dome could be completed in time—and Celli felt responsible for it. She and Solimar had naïvely brought the treelings here fifteen years earlier, glad to see them thrive in the nebula light, how swiftly they grew.

That was during the heady construction days of Fireheart Station. The Roamers were expanding their food-production systems to accommodate the station's increased population, and as green priests, she and Solimar were happy to help with agriculture and communication. They sent messages wherever needed.

Once Kotto Okiah had come up with his grand idea for the Big Ring experiment, she and Solimar were busy sending hundreds of instant communications to Roamer clans, to Newstation, and across the Spiral Arm in hopes of garnering support and funding. Together, they had kept extremely busy, consumed with the dynamic success of Fireheart. They served a necessary purpose, which was perfectly suited to their abilities—telink was the only way to send messages through the turbulence of the nebula. Celli and Solimar had felt so needed. They were happy with what they'd been doing.

Somehow, the point at which the trees could have been transplanted and saved passed them by. Bathed in the radiation of the blue supergiant stars at the heart of the nebula, the worldtrees had grown at an astonishing rate. Now it was much too late. Kotto's two research assistants had proposed an emergency solution, and it just might work.

But Celli and Solimar still had duties to do.

They had transmitted messages through telink, spreading Kotto's idea of infiltrating the lair of the Shana Rei. She and Solimar helped to arrange the CDF and Solar Navy attack, and soon the strike force would arrive, ready to hit the creatures of darkness from a point of possible vulnerability.

Solimar stroked the giant trunk. "We haven't been this busy in five years." He winced at the pain in his back and shoulders.

All day long they filtered communications that came in, listened to discussions throughout telink, talked to other green priests, and heard the reports of Shana Rei attacks. As they communicated with the green priests, they imparted their dismay about the trapped worldtrees. Even if the expanded dome were completed in time, it was only a temporary solution.

Each tree was part of the overall verdani network, but Celli and Solimar felt closer to these particular trees, *their* worldtrees. Green priests were also one vast network, countless human minds that could all tap into the forest database, and now they all felt the same pain.

Outside in the nebula, the Roamer engineers continued to build around the terrarium, working frantically.

Meanwhile, the restored Fireheart operations continued at full speed. Chief Alu had focused on power-block production so they could fulfill long-standing orders. Isotope factories packaged exotic materials to be sent to research stations and experimental reactors on far-flung colonies.

And now the CDF and the Solar Navy were on their way to fight the Shana Rei through the hole in the nebula.

Celli knew the expanded greenhouse dome would take at least two more weeks to complete. Exhausted and filled with visions, she withdrew her hands from the bark and sat back. Solimar gathered her into his arms, holding her against his broad chest. They lay together in silence, leaning against the trunks and listening to the stir of worldtree fronds as nebula light poured in. The trees couldn't stop growing.

As Celli looked up at the swatch of stars and colorful gases through the crystalline dome, she heard a loud, thin *crack*, and she saw the first hairline fracture zigzag across the stressed greenhouse pane.

CHAPTER

87

EXXOS

In turmoil, the Shana Rei were more intractable than ever—and more dangerous. Sixteen of their shadow clouds had collapsed out in the universe, forced to coalesce by some incredibly powerful outside force, until in a flash of painful light the clouds ignited to become new stars.

Exxos and his robots wanted to keep killing humans on planet after planet, but for all their inconceivable powers, the creatures of darkness were in a manic, unfocused rage, simply preying on things that were helpless. Capriciously destructive, they broke down and disassembled ten thousand Exxos robots—robots they themselves had just created—degrading the dark matter that comprised them and unmaking them into nothingness again. The Shana Rei had created them, and the Shana Rei could reverse creation as well.

Exxos argued, but the shadows would not listen. It was a stupid and pointless waste of materials, and he needed to make the Shana Rei see how foolish they were being. Considering the incomprehensible force that fought against their chaos, Exxos feared the creatures of darkness would shy away from the kind of massive attack they had done on Earth. And if the robots suffered damage and losses in such a battle, would the distressed Shana Rei be willing to restore them, as before? He wasn't even sure the shadows would replace the ten thousand robot victims they had just maliciously eliminated.

These allies were maddening.

He had to find a less risky way to spread death among human populations, one that did not require gigantic robot fleets. The shadows' interest in Tamo'l and her research at Pergamus gave

Exxos an idea, and he knew the Shana Rei must already see the possibilities.

The robots knew how destructive those virulent pathogens could be. Humans were vulnerable—terribly vulnerable. And the tangled, wire-thin connections into Tamo'l granted the Shana Rei access to a previously unknown deadly weapon.

In the turbulence of the lightless void, the Exxos copies linked together and attempted to focus the frenzied inkblots. "Your energies are wasted in destroying my robots. We need to keep killing *humans*," Exxos insisted. "Think of your priority. Now is the time we should continue our attack."

One of the smudged inkblots hovered in front of his optical sensors, its singular eye blazing but unfocused, as if it were going blind. "It is impossible. With Eternity's Mind, the pain of human sentience is no longer our priority."

"You have more than one priority," Exxos said. "And I have an efficient way to wipe out the human race without exposing us to further dangerous engagements." Neither the robots nor the Shana Rei wanted to endure the wild destruction of hundreds of sun bombs again. "We can make the humans extinct if you will assist in one more battle. A small battle, but a necessary one."

The creatures of darkness swirled about like bat wings. "What battle? How would this be possible?"

"With the diseases at Pergamus. You already know about them. We can go there, seize Tamo'l, and take the stockpile of deadly viruses. If we unleash them, we would spread death throughout the human-settled planets. We could kill them and keep killing them across the Spiral Arm, without any further effort from you. It would be a self-propagating extermination. The hundreds of plagues would kill them all."

"That is not as satisfying as overt destruction," one of the inkblots said.

Exxos agreed. "Nor is it as immediate, but it *will* produce the results we seek. It will kill many of them quickly, and that will provide relief to the Shana Rei. Meanwhile, we will still be able to hunt down and wipe out the rest. More personally."

The shadows were disorganized, agitated, and unreliable. Exxos was growing increasingly frustrated with them. In a thought that rippled across nearly a million identical robot minds, he wondered if it might be time just to trigger the entropy-freezing plan, to shatter and shut down the creatures of darkness and cut his own losses.

But not yet. He still needed the Shana Rei to accomplish other goals, and before the shadows were exterminated, he had to have as many robot counterparts as possible. He still required these insanely powerful allies. For now.

"Only one attack on Pergamus," he pushed. "We know from Ta-mo'l that the planet has few defenses, so our victory there will be easy. Through her eyes you have already seen the disease stockpiles locked in their vaults. And when we unleash those plagues on populated worlds, you know what those diseases will do."

In fact, Exxos wasn't sure whether or not the shadows understood pathogens and mortality rates. "Trust us," he said. "I have proved that we understand your need for destruction, so let us achieve that destruction for you. If we remove the agony of sentience by killing humans and Ildirans, you will then have more strength to fight Eternity's Mind. Think how it makes sense."

The creatures of darkness were so chaotic that Exxos was not sure they could understand cause and effect, but he hoped they would listen to him.

Finally, the pulsing inkblots agreed. "Yes. We will engulf Pergamus, seize the deadly diseases . . . and destroy the rest. Then we will loose all the plagues on humanity."

"Good," Exxos said. "That is a perfect plan."

88

TASIA TAMBLYN

After the heart-wrenching dismay from the destruction of Earth, Tasia found some joy in visiting her brother at Academ. Not only was Jess family, the two of them shared many experiences—wonderful ones as well as terrifying ones. They had both witnessed the destruction of worlds . . . more than once, in fact.

Rlinda insisted on joining Tasia and Robb as they shuttled over to the glowing comet. Most of the students had transferred away as a precautionary measure against the increased wental activity, but Jess and Cesca had stayed behind. Jess had sent Tasia a mysterious message. "I have a mission for you—I know you can help out."

Rlinda shook her head as the *Curiosity* docked in Academ's landing bay. "Strangeness after strangeness." She looked at the oddly shimmering ice walls. "I'd prefer a boring retirement where all I have to do is manage a restaurant and worry about Zachary Wisskoff insulting the customers." She sighed and looked at the silver capsule in her wide palm. "BeBob was always a calming influence. I'm glad he's resting in peace, but I wouldn't mind having him around right now."

The comet seemed alive and vibrant, and when Tasia inhaled, she smelled ozone in the processed air. Even if the elemental beings were allies, it was probably best that the Roamer children had gone back to Newstation. A few determined students and Teacher compies remained inside the comet, but Academ was mostly empty.

When Jess and Cesca came to greet them in the landing bay, Tasia ran to give her brother a hug. He wrapped his arms around her and swung her in an arc in the low gravity. Tasia felt like his young sister again, a spunky teenager at the family ice mines on Plumas.

"I see you're still getting into trouble," he said, "and leaving plenty of problems in your wake."

Robb looked around, blinking against the glow in the walls. "I remember when you two were charged with all that wental energy."

"It's not the same this time," Jess said. "The wentals are different now."

Cesca interrupted, "Everything is different since the Elemental War. I wish the wentals were back and strong. Then they could be fighting the Shana Rei with us."

Tasia said, "The Shana Rei are more dangerous than the hydrogues ever were. They're everywhere."

"We'll see if we can do something about that." Jess and Cesca led them through the empty corridors of Academ.

"These wentals are pure," Cesca insisted. "We can sense it, and there's something they need us to do."

Jess turned to his sister. "Something we need *you* to do, in your ship."

"We have the *Curiosity* and *Declan's Glory*," Rlinda said. "What do you need?"

"The wentals want you to deliver something to Fireheart Station."

Tasia and Robb looked at each other, then at Jess, raising their eyebrows. "Sure, we should make a trading run anyway."

Rlinda broke in, "It'll be good timing. You've heard the news? General Keah and Adar Zan'nh are bringing a giant military force there to kick some Shana Rei butt."

Robb held up a hand. "You're agreeing awfully fast. We don't even know what the mission is yet."

Tasia rolled her eyes. "If Jess asks, you know we're going to do it, Robb."

He sighed. "I suppose."

When they reached the main office, KA was attending to administrative details, securing files and temporarily shutting down the school. The office walls were bare ice, and the frozen wall glowed.

Cesca set an empty liter-sized canister on the desk, while Jess stepped up to the wall of ice. "This is what we need you to deliver to Fireheart."

He drew a square on the ice wall with his fingertip. The wentals reacted and melted a line of water in an eight-inch cube. Jess reached in to pull a perfectly cut block of ice from the wall. It held itself together through the will of the wentals, and once the cube was removed, the comet wall reshaped itself to fill the socket, leaving a smooth surface.

"Take this to the terrarium dome in Fireheart. The two green priests need it." Jess carried the block to the liter container, and the wental ice thawed of its own volition. Like an amoeba, the water flowed into the canister and filled it precisely.

Rlinda grabbed the container. "I'll deliver it. I've known little Celli for years."

"We'll take both ships and round up a load of special isotopes and new power blocks while we're there," Tasia said with a grin. "Sooner or later we're going to distribute through Handon Station. Kett Shipping has to support Xander and Terry, you know."

"I'm not sure how much is left of the company," Robb said. "I wonder how many of our ships got away from Earth. . . ."

Rlinda said, "We'll consolidate whatever we have. After all"— she held the container of wental water close—"Kett Shipping is still around as long as I'm still around. And the shadows haven't gotten me yet."

89

LEE ISWANDER

After being shunned by the Roamer clans, Lee Iswander returned to his extraction operations and pondered what to do next. The price of ekti was already falling—a good thing for the customers, he supposed, but certainly bad for business, his business in particular.

Iswander had been through it all before, and he had survived.

Alec Pannebaker looked distraught when Iswander arrived back at the facility, alone. The deputy's usually optimistic nature was more introspective. "I thought you should know, Chief—we've lost twenty-five workers in the past four days. Some gave notice, took their pay, and departed in their own ships. Others just disappeared into the night." He shook his head. "Damned unprofessional, if you ask me—complete lack of courtesy. I have enough people to run the crews, though, and we've kept producing ekti while you were gone."

"If we could only find a place to sell it . . ." Iswander said, disappointed with the bitterness in his voice.

Pannebaker scowled. "After all you've done for them, Chief, I'd hoped for a little more loyalty."

"I'd hoped for a lot more of everything. But I've run industries most of my life. There are unreliable employees and good employees." He looked up at his deputy. "You're one of the good ones, Mr. Pannebaker, don't ever forget that."

Pannebaker scratched his goatee, embarrassed by the compliment. "Well, I've always liked to take risks and do daredevil things." He forced a grin. "I never thought that staying by your side would be a risky thing."

Iswander studied the summaries of their operations, the daily

work logs. Ekti production was down—no surprise, due to the reduced workforce and, quite likely, because of diminished enthusiasm
among the employees. But it was still a respectable output of stardrive
fuel waiting to go to market. Surely somebody would need it.

He turned to go. "I'll be in my quarters, Mr. Pannebaker. I have
some business-development plans to write down."

"If you need a sounding board, sir, I'd be happy to listen. A lot of
our workers, even the loyal ones, want to know what's next. Iswander Industries has poured everything into these bloater-extraction
operations, but you always have another innovative idea up your
sleeve."

"You're right, I've had plenty of ideas in the past. Thank you for
your faith in me." Iswander wondered just how many brilliant and
innovative ideas one man was allowed to have in a lifetime.

He reached his quarters, which were cold, dark, and empty.
Londa had been away on Newstation for some time, and now this
place was his alone.

He scolded himself for his defeatist attitude. He still had money
squirreled away from his past investments; he had knowledge and
expertise and—as Pannebaker had just shown—he had good people
to implement his plans. But he just wasn't sure he had the energy to
start all over again.

He sealed the door, looked at the bright, clean rooms, and lifted
his chin with determination. He recited the mantra that he had said
aloud so many times in recent weeks. *A successful man fails more
times than an average man bothers to try.*

His workers believed in him—otherwise why would they have
followed him after Sheol? Why would they have stayed after the
terrible accusations leveled against him? Inertia? Yes, they had faith
in him, and so did his wife and son. He knew it, and he loved them
for it—even though he rarely showed his affection or his pride.

That was a failing on his part. A good leader always had to
encourage his troops, to acknowledge the things they did for him so
they would remain loyal. It was part of being a leader, but it was
also part of being human. Perhaps Iswander had spent far too much
time working on the former and not the latter.

He had taken his wife for granted, because she wasn't the sort of driven person he was. Now these quarters felt hollow, mere *rooms* instead of a *home*. He looked at the walls and saw the art prints there, the stylish furniture, the colorful decorations, the well-maintained kitchen unit, their bedchamber, all of which carried personal touches he had not bothered to notice before. These were not just quarters for sleeping during down time. Now that Londa was gone, the place was a museum that reminded him of what normal life should be. Oh, he knew Londa remained just as devoted to him as ever, and that she loved and adored him. He hoped she was happy where she was.

Arden was also his future, his hope. The young man was growing stronger, even though he likely did not enjoy the pressures heaped on him at Academ. Iswander believed that giving a person an easy road to success was also a road to disaster; Arden would understand that someday.

He made himself tea and heated a packet of spiced protein noodles, knowing he needed to eat, even though he didn't have much appetite. He sat in the empty chamber, chewing and thinking.

Elisa Enturi was also an exceptionally loyal worker, but sometimes loyalty could go too far, and now she was gone, too. Considering what she had done, he'd been forced to banish her, but if there had been any way to salvage the situation he would much rather have her here now. . . .

Nevertheless, he could rely on his own skills. He resolved to do so without feeling sorry for himself. Lee Iswander would find some way to reinvent himself. He would regain his respect in such a way that even the Roamer clans would have to admit that it was the greatest comeback story ever told . . . whatever that turned out to be.

Although he wasn't tired, Iswander knew he needed to sleep. But after he dimmed the lights, he just sat in the shadows and stared out the windowports, watching the extraction operations: pumping rigs, tankers, inspection pods, ekti-transport arrays. The activity gladdened him.

From this distance the operations looked marvelous, vibrant and successful. They were all he had now—along with his wife and son. Londa and Arden were his real legacy, and he had to leave them something worthy of the Iswander name. For now, he would tell his crews to keep working, to produce as much ekti-X as possible, because that was what *they did*. That was where they excelled.

Until his final chance fell apart, he was determined to squeeze every last drop of profit from these operations.

ELISA ENTURI

Relleker was a mess, as Elisa had expected. After learning about the salvage operations, she had flown here to join Xander and Terry's crew. She knew she could do the work; in fact, Elisa was convinced she could do anything that was necessary—preferably for someone who appreciated her efforts.

Unfortunately, doing "what was necessary" had led to her current situation, made her an outcast and an exile. A flare of anger toward Lee Iswander crossed her mind, only to be replaced by sad resolve. She had pondered much during the flight from Newstation to the Relleker system. Though it pained her, she couldn't deny that Iswander had made the proper decision to save himself and his company. He needed to have a scapegoat, a sacrificial lamb. And that was Elisa.

Still, it hurt her. Everyone was howling for her blood anyway, so he had made the right choice. With cold objectivity, she knew she would have done the same in his shoes, although she believed *loyalty* should be a commodity more valuable than profits.

But if Iswander had stood by Elisa, what then? He would have taken the fall along with her, and if he had refused to turn her in to the authorities, then there might well have been a war—one that she was sure Iswander Industries would lose.

No, allowing her to slip away and stay free was probably his best choice as well as her best chance in the long run, because she didn't have any good chances at all. . . .

Elisa had to make her own future, and in order to do so she would call in other favors. She had certainly earned enough of them during her years of hard work. By granting Xander Brindle and

Terry Handon exclusive ekti-X distribution rights, she had made them a fortune. They owed her. . . .

The planet Relleker was damaged and dead, its cloudy skies stained black. Smoke and wildfires still raged across the continents after the robots' devastator bombs, and only radioactive wastelands remained of the cities. The wreckage of ships created an obstacle course in orbit. As she flew in, she scanned the debris of CDF Mantas, the shrapnel of thousands of private and commercial vessels. She doubted many had gotten away.

Among the orbiting junk, she spotted more than a dozen active ships rounding up the largest remnants. She eavesdropped on their comm channels and, as expected, identified them as Roamer salvage ships, tugs gathering semi-intact vessels and large hull sections, which would be delivered to Rendezvous. Exosuited figures flitted about, stripping out engine components, disengaging large modules, and setting them free so they could drift to corral points.

Elisa maintained radio silence as she cruised closer, still observing, still listening. One group of people herded small drifting objects and arranged them in a stable array, tethered together. For a moment, judging by their general shape, she thought they were large ekti cylinders; then she realized they were human bodies, stiff corpses retrieved from the destroyed ships, now frozen in space.

Elisa guessed she would have to start at the bottom if she meant to work for Xander and Terry. Maybe there was no deeper bottom than being forced to retrieve cadavers and stack them in space. If she were asked to do that, she would accept the job, because she had to start somewhere . . . but she would demand respect, no matter what. She had lost too much already.

So many Roamer ships were flitting around the reclamation operations that no one noticed Elisa at first; they all simply assumed she had come to work just as the rest of them had. A smiling but harried Xander Brindle came over the general comm channel. "It's slim pickings around here, and a lot of these ships are just lemons—but we're going to make lemonade, to use a sour old cliché." He chuckled at his own joke.

Terry Handon's voice broke in, "I hate to point out, Xander, but there'll be a lot more salvage at Earth."

Xander balked. "I'm . . . I'm not ready for that yet. Thank the Guiding Star that my parents and Rlinda Kett got away."

Terry came onscreen, taking a seat next to his partner in the *Verne*'s piloting deck. "But about five billion people didn't."

Elisa frowned. Something had happened on Earth? She had been out of communication contact since leaving Newstation. After she tapped into the appalling database reports and learned of the Shana Rei attack there, she decided it was time to announce herself. "If you need someone to manage operations at Earth, I'll do the job, Xander Brindle—you know I'll do it. Put me in charge if no one else wants the responsibility."

On the screen, he recognized her with a surge of astonishment. "Elisa Enturi, what the hell are you doing here?"

"I'm joining your salvage operations. I am no longer employed by Iswander Industries. I gave you ekti-distribution across the Spiral Arm, and now I request the same consideration in return. I need a position." She hardened her expression and leaned closer to the screen. "You know I'm competent. Let me work for you."

Terry cringed. "Not in a million years!"

"I was looking for a slightly less permanent position than that," she said.

A bearded old clan leader broke in on the comm channel. "Shizz, Xander—you know who that is? Suck it down a black hole, that's Elisa Enturi! The bitch wiped out the clan Duquesne operations. She's got blood on her hands, and a price on her head."

Elisa was immediately alert. "Clan Duquesne provoked me, and it's none of your business."

"It is our business," Terry said. "All the Roamer clans want you brought to justice. We have to take you in."

Xander was flushed. "You attacked and tried to kill my parents!"

More than twenty Roamer ships raced toward her vessel, converging in among the debris. They were not large battleships, but she knew that every Roamer craft had significant defensive weaponry. All their systems were activated.

But Elisa's ship had weaponry too.

ZOE ALAKIS

Tom Rom's new Klikiss samples were interesting, but useless for Zoe's purposes. The royal jelly specimens taken from alien cadavers were ineffective as a treatment for the more virulent strain of the Onthos plague.

Safe inside her sterile chamber, Zoe studied the records again. Tom Rom had taken many images of the Klikiss ruins on Llaro, but she didn't care about Klikiss architecture, culture, or history. With the insect race gone from the Spiral Arm, what did that matter?

What fascinated her was the alien plague itself, the viral specimen he had brought in his own bloodstream as the plague raged through his body; it was the closest he had ever come to death, and he had done it for her. Responding to news of the exotic disease spreading through the derelict Onthos space city, he had arrived too late. Every member of clan Reeves was dead, and the only infected person still alive had been Orli Covitz. Zoe didn't know the details, but he had obtained the specimen from Orli, and gotten infected in the process.

True to his promise, he had used his last efforts to return to Pergamus and give Zoe what she'd requested—this sample, which she now held in her hands.

Though it went against her better judgment, she studied the specimen inside her sterile dome. Tom Rom would have been extremely upset if he knew the risk Zoe took when she transferred a sealed vial teeming with the mutated plague organism.

She had already studied the medical data from clan Reeves, as well as ancient archival information about the original Onthos epidemic, all of which she had gained from King Peter and Queen

Estarra in exchange for the Pergamus database on Prince Reynald's illness. His debilitating microfungus infection was far less interesting to her than the Onthos plague, but even though the Confederation had destroyed Rakkem as promised, Zoe disliked the idea of making bargains. It left her vulnerable, and she didn't want to give up proprietary information.

Zoe kept the sealed plague specimen in her private chamber. Although she wore gloves and a breathing mask, she knew that would not be sufficient if the specimen got loose. She normally kept herself so protected, so perfectly clean against all deadly organisms. Now that she had this sample vial right in front of her, she felt as if she were facing a monster. It gave her a secret thrill.

She admired the rare plague organism more than she liked to admit. Of all the germs, viruses, and parasites that proliferated by killing human beings, this one was the most perfect lethal organism—and Pergamus was filled with lethal organisms. Zoe had been obsessed with pathogens for most of her life. How could she not be enthralled with this one?

Zoe was annoyed to be disturbed from her study of the marvelous specimen when the perimeter sensors around Pergamus set off alarms. She wondered what intruder was bothering them now. Probably some pathetic dying person who wanted her to offer a magic cure, as if Pergamus sold such things like Rakkem did. The Pergamus mercenary forces always managed to drive the intruders away. Nothing good ever came of unannounced visitors.

The alarms were louder than ever, more insistent, and Zoe caught her breath as she glanced at the screen. In an image taken from orbit, she saw a gash open up in space. Inky black shadows spilled out like the oozing blood of night, and black hexagonal cylinders came through, surrounded by a cocoon of shadows.

A sharp cold flowed down her spine. Tom Rom had warned her of the Shana Rei threat, but Zoe had never taken it seriously. Not here. Now she stared in disbelief. The threat couldn't possibly be real.

Like angry hornets from a smashed nest, black robot ships swarmed out by the thousands. Her mercenary fleet shouted alarms, and Pergamus facility-lockdown systems engaged. Klaxons rang out, and flashing magenta lights strobed through the corridors and sealed labs, calling everyone to full emergency status.

Tom Rom's voice crackled across the open intercom, barking orders to the mercenary ships. "Stand your ground—attack the intruders! Do not let them approach Pergamus." His command was bold but absurd. Her mercenary fleet was only large enough to drive away curiosity seekers; they could never stand against this.

To their credit, five mercenary ships plunged toward the robot vessels, opening fire. Their jazers even destroyed two robot ships before the defenders were vaporized—all of them. Her other ten perimeter patrol ships turned about and fled the system.

The shadow cloud headed straight for Pergamus.

Zoe was aware of what had happened at Earth and Relleker. The black robots had devastated those planets, obliterated every city on the surface. The small Pergamus outpost didn't stand a chance.

The Shana Rei cloud expanded as it came closer. The first group of robot ships plunged into the poisonous atmosphere, but they did not open fire, did not drop devastation bombs. This was obviously a different kind of assault from before. The invaders did not mean just to destroy—not at first. The black robot ships were descending to the surface for some other purpose.

Zoe felt a deeper cold of terror and anger as she guessed that they intended to seize the assets of Pergamus. All the plague samples.

Tom Rom's face appeared on the screen. "I am coming for you, Zoe. I'll get you out of here—no matter what it takes."

Then she heard the first explosion. It resonated through the main outer dome—but it was not from a robot attack. Tom Rom had detonated a shaped charge that blasted through the first of the seventeen decontamination locks. He was breaching the barriers. He was going to rush inside her sterile dome and save her.

She knew he would.

She got ready.

92

GENERAL NALANI KEAH

It felt damned good to be flying the *Kutuzov* alongside the Solar Navy warliners again. General Keah felt strong and confident as she looked out at the forty-nine magnificent alien ships, with their exotic design and extended solar-sail fins. After the ass-kicking she had received at Earth and Relleker, she needed some real payback.

Sitting on the bridge of her Juggernaut, she let the excitement and anger build. She leaned forward to address the screen image of Adar Zan'nh, who stood in the command nucleus of his own flagship. "I feel good about this, Z. It'll be a sucker punch to the damn shadows—a real kick in the balls."

Zan'nh seemed confused by her comment. "I'm not certain that such anatomical references are applicable to the Shana Rei."

"It's a metaphor, Z. Don't be so literal." Come to think of it, she had never asked about the testicular arrangement of Ildirans either, although she supposed the appropriate parts must be similar, since they could interbreed with humans.

The *Kutuzov* and the *Okrun* were the CDF's two remaining Juggernauts, and she had forty-five Manta cruisers that were functional enough to fight. After the retreat from Earth, CDF engineers had worked around the clock, using the commercial spacedock facilities at Theroc to make repairs. She had made her priorities clear. "It doesn't have to be pretty, but it does have to work—at least for one more engagement." All of her soldiers knew the stakes.

They had rounded up a good portion of the ships that were still available to fight for the Confederation. Some remained at Theroc to defend the capital, but Keah—and everyone else for that matter—knew that *all* of the remaining defenses would not be sufficient against a frontal attack from the Shana Rei. They had to defeat the shadows some other way, and this was it. The mission into the void would be an all-or-nothing gamble. They would never have a second chance to hit the Shana Rei by surprise.

A substantial and intimidating fleet of nearly a hundred battleships, Confederation and Ildiran, was on its way to the nebula. Ahead of them, Fireheart blazed in its ionized splendor, and at its core burned a cluster of gargantuan stars that ignited the entire sea of gases.

"Approaching the dust boundary, General," said Lieutenant Tait. "It might get a little bumpy."

"Plenty of Roamers fly through with their junk-heap ships all the time," she said. "Stay steady and keep our shields at full strength."

The Ildiran warliners retracted their solar-sail fins, and the strike force plunged through the boundary where photonic pressure from the core stars had piled up interstellar dust. The passage was somewhat rough, but the hundred ships held on and passed safely through into the diffuse sea.

Keah snorted. "That was nothing more than potty ripples compared to getting away from Earth a week ago."

"When you put it that way, General . . ." said her first officer.

She had seen a diagram of the Roamer facilities inside Fireheart Station, but she was even more impressed when she saw floating frames covered with stretched-out energy films for power blocks, huge scoops to harvest exotic isotopes, as well as the scientific, admin, and habitation units.

"Radiation levels are high, sir," said Sensor Chief Saliba, "but tolerable, with a little extra shielding."

"Roamers live here all the time," said Keah. "If we find a way to face the shadows, a little ambient radiation is going to be the least of your concerns."

No one disagreed with her.

Alongside the CDF fleet, the Ildiran warliners cruised along in perfect formation. Keah was surprised that Adar Zan'nh didn't show off with fancy skyparade maneuvers. She had fought many engagements with the Adar; she respected and even liked him. They were colleagues as well as rivals.

"We're about to go down in history, Z," she transmitted as they flew toward the admin hub. "You think I'll be part of your Saga of Seven Suns?"

"If anyone survives to record it," said Zan'nh. "We brought five rememberers, including Rememberer Anton. I hope that some are able to chronicle the event for the sake of history."

"Right . . . for the sake of history," Keah said. "Not to mention that it would be nice to survive."

"That as well," the Adar said.

Some of the military ships approached the Fireheart admin hub while Admiral Haroun's *Okrun* patrolled the nebula and circled the black maw where the nebula gases disappeared. General Keah and Adar Zan'nh went aboard to meet with Station Chief Alu and review the images Kotto Okiah had taken in his scout expedition, where he'd found the dormant Shana Rei hiding in their void.

Keah entered Chief Alu's designated meeting room, joined by Adar Zan'nh and the human historian Anton Colicos, who captured an image of both Keah and Zan'nh. "For posterity. You know that this could be a pivotal expedition."

"I hope it's a damned successful one," Keah muttered, then looked around the room. Howard Rohandas and Shareen Fitzkellum were sitting there for the meeting, both of them clearly nervous. Keah was surprised. "They're just kids!"

"Intelligent and innovative ones," Shareen said, indignant. "Believe me, you'll want us along with you when you go in there."

"We have studied all the void data more than anyone else," Howard added. "We're your best assets."

Keah snorted. "I never agreed to take two teenagers aboard the *Kutuzov*."

"But you will," Shareen said. "No one knows that other dimension better than we do. We've studied every bit of data that came back from Kotto's survey craft. We've been analyzing it ever since."

Howard said, "Kotto wouldn't let us go along last time, and maybe we could have saved him. We won't make that mistake twice."

"Before our strike force enters that dimensional space, we will want to know the hazards Kotto Okiah found," said Zan'nh. "I understand he did not survive? We should be prepared."

Keah nodded. "Right. How do we protect ourselves against whatever the shadows used to fry Kotto's brain?"

"The Shana Rei didn't cause the surge in him," Shareen said. "That was another thing entirely, a different presence . . . separate from the shadows. Something he called Eternity's Mind."

"It's quite clear from the mission records," Howard added. "He intentionally sought it out."

Keah muttered, "Great, another threat to look forward to."

Zan'nh looked over at her. "Are you having second thoughts about the mission, General? Should we perhaps send only one battleship into the void and see what happens?"

"That would defeat the purpose of a full-on surprise attack. This isn't the time to dip our pinky toes into the water."

Shareen said, "I was worried about all of us being zapped by Eternity's Mind, like Kotto, but he survived in the void for a long time without being affected. It wasn't until he intentionally connected to that other presence, opened himself to a flood of knowledge, that he was harmed."

"If we do not initiate a contact with Eternity's Mind, we should be safe," Howard said.

"Hell, I'm only interested in the Shana Rei," Keah said. "And for an opportunity like this, we'll take the risk. It's the best chance I've seen so far." She swallowed in a dry throat as she thought of her failure to protect Earth.

"We can thank Kotto for it," Shareen said. "And Howard and I *are* going along."

Keah looked at the two. "All right, if you two can contribute, then I'll let you come along. But I can't guarantee your safety any more than I can promise any of my soldiers will come back alive."

Shareen nodded. "And we still want to go along."

Keah turned to the Adar. "Well, Z, let's rally our ships and make our plan. Next stop, into the void." She gave him a hard grin. "How else are we going to get the Shana Rei?"

RLINDA KETT

The *Voracious Curiosity* and *Declan's Glory* headed off to the Fireheart nebula on the mission Jess and Cesca had given them. Even though the two ships flew close together, they had no direct communication while using the Ildiran stardrive. In an emergency, either pilot could send an alert pulse, and they would drop out of faster-than-light travel, so they could confer.

Rlinda carried the glowing wental water that they were supposed to deliver. She knew how important and how powerful the liquid was, and she hoped the green priests would know what to do with it.

Flying alone in *Declan's Glory*, Rlinda found herself stroking the capsule of BeBob's ashes. She still had trouble believing her favorite ex-husband would drop dead of an aneurysm as he crossed the street. "A strange ending after all the crazy adventures we both survived, BeBob." She shook her head, then placed the capsule on the console in front of her.

Since that time, Rlinda had lost some weight, and she had grown much older. But she knew that Captain Branson Roberts would still have found her attractive. He'd been wiry, scruffy, even goofy-looking, but she loved him anyway. "How I miss you now . . ."

Alone in her ship, Rlinda had a lot of time to think, and too much thinking time was not necessarily a good thing. She had so many memories, so many things to do, and not a lot of regrets (but some). She generally lived in the present; she loved life and decided to make the most of it. She stuck to that. Rlinda was a sociable person, but now she was in a big empty ship. She leaned back in the expanded piloting chair, regarded the silver capsule. "I don't like to sit around feeling sorry for myself or mulling things too much."

She got up and went to the *Declan*'s woefully insufficient galley and looked in dismay at the stored food there. "How can anyone survive with this?" She glanced back at the capsule, knowing BeBob had never paid much attention to food, despite her best efforts to get him to appreciate the finer things. "Well, I'm a resourceful person, and I can make the best of it. Certainly enough to cook a meal for one."

Eventually, she decided to tear open several prepackaged meals and deconstruct the ingredients so she could cook up something edible. She managed that . . . just barely.

As she ate, she thought about Prince Reynald, whom she affectionately called "Raindrop." She had helped the young man see the best medical specialists on Earth, but from the reports she'd heard, he was growing much worse, and there was no cure in sight. Unlike BeBob's sudden unexpected death, poor Raindrop's suffering was long and drawn-out . . . and woefully premature.

She sighed, thinking of the dear boy. She tapped a finger on the silver capsule. "Once we're done at Fireheart, BeBob, I'm going to see him on Theroc, just to give him a hug if nothing else." She wiped her mouth with a napkin and gathered up the dirty dishes from her not-awful meal. "And I owe Xander and Terry a visit, too—we should see their new trading hub at Rendezvous."

In fact, she needed to do a lot of things, and Rlinda decided to keep a list—a bucket list, she supposed. She pocketed the capsule again. "You never know how long you might remain alive. A bucket list is something to take seriously." There were so many things she had wanted to do with BeBob.

That was the problem with being alone—having too much time to think.

Two days from Fireheart Station, Rlinda detected something ahead that was strange enough to catch her attention. "Anomalies" often turned out to be dangerous, and she considered just racing past without drawing any attention to herself. But she also wanted to know what it was.

Nearby, Tasia and Robb cruised along in the *Voracious Curiosity*. Rlinda had no doubt they were having a fine time together. She sent a communication ping for the *Curiosity* to drop into normal space again so they could take a quick look at whatever had distorted their sensors ahead. She shut down her own stardrive, and the *Curiosity* dropped out immediately thereafter. Robb and Tasia had spotted the anomaly, too.

When the ships found themselves drifting close to an uncharted dark nebula, the roiling shadow cloud struck fear in Rlinda's heart. "Never should've stopped," she said. "Better get out of here before they detect us!"

"Wait," Tasia interrupted. "Something's happening. Look at the fringes, use Doppler scanners."

"It's collapsing, not expanding," Robb added. "The implosion velocity is off the charts."

Rlinda realized that the large black nebula was indeed condensing, its outer fringes falling inward, as if surrounded by a giant clenching fist. Rlinda could see one—and only one—of the long ebony cylinders inside. The fearsome Shana Rei ship was broken, its long crystalline sides cracked, shattered.

In the middle of the collapsing gas cloud, a ruddy ember shone out as nuclear reactions ignited inside a proto-star, brightening as more and more dark matter fell into the center of mass, adding fuel. The new star began to burn.

"Shizz, would you look at that!" Tasia said. "A hundred sun bombs wouldn't blast away that much of a shadow cloud."

"It's not sun bombs," Rlinda said. "Some other force is crushing that black nebula."

"Whatever it is, I'm rooting for it," Robb said. "Anything that squashes the Shana Rei is a friend of mine."

The two ships took extensive images so they could show the Roamers at Fireheart Station, but Rlinda was impatient. "Nothing more we can do here. Come on, we've got a mission to finish."

"Agreed," said Tasia.

They broke communication and activated their stardrives again. *Declan's Glory* and the *Voracious Curiosity* streaked away from the dying shadow cloud and headed toward Fireheart.

ARITA

Arita's fascination with exotic plant and animal (or "other") species had begun at a young age. She had studied everything about
the Theron worldforest, from the tiniest insects to the enormous
worldtrees. She was fascinated by the wondrous possibilities of
biology—and now she knew that somewhere, in one of those countless specimens, lay a cure for her brother.

In the past two years, she had traveled to see other peculiar life-
forms the Spiral Arm had to offer. She'd studied the Whistlers on
Eljiid, and she'd been to the hanging kelp-vine gardens on Atoa;
she'd seen centuries-old hive mountains built by myriad tiny arach-
nids. Each new discovery fascinated her.

But the bloaters were something else entirely.

Garrison Reeves flew the *Prodigal Son* to an extraction operation
near Ikbir run by clan Kellum. "They'll be amenable to unexpected
visitors," he said.

"Unlike the Iswander operations, where Elisa nearly killed us,"
Orli said.

En route, Arita spent a lot of time getting to know Orli, feeling a
close kinship with the other woman. They both felt that powerful
awakening presence in the cosmos; they both heard the throbbing
voice inside their minds. It seemed ominous, yet supportive; infinitely
wise, yet also lost . . . and there was desperation as well as pain.
Arita didn't know what to do.

When the *Prodigal Son* arrived at the busy Kellum extraction operations, Collin cradled his potted treeling so he could transmit his
observations back to the other green priests. He had never been
away from Theroc before, and everything amazed him, but he tried

to do his job in maintaining communication with the other green priests.

Seth and DD pressed close to the windowports, both eager to see. Nearly a hundred Kellum ships hung among the drifting nodules. Pumping apparatus like enormous metal mosquitoes pierced the bloater membranes to harvest the stardrive fuel inside. Arita saw bright illumination banks and the darting lights of scurrying tugs and cargo haulers, tank array frameworks, a headquarters ship.

Garrison activated the comm. "Calling Kellum ops. This is Garrison Reeves in the *Prodigal Son* with Orli Covitz and Arita, daughter of the King and Queen, as well as a green priest and a few other visitors. We're here to have a look at the bloaters, if you don't mind."

"Garrison and Orli, by damn!" said a gruff, bearded man on the comm screen. "If it wasn't for you, we wouldn't have found this cluster. Come in and keep us company. We'd be happy to show the Princess around, if there's something she'd like to see."

As the *Prodigal Son* headed toward the Kellum headquarters ship, Orli and Arita were far more interested in the bloaters. Orli rubbed her temples. "Can you hear it?"

Collin closed his eyes, held his treeling, and concentrated, but shook his head. "Nothing."

Arita didn't need to make much effort. "It's there—not exactly words, but thoughts and images."

Orli added in a rush, "I sense a great grandeur, but also fear. Even pain."

"Something's hurting them," Arita said.

"Is it the Shana Rei?" Seth said. He turned to DD. "Are there any shadow clouds nearby? I want to hear what they're hearing."

The compy said, "The *Prodigal Son* only has basic sensors, Seth Reeves. I cannot pick up whatever Orli and Arita are hearing."

Arita stared at the hundreds of quiet, drifting nodules, formless sacks in a main cluster with outliers extending like bread crumbs off into space. Orli came up beside her at the main windowport. "The outliers eventually connect to other bloater clusters across interstellar space. There's no telling how many there could be, or how far they're linked."

"Like the trees in the worldforest mind," said Collin.

Arita stared at her friend. "Very much like that—only bigger."

Once their equipment was in place, the Kellum operations had expanded with reckless energy. Zhett Kellum and Patrick Fitzpatrick had deployed every possible piece of machinery to extract ekti-X from the bloater sacks. In only a short time they had already harvested nearly half of the cluster.

Orli's face showed a deep concern. She whispered to the windowport, at the strange silent nodules. "What are you trying to say to us? We're here. What is it you want?"

Arita gritted her teeth, trying to concentrate, shoulder-to-shoulder with Orli. She felt a booming need . . . and an anger, and a knowledge that she could not grasp. "These bloaters are more than sacks of stardrive fuel."

Roamer scout pods flitted around. Several small ships escorted the *Prodigal Son* to where the operations were busiest.

Suddenly one of the nodules sparked and flashed, triggering an adjacent flare. Then several others across the expanded cluster blinked with bright flashes. With each flare, Arita felt the connection in her mind intensify.

While she stared in deep concentration, Arita thought about what Collin had said about the interconnected trees in the verdani mind, the clusters of bloaters, the sparkling signals, and she caught her breath. "I know what they are! The bloaters aren't just drifting plankton. They are . . . giant *cells*, like neurons. Millions of them connected in a network across space."

Orli's mouth dropped open with understanding. "That's it! They're cells, all interconnected into a large . . ." She fumbled for words.

Arita answered for her. "It's a *mind*. An immense mind spread out over the galaxy . . . and now it's finally awakening."

CHAPTER

95

EXXOS

The shadows descended upon the disease library of Pergamus, but they let Exxos do the dangerous work.

The black robot fleet, with thousands more ships than were necessary for such a small target, closed in to capture the virulent specimens held inside the domes. Exxos had promised the Shana Rei that this one relatively minor sortie would give them a lethal biological arsenal to kill more victims than dozens of planetary massacres like Relleker, Wythira, and Earth ever would. Although he and his counterparts relished the feel of actual blood on their pincers and the sound of screams, merely inflicting death was a sufficient reward in itself.

To achieve their objective, the robots needed to keep the disease specimens intact, but the human personnel in the facility were all fair game. Exxos did not plan to leave any of them alive—except for Tamo'l, who was already connected to the Shana Rei. She would be retrieved alive and then imprisoned inside an entropy bubble like Rod'h, where she would be analyzed, tested . . . dissected if necessary.

The other victims, though, were going to be mere sport.

For a world containing so many dangerous specimens, Pergamus had laughably insignificant security, and the black robots would easily dismantle it all. The black ships swooped in, opening fire. The mercenary ships were there to scare away occasional interlopers, not a full military fleet. Some of the defenders took potshots, racing in and opening fire, but robot ships overwhelmed them and tore them to shreds. The rest of the mercenaries fled without even trying to put up a fight.

Exxos knew his primary goal was to retrieve the biological specimens from the laboratory domes. His secondary goal was to kill the
researchers, while the lowest priority was to chase down the few
straggler mercenaries. He realized, however, that he had more than
enough robot fighters to accomplish all three of those goals. Therefore, a hundred Exxos counterparts streaked after the fleeing security ships and hunted them down one by one.

The shadow cloud swelled in space, looming like an eclipse over
Pergamus. The hex cylinders waited there, pulsing with entropy. The
Shana Rei throbbed out, calling to Tamo'l, who was trapped inside
one of the domes below. She struggled to drive them away, but Exxos
would find her. If not, the shadows would simply come in and
engulf her, as they had captured Rod'h.

This isolated planet had no standing military force, and the
creatures of darkness could have taken their time and englobed the
entire world in hex plates as they had done at Kuivahr. But that was
not necessary. Exxos and his robots would achieve their goal with a
straightforward ground assault. Hundreds of angular ships swooped
down to the surface.

The toxic Pergamus atmosphere would not bother them. The
angular vessels landed on the desolate landscape, and the beetle-
like robots emerged from their ships and advanced on clusters of
finger-like legs. The soft and fragile humans who huddled inside
their domes had no place to go, nowhere to run. Crimson optical
sensors glowed bright as hundreds of Exxos advanced toward the
complex.

As he moved toward the surface domes, Exxos picked up different communication bands, heard the shouts for help, the frantic distress signals, all of which were pointless. He filtered through the
overlapping conversations, used them to identify specific targets—
although that mattered little, since Exxos intended to conquer it all,
kill them all.

High above the planet, robot ships surrounded the Orbital Research Spheres, which also contained deadly plague specimens worth
retrieving. Nothing would be wasted. Each such disease would have
its use. The scientists trapped inside shouted for rescue, but the black
ships closed around the spheres. Robots would slice open the satel-

lite labs, kill the scientists with explosive decompression, and take whatever they could find.

Then Exxos realized that the panicked ORS transmissions were more than the mere fear of capture. One of his counterparts— another robot that was exactly *him*—on the outside of an orbiting sphere, worked at disassembling the airlock hatch. Other robots swarmed over the laboratory globe.

Then they simultaneously understood that the emergency sterilization procedures had been initiated inside the spheres. The countdown was nearly finished.

A voice from the surface crossed the comm, addressing the trapped ORS scientists. "This is Tom Rom. I appreciate your efforts. There is obviously no escape, but we dare not let your specimens fall into enemy hands. The flash will be swift."

The scientists screamed, and then sterilization bursts rippled like blossoms of intense energy, one after another after another. High-intensity gamma-ray bursts flooded the orbiting laboratories, vaporized the humans inside, destroyed the equipment, and annihilated every single microorganism. By the time the robots broke through the hulls, the laboratory spheres were dead and completely useless. Exxos was infuriated.

Now, on the surface, as he stood outside the nearest dome, he extended his cutting tools and powerful pincers, meaning to rip through the metal walls to reach their specimen vaults before the prizes could all be disintegrated.

Four humans in silvery exosuits emerged from the dome. Carrying long jazer-pulse rifles, they opened fire on the encroaching black robots. Exxos felt three of himself die, all circuitry overloaded; even their shielded cybernetics could not withstand the jazers. But many more robots surged forward, and the desperate human defenders fell back and continued to fire. They killed four more robots before they themselves were torn to ribbons of flesh and protective fabric.

Exxos continued cutting through the armored wall of the lab dome, ripping through the metal plates, slicing apart structural beams. He didn't bother to use the sealed doors, which might have been booby-trapped. Instead, the robots tore directly through the wall, and as soon as they breached the barrier, poisonous atmosphere flooded in.

Exxos and his counterparts marched inside, where they would find all the biological weapons they needed to obliterate the human race.

CHAPTER

96

TOM ROM

The robot invasion force swarmed over the Pergamus domes, and Tom Rom could do nothing to stop them. With such numbers and weaponry they would easily blast and tear their way through any armored walls. The trapped researchers were desperate to find some way to evacuate, yet they had no place to go. Saving them was not Tom Rom's priority.

But he would save Zoe—at all costs.

Barricaded behind seventeen quarantine layers, isolation doors, and airtight barricades, she should have been the safest person on Pergamus, but Tom Rom saw the robots' relentless march, watched how they peeled open the research domes like ripe fruit. No, even her central isolation dome would not protect her. He had to rescue her. He didn't have much time.

Since he had helped develop and install the interlock systems himself, he could at least override the flash-sterilization procedures designed to purge all life inside each dome in the event of a breach. Feeling the urgent need to get to Zoe, he deactivated the sensors so that when he blasted through the walls, he wouldn't trigger a complete self-destruct.

He pressed a shaped charge against the next interlock, applied protective dampening seals to his ears, then retreated to safety. After he heard the thump of the explosion and the groan of collapsing metal, he raced back in before the smoke had cleared. He used a makeshift crowbar to peel away the breached barricade. Then he ran to the next wall, applied another charge.

Fifteen layers to go.

High above, the shadow cloud eclipsed the sky, much different from the Shana Rei threat he had experienced at Kuivahr. Here at Pergamus, the creatures of darkness did not try to encapsulate the planet. Instead, the black nebula simply loomed there while the robot marauders did their work.

Hordes of beetle-like machines scuttled across the landscape. Tom Rom pushed aside any debilitating panic that would interfere with his efficiency. No time for that. There were so many steps—so many impossible steps—involved in getting to Zoe.

He broke through three more walls, kept pushing his way deeper.

And even after he broke through all those protective barriers, he still had to take her back out, get to his ship, then escape from Pergamus, in the midst of an overwhelming attack.

He blasted wall after wall, ever closer to the center. On the intercom he said, "Five levels to go, Zoe. Be ready." He systematically worked his way through more layers.

Zoe had emerged from her dome only two times since sealing herself inside: the first time, when she'd flown up to the Orbital Research Sphere to see him as he lay dying from the Onthos plague, and the second time when she had gone to Theroc to bargain with King Peter and Queen Estarra for Iswander's plague data.

This time it wasn't by her choice. Tom Rom would force her to go, if necessary. He had to take her out of here.

He blasted through the next barricade, and the next. The smoke, residual explosive fumes, and hot metal made it hard for him to see or move. Tom Rom burned his hands as he pried the wall away, but he didn't feel the pain. He kept moving, muttering under his breath, "I'm coming, Zoe."

He realized that the black robots could have just vaporized the entire facility from the air, but instead they pursued a ground assault. Therefore, he concluded that they had come here to steal the deadly diseases for some purpose of their own. He understood how lethal the specimens were and realized that these enemies of humanity would likely use them to kill billions. He felt obligated to stop them, if possible—but only after he saved Zoe. She was his first priority, and he didn't even consider rationalizing why.

When the robot attack had first begun, Tom Rom used the admin console to prepare the Pergamus defenses. He triggered the sterilization shutdown routines for all the Orbital Research Spheres, because he knew they were easily vulnerable. He was deaf to the pleas of the isolated researchers in space; their lives had been forfeit from the moment the shadow cloud arrived, so he wasted no time with guilt. Tom Rom decided they would prefer a gamma-ray flash to being torn apart by Klikiss robots. When the orbiting labs detonated, the deadliest Pergamus specimens were eradicated.

Here on the surface, hundreds of black robots had already broken into the first armored dome, a section devoted to cancer research. Cancer was a disease deadly to humanity, but not contagious and nothing the robots or the Shana Rei could weaponize— but they didn't know that yet. He would let the robots be distracted while he rescued Zoe.

After blasting through the next sequence of levels, he used the intercom, shouting to be heard over the constant alarms. "Zoe, stay away from the hatch—I'm going to blow it open. Take whatever shelter you can find." He gave her a few seconds, but he could afford no more time.

When the blast tore down the final wall, he charged in, ducking low through the smoke. Previously, in order to join Zoe, he had needed to endure hours of decontamination procedures. Now he had forced his way through all seventeen barriers in less than twenty minutes.

While the smoke cleared, Zoe rose from behind the shelter of her desk, scrambling to put a breathing mask over her face. She looked pale. "I don't want to leave here."

"I know." Tom Rom grabbed her arm. "But you have to. I won't let these things kill you."

She didn't resist. She simply needed to hear him tell her this was their best, their only choice. She grabbed a small duffel that she had stuffed with a few things she insisted on taking along. "Then I'm ready." She was shuddering. "I thought this place would stay protected and safe."

Tom Rom said, "Now it's neither. We'll have to go out on our own. You and I have survived that way before. We can do it again."

She groaned. "But Pergamus . . . all those years, all those specimens. We can't just leave my collection!"

Tom Rom urged her toward the hole in the wall. "But we will. We've got to get to my ship."

They were probably already out of time—and yet, realizing why the robots must have come here, a heavier responsibility made him hesitate. "Wait for me, Zoe," he called, and ran to the main controls inside her central chamber. Time to set the sterilization routines throughout all the facilities.

He knew the access and emergency triggers, and he couldn't let these specimens fall into the hands of the inhuman enemy. He set the self-destruct mechanisms, timed vaporization blasts that would erase every cell, every virus, and every data set in the domes.

When designing the system, Tom Rom had required each dome to be triggered separately, so that a lone terrorist couldn't destroy the entire facility in a single attack. Now, though, the interlocks worked against him and caused a maddening delay. His fingers were trembling, but he steadied himself. He didn't have time for panic. Panic could cause mistakes.

When each of the fifteen domes was prepped, he adjusted the countdown to give enough time to reach his ship—barely enough time.

Overhead, the Shana Rei shadow cloud loomed in the sky as if intending to smother the planet. Black tendrils reached down toward the surface.

He joined Zoe out in the corridor and forced her along. Running, they ducked through one blasted wall after another. Carrying her duffel, she was disoriented, but not just from the terror and the chaos. She simply hadn't been outside her chamber often enough to know the layout of her own research dome.

"My ship's engines are powerful, and I know how to fly. I have the incentive." He gave her a hard look. "I have to warn you, though, we could just as well die on our way out."

Zoe ran along. "You'll save me."

He steeled himself and silently swore that he would not let her down.

97

XANDER BRINDLE

The Relleker salvage field was already a disaster, but Elisa Enturi's arrival made the situation worse. Xander felt a deep chill go down his spine. He turned to Terry. "What the hell is she doing here?"

Terry was aghast. "Kett Shipping broke all ties with Iswander Industries because of her—and now she wants . . . a job? We're just supposed to forget everything she did?"

Roamer salvage ships closed around Elisa's ship, which hung there, waiting. Xander couldn't comprehend what she could have been thinking.

"Our unemployment situation isn't that desperate," Xander muttered. He gathered his courage and opened the comm. "Elisa, I don't know what you had in mind, but you're an outlaw and a murderer. There's no place for you here."

A grizzled, hatchet-faced old woman, Annie D, grumbled on the comm screen, "Take her into custody and haul her ass back to New-station where she can face justice. We've got enough ships." Annie D wore an eyepatch over her right eye, which she had lost due to ocular cancer. Med techs could have replaced the eye, but she seemed to prefer the affectation of the patch. Now, her visage looked fierce.

From his battered ship, old Omar Selise barked, "Stand down, Enturi—we outgun you twenty to one, and we have no incentive to exercise restraint. The Duquesnes were friends of mine."

As more ships surrounded Elisa, she activated her own defensive weapons. Xander was surprised at how utterly unrepentant the woman seemed. "You can try to capture me, but you won't be happy with how it turns out. I did not come here for a firefight. I offered my services to work."

Xander opened the comm and used his most reasonable voice, which he doubted would be sufficient. "Elisa, we'll escort you to Rendezvous, see that you get a fair hearing. No need for shooting."

Terry added, "Would you rather serve a prison sentence or have your ship join the shrapnel here at Relleker? These people are ready to shoot."

In response, Elisa opened fire—at the *Verne.*

"Whoa!" Terry said, holding on.

Linked to the piloting controls on full standby, OK reacted even more swiftly than Terry or Xander could. He put the *Verne* into a corkscrew spin and accelerated upward so that Elisa's deadly blasts streaked past. One jazer beam skimmed the shields, while the others missed them entirely.

"Excellent work, OK." Terry looked ashen.

Xander was impressed. "Good thing we paid for all those new systems."

The other Roamers began to open fire as Elisa accelerated away.

The compy reported, "I should inform you that Elisa Enturi's weapons were not set to low-intensity or damage-only bursts. That shot was meant to kill. We would have been destroyed if I had not evaded."

"Well, thank you very much," Xander muttered.

Spinning about, Elisa's ship raced through the Relleker debris field, heading out of planetary orbit. Seven Roamer ships pursued her, ready for the kill.

"I would have been a good asset to your operations," Elisa shot back to the *Verne,* her voice icy. "I would have made you great profits. I already *did* make you great profits." She dodged the sharklike wreckage of a robot ship, then swooped around, opening fire so that she incapacitated Annie D's craft. The two Selise ships closed in, taking potshots, presumably to damage Elisa's engines and stop her ship, but their aim was terrible. Elisa dodged and flew, racing toward the sparser debris in outer orbit, where she could accelerate harder.

Xander looked at Terry. "We did invest in the best engines money could buy. Let's see what the *Verne* can do."

"You're on!" Terry said.

"Shall I pilot?" OK asked.

Xander and Terry both shook their heads. "Not on your life."

The *Verne*'s acceleration was powerful, but smooth, like a velvet glove shoving them back into their seats. They swiftly overtook the other pursuers and raced past them. Xander used all of his concentration to fly. Fortunately, the *Verne*'s delicate response systems and improved maneuverability were just as good as the enhanced speed.

Terry worked the weapons grid, worried. "I was planning to test all these systems out, but under controlled circumstances." He let out a quick exhale. "I suppose there's no time like the present."

OK also studied the full systems displays. "All modules optimal. Our jazers should be sufficient to knock out her engines. Our targeting systems are highly calibrated."

"Good, then this should all be over in just a few minutes," Xander said.

The *Verne* leaped ahead like a greyhound reaching the end of a race, closing in on their quarry. Elisa's ship soared out of the planetary system, dodging the Roamer weapons fire and pulling away from the pursuers. Xander was surprised at how well she was doing. He doubted her engines were superior to any of these ships', but she did have one thing in her favor—she had nothing left to lose. She was willing to burn out all of her systems just to get away.

Xander didn't plan on letting her do that. They closed in on her ship, and OK and Terry enlarged the targeting cross. "Last chance, Elisa," he called.

"You owe me," she said back, "but I don't owe anything to you. We're clear."

Behind them, one of the reckless pursuing Roamers squawked with a distress emergency. "Damn! We just got winged by spaceship debris. We're damaged, leaking air! Life-support systems failing."

Xander gritted his teeth. It was instinctive to turn around and help any other ship in distress, but he kept his eyes forward, focusing on Elisa. There were plenty of other ships that could help the damaged craft. But if Elisa got away, she might never be brought to justice.

"Ready to open fire," Terry said, swallowing hard. "You sure about this, Xander?"

"I'm sure, but let's try not to blow her out of space. I'd much rather see her make excuses in front of a clan jury."

Xander accelerated the *Verne*. Elisa's ship had reached open space, far enough from all except for the last few hulks of Relleker ships. Xander recalled, just for a fraction of a second, how Elisa had approached them at Ulio Station, offering two young traders the deal of the century—exclusive distribution rights to ekti-X. This woman had made a fortune for Kett Shipping, but in the end, just as Rlinda feared, the money had blood on it.

Together, he and Terry activated the firing controls.

Elisa seemed to sense the oncoming barrage. She adjusted course at the last instant. Instead of a direct hit on her engines, the *Verne*'s jazer blasts hammered her shields at full force, caused them to collapse, and then scored her lower hull.

But she impetuously activated her stardrive, and the engines flared even as the *Verne* closed in. Battered, damaged, yet still functional, Elisa's ship flashed away into lightspeed, escaping into trackless infinity.

An instant later, the *Verne* flew through the empty spot in space where her ship had been. In frustration, Xander slammed his fist on the control panel.

OK announced, unnecessarily, "She escaped."

"She didn't have time to set a course," Terry said. "Who knows where she went."

"We might get lucky," Xander muttered. "Maybe she accidentally flew into a black hole."

Shaking his head, he eased back on their engines, spun around, and headed toward Relleker, in case some damaged Roamer ships still needed assistance.

ORLI COVITZ

Bursting with their new understanding about the bloater clusters and the enormous, sentient mind they comprised, Orli was excited to meet the Kellum production staff. They headed up to the bridge of the large ship that served as the ops center for the Kellum extraction field.

As soon as they reached the old bridge, a blustering Del Kellum came in to greet them. "We used to have a giant skymine at Golgen with big skies and all the elbow room you could want. We're a lot cozier aboard a bunch of mothballed ships, but, by damn, it's much easier to harvest ekti-X from bloaters than in the clouds of a gas giant."

Orli burst out, "But there's something you don't know! These bloaters are more important than you think."

Arita nodded briskly. "Orli and I just figured out what they really are."

Zhett looked out the bridge windowport, made a broad gesture with her hand. "The bloaters are appearing everywhere, like naturally occurring fuel tanks. The clusters aren't even hard to find. Cheap ekti will be commonplace before long."

Patrick was more serious. "That's why we'd better bank a decent profit soon."

"Everybody needs stardrive fuel. We can still make it economically feasible if we keep our operations efficient," Del said, then added with a snort, "Remember, we weren't making much money at our Kuivahr distillery either."

Outside, as the ships and extractors flitted among the bloaters, another sequence of bright flashes ignited in the nuclei of the nodules. Orli flinched and then smiled with wonder, while Arita gasped beside her, grabbing her arm to share the connection. A wide-eyed Collin clutched his treeling and muttered reports to all the connected green priests.

Orli pointed out the windowport. "Did you see that? The bloaters are part of something that's bigger than we can imagine. They're gigantic cells with nuclei, parts of a coalescing mind."

Arita nodded. "Those flashes are like neural impulses, a sequence of thoughts as the great mind awakens. It's an emerging cosmic sentience—I don't know how else to explain it. Those scattered chains and clusters of bloaters are akin to ganglia."

Zhett laughed out loud at the idea, while Patrick remained skeptical. Del just blinked as if trying to be sure he had heard correctly.

DD interrupted, like a small compy lecturer. "Shana Rei shadow clouds have spontaneously appeared throughout the Spiral Arm. We know that more bloaters are also appearing, and they are demonstrably connected across interstellar space in huge, diffuse structures. We have also seen recent reports that some of the Shana Rei shadow clouds are collapsing spontaneously, as if from an external force. Perhaps there is a connection."

"There is definitely a connection," Orli said. "It is Eternity's Mind, and it's awakening. It made us both understand. Just as the Shana Rei returned, so did this cosmic sentience—and it's the only thing strong enough to fight the shadows."

Del Kellum made a loud rumbling sound in his throat. "By damn! Are you telling me these bloaters are . . . the mind of God? And we're waking it up?"

Orli's voice was firm. "We're trying to tell you that it's huge and it's aware—and it's also aware of us, and of the Shana Rei."

"And it's on our side," Arita said.

As if the great diffuse mind could hear their conversation, the nearby bloaters sparkled in sequence, brighter than before. Strobing lights raced around the cluster, like a flurry of thought. With the flashes, Orli felt a shudder go through her mind and body like a lightning bolt connected to her brain. She reeled, nearly overwhelmed.

Garrison hurried over to support her, but for the moment she was so inundated with energy and wonders that she couldn't talk. Orli clenched her teeth and closed her eyes, but she still felt all the colors and flares swimming around her mind. Behind her closed eyes she saw deep crimson and bright scarlet swirled with black and gray, then sparks of brilliant intensity. She did feel a connection. A communication.

A year ago, she had nearly died from the Onthos plague, weak, delirious, and she had survived only by immersing herself in bloater protoplasm. Orli still remembered that heady, mysterious baptism, and now the same sensory flood was happening again. When she had been swallowed up in that embrace, Orli had touched a part of the immense slumbering mind. Now, that mind continued to make contact with her.

Arita seemed just as entranced, and the two women connected as well, although they didn't understand how. But they each realized that the space mind was being extraordinarily careful in its contact with them, attempting to control itself so as not to harm them.

Without words, Orli understood that Kotto Okiah had encountered a similar thing, opening himself to whatever Eternity's Mind wanted to share—but his brain had been wiped out by the enormity of the imparted knowledge. The bloaters and their connected sentience now struggled to show restraint in an effort to communicate with Orli and Arita. She understood that the entity was also attempting to touch the Ildiran *thism* network, as well as the verdani mind that struggled against the Onthos blight—also a manifestation of the shadows.

Now that Orli was more aware of the threat to the cosmos, she could grasp the extent of the Shana Rei infiltration into the real universe—and what she saw terrified her. The space mind was fighting back with inconceivably powerful defenses, crushing the emerging shadow clouds and burning away the darkness.

But the shadows were everywhere . . . *everywhere.*

Orli also realized something else: even though Eternity's Mind was awakening and should have been increasing in power, it experienced constant stabs of pain, ripples of debilitating agony. Something was harming its components even as it tried to save the cosmos.

Another great flash from the bloater nuclei, and suddenly Orli's connection was broken. She blinked and collapsed into her seat in the Kellum HQ ship. Perspiration covered her. Beside her on the Roamer bridge, Arita was also reeling. They shared their thoughts, connected with the pain of the bloaters, the growing mind.

DD hummed in front of her, concerned. "Would you like a drink of water, Orli Covitz?"

But she shook her head. Arita had the same reaction. Collin was deeply concerned, stroking her forehead. "Can you explain?" he pressed. "What did you just experience?"

Arita looked at Orli and asked, "Why is the space mind in pain? It's struggling to fight the Shana Rei, but all that pain . . ."

As Orli stared through the windowport of the Kellum operations center, looking at the extraction operations, she did understand. "Eternity's Mind is in pain because it's being systematically slaughtered."

Outside, the Roamer ships finished draining another bloater sack, filling their ekti tanks and then towing away the flaccid discarded husk.

"Cell by cell," she said. "And we're the ones killing it."

ZOE ALAKIS

Somehow, they made it to Tom Rom's ship.

The robot assault on the Pergamus installation continued, like a murderous swarm of mechanical insects tearing apart a rival hive. They broke into a third research dome, and the screams of the scientists and disease techs inside reached a crescendo, then fell silent as the sudden influx of unbreathable atmosphere killed most of them, while others fell victim to the marauding robots.

"Hurry!" Tom Rom pulled Zoe's arm as they raced aboard his ship. She nearly dropped her satchel of rescued belongings, the only thing she took from Pergamus. All the rest would be destroyed; she knew it.

"I set the timer. The sterilization blasts will go off in only a few minutes," he said, "and I need to get you to a safe distance."

Zoe saw the mayhem behind them, thousands of skittering robots and the looming shadow cloud in the sky. "What *is* a safe distance? And where?" She did not mean to be sarcastic.

"Leave that to me." He urged her into the back compartment to find a secure place as he grabbed the piloting controls.

Zoe felt disoriented and numb. Perhaps it was shock, not just from the violence all around her, but from the singularly horrifying idea that she was out of her sterile sanctuary, that she had already been exposed to the countless lethal organisms on the outside. Even after all this fighting, even if Tom Rom managed to escape the attacking robots, the universe itself was still hostile to human life. The smallest microorganisms would attack her, unseen. Everything wanted to kill her.

But she could not fault Tom Rom's decision. By escaping, they would live for another day at least. That was the mantra she and Tom Rom had gone by when they'd left the ruins of Vaconda two decades ago, when her entire life had changed.

Black robots began to cluster outside the hangar as Tom Rom dropped the barrier field and raced forward for takeoff. His ship lurched ahead, and the heavy-thrust engines kicked in, but the robots were swarming toward them. Though the beetle-like machines looked hulking and sluggish, they moved with surprising agility.

His ship plowed down dozens of them on his way out of the hangar. Smashing their metallic bodies and scattering segmented parts, he rose up into the fume-filled sky of Pergamus. But Zoe saw they weren't free yet.

Several robots on the ground spread open their carapaces, extended metallic wings, and launched themselves into the air after the escaping ship. Tom Rom was able to dodge and use his weapons at the same time. He picked off the nearest robots that threatened their flight, then concentrated on getting away.

The Pergamus sky was full of angular black ships, and they closed in, seeing him as prey. The robots had not let any other Pergamus ships get away, and they had no intention of letting this one slip through, either.

Zoe was thrown to the deck as Tom Rom made a barrel roll to avoid enemy weapon blasts. She slid against the back bulkhead, skinned her knee. He called over his shoulder, "Strap yourself in! I don't want to worry about you right now."

Zoe picked herself up, tried to balance on unsteady legs. "You always worry about me."

She lurched to the rear compartment, retrieving her satchel with its packed specimens. She stowed it by the engine wall and secured it with a strap to the deck; then she fought her way back to the cockpit, dropping into a seat near Tom Rom, fighting against the acceleration and the jarring evasive maneuvers as he tried to get away. Her body felt lighter now, and her heart was pounding; adrenaline sang through her bloodstream. She was terrified, but this was also exciting. She felt startlingly alive!

She wondered if this was why Tom Rom enjoyed the perilous tasks of collecting specimens for her. But with Pergamus destroyed, her samples, her data, her collection would be wiped clean. She would either have to start a new facility from scratch, or simply give up. Tom Rom wouldn't let her give up. At least she had managed to save that rarest and deadliest of microorganisms, the Onthos plague.

A metal swarm of robot ships closed in. Tom Rom chose his targets with great precision and opened fire—not to defeat the robots but to blast a hole in their cordon so he could fly through. Still, the ships came racing after them.

The first countdown ended, and one of the research domes below flared bright as the gamma-ray sterilization burst obliterated everything inside and wiped out the encroaching black robots within a hundred-meter radius. Tom Rom didn't even flinch from the nearby blast, but the robot pursuers reeled in identical surprise, as if all of their cybernetic minds were somehow connected. Tom Rom took advantage of the disorientation among the enemies, and he altered course and accelerated away, looking for a chance to streak upward.

Then the second dome thumped with the sterilization protocol. The Shana Rei cloud kept growing larger in the sky. Pseudopods pushed down toward Pergamus as if to engulf the research domes in black fog.

Tom Rom roared along the surface, putting distance between himself and the research station. Hundreds of robot ships came slavering after them.

The third research dome collapsed under a sterilization burst.

"All specimens had to be destroyed," Tom Rom explained to her. "We can't let the black robots and the Shana Rei turn them against the human race."

"Such a loss," Zoe said. "But that is why we designed the emergency protocols." She had the utmost confidence in him, but her heart was heavy. She felt as if she were leaving a significant part of her soul behind.

As he raced away, Tom Rom's face was drawn, his jaws clenched, his focus hyperacute. He flew the ship as she had never seen anyone fly before. After he had gone more than a hundred kilometers away from the Pergamus outpost, racing low over the bleak and rugged landscape, he angled upward in a steep climb. He spoke clipped words in the high Gs. "I hope we're far enough from that shadow cloud so our ship can reach orbit. From there, I'll activate the stardrive and get you out of here."

In the chase, he had eluded many robots, but more followed, sticking close with a ruthless mechanical determination. Another fifty robot vessels dove through the sky, closing in on this one insignificant ship. Zoe wondered why they felt she and Tom Rom were so important . . . or maybe they just didn't want to let even a single target escape.

Tom Rom gambled, adjusted the fuel supply in their engines, then dumped part of the reserve into the reactor chamber, which gave his vessel an unexpected turbo boost. He lurched ahead of the robot ships, disorienting them. Their energy blasts went wild—but even more robots swooped in front of them just as their ship reached the edge of the atmosphere. The robots opened fire, and Tom Rom couldn't dodge them all. A blast struck the starboard engine, and an explosion rocked the compartment. Shrapnel and deck debris flew in all directions. Zoe cried out, holding on to her seat.

Tom Rom struggled to keep flying. His hands raced over the controls, activating emergency systems. "Just a minor hull breach," he said. "I've sealed it from the outside with an automated slider plate, but we've lost one engine. My speed will drop unless we can get to high orbit."

"They're coming too fast for that," she said.

The robot ships closed in with a vengeance, sensing a kill, and Zoe didn't think they were going to let Tom Rom have his way.

Behind them, she saw the shadow cloud swelling into the Pergamus atmosphere as if it thrived on the poisonous gases. The nebula looked like a sluggish sea creature, an ebony starfish folding over the remaining domes of Pergamus as if it meant to absorb them.

Another sterilization blast finished its countdown and seared a hole through the shadow cloud, but the Shana Rei quickly healed the gap and pressed forward.

More robots closed in on their fleeing ship as Tom Rom soared at high acceleration up to the fringe of space. Zoe saw with astonishment that he had tears pouring down his face, and she knew he was heartbroken, convinced that he had failed her. She wanted to reach out and clasp his shoulder, or maybe just hold him if they were both going to be vaporized.

But he hadn't given up yet—and so neither would she.

He blinked and stared ahead, abruptly changing course. "What the hell?"

Space in front of them was suddenly filled with flying objects, huge gray-green organic nodules with broad wings. Breathtakingly huge organic mantas swooped in, appearing out of the interplanetary emptiness, flying on bizarre extended flaps that somehow caught light or cosmic rays, or just sailed on ripples of gravity manipulated by their own internal forces.

"Bloaters!" Tom Rom said. "I've heard of the metamorphosis, but . . ."

Like a flock of strange flying plankton, the transformed nodules closed in to attack the shadow cloud.

100

ADAR ZAN'NH

Solar Navy warliners and CDF ships gathered at the verge of the dimensional opening, where colorful nebula gases streamed down into the blackest trapdoor of the universe.

As the fleet waited on the brink, Adar Zan'nh stood at the rail of the command nucleus. His crew betrayed anxiety and tension, but he made a physical effort to draw the strongest strands of his own *thism* to shore up the confidence of his fighters.

From the *Kutuzov*, General Keah transmitted, "You ready for this, Z?" She showed him a cocky, determined grin, but he saw her swallow hard.

"Once more into the breach," Anton Colicos muttered in the command nucleus. Zan'nh did not recognize it as a quote from the Saga of Seven Suns.

He reminded himself of the massacre at Wythira, the battles he and Keah had faced at the Onthos system, the surprise Shana Rei attack at Plumas, the destruction of the Hiltos Lightsource shrine, the mindless mob uprisings in Mijistra . . . all the terrible things the poisonous shadows had done to the Ildiran race.

He was angry enough. He was strong. "It must be done." The Solar Navy and the CDF would strike a blow for revenge—a significant one, he hoped. He said to his entire maniple, "Forward. All helmsmen, match speed into the void and keep our forces together. General Keah, will you join us?"

"You bet your ass, Z."

He frowned. "I have no intention of making such a wager, but I understand what you are saying."

The ships entered the void. Zan'nh braced himself, and his crew fell silent, holding their breath. Rememberer Anton's eyes were full of fascination. Even the log recordings from Kotto Okiah's expedition gave only sketchy data about what lay inside that vast empty dimension. But if the Shana Rei went to ground there, it was a chance for the Solar Navy and the CDF to strike a mortal blow. . . .

Once they crossed the threshold into that darker universe, Zan'nh felt the immediate change around him. It wasn't that the strike force was lost, but after the warliners crossed into the void, he no longer felt connected to the overall *thism* network. The Mage-Imperator was always there with strength and confidence that every Ildiran could feel. Here in this void, suddenly Adar Zan'nh and the Solar Navy crewmembers went deaf to the rest of their race. They could only feel the group of soldiers accompanying them.

It would have to be enough.

He transmitted across the open comm lines to all Solar Navy ships. "Be reassured. We are here, and we are intact. Though we may be cut off from the *thism* outside, we have our own thoughts and strength. There are more than enough of us to share our mutual energy. We will keep each other strong. *I* will keep you strong." He raised his voice. "We must move forward and destroy the darkness."

General Keah transmitted from the *Kutuzov,* "We're here too, Z. All for one, and one for all."

Their sensors became strangely disoriented, without any anchor points or reference guidelines. The sensor technicians scrambled to adjust, but their dismay was clear.

"Our ships can use one another as reference points," Zan'nh declared. "We will establish our own orientation. That is all we need to know."

"We need external images for the historical record," said Rememberer Anton.

On the Juggernaut's bridge, Kotto Okiah's two young lab assistants stood near the General. Howard said, "Even without reliable points of reference, we can maintain our relative positions. As long as our navigation systems keep track of where we're going, we should be able to find our way back out."

"We'll drop breadcrumb buoys as well," Shareen added. "That's what Kotto did."

The Solar Navy and CDF ships forged into the confusing nothingness. By instinct, Ildirans were repulsed and terrified by the absence of light, but this tactic might be the only way they could strike at the heart of the darkness—the only way they could go directly to the Shana Rei.

"Align our course with the records taken by Kotto Okiah's survey craft," Zan'nh said. "Keep our weapons ready."

"And your eyes open," Keah added.

He didn't know what would happen if a firefight occurred in this bizarre antidimension. If the strike force had to scramble in retreat, would they be able to race back to the opening and escape into the Fireheart nebula?

The *Kutuzov*'s green priest shook his head. "I can't use telink. My treeling can't find the rest of the verdani mind. I don't like it in here." Nadd sniffled.

The emptiness around them was breathtaking and oppressive. The void's complete homogeneity was unsettling, and they flew onward for an unmeasurable distance—until finally they encountered a change in the smooth blackness, where knots and cracks of a deeper darkness were overlaid upon the emptiness. This was what Kotto had found.

"Heads up. I think that's what we're looking for," called General Keah. "It certainly seems suspicious."

Zan'nh studied the readings displayed on the sensor screens, seeing a different sort of blackness etched upon midnight. He was sure he could see dark objects, geometrical shapes. As the combined fleet approached, the resolution grew clearer.

Shana Rei hex cylinders.

He drew a deep breath. "Yes, I believe this is it."

Ahead in the strange distorted field of the void he could discern the long sharp-edged manifestations of the creatures of darkness, like broken black lines against the membrane of the void, scattered about in a number that was difficult to count.

"They look like the bodies of crushed spiders," Keah said. "And I don't like spiders."

Zan'nh compared them to the shadows of shadows, imprints on the void from a much more powerful presence in realspace. By now, the strike force was coming up from the unprotected flank of the Shana Rei.

Zan'nh said, "I am concerned that our presence might alert them, particularly these electromagnetic communications."

Keah rallied her CDF ships as well. "You're right, Z. They haven't noticed us yet, so this is our chance. I say we let the Shana Rei bastards have it with everything we've got. It is supposed to be a surprise attack, after all."

Zan'nh didn't hesitate. This was the reason they had come. "I agree." He transmitted to all of his warliners. "Prepare laser cannons and sun bombs. We will blanket their ships and hope that it hurts them."

"Hell, let's hope that it *kills* them." Keah called out to her ships, "Commanders, bombs away!"

The CDF ships and the forty-nine warliners opened fire on the unsuspecting Shana Rei. Laser cannons blazed with a flash and crackle, weaving a tapestry of coherent light inside the void. Gunports spewed out sun bomb after sun bomb, hundreds deployed even before the first ones detonated, all of them targeting the ill-defined cluster of crushed-spider artifacts. Purifying light flared out in a cascading shout; blaze built upon blaze.

The Solar Navy ships wheeled about as sun-bomb detonations seared across the void. "General, I suggest we pull back to a safe distance so we can assess," Zan'nh said. "We don't know the consequences of what we just did." His warliners withdrew with all possible speed, so they could watch.

The CDF ships raced after the warliners as they withdrew, and General Keah gave a long, loud whoop of delight.

101

TAMO'L

As the attack on Pergamus continued and the black robots tore into the research domes, Tamo'l remained alone in her isolated facility. The robot attackers had not found her yet . . . or maybe they were intentionally ignoring her, since the Shana Rei had already contaminated her.

Tamo'l felt sick, certain that the dark mental link through her mind had drawn the attention of the shadows. They had slithered into her thoughts, forced her to reveal the countless disease specimens kept at Pergamus. That was why they had invaded here. She could feel it.

Overhead, the shadow cloud knotted the poisonous sky, and tendrils of darkness reached down to smother what remained of the medical facility. Tamo'l could feel an icy hollowness in her heart, knowing she wouldn't survive. Even with her supposedly impervious halfbreed genetics, the Shana Rei had found a way inside her. They had looked through her eyes. They had used her hands and her mind to find the secret stockpile of death.

Nearby, a research dome self-destructed with a silent bright flash of searing gamma rays that annihilated everything within the blast radius—disease specimens, personnel, and any black robots in the kill zone. In her own dome, she could see the countdown dropping to zero. Within minutes her lab would be vaporized, too.

At least she wouldn't be able to cause further damage.

Just before the shadow cloud covered the domes like a giant hand, Tamo'l saw the skies filled with battle, swirling robot ships and flashes of weapons fire as a lone vessel tried to escape—Tom Rom, she wondered? Probably.

Then she experienced a moment of confusion and surprise when other creatures appeared high overhead—swift and swollen, bloaters in their flying phase with flat wings outstretched. The bloaters soared in and around the creatures of darkness, like birds of prey harrying the encroaching black nebula. The Shana Rei recoiled and fought back, but the bloaters were relentless. The strange flying creatures seemed to intimidate even the shadows.

Tamo'l glanced at the countdown. In less than a minute she would be obliterated in an instant of purifying light.

She had been born a halfbreed, developed as part of the Dobro breeding program. To make amends for the horrors she saw there, she had devoted her life to helping the leftover misbreeds, certain that they possessed some spark that the rest of the Ildiran race didn't see. She had accomplished much for them . . . but not enough. Tamo'l had never imagined she would become a pawn of the Shana Rei.

She longed to know what had happened to Mungl'eh, Gor'ka, Har'lc, Alaa'kh, Pol'ux, and all the others. Had they all gotten away from Kuivahr, as Tom Rom promised? Or had they, too, been absorbed by the shadows there?

Half a minute left on the countdown. She gritted her teeth and drew deep breaths, preparing herself.

A fourth laboratory dome went down with a flash and a thump. All the deadly specimens would be eradicated in a pitiless but necessary annihilation. She knew the robots and the Shana Rei would not capture these diseases to unleash upon the Spiral Arm. Everything in Pergamus would be gone—along with her.

But the shadow cloud had a mind of its own. Formless black arms reached down to the last of the laboratory domes—her dome. Tamo'l could feel the shadows like obsidian spikes in her mind as they roiled in with a sinister swiftness. She felt them reaching around and into the dome . . . coming for her.

Tamo'l became airborne and disoriented, engulfed in a protective bubble. She screamed and tried to escape, but she had nowhere to go. Only seconds remained in the countdown—but the shadows had her now. They had her mind, they had her *thism* strands, they had her telepathic connection with Rod'h.

She heard her brother's mental shout, cursing the Shana Rei, howling in his own pain and despair.

Then the inky pseudopod swept her away, stealing her into the shadow cloud even as the sterilization systems vaporized the dome where she had done her research. But Tamo'l was no longer there. She knew that the entire research station and disease library was destroyed, nothing left but radioactive rubble and contaminated scraps that would do no enemy any good.

Even as it retracted, the shadow cloud still fought against the merciless harassment of the flying bloaters. The black nebula collapsed, and then the entire shadow cloud withdrew into its own universe.

Where they were already under attack!

Tamo'l found herself in an empty sensory wasteland, a black entropy bubble where she drifted without any context at all. She despaired—and then she saw her brother.

Rod'h groaned. "No, not you! They should have left you alone."

Tamo'l was glad to see him, but her joy was snuffed out like a small flame in the wind. "At least now we're together," she said, "and safe."

Gigantic lights of another nearby battle slashed the protective shadows, a powerful attack . . . here in the void.

"Safe?" Her brother's voice came from a great distance. "I am sorry that you are here with me—but maybe we can fight in a different way. Together."

102

MAGE-IMPERATOR JORA'H

Even inside the Prism Palace under the seven suns, Jora'h was lost in dreams of a darkness that rose up inside his mind. He didn't even remember falling asleep. He and Nira had been attending a lavish midday meal surrounded by noble kith, court functionaries, and attenders. The bright sunlight seemed unduly harsh, grainy, as if molecules of blackness speckled the air around them.

Jora'h remembered looking at Nira. She had smiled at him, said something about Gale'nh, her son . . . and then the Mage-Imperator lost her. He lost himself. He found himself alone in his mind, swimming through a crisis, entangled and strangled by the lines of *thism* that should have been a safety net. Instead, the cords turned dark, like razor wires that swept around him, capturing his arms and legs, wrapping tight around his torso. Other strands encircled his neck like a garrote.

Jora'h knew he was dreaming, but that didn't help him escape.

Far out in deep space, he could feel the throbbing strength of the awakening cosmic mind. He could sense the squirming pain among the Shana Rei as their dark nebulas collapsed and the shadows retreated into the dubious safety of an unreal void. But the creatures of darkness fought in any way they knew how.

As their shadow clouds were crushed into newborn stars, the Shana Rei struck out in other ways. They pressed for any weakness, any chink in the mental armor of the Ildiran race. Somehow, they knew how to find Mage-Imperator Jora'h.

From within, the darkness swelled and engulfed him. He was drowning in a black static of shadows. He thought about Nira's son Rod'h, captured by the Shana Rei and placed in an endless agony of isolation that he could not endure, yet somehow did. He caught an echo of Rod'h's screams, as well as Tamo'l's, but as he responded with frustrated outcries that had more to do with his own helplessness than with any actual pain, he knew Rod'h couldn't help him.

Instead, he struggled to find Gale'nh, who had once successfully resisted the shadows and was possibly immune. But Jora'h was helpless—and the shadows had him. . . .

He woke to shouts and astonishment. The blackness cleared from his vision like a dark veil ripped away, exposing him to blinding light. He felt weak hands flailing at him, beating against his arms, and he saw that he was standing over Nira. His hands were locked around her throat. He was squeezing tight, strangling her. Her eyes bulged out; her lips were dark and discolored, and she twitched, no longer able to fight.

He recoiled, tearing his fingers away to release her, lurching backward and staggering against the wall. Nira dropped to the floor as if her joints had become liquid. She gasped and sobbed, sucking in air as she crawled away from him.

Jora'h saw blood on his hands, blood on his robes—and he looked up to find Muree'n and Yazra'h both there, holding up crystal-tipped katanas that were also dripping with blood. They directed their pointed weapons at him, their faces frozen with uncertainty and fear.

They were ready to kill him!

Jora'h sprawled backward onto the polished tiles, lifting himself on his elbows to face them. He heaved great breaths.

Yazra'h stayed Muree'n from delivering a death blow. "Wait." The two warrior women gripped their weapons, ready to strike him down if he flinched. Three other guard kithmen had dragged a panicked Prime Designate Daro'h into an alcove, surrounding him with drawn weapons, ready to fight against anyone who might try to kill him—against Mage-Imperator Jora'h, if he became wild and murderous . . . again.

Jora'h saw that the courtiers, attenders, and noble kithmen inside the Prism Palace chamber lay dead, slaughtered. He saw a broken weapon, a long table knife, lying next to him.

He gasped. A crushing weight filled his chest, and he could barely breathe. Had he done that . . . all by himself? One weapon killed so many? Or maybe the Shana Rei had possessed other Ildirans too. It had been a massacre.

Nira pulled herself into a sitting position, shaking and sobbing, wheezing to fill her lungs. When she looked at him with abject fear, Jora'h felt empty and cold. He had never imagined that this woman, whom he loved more than anyone or anything else in the Spiral Arm, could ever see him that way. He had tried to kill Nira! How had his vulnerability to the shadows been so profound that he would try to kill his beloved?

The Mage-Imperator recoiled, turned away, and retched.

Weak with relief, or perhaps despair, Nira collapsed the rest of the way into unconsciousness.

Yazra'h had yelled for medical kithmen, and running footsteps thundered down the corridors, doctors along with more guards.

Daro'h also stared at him, clearly terrified by the bloodshed he had seen and the prominent shadow that had so obviously manifested inside his father's eyes. The Prime Designate must also realize that if they did have to kill Jora'h because he was irrevocably contaminated, then he would become the next Mage-Imperator. Would Daro'h be any stronger against the creatures of darkness?

Jora'h hauled himself to his feet. Muree'n still held her katana, but she backed off, watching him warily. The Mage-Imperator knew that the poisonous blackness was inside him, inside the *thism* and inside all Ildirans. He had to get it *out,* somehow. He had to purge himself. He dared not let the contamination continue, or else his entire race would die.

With Nira unconscious, and all the others in the bloody banquet chamber afraid of him, Jora'h pondered the old stories about the Shana Rei. For so long, mad Designate Rusa'h had insisted they follow the old story of Mage-Imperator Xiba'h, who had burned himself to summon the faeros.

But there was another story he should have heeded more closely. Jora'h remembered the dark tale of the possessed Ahlar Designate and how he had freed himself when he tried to murder all his children.

Without explanations, Jora'h strode out of the banquet chamber, ignoring the questions and the outcries that followed him. He fled back to his private rooms, where he would lock himself inside. He knew what he had to do.

ARITA

Arita had never been so convinced or so determined in her life. Eternity's Mind had spoken to her and conveyed the same message to Orli Covitz.

Now it all made sense—from the confusing tangle of images and whispers, the retreat of pain and uncertainty. The bloaters drifting through space were coalescing, somehow manifesting out of the fabric of the cosmos, at the same time that the Shana Rei were striving to *unmake* creation. But that vast space mind, an organism of interlinked cells as large as the galaxy itself, was being decimated by human ekti harvesters. By draining the stardrive fuel and killing those bloaters, those "brain cells," the extraction operations were slowly but surely attacking Eternity's Mind like a disease.

And that sentience might be the only thing powerful enough to stop the Shana Rei from uncreating the cosmos.

Arita shivered as she stared at the Kellums. "You have to stop harvesting the bloaters. Stop draining them. You're wounding our greatest potential ally!"

Orli's voice also had an urgent edge. "She's right. Every bloater you drain weakens the neural network, damages the connected cells."

"That mind won't save just *us,* but the universe itself," Garrison said. "Think of what the Shana Rei did to Earth, to Relleker, to the Ildiran planets. That's only a start. We know what the shadows intend to do to . . . everything."

Orli looked sickened. "Once Tasia, Robb, and I told the Roamers about the source of ekti-X, we triggered an avalanche of bloater harvesting." She blinked, dismayed. "*We're* the ones who provoked this new mass slaughter of the clusters."

Garrison said, "It wasn't your fault."

Arita turned to her green priest friend, who grasped his treeling. "Collin, you have to send the message far and wide through the telink network, so all the green priests know. We have to convince them, and convince all the ekti harvesters!"

Arita knew it would be a tough sell to the more extensive Roamer commercial operations, but she had another option. She rarely had to draw on her connection to her parents, but now was the time. "And most importantly, let the King and Queen know. Bloater extraction has to cease across the Confederation, immediately! They need to order at least a temporary moratorium until we can prove to everyone what this means."

Collin was breathing hard, amazed for Arita's sake, glad that after her many years of feeling discarded and inadequate, now she could connect to an immense new sentience. Now they both understood what it meant. "I will tell them. I'll make sure the King and Queen know how urgent it is." He drew a deep breath. "I once was sure that the verdani mind was the greatest consciousness the universe had ever seen, but this is so much more."

With a deep frown, Zhett stared out at the Kellum operations, placing her hands on her hips. "So you're telling me that we're both awakening and killing God, at the same time."

Orli said, "We're *saying* that you have to stop the bloater harvesting. Each operation like this is sabotaging a powerful weapon against the creatures of darkness. We know it. Arita and I both know it."

"But that's a fortune waiting out there, and we spent our last pennies on this gamble!" Del said. "By damn, we just got running at full capacity . . ." Looking at Arita's expression and a similar one on Orli's face, he wrestled with the decision.

Zhett heaved a sigh and slammed a fist on the comm channel. "All Kellum workers! Withdraw from the bloaters—take a break. Cease all ekti extraction immediately until further notice." She looked around at the others on the main deck. "We can take a breath while we figure this out."

A flurry of confused responses came back, some of them angry. Marius Denva was quite insistent on finishing out their shift and filling one last array. Patrick fielded questions. "We're not happy either, but we have to do it. Temporary moratorium—deal with it."

"All those flashes in the nuclei—are they more dangerous than we thought?" Denva said.

DD interjected, "We know the bloaters are indeed highly volatile, and an explosion could travel throughout the cluster and obliterate all operations."

Orli added, "Those active flashes make the extraction field more dangerous. It's an awareness spreading through the neural network of Eternity's Mind as it becomes more conscious, and the flashes will increase—if we don't kill all the brain cells first."

Arita considered, then smiled at Zhett. "If that's the reason they need to hear, then tell them it's too hazardous—too hazardous for the whole universe."

Seth swallowed hard. "My mother set off the first chain reaction when she was chasing us. That wiped out a whole bloater cluster."

"And she destroyed another cluster when she hit the clan Duquesne operations," Orli pointed out. She had been there to see the aftermath herself. "Each one of those large-scale explosions wiped out hundreds of bloaters—what kind of damage did that cause?"

Arita gasped. "It might have been like a . . . a stroke to the space mind. We can't let that happen again."

Collin released his treeling, and his face was filled with hesitant hope. "I've informed the King and Queen through the verdani network. Green priests are spreading the word with great urgency. I stressed how much you want this, Arita. Your parents didn't waste any time—they issued an immediate decree that places all bloater-harvesting operations on hold, under threat of the strictest penalties."

Del, Zhett, and Patrick paced the bridge of the HQ ship. "We'll have to shut down our work for now. If we refuse an order from the King and Queen, by damn, that could cause war to break out between the Roamers and the Confederation."

Zhett added, "The Shana Rei have hurt us too, and if this space-brain thing is fighting against them, I'm not going to do anything to help out the shadows."

"If we're the only ones who stop harvesting, it won't help," Patrick said. "Most clan operations don't have a green priest. *We* don't have one. It'll take a long time for word to spread."

Garrison's expression hardened. "The biggest operations are still run by Iswander Industries. He's extracting bloaters by the hundreds."

Arita turned to Collin. "Does Iswander have a green priest? Wasn't Aelin with him?"

"Aelin died at Ulio Station," said Collin. "I have no contact with the Iswander complex. We have no way of sending a message, and he will keep harvesting and killing the bloater cells as fast as he can."

Orli straightened, looking at them all. "*We* know exactly where the Iswander operations are."

Garrison had already risen from his seat in the HQ ship. Zhett Kellum had also made up her mind. "I saw the damn shadows at Golgen and again at Kuivahr, and I'm going to do what I can to fight them. We know where a lot of other clan operations are. We can take fast ships and tell them they may be destroying our only chance against the Shana Rei. We'll deliver the Confederation command—and twist arms if they won't listen." She looked at her gruff, bearded father. "Dad, you're going with us. You're a former clan Speaker, and the Roamers will listen to you."

"Good point, my sweet."

Garrison turned to Orli and Seth. "We'll take the *Prodigal Son* straight to the Iswander operations." Arita and Collin hurried to follow him back to the ship. "One way or another, we'll make him stop."

GENERAL NALANI KEAH

The detonations looked beautiful against the infinite black void, sun bomb after sun bomb washing over the crystalline shadows. Even with the *Kutuzov*'s protective filters, the flares still burned her eyes.

And it felt damned good.

Keah smiled. "Even when you try to hide in another universe, there's no place where the sun don't shine."

Her soldiers cheered and whistled. Sensor Chief Saliba just shook her head. "How can I work with this? These readings make no sense!"

The void itself seemed to echo, ricochet, and enhance the sun-bomb blasts, sending nova light into the deepest shadows where even the corners had no corners. Howard and Shareen were bursting with joy on the Juggernaut's bridge. "That's a blow for Kotto!" Shareen said. "Wish he could have seen it."

Howard said, "Looks like the strike was very effective."

"Damned right it's effective." Keah turned to the helmsman. "Let's head back out to Fireheart Station." She lounged back in her command chair. "Where does our arsenal stand, Mr. Patton?"

The weapons officer received reports from the other ships in the strike force. "We used approximately half of our restored sun-bomb complement, General. Our laser-cannon batteries are substantially drained, but they'll recharge in a few hours."

"Then let's hit them again," she said. "No harm in a little over-kill. Don't take anything for granted."

Adar Zan'nh interrupted across the comm, his transmission edged with static. "General, are your sensors picking up the same readings?" The Adar's brow was furrowed, his voice grim. "We may need to brace ourselves."

She glanced at her technicians, then turned back to the screen. "Our sensors are so overloaded we can't see much of anything at all, Z."

Lieutenant Saliba cried out, "General, the void is folding, crystallizing—it's the Shana Rei!"

On the main screen, the blackness consolidated as long lines formed hexagonal cylinders. Obsidian plates manifested while the creatures of darkness returned to the void from wherever they had been in realspace.

Keah felt a shiver run down her spine. "Better launch a few more sun bombs after all, Mr. Patton." She swallowed hard. "And then haul ass for home."

Another round of blasts knocked apart the emerging hexagonal cylinders, but they recoalesced as the CDF ships beat a hasty retreat. The Solar Navy warliners fired their aft laser cannons, tracing destructive lines across the shadows, but even more black hexes emerged after them.

"Hard about and let's get out of here," Keah said. "Can we find our way back to the opening, Lieutenant Tait?"

"We've got the breadcrumb pingers to follow."

"Then get us back to that doorway."

The *Okrun* launched two more sun bombs as the hex cylinders hurtled after them. "I can stay and fight if you need me to, General," Admiral Haroun said. "It'll give you time to retreat to safety."

"If we don't find a way to stop these things, there'll be no safety out in Fireheart either," Keah said. "Follow us—we're all in this together."

The Shana Rei looked blacker and more malignant inside the void, which was their natural habitat. Shareen looked at Howard with a stunned expression. "That attack should have wiped them out. It should have hurt them to the core!"

"I think it hurt them, but maybe not enough," Howard said.

Giant hex cylinders hurtled after them. Keah grumbled as they raced out of the angry void, heading toward the doorway in space. "A little more speed if you please, Mr. Tait."

The helmsman overrode the safety systems, and Keah could feel the added acceleration. Alongside, the Solar Navy warliners raced along, keeping pace—and the infuriated Shana Rei closed in from behind.

"They're gaining on us, General," Tait said.

"Maybe we can lock them inside the void somehow," Shareen suggested. "If we close the doorway into Fireheart, they'll be trapped here."

Keah wasn't so convinced that would matter. "The shadows can pop in and out of realspace whenever they like. I'm not sure we'd stall them for long."

"And they're right on our tail, General," said the first officer.

Adar Zan'nh and his warliners kept firing their laser cannons, barely holding off the Shana Rei. "Our batteries are nearly depleted, General. We must leave here soon." His transmission was plagued with more static as the entropy closed in.

The rippling aftereffects penetrated even the CDF shields, and at their stations, the *Kutuzov* bridge crew yelled as half of their systems failed. Keah prayed that her flagship wouldn't degenerate into a confusing gasp of malfunctions before they could get back into realspace. "Keep up the pace, Z! Just a little farther. There's a surprise for them right on the doorstep. Shareen just reminded me of it."

The Shana Rei lunged closer, but at least they didn't launch their black robots inside the void. The hex cylinders were surrounded by a thickening cloud of shadows that had folded into the void, which now extended toward the strike force. One of the lagging warliners tumbled out of control, disoriented, its lights dimming. Ildiran distress signals were swallowed up in a garbled disarray of transmissions.

Ahead in the featureless black emptiness, her navigator suddenly spotted a gash of light hovering in space, a colored flare of diffuse nebula gas that evoked another cheer from the crew. But the angry black hex cylinders careening after them did not seem intimidated.

Adar Zan'nh said, "Perhaps we should block the gate, use the last of our enhanced weapons to prevent the shadows from attacking Fireheart Station."

Keah steepled her fingers as she sat on the edge of her command chair. "I have another idea, Z. Trust me—if this doesn't work, we can always fight to the death later."

"I would be glad to have another alternative, General."

"Twelve sun bombs remaining on the *Kutuzov*, General," said the weapons officer. "But once they're gone, they're gone." Dr. Krieger's facilities certainly weren't going to be manufacturing more, and it would take some time before weapons factories elsewhere in the Confederation could pick up the slack.

"We have two more warheads in reserve," Keah said, "and I want to trigger those first. Keep the rest for a rainy day." She flashed a hard grin. "Kotto Okiah left them right here for us."

The CDF ships shot out of the open gateway back into the Fireheart nebula, with the Solar Navy warliners following close behind. The emanating ripples of dark entropy caused one of the Mantas to fail, its systems shutting down—but with its momentum, it continued straight out through the gap.

The *Kutuzov* was there watching, and when the last CDF and Solar Navy ships had rushed out of the void, she activated the standby systems of the two sun bombs Kotto had left on the threshold. As the hex ships raced toward the opening, she detonated the nova explosions, and their effects from deep inside the void rippled and resonated and fed back upon themselves. The flares were even more intense than what she had seen before, as if the explosions were enhanced on the boundary between reality and nothingness.

The brink of the void was already unstable, and as the CDF ships and Solar Navy warliners soared out into realspace, Keah watched the hole in space collapse like a mouth closing, a scar healing—leaving the Shana Rei trapped behind in their void.

The rest of the CDF and Solar Navy ships flew out into the vast nebula.

Keah was sweating, her heart pounding. Heaving a deep breath, she forced unrealistic humor into her voice. "Well, that sure got their attention."

ELISA ENTURI

She survived the transfer—just barely. The stardrive activated and lurched her into lightspeed at the moment the *Verne* opened fire. Elisa's ship suffered extreme damage—she knew immediately that it was bad. One of her in-system engines dropped offline, and she felt the explosion resonate through the ship.

"Hold together!" she shouted, as if she could threaten the hull into maintaining integrity. If the structural plates failed catastrophically, she wouldn't have enough time to know it.

Elisa slammed her hand on the controls. Brindle and Handon had tried to kill her! She was so angry she was shaking, and she didn't bother to set a course. Not yet. Her ship flew off into nowhere.

Elisa had never been a warmhearted person—she knew that—but she was reliable and trustworthy. She counted on others the way they counted on her, and she'd been lulled into a false confidence. She had come to Relleker offering her services—and Brindle and Handon had tried to destroy her. The only thing that felt worse than the betrayal was a sense of her own stupidity. What had she been thinking?

Now, she felt a throbbing inside her skull as she recalled Xander Brindle's last threatening transmission, how the *Verne* had opened fire. Bastards! Traitors and murderers. She could have helped make their new business operation into a guaranteed success.

"Bastards . . ." she whispered again. There was no one to listen. Everyone who mattered to her had been taken away.

As her ship flew on, she ran diagnostics, assessed the damage. Her hull had held together, just barely, but it would not withstand any further stresses. Some of her fuel was leaking, but the ship still had enough to reach plenty of basic destinations . . . if only she could figure out where to go. She didn't dare return to Newstation.

She wanted to reset the clock, reset her life. Everything that had previously mattered had been burned away. She had already changed her name from Reeves back to Enturi, reclaiming her original surname and erasing any connection to Garrison. Now, though, as she flew away, the name Enturi also made her think of her old family back on Earth—losers, screwups, parasites. How her life would have been different if she hadn't been forced to spend so many years dragging them along as baggage. They probably resented her for abandoning them, for refusing to give them a handout in their time of need.

Well, Earth was destroyed now, and she could just imagine them calling out her name at the end, demanding that she rescue them when the robots and the Shana Rei closed in. Their loss presented no great problem to the universe.

Elisa had once thought that overcoming difficulties was a mark of her character, that adversity made her stronger. If that was true, then she must be strong indeed.

She called up cockpit images of Seth. She still retained a library of her son's photos, although she had edited them to remove vestiges of Garrison, whom she no longer wanted to see as part of their family. In truth, she had lost Seth too. The workers and teachers at Academ had denied Elisa her rights to her own child—but Seth had fought against her, too, as did Lee Iswander's son . . . and even the wentals! The whole Spiral Arm had turned its knives on her.

Good riddance to all of them.

After pondering for more than a day while she drifted between star systems, Elisa made up her mind that she would *take* what she needed. It was her due. She could wallow in misery and let herself be stepped on again and again, or she could go back and play the one remaining card she had left.

Lee Iswander owed her far more than Xander Brindle and Terry Handon did. It was her last chance. Before she gave up entirely, she would go back and see if he could change things, if he could prove himself to her again.

With hot tears in her eyes, Elisa adjusted course and performed a final status check on her stardrive and the amount of ekti remaining in the reactor chambers. She decided the ship would get her there. Nursing the engines, double-checking the integrity of the damaged hull, she guided her ship away. . . .

In less than a day she returned to the bloater-extraction operations with the tank arrays being filled by halfhearted workers. The bustle seemed lackluster to her now, or maybe she just saw it without the illusion of excitement she had felt when she was in Lee Iswander's good graces. The industrial activity seemed quieter, the number of ships and workers less than before. Some unreliable Roamer workers must have abandoned Iswander when times got tough. Elisa felt indignant on his behalf—she would never have abandoned Iswander . . . if he hadn't cast her out first.

She flew in, seeing drained and discarded bloater husks drifting loose, as if there weren't enough people left to corral them. The pumping operations continued at full speed, but the ekti-X tanks were piling up for distribution. Three full arrays were ready to be shipped, and other tanks were corralled in stockpile groupings. Iswander was probably unable to sell it. Elisa had seen how he was blackballed at Newstation. By now, there would be so many other upstart ekti producers that any buyers could simply brush him aside.

Once again, the man would be ruined. Elisa could have helped him. . . .

He was a fighter, though, and Elisa wanted to fight at his side—if he would have her back. They belonged together. She had her pride, and she hated the fact that this was her best option. Elisa did what she had to do.

Even though the security had become lax, her arrival was soon noticed. She ignored the comm inquiries and transmitted directly to Lee Iswander. "I need to speak to you in person, sir."

When his face came on the screen, she was shocked to see how drawn he looked. He had dark circles under his eyes. Iswander no longer looked strong and confident; instead, he seemed at least partially broken. "Elisa, I told you to go. You are not welcome here. I can't have you at my operations."

Seeing him like this caused a deep ache in her heart. She had meant to shout and demand her rights, but now he just looked weak.

Elisa was not weak, though. "You have to take me back," she said, but her determination lasted only an instant. Her vision blurred. "You have to take me back!" she repeated. "I've got nowhere else to go."

106

XANDER BRINDLE

After the "unpleasantness" with Elisa Enturi, Xander and Terry decided it would be a good idea to go back to Rendezvous, hauling the next batch of salvage hulks with them. That woman's arrival reminded Xander that even though the Shana Rei and the black robots were out to eradicate the human race, there were also plenty of dark and evil people out there, too.

It wasn't just Elisa driving him away from Relleker, though. The planet below was completely dead, and it sickened him to see so many ruined civilian ships wiped out in orbit.

"I think our place is at Handon Station, so we can make sure it's run properly," Xander said. He gestured out the *Verne*'s front windowport. "We're executives. We have people to do this sort of work."

Terry nodded. "We should be there."

OK sat at the helm controls awaiting orders. "I would be happy to monitor the ships to be dispatched to Rendezvous. Shall I compile an inventory of the most viable Relleker salvage ready for delivery? With the tethers holding them together, we should be able to transport the entire batch."

"You do that, OK," said Xander.

Terry added, "With all those expensive modifications we made, now we're using the *Verne* as a space tug!"

The compy diligently did his work, as Xander contacted Annie D, Omar Selise, and the other salvage workers. Omar responded, "You two go back to Rendezvous and make sure the repair yard is ready to put the pieces back together. We'll keep gathering spare parts."

Annie D added, "We should already have enough components to build at least ten new ships for the open market."

OK interjected, "If my assessment is correct, the currently salvaged components can be reassembled into at least nine standard cargo vessels. I am assessing various ship designs to make the best use of our resources."

On the screen, Omar fixed his gaze directly on Xander. "And you tell me what else you find, you hear? I'm counting on you for my grandson."

"I'll let you know," Xander said, in a rush to end the conversation.

In the weightless ship, Terry pulled himself into the piloting deck with his legs drifting behind him. He swung into the chair. "What was that about?"

Xander talked quickly. "We have to distribute responsibilities if we're going to run a big operation. You don't need to know every administrative detail."

Terry chuckled. "Nor do I want to."

As they prepared to depart, the last salvage hulls were securely tethered together. With its enhanced engines, the *Verne* could tug them using boosters, hauling all that salvage to the Rendezvous asteroid cluster. The setup reminded him of the old-fashioned custom of tying tin cans on strings behind a newlyweds' car. When the load was ready, the *Verne* accelerated the collection of wrecked ships.

In the previous several days, Xander had studied the medical reports OK had scouted. Terry kept himself so busy monitoring the debris field that Xander had opportunities to do the work out of his partner's view. He was no medical expert, but from what he could tell, the spinal-restoration research showed promise. As far as he was concerned, the experimental treatment might be worth the risk, despite the small possibility of bad side effects, but he hadn't mentioned it to Terry yet. He knew his partner would have a knee-jerk reaction against it, but Xander wouldn't listen to his excuses. Rather, he intended to gather all the data, compile his arguments, and present his case—then see what would happen.

At least four times during the flight back to Rendezvous, Xander tried to raise the idea, but he always backed down, convinced he should double-check just a few more details.

Terry sensed something was off, but did not press Xander for details, letting him take his time. Xander had never known Terry when the other man could use his legs; the degeneration had set in while he was only a teenager. By now, Terry was so accustomed to his life that he didn't bother with wisftul dreams of running across green fields. But if Xander could give him that . . .

The *Verne* returned to the asteroid complex, and when they arrived, Xander was pleased to see the traffic. At least five more ships had joined the work of Handon Station.

"We're on our way to become the new go-to supply station and repair yard," Xander said brightly.

Rajesh Clinton responded as soon as they arrived. "I'm glad to see you two! I agreed to take over when Garrison had to leave, but I never meant to run the show. Do I at least get a raise? Or maybe profit-sharing?"

"A raise," Xander said. "We'll discuss terms later." The money meant little to them, considering Terry's fortune, but Xander was reluctant to squander it, even so. He had to keep watch on his partner's business interests.

Above the main Rendezvous cluster, the *Verne* detached the towed salvage hulls and components, and Xander called out for clan teams to suit up and help separate, clean up, and inventory the wrecks. Terry was already in the back compartment prepping his exosuit. "I'm going out to monitor operations. I can make sure all the pieces are distributed and get work crews started on them right away. We've got a reputation to build."

Xander said, "I'll dock the *Verne* and head inside the main asteroid for admin work."

Terry chuckled. "You've never volunteered for paperwork before!"

Xander forced a smile. "I can see how much you want to go outside. You know what you're doing."

Suited up, the other man cycled through the airlock, skimming out into space where his useless legs were no hindrance at all. Terry jetted around like a silver fish, moving from wrecked hulk to engine component, nudging them, using heavy impellers to shove the massive objects into place.

Xander watched him, saw how easily he moved, the grace he demonstrated in zero gravity, and he wished he had half as much finesse working out in space. Once again, he tried to convince himself that Terry would really want the risky proposed cure.

CELLI

From within the stressed terrarium dome, the two green priests had a perfect vantage to watch the CDF and Solar Navy strike force rush back out of the void. Wide-eyed, Celli whispered to Solimar, "Did they just lead the shadows back to us?"

Solimar stepped closer to the crystalline plates of the greenhouse dome, pressing a hand against his back, which ached due to sympathetic pain from the agonized trees. The long hairline crack had been sealed and reinforced, but other weaknesses would surely manifest soon; even the original girders were at the limits of their material strength. The new arcs of the expanded dome had been completed, but the Fireheart factories could not produce sheets of reinforced crystal quickly enough. Only one wedge of the larger dome had been completed.

When General Keah detonated the sun bombs on the threshold, the flare of light at the boundary somehow cauterized the wound in the universe. Inside the terrarium, the bent worldtrees shuddered, and the pain of their existence resonated through telink and into the verdani mind. Celli felt the hurt in all her bones and muscles.

The Roamer work crews on the new dome framework raced away, evacuating to the main admin station. Celli watched them go, wishing they would come back. "Keep working," she whispered. "Don't leave us." At a minimum, they still had a week of work to complete the project and let the trapped trees have a little more room.

Meanwhile, the battered *Kutuzov, Okrun,* and the Mantas headed toward Fireheart's main admin hub. Solar Navy ships swooped around the heart of the nebula, extending their solar-sail fins. The supergiant core stars seemed intensely bright, as if defying the shadows.

Inside the terrarium, the two worldtrees strained and groaned, and Celli gasped as she heard a loud creaking, splitting sound up above. Another lightning-bolt crack extended across the main crystalline dome.

Solimar said in a deep and concerned voice, "The new dome may not be finished soon enough. Someone will force us to leave—very soon, Celli."

"No! The trees are part of us, and we're part of them."

"But I won't let you die for them. The dome is going to fail."

The trees shuddered again, and Celli wrapped her arms around the nearest trunk, as if to extend comfort while drawing support from the worldforest mind. For the next few hours, she lost herself, just existing there as she saw through millions of leaves on dozens of planets. . . .

Then a dark, cold ricochet passed through Celli's thoughts. Suddenly more alarms shot across the Fireheart comm systems. She groaned with dread.

Three Roamer scout ships raced in through the boundary of the nebula, transmitting urgent signals. Far outside in space, two new shadow clouds had unfolded from the emptiness, enormous black blots that converged on their target from a different direction. Even though the Big Ring's gap into the void was sealed, the Shana Rei created their own access point. The ominous black nebulas expanded into realspace—and then poured toward the Fireheart nebula like a thunderhead composed of the darkest smoke.

Station Chief Alu sounded a preemptive evacuation order for all personnel. "Fireheart is not a place you'll want to be in the next few hours—follow your Guiding Star and get out of here. We can't fight the Shana Rei or their robots."

The ships and industrial operations became a storm of activity; workers and transport pods began to move, abandoning the energy-film farms and the isotope-gathering scoops. Solimar grabbed Celli's thin arm. "This is it—we can't stay. The trees can't be moved, and the shadows are coming. You know what the Shana Rei will do here."

"I know," Celli said, "but we can't just abandon them!"

"We have to," Solimar said.

She knew he was right. For so long she had held out hope of finding some kind of desperate solution, and the new dome was being built. She clung to every last moment.

"If we stay here, then we die with them," Solimar said.

Green priests could pour themselves into the worldtrees, link their thoughts and souls with the interconnected verdani mind. At the moment of death, they could flood into the stored thoughts and experiences and achieve a sort of immortality. Celli's green priest brother Beneto had done it.

But she was still young, as was Solimar. They had so much of their life ahead of them. "Even if we wanted to leave, we wouldn't make it out in time," Celli said in a dull whisper. "We have to stay here."

"We have our shuttle," Solimar said. "If we get to the admin hub or one of the CDF warships, they'll take us with them." He swallowed hard again. "If you want to go?"

"If I want to go . . ." Celli repeated. "It doesn't seem right. The trees are trapped here, even if we're not."

As the two shadow clouds bled into the blazing lagoon of Fireheart gases, the worldtrees shuddered again and flexed their bent trunks as if preparing for one last battle.

Two more of the crystal panes overhead split as cracks formed across them.

108

GENERAL NALANI KEAH

After all the destruction they had just heaped on the Shana Rei inside the void, General Keah should have been dancing in triumph. She had seen hex cylinders crumbling under the barrage of sun bomb after sun bomb, and they had even sealed shut the dimensional doorway so the shadows couldn't come after them—at least, not from that direction.

The Solar Navy and CDF ships were out in the Fireheart nebula now, temporarily safe, but Keah didn't feel good about this. She knew it wasn't over yet . . . not even for today.

Shareen Fitzkellum and Howard Rohandas both seemed stunned after their narrow escape from the Shana Rei. They tried to cover it with excitement, but Keah could see their battle shock, the realization that they had both nearly died in space. Those kids didn't belong on the bridge of a battleship in a war zone. At Keah's direction, the *Kutuzov* flew directly toward the Fireheart admin hub. "Let's off-load the civilians and continue our patrol."

"But we should stay with you," Shareen insisted. "We want to fight the shadows."

Keah wouldn't hear of it. "I'm responsible for enough people. I'm at my limit. I can't handle two more." As the *Kutuzov* docked at the Fireheart admin hub, she urged them to the disembarkation deck and escorted them aboard the admin station personally.

Less than an hour after the *Kutuzov* returned to patrol with the other CDF and Solar Navy ships, new shadow clouds appeared outside of the nebula. The pair of amoeba-like masses threatened the Fireheart nebula from a different direction, now that the main doorway into the void had been sealed again.

She had barely had a chance to get to her quarters, longing for a shower and a change of uniform, when her first officer shouted on her personal comm, "General, *two* incoming Shana Rei clouds! We need you on the bridge."

"Oh shit," Keah said, then she began to run. "Battle stations! Contact the Solar Navy to coordinate our defense of the station."

The General made it up to the bridge in record time and dropped into her command chair. The Roamers were already evacuating. "While we give these people time to get away, we're going to confront the shadows head-on." She drew a deep cold breath. "Mr. Patton, I hope you found a few more sun bombs for us to use."

"Only a few, General . . . only a few."

Admiral Haroun contacted her, wearing a grim expression. "The situation looks dire, General. Thank you for the many opportunities you've given me. If this doesn't turn out well, it's been a pleasure serving under you."

"Stop jumping to conclusions, Admiral. We've still got some fight left in us."

"Yes—as do the Shana Rei."

When Keah looked at the screen, her throat went dry. "And so, obviously, do the bugbots." As the two shadow clouds encroached into the nebula, tens of thousands of robot attack ships also poured in.

She raised her voice. "All right people, we know what to do. We've had a hell of a lot of practice at this." She glanced at the tactical screen, contacted the Solar Navy warliners. "I don't think the shadows learned their lesson, Z."

The *Kutuzov* left Fireheart's main station behind as evacuating Roamer ships scattered across the nebula, flying as far from the Shana Rei as they could.

Keah settled into her chair, wove her fingers together into a tense knot. "No sense waiting, Mr. Patton. Launch our first volley of sun bombs."

The Juggernauts and Mantas spat blazing fireballs toward the oncoming shadow clouds. The Solar Navy warliners spread out in formation.

Fireheart's central cluster of hot stars blazed intensely, but the shadow clouds were impenetrable. Even the detonation of the sun bombs did not wash away the darkness.

Robot marrauders swarmed in and destroyed the power-film farms, but workers had already abandoned the operations. Another volley of blasts detonated the isotope storage tanks.

"I think we pissed them off," Keah said.

"We're down to our last twenty sun bombs in the whole battle group, General."

Keah stared at the thousands of robot ships and the enormous hex vessels that protruded from the shadow clouds. "Then let's make those last ones count." The words sounded flat even to her own ears, but her crew muttered a dutiful cheer.

Firing laser cannons, the Solar Navy warliners drove forward in perfect formation, as usual—then suddenly the Ildiran ships scrambled about in disarray as if they had all been jolted. They broke formation, which Keah had never seen them do. The warliners flew erratically, out of control, and all their weapons fire ceased.

She hit the comm. "Z! What the hell's going on? I need you at my side. It's the only way we'll survive another ten minutes."

On screen, though, she saw Adar Zan'nh. His face looked drawn, his lips pulled back into a rictus, his eyes wide. In his command nucleus, the Ildiran crew began to shout and moan, frantic. Several collapsed to the deck, as if they had received mortal wounds.

Zan'nh yelled, "Not the Mage-Imperator!" His hand was spasming and his entire body twisted as he collapsed. On the screen, Anton Colicos looked astonished; his face had gone white. The Adar barely managed to reach up and terminate the communication, and the Solar Navy maniple fell apart.

Keah felt sick with dismay, and she slumped back in her chair. "We're on our own."

Fighting to the last, her surviving ships plunged into the oncoming wave of robot ships.

109

MAGE-IMPERATOR JORA'H

The darkness within choked him like a black poison. If it could hide inside the Mage-Imperator, then that same deadly toxin could seep into all Ildirans—manifesting in violence, hatred, and death. Jora'h was supposed to be the strongest of his race, and if the creatures of darkness had managed to possess and corrupt him, then the rest of the Ildirans had no hope.

Strong. He had to be strong. For himself, for his people, for Nira. But how? There was a way. . . .

Shuddering as he staggered into his quarters in the Prism Palace, Jora'h felt violently ill, but he forced control on himself. His hands ached, and he could feel his fingers trembling—fingers that had recently been wrapped around the throat of his beloved Nira, and the Shana Rei had possessed him so thoroughly that he couldn't even remember doing it. Jora'h had been deaf to her screams, her pleas. He hadn't been aware of himself as he murdered the other noble kithmen at what should have been a quiet meal in the banquet hall.

He closed his eyes but could not forget the disgust he had seen on Muree'n's face when she saw what he had done. The black taint was inside him—and he had to get it out.

He heard attenders and guards hurrying down the hall, calling after him, but he sealed the doors to his chambers. He needed to be alone for this. He didn't dare let anyone near him—not because they might harm him, but because they might *stop* him. Jora'h had a different kind of duty to perform for his people.

The *thism* inside him was tangled, and he could feel shadows like cold eels swimming in his bloodstream. A black static hovered around the fringes of his vision, and because Jora'h was the nexus of the *thism,* all the darkness came through him. There was no avoiding it, and the Ildirans were helpless unless he could do something.

Unless he was strong enough to do what must be done.

He heard pounding, shouts outside, but he had secured the door with heavy locks. Until now, he hadn't even realized there were locks on his door. The Mage-Imperator always had guard kithmen to protect him, and he had never needed to lock himself away. Then he remembered that the locks were only recently installed by Rod'h—a defensive measure that Nira's son had taken when the mob attacked Prime Designate Daro'h. As he thought of that, his heart ached with more guilt: Rod'h had seen the grim reality before the Mage-Imperator would admit it. And Rod'h had paid the price, swallowed up by the Shana Rei.

The words of the attenders and guard kithmen were muffled from behind the door. Jora'h ignored them and went to stand in the center of his room, where bright light poured through the curved crystalline walls. In this place he had spent many warm and happy times with Nira. This chamber was the heart of the rebuilt Prism Palace, where he had learned to believe again that the Ildiran Empire would grow and stay strong.

But now the shadows were inside him, and he had tried to kill Nira. This had to end.

His movements were jerky, as if black threads were tangling his muscles, preventing his smooth bodily control, but he forced himself to keep moving. For so long he had pored over the Saga of Seven Suns, listened to Rememberer Anton, tried to find some hidden revelation as to how he could fight this insidious enemy.

Following the old story, mad Designate Rusa'h had sacrificed everything to call the faeros, and the fiery elementals had indeed joined the fight against the Shana Rei at Earth, but Earth was still destroyed and the creatures of darkness remained as strong as ever. The alliance with the fiery elementals had been a mistaken hope. Yes, the fireballs had helped fight the Shana Rei in their previous encounter, when the faeros were stronger and the shadows weaker. Now, though, the creatures of darkness seemed invincible.

He had wasted altogether too much time studying the tale of

Mage-Imperator Xiba'h, when the true key to saving himself from the inner blackness lay in the tale of the Ahlar Designate. That was what Jora'h needed to follow now.

In the brightest sunlight, he picked up a thin crystal picture frame, a flat glassy plate that held an image of Nira. He smashed the frame into shards, letting the etched image fall free. "I am sorry, Nira, my love." Then he expressed a deeper, silent apology toward all of his people before holding up the jagged broken edge. His hands were shaking, but he wasn't afraid of his decision. The Shana Rei were what he feared, and he had to get them out of him.

As he grasped the broken shard with its razor-sharp edge, yellow sunlight glinted from the surface, which heartened him, although the crystal seemed to reflect the bright light away from him.

"I'm sorry, Nira," he said again, then drew the jagged edge down his inner arm, slashing open the skin and muscle, slicing his major arteries. Blood spilled out more quickly than the pain came. Before he could lose his resolve, he switched the crystal shard to his other hand. His fingers were bloody, and the edge was slippery. He cut again, plunging deep in a long gash on his other arm, opening his blood vessels wide.

When it was done, he clenched his fists and held his arms in front of him. As his heart kept beating, he could see the pulses in the flowing blood, like swift tides coming and going. Red liquid spilled out of his arms, ran down his hands, and pooled on the floor, spreading out in an ever-widening puddle.

But it wasn't just red. The familiar scarlet was swirled with black tendrils. More and more of the Mage-Imperator's life spilled out, drawing out the darkness like leeches. Black swirls escaped from his body. They writhed and twitched, and Jora'h clenched his hands tighter to force more blood out.

Within minutes his vision dimmed. He hadn't known he had so much blood inside of him, but it continued to flow . . . still tainted with the darkness in the *thism*. But he had to get it all out. All of the blood. All of the life.

It continued to spill from the gashes, and the suns shone down on it, highlighting the contamination. All of the poison blood had to be gone—all of it.

His blood flow decreased, weaker now. His heart barely pumped, but he didn't call for help—he couldn't.

Daro'h will be a good Mage-Imperator.

His vision and his soul grew darker as the light washed away, spilling out of him just as the blood did. But the darkness that came next wasn't a poisonous shadow brought on by the Shana Rei, but by a different kind of end, a different kind of darkness.

Jora'h let out a long sighing breath, sure that the last of the shadows was gone from him, gone from the Ildiran race. The *thism* was clean at last . . . and he let go.

LEE ISWANDER

Facing Elisa again, Iswander felt gravely uneasy. After docking at the admin hub, she had emerged from her ship—a stolen Iswander ship—and commanded the technicians to make the necessary repairs, as if she were still their supervisor. Then she presented herself inside the control center. The operations personnel stared at her with a kind of horror, but they looked sidelong, waiting to see what Iswander would do.

He seemed to be out of options. "I am not pleased to see you, Elisa. I gave you a chance to make a clean break. By coming back here you are putting all of us at risk."

"This is where I belong, sir, no matter what else happens. You need me, and I need you."

"I don't know what I need, other than to be treated properly in business, and to earn a fair reward for hard work and innovation." Iswander sounded defeated. "That no longer happens."

Alec Pannebaker charged into the control center. "You killed all those people. What the hell were you thinking? Why can't you just go away and leave us alone to clean up your mess?"

She gave him a withering stare. "The bloaters were my discovery, freely given, Alec. For better or worse, there would be no ekti-X operations if not for me—and now I've come home."

Iswander sighed. "She can stay here, Mr. Pannebaker—provisionally. She knows the risks and the consequences." He narrowed his eyes and hardened his voice. "But I will not defend you if the Confederation comes to arrest you."

"I have never needed your defense. I can take care of myself. What I need is your faith in me."

He didn't answer for a long time, then he said in a low voice, "That's something you will have to earn again, and I don't know if it's even possible."

"Then I'll prove you wrong. Give me work to do. Assign me to a crew, and I'll demonstrate my worth to your operations."

Though Iswander felt backed up against a wall, he could not deny her. She made him uneasy, even fearful, but she was *Elisa*. He didn't want to admit it, but he did owe her, and if she chose to call in that chip, then she gave him no choice. He didn't want to admit that part of him was glad to have her back. He realized it was a risky decision, but under these circumstances he could not see any better decision available to him. "Mr. Pannebaker, see to it. Elisa knows what to do. If she's going to be here, at least let her make herself useful."

The normally cocky and good-natured Pannebaker was obviously displeased, but he gruffly took Elisa away with him.

Mostly silent, Iswander monitored his operations for hours, feeling all alone inside the control center even with his support personnel around him. They did their work, but they sounded subdued. He scanned the daily report and noted that seven more workers had sneaked off, all of them members of Clan Tavish. Iswander couldn't hold them here against their will, but he wished they would at least have the courtesy of informing him of their departure. He didn't need to hear their reasons, because he knew all the reasons. There would be no talking them out of it, and he wasn't sure he should even try. What could he offer them anyway? How could he convince them to stay? He didn't even know how long he was going to be in business here, or if there was even a point to doing so.

But he wouldn't give up. That was the point.

He would find some solution, find a new way to resurrect his stardrive-fuel operations, or he would find something else to do. That was what Lee Iswander did. And even if these ekti-X operations were going to collapse, they still belonged to him. Through innovation and development, he had made a vastly lucrative operation out of the wandering bloaters. He wouldn't let it go . . . even if it seemed to be fading on its own.

Despite the diminished work crews, ekti extraction continued at full speed, even if continuing to harvest the bloaters was a losing proposition with no means to bring the fuel to market. How could he dispose of all the canisters they had already stored? He hoped he didn't have to just dump it in space as worthless.

That thought made anger rise within him. He would never do that! The Roamer clans could insult him all they liked, and they could refuse to do business with him, but they could not erase what he had accomplished. Even now, the Roamers were copying him, making their fortunes while destroying his. Even as they invested heavily in their own operations, they would know—if only in the back of their minds—that they owed it to him.

Then the *Prodigal Son* arrived, piloted by Garrison Reeves—one of *his* ships, an Iswander cargo vessel that Garrison had stolen when fleeing Sheol. Iswander could demand it back, he supposed . . . but he wouldn't be so petty. He was shocked that Garrison had returned at all.

As soon as they transmitted their identification and flew the ship toward the control center, Elisa strode back in, enraged. "He's got Seth with him. That's my son!"

Iswander was annoyed with her behavior. "Your domestic problems are not my priority, Elisa. You brought enough troubles with you. Why did those people come here?"

She blinked. "I didn't bring them. I've been looking for them ever since they took my boy away from Academ, away from me. I'm surprised they would show their faces."

Iswander went to the comm station as the *Prodigal Son* drifted in among the bloaters. His words were sharp and clipped. "Why are you here?"

Garrison answered in a calm, professional voice. "On orders from King Peter and Queen Estarra, ships are traveling to all known ekti-extraction fields with an urgent message. We knew where to find you, so we came here."

Iswander straightened with surprise. What did a man like Reeves have to do with the King and Queen?

Orli Covitz came on the screen, and Seth joined them. Elisa flinched, but Iswander grabbed her arm, forcing her to remain quiet before she could blurt something stupid. Orli said, "The bloaters are not what you think. They are valuable, sentient, and they're fighting against the Shana Rei."

Another young woman appeared next to a male green priest about her age. "I am Princess Arita. The command of the King and Queen was issued throughout the worldforest mind, but since you have no green priest for communications, we had to come in person. Your bloater-extraction operations are damaging Eternity's Mind. It has to stop, or the Shana Rei will destroy us all."

Pannebaker returned to the control center. "What the hell is going on, Chief? Who do they think they are?"

Arita continued, "By order of the King and Queen, you must stop harvesting the bloaters immediately. Your operations are hereby shut down."

111

RLINDA KETT

When their two ships finally reached Fireheart, all hell was breaking loose. Clouds of darkness had cracked open the blazing cauldron of the nebula—and they had to get to the green priests and the terrarium inside. Giant Shana Rei hex ships emerged from the two swelling shadow clouds, and thousands of robot battleships swooped in to harass the ships and facilities.

"Oh hell, I've seen this show before," Rlinda transmitted. "Never wanted to see it again."

Tasia's response from the *Curiosity* was clogged with static, partly from the nebula's ionization and partly from the entropy backwash of the Shana Rei. "This doesn't look like a place we want to be."

"We'd be crazy to go in there," Robb said.

"I agree," said Tasia. "Setting course now."

Rlinda had the container of wental water. "I'll do what needs doing here. You two keep my *Curiosity* intact, go join Xander and Terry, make something of yourselves. But Jess and Cesca asked me to deliver the wentals, so it's got to be important."

Tasia responded with a rude snort. "You don't get to have all the fun."

Escaping Roamer ships plunged through the dust boundary at the edge of the nebula and flew helter-skelter into space. Many were pursued by robot ships, but the pilots flew erratically enough to avoid destruction.

The comm channels were awash with the urgent chatter of distress calls. As she flew into the bright gases, Rlinda saw CDF battleships inside the nebula, as well as Solar Navy warliners that were all reeling out of control. Focused on her mission, she spotted the glint of the terrarium dome. Not much time—the battle was raging all around. Rlinda muttered under her breath, "I hope they know what to do with this wental water."

"Right now, maybe the green priests just need to be rescued," Tasia responded.

"In that case, I'm at their service. On my way."

In the space battle within the nebula, vastly outnumbered CDF Mantas crashed into the robot ships. Angular black vessels were torn to scrap metal by a flurry of jazer blasts, but four Mantas also exploded under the barrage of return fire. The Ildiran ships swirled about drunkenly, taking heavy fire—against which they failed to respond.

Urgent distress calls came from the Fireheart admin hub. Shuttle craft and shielded inspection pods were flying out, desperate to get away, but they were short-range ships and far too slow to escape. The black robots picked them off.

Tasia transmitted, "Shizz, look around the nebula. What happened to the giant hole in space from the Big Ring? It's gone!"

On the screen, Robb looked at her in surprise. "With everything going on, *that's* what you're wondering about?"

From the admin center, Howard Rohandas sent a priority transmission: "We're in the laboratory module. We have all of Kotto Okiah's data as well as the results from the mission exploring the void."

Shareen interrupted him, "And it all comes free with any rescue. Any takers? Please?"

Tasia said to Rlinda, "If you're going in there, then so are we. After all, we got away from the battle of Earth. How hard can this be?"

"I won't argue with that," Rlinda said. "Kett Shipping always does its job. I'm heading to the greenhouse dome, and I'll rescue those priests, one way or another."

Declan's Glory split away from the *Voracious Curiosity*. As both ships dove into the embattled nebula, flashes of detonating sun bombs illuminated the swirling gases, momentarily brighter than the core supergiants. Many Roamer facilities were already obliterated, and black robot ships circled back to destroy the rest.

As the encroaching shadow clouds sliced into the nebula like executioners' blades, *Declan's Glory* and the *Voracious Curiosity* flew faster and deeper. Rlinda gripped the silver capsule in her palm, as if it were a talisman. "Come on, BeBob. Give me strength."

She flew straight toward the terrarium dome, which was surrounded by contruction girders and a partially finished expansion. As she closed the distance, she could see the crowded trees pressing up against the crystalline plates. Obviously, the outer dome wasn't going to be finished after all. She hoped Celli and Solimar were still inside the greenhouse, otherwise this would be a wasted effort. On the other hand, the two green priests would have been smart to evacuate long before now.

But why did they need the glowing wental water? Rlinda had enough experience with the water elementals during the previous war that she wasn't going to second-guess.

Declan's Glory docked at the greenhouse. She had to complete the process herself because no one responded to her calls. She bounded out of her ship, glad for the low gravity as she carried the sealed cylinder. "Celli, Solimar! I've got something for you." The wental water felt warm, fizzing with energy. "Celli!" She raised her voice. "Come on, girl."

The main greenhouse chamber was filled with thrashing, restless worldtrees. The gold-barked trunks had expanded and partly split. Some thick branches were broken and dangling. Overhead, the crystal dome showed obvious spiderweb cracks spreading out, and Rlinda felt sudden dread. She had walked right into what would surely be an explosive decompression.

The two green priests were on the ground against the trees and they lurched to their feet, staring at her in shock. Both of them moved as if they, too, were in terrible pain. "Why are you here, Rlinda?" Celli cried. "You have to go!"

"You two have to go with me." She grabbed the young woman's arm. "Come on, we can fly out in time."

"We won't leave the trees," Solimar said in a hard resigned voice. "We'll stay in the verdani mind to the end."

Celli groaned. "You should be evacuating with everyone else! Leave us—it's over here."

Rlinda held up the container of throbbing water. "I had to bring this. Jess and Cesca told me you needed it. The wentals insisted."

"But what . . ." Solimar asked.

Celli's eyes brightened. "Wental water . . . and the trees! Yes, Rlinda—*yes!*" She snatched the container out of Rlinda's hands. "This is exactly what we needed."

Solimar looked at Celli, as if they both shared a deep secret. "Yes, that would work. Far better than just dying here."

"Glad you agree," Rlinda said. "Now let's take the water and get out of here. I can't guarantee my ship can outfly those bugbots, but I'll give it my best—and that's usually good enough."

"No. Now, more than ever, we're staying here," Solimar said. "Leave us. We'll be fine."

Celli urged, "The wental water won't help you, Rlinda, so you have to get away." She looked up at the towering, stunted trees. "But we have what we need."

TOM ROM

Harassed by the manta-like bloaters, the embattled shadow cloud withdrew from Pergamus and folded back into the void, leaving nothing behind. The bloaters swirled around in empty space, destroying a few straggler robot ships that had been abandoned by the Shana Rei, and then the strange flying creatures also departed, as if they had accomplished their mission.

Tom Rom and Zoe were alone near a dead planet. His damaged ship drifted at the edge of the star system, undetected—and that made them safer than they had been for some time. He and Zoe had survived. He had saved her. Again. As he always intended to do.

As his body shook in the afterwash of adrenaline, he turned to glance at her. Zoe seemed pale and strained, but she was too strong to be terrified. He had raised her to be strong, throughout terrible adversity, but right now she looked so vulnerable sitting there in the back compartment. Dragged out of her sterile dome without a protective suit, she seemed naked and exposed, but she took heart by being next to him.

"I promised I'd keep you safe," he said. "I told you we'd get away from Pergamus, that I'd save you from the Shana Rei and the robots."

She swallowed and nodded. "I can always count on you, Tom Rom. Where will we go now?"

"We'll find a place—we always did before. We'll be starting over."

Her shoulders shuddered and her body was racked with sobs. "But it's all gone. My wonderful Pergamus—all my data, the research I spent years compiling. My collection!"

"We're still alive." He sounded firm. "Our engines were damaged, but I can probably implement repairs. I know enough about stardrive functionality. I'll patch us up, and we can make it to some trading outpost. We'll find a place."

He didn't remind her that Ulio Station was gone. Earth was gone. Other colonies were under attack. Tom Rom knew that the shadows were intent on eradicating human civilization, and so wherever he and Zoe went, they might still find themselves hunted down, targets.

He would take her someplace alone and safe where they could regroup. He looked out at the emptiness of space, and the scarred planet was just a pinpoint in the distance as the ship limped away. During the escape, he had been hyperfocused, his reflexes sharpened to amazing speed and accuracy; his thoughts had no room for panic, worrying only about the next half second of survival. He was completely consumed by dedication for Zoe, knowing she was with him, knowing he had to survive, that the ship had to survive—for her. And he had done that.

But he had also faced the awful black cloud, the swarms of deadly robot ships. Even he could not believe that they had gotten away, and now the moment of calm paralyzed him.

Zoe shook his shoulder. "Tom Rom, are you all right? What's wrong?"

He realized to his embarrassment that he had slipped into exhausted unconsciousness, and their damaged ship had continued drifting in space. He woke up, shook his head. "I'm fine." He placed his hand over hers as it rested on his shoulder—and realized with a start that she was *touching* him.

Zoe realized it too, but didn't withdraw, just kept her hand there. "Should we go back to see if there's anything left of Pergamus?"

Tom Rom was certain the planet would just be a blackened wasteland, but she had asked, and so he did as she requested.

Since his ship had suffered great damage, he didn't dare take them into the atmosphere, but instead, they ran intensified scans from orbit so Zoe could see with her own eyes the broken research domes, the blackened landscape. Viewing the images, she shook her head, her dark eyes shining with tears. "It's all gone then. My specimens, my data . . . my reason for building it . . ."

"Not all of it." He let himself show a relieved smile. "I'm not one to allow for a single point of failure. We've been threatened before, and I always protected you. When the Confederation learned about Pergamus, I realized we might have to abandon it, so I took precautions. I kept a complete data backup. Not the actual specimens, but all of your cures and treatments, your studies, your data—everything. I have the complete library files on board this ship."

Zoe's eyes went wide, then filled with tears. "You did that?" Her brow furrowed. "But what if you had lost your ship? What if someone had captured it? All that data could fall—"

"I protected it, and now it's still yours."

Zoe shuddered and collapsed in her seat. As Tom Rom guided them away from Pergamus, he knew they were on their own—as they always were—and he would find a solution. Because he always found a solution. "I don't leave things to chance."

"I have something, too." She nodded. "I should have known that I didn't need to smuggle the sample vial out with me."

He was instantly on his guard. "What sample vial?"

She rose, looking shaky, and left the piloting deck. She went back to the damaged engine compartment where she had stowed her package of rescued belongings. He hadn't asked her why she would insist on bringing a satchel of keepsakes. Knowing Zoe as well as he did, he couldn't imagine what she considered so important, and now he followed her to the back with a growing sense of dread. A sample?

Zoe's face dropped into dismay as they reached the compartment where the explosion had occurred. While they were under fire from the black robots, the interior shielding had surged, causing a power block to overload. The blast had smashed Zoe's satchel, torn its fabric, and strewn the contents about the deck. She crept forward, concerned.

Tom Rom drew in a long, heavy breath. What had she lost? What kind of specimen?

She seemed oddly stoic when she picked up a smashed vial. He saw blood—but it was an old sample, not hers. "It's your original blood," Zoe said. "The Onthos plague . . . I didn't want to leave it behind."

A deep dread filled him. The blood was on her fingers, but she had already been infected just from the recirculated air. And he had been exposed, too. "Oh, Zoe . . ."

"I suppose I'll be studying it more closely than I ever imagined," she said.

Tom Rom felt suddenly, devastatingly helpless. "I . . . I still have the data on the Onthos plague." But all the treatments used on him had been vaporized at Pergamus—and even those royal jelly treatments were no longer effective, since the plague organism had mutated. The new strain was proof against even the cure that the Pergamus researchers had worked so hard to develop.

Because he had already survived the plague, he might have immunity. He hoped he remained healthy long enough to care for Zoe at least.

He wiped the blood from her fingers. She seemed in shock. He wrapped his arms around her and led her back to the piloting deck. "It'll be fine," he said. "You'll be all right. I'll take care of you."

She gave him a bleak smile. "I know you will."

CHAPTER

113

TAL GALE'NH

Gale'nh reeled when he saw the massacre in the banquet hall. The Mage-Imperator had slain all those courtiers and noble kithmen with his own hands, and he had even tried to strangle his beloved Nira, Gale'nh's mother!

Yazra'h's voice was cold. "If the Mage-Imperator has fallen to the creatures of darkness, then we have all fallen. Ildirans are now a race of shadows."

After Jora'h fled to his chambers, Nira coughed and choked, rubbing her throat and struggling to recover. Her voice was raspy. "Don't give up hope! We have to save him."

Gale'nh felt as if ice water washed through his veins. "He begged me to teach him how to fight the Shana Rei, but I couldn't give him what he needed. I didn't know how." He clenched his fists. "I didn't know!"

"He is desperate and in despair." Nira forced the words out of her damaged larynx. "Save him!" She went into a long coughing spasm.

"We can all feel it." Yazra'h thumped the end of her katana on the bloodstained tile floor, but she didn't know how to fight an intangible enemy like this.

Nira finally got her voice under control again. "I'm afraid Jora'h is going to do something foolish. We dare not leave him alone."

"Come! If the Mage-Imperator needs us," Gale'nh said, "then how can we respond other than to offer everything we have?"

Yazra'h said, "If we are going to die, I would rather die fighting the shadows, than be paralyzed with misery."

Though weak, Nira forced herself to her feet. "I have to be with Jora'h."

Attenders and guard kithmen followed them, but Muree'n and Yazra'h raced ahead, while Gale'nh helped his mother hurry. Because he was a halfbreed like Muree'n, he didn't feel the *thism* with the same clarity as did other Ildirans, but he felt the dread and the violence—and then came slashes of pain. He staggered.

As they reached the Mage-Imperator's private chambers, Yazra'h reeled against the crystalline wall. The other Ildirans lurched to a halt as if shock waves had ricocheted through the *thism*. Nira couldn't feel any of it, and yet she knew. "No—Jora'h!"

Gale'nh yelled back down the corridor, "Call for medical kithmen." In his heart, though, he knew that the contamination of shadows was not something a doctor could treat.

The Mage-Imperator had barricaded the doors, and even though attenders and workers pounded on them, he did not respond. Yazra'h knocked the attenders aside and began to batter against the locked door. "Father, let us in."

"Jora'h, please!" Nira cried. Her voice was raw and painful, and yelling made her bend over, coughing again.

Sudden waves of pain rippled through the *thism*; then another telepathic lightning bolt shuddered into them all.

"He is hurting himself," Yazra'h yelled. She and Muree'n redoubled their efforts against the barricade.

Gale'nh joined them trying to break down the thick door. He himself had found the strength to survive the Shana Rei, and surely the Mage-Imperator was stronger than a mere halfbreed military officer.

Finally, the murky crystal cracked; the locking mechanism broke. Yazra'h slammed her body against the door, and Muree'n kicked the fragments aside. Gale'nh and the others surged into the bright chamber.

Nira cried out when she saw Jora'h, and Yazra'h froze with Muree'n beside her.

The Mage-Imperator had collapsed in the center of the room in a pool of bright sunlight and crimson blood. He clutched a broken crystal shard in one damaged hand next to a framed image of Nira. His slashed forearms spilled his lifeblood in a widening red lake on the floor. His skin looked chalky, ghostly pale. He did not move, did not seem to breathe.

Gale'nh bent over to cradle his shoulders. Nira was beside him. "Jora'h!" she wailed, touching his face. "Jora'h, don't leave me."

Blood oozed out of his mangled arms, but very little was left inside him. Gale'nh remembered the terrible story of the Ahlar Designate, who had bled himself to death to get the shadows out of his bloodstream. He realized that was what Jora'h had been trying to do.

A whisper of words came out of the Mage-Imperator's mouth. "It was necessary."

The Ildirans were panicked into near catatonia as the Mage-Imperator was dying. Medical kithmen staggered into the room, but they were just as frozen, just as terrified.

With the faintest remnant of his voice, Jora'h said, "Is it running true? Is my blood . . . ?"

On the floor Gale'nh saw that some of the spilled blood had swirling undercurrents of blackness, threads of shadow that darkened the crimson . . . but the last trickles from the wounds in his arms were red and pure.

"He has lost too much blood," said one of the medical kithmen, staring in shock. "Too much for us to save him."

"You can save him because you must," Yazra'h snapped.

"But we have nothing. If he is tainted—"

Gale'nh looked up. "Take mine! Use my blood to save him."

Nira whirled to face Gale'nh. "Will that work? Can he take your blood?"

The medical kithmen said, "The Mage-Imperator can accept blood from all Ildirans. But if it is tainted again . . ."

"It's not tainted," Gale'nh said. "I survived the shadows. I was strong enough, and he needs my blood. He asked for my help. I did not know how to help him then, but this will give him what he requires—from me. I think it carries immunity."

Jora'h seemed so still, but Gale'nh knew that the Ildiran leader clung to life because once a Mage-Imperator died, all of his people would fall into paroxysms of grief and helplessness.

"We do not have much time." Muree'n grabbed the doctors and plucked the sharp-edged fragment out of Jora'h's hand. "Take my brother's blood. Do it now—or do I have to open his veins myself?"

Gale'nh bared his arm. "Save him. My blood should grant him immunity. If he's purged himself of the shadows within, then it may be the only way for the Ildiran race to survive."

The doctors swarmed around him and Jora'h. They hauled the Mage-Imperator out of the pool on the floor, as if fearing that the tainted blood might contaminate them.

Gale'nh felt the sharp jab of needles piercing his arm, but he closed his eyes and thought of the light, thought of how he himself had pushed the shadows away from him. As his blood flowed into Jora'h, he made up his mind to give everything, every drop of his life, if that was what the Mage-Imperator needed.

114

ROD'H

The blackness inside the entropy bubble seemed darker and more painful than before. He feared more for Tamo'l than for himself. Rod'h had endured his own agony for so long, and he had refused to give the Shana Rei and Exxos the information they demanded. He had wanted to die so many times, but they kept him alive, re-creating him without diminishing the torments to his psyche.

Death would be surrender, and he had tried to surrender . . . but he was still here. And now they had trapped Tamo'l as well.

He'd been unable to stop the black robots from savaging the research domes on Pergamus. Exxos had gloated to Rod'h over the plan as they approached the plague library, revealing how they would seize all the deadly organisms and spread them throughout the Spiral Arm. But the disease stockpile had fail-safe systems that prevented the robots from obtaining any samples. Those safety systems had not protected Tamo'l, however. The shadows had seized her at the last moment, swept her away from the sterilization blasts. They had taken her prisoner, just as they held him.

Rod'h hoped he could use that. Maybe they could do something together. Now that his sister was here, perhaps they could find some way to join their abilities, to fight back. They were both halfbreeds, and they had unexpected ways to resist. The Shana Rei were not omnipotent, and Rod'h had begun to notice cracks in their invincibility, failures, small defeats.

Inside the unrelenting darkness, he saw a faint spot of light. Rod'h had witnessed the shadows writhing, felt the clenching fist of some vast mind as gigantic thoughts squeezed the shadow clouds and shoved many of the Shana Rei back into the void, imploding others, igniting stars, and sending the creatures of darkness on the run.

The Solar Navy and the human military had attacked them from within the void, unleashing a ferocious storm of sun bombs directly where the shadows went to hide, and the creatures of darkness were badly wounded.

Yes, he could still experience hope.

Tamo'l floated with him here now, her arms outstretched, her pale face filled with empty horror. "Where are we?" Her voice came from a great distance. "What are they going to do with us?"

Rod'h wished he had a better answer. "We are nowhere—there aren't any definitions that make sense. And they won't let us go." He paused for a long moment. "We are now their test subjects, but we can learn from them, too."

"Learn? What can we know about the Shana Rei?" She seemed lost. "They were inside me, Rod'h. And now I . . . am inside them."

"You and I can see the shadows in ways that no one else can." He felt the energy trembling within him, a change from the crippling helplessness. "They are afraid of something—a powerful mind has been fighting them, hurting them from the outside."

Tamo'l let out a long moan. "I'm not as strong as you, and not as strong as Gale'nh either. The shadows found a way inside me. They used my mind. They saw through my thoughts."

"But they're being beaten now," Rod'h said. "Many of their shadow clouds are collapsing."

Tamo'l shook her head as she drifted in the empty prison. "It won't be enough. I saw them attack Pergamus. There are millions of robots. . . ."

Suddenly, they felt ripples in the void, an agony that seemed to tear the Shana Rei apart. Even here, far from the core of the battle, Rod'h could feel exotic defenses out in the universe. He wished more than anything that he could find some way to assist the others fighting the shadows. "Come closer. Try to join your mind with mine, like when we were children."

She tried, and he was able to extend his own thoughts to connect

with hers, to share strength with his sister. And as he strained, con-
centrating so hard that his head throbbed, he also felt Osira'h . . .
and Gale'nh, and Muree'n. All far away. And even Nira, their
mother, who had not been able to connect before.

They all understood that he and Tamo'l were here, lost. So close
to him, so infinitely distant, Tamo'l asked, "We are both trapped,
aren't we, Rod'h?" When his sister looked at him, her eyes seemed
to glow in the darkness.

He would not lie to her. "I know of no way we can escape, but
I'm more intent on finding a way that you and I can fight. We are
here inside the heart of the shadow clouds." He raised his voice.
"They must be vulnerable somehow. We've got to find a way to
make a difference—to strike them from inside."

Tamo'l drifted close, but because of the physical vagaries of the
entropy bubble, no matter how near they were, they remained separated. Rod'h reached out, and he saw his fingers extended. She
clutched at him, but they could not connect. They remained apart,
as if divided by a cruel fold in dimensional space.

"We're still together, regardless." Rod'h did not let himself feel
defeat. "You are my sister. I can sense our halfbreed siblings out
there. They know we're thinking about them."

Tamo'l said, with a lilt of wonder brightening her voice, "And the
misbreeds—I can feel them, too."

Right now, he knew the shadow clouds were plunging into the
Fireheart nebula. The creatures of darkness had been wounded from
the surprise attack inside the void, and now they were retaliating.

In a distant muffled fashion he watched the Solar Navy ships and
the Confederation Defense Forces. He saw the Roamer facilities, the
blazing supergiant stars . . . and the encroaching shadow clouds kept
growing, ready to swallow it all. But he and Tamo'l were trapped
here.

In the black walls of their prison, Rod'h spotted a flurry of inkblot smears, black shapeless forms that were the Shana Rei. Their
representational eyes glared at him and Tamo'l. When she cringed,
he realized that this was the first time she had seen the creatures of
darkness manifest themselves.

As the shadow blots throbbed, other forms appeared, identical and angular robots, four copies of Exxos. They loomed closer, approaching Tamo'l. Rod'h struggled, trying to reach her, but they ignored him. They had come for his sister, not for him.

Tamo'l couldn't move, couldn't escape. He knew exactly what Exxos meant to do to her, because they had torn apart his body and mind enough times, then spliced them back together again, letting him keep all the memories of the pain.

Tamo'l screamed, and even though Rod'h could see her, right there, she might as well have been in a different universe. The robots came at her from four sides.

But something changed suddenly. The Shana Rei stared at them for a moment and then winked out of existence. An instant later, just as the robots extended razor pincers toward Tamo'l, they were yanked away as well.

The Shana Rei and the robots continued their attack in the Fireheart nebula, leaving Rod'h and Tamo'l alone in the dark, while the rest of the battle raged in the real universe, completely out of their reach.

115

TASIA TAMBLYN

After all their years fighting in the Elemental War and now flying for Kett Shipping, she and Robb worked together like a perfectly tuned machine. After letting *Declan's Glory* peel off for the terrarium dome, Tasia plunged toward the central Fireheart complex, following one of many distress calls.

In the nebula battlefield, sparkling starbursts marked the detonations of fleeing ships, flashes of laser cannons and jazers wiping out robot attackers, even sun bombs that scooped divots out of the encroaching shadow clouds.

"Remind me again why we came here?" Robb asked.

"Rlinda had to make a delivery," Tasia said.

She managed to dock the *Curiosity* at the admin hub amid robot ships, sun-bomb explosions, and blasts from CDF battleships. She and Robb picked up Fireheart stragglers, including Shareen Fitzkellum, Howard Rohandas, Station Chief Alu, and the last dozen or so Roamers who needed an evacuation ship.

Alu scrambled aboard. "Thank you, thank you all! Now let's get out of here. Keep us safe!"

"That's a tall order," said Tasia, "but we'll do our best."

"We sounded the evacuation," Alu gasped as he scrambled aboard, "but the shadow clouds came so fast. They're after us for revenge."

Shareen continued to explain, "We went into the void with a strike force and hit the shadows where they were most vulnerable, hammered them with sun bombs. We destroyed a lot of hex cylinders."

"Just enough to piss them off?" said Tasia.

Howard looked sheepish. "I can't dispute that."

Lost and aimless, the Solar Navy warliners were being decimated. Tasia saw four Ildiran ships fall as black robots tore them apart. Many didn't even bother to fight back.

"The Ildirans are just reeling," Robb said. "What's wrong with them?"

General Keah was not ready to give up, though. Her CDF ships kept blasting away as if they didn't realize, or didn't care, how badly they were outgunned.

The *Curiosity* shuddered as energy bursts erupted around them. Robb and Tasia worked together smoothly, without talking. They reacted in perfect synchronous moves, dodging an oncoming, out-of-control robot ship that opened fire with great verve but minimal accuracy.

Tasia activated the comm. "Rlinda, are you there? Are you safe?" She felt an empty sadness when *Declan's Glory* didn't respond. Finally, more than a minute later, the big woman said, "Define safe."

A nearby explosion knocked out half of their shields. The *Curiosity* spun out of control. The passengers shouted in panic, and Howard and Shareen tumbled together across the deck. Because Robb and Tasia were strapped in, they managed to stabilize the ship.

Robb said, "I think it's time to go."

As the ship soared out of the nebula on a trajectory away from the two shadow clouds, Howard and Shareen picked themselves up from the deck and came to the piloting compartment. Several of the *Curiosity*'s control panels had gone dark, and a shower of sparks flew up from another, but Tasia nonchalantly bypassed the circuits, then shut down extraneous components. Robb kept flying.

With a gasp, Shareen pointed out the front windowport. "Look at the first shadow cloud!"

One of the black masses clenched and convulsed, as if recoiling. Diving in from the outside fringe of the nebula, an unexpected swarm of flying nodules arrowed straight toward the nearest shadow cloud, like birds of prey.

"It's bloaters," Tasia shouted. "They're bloaters!" She remembered seeing the cluster at the Iswander extraction field, but these bloaters had transformed, come alive—and they sent out ripples like gravitational waves that stirred the Fireheart gases. The invisible force was directed toward the amoeba-like shadow cloud, crushing the darkness like a fist.

"Looks like we're not the only ones fighting," Robb said.

The black swirling cloud collapsed, falling inward. As the cloud crumpled under its own mass, the flying bloaters followed it in, vanishing into the last remnants of darkness, like moths to a flame.

"Hang on!" Tasia said.

One gigantic shadow cloud still remained.

So far the *Curiosity*'s engines hadn't been damaged, and she wrung out every last bit of acceleration, dodging as the bright nebula tore itself apart around them.

116

CELLI

The crack widened in the glass of the terrarium dome overhead, splitting sideways and forking into several branches. The brittle snapping sound was even louder than the rumble of shock waves from nearby explosions.

Outside, a panoply of flashes marked the ongoing space battle, but Celli could focus only on the groaning trees. She could feel it in her muscles and bones, dreading the imminent disaster when the dome failed.

Rlinda Kett was bursting with urgency. "We all have to get out of here. Now, dammit!"

With growing wonder, Celli embraced the warm, pulsing glow of the wental water. "No, *you* have to go."

Solimar folded his hands over hers on the wental container and looked up at the trader woman, hopeful now. "Believe me, Rlinda— this is why you came here. You've done your part. Now, run to your ship. Celli and I can't do what we need to do with you still here."

With a groan of frustration, Rlinda looked up at the lengthening cracks in the dome overhead; then she turned and ran.

Now that she no longer needed to worry about the other woman, Celli felt her heart swell with elation, as well as terror . . . but she had lived with terror for a long time. Now the wental water gave the two of them an opportunity to save these trees, to save themselves . . . and to change forever.

Taking the wental cylinder, they knelt before the pair of suffering trees. Once the terrarium dome shattered, the trees would be killed, but now the wentals gave them another option.

"We will be magnificent," Solimar said.

Celli was breathing hard with wonder. "We'll soar through the universe. It will be perfect."

The metamorphosis would destroy the greenhouse, but it would allow the transformed trees to fly free. There was a finality to their symbiosis with the trees. Celli and Solimar would never be able to touch each other again, to make love, to sit side by side with skin touching skin as they looked out at the swirling nebula.

But they would be more . . . so much more.

Above, the crystalline ceiling split with a much longer fissure, enough that a scream of escaping air whistled through the gap. It was going to fail within seconds.

Celli poured the wental water around the base of the two worldtrees. The elemental liquid seeped into the soil and into the roots, swelling into the trunk like lightning. She and Solimar kissed, ignoring the escaping air as the dome crack split farther. A great wind roared through the greenhouse.

They touched one last time, let their fingertips linger, and then they turned back, each facing the enormous bole of a worldtree. Inviting and welcoming, the gold-barked trunk split open, forming an opening for them to enter.

Escaping air rushed and swirled inside the terrarium. Mulch and debris from the crop fields swept up in small whirlwinds to vanish through the fissures in the dome.

Celli climbed inside the waiting tree, which was like a perfect cocoon. As she backed in, she took one last look at Solimar, who had also found his home inside the heartwood. Her eyes met his—and then the tree gap sealed shut again, its pristine wood folding over her.

She could feel the fibers lacing around her like a mesh that became part of her green skin, then dipped into her muscle tissue, her nervous system, her bloodstream. The wentals reproduced and flooded through the water inside the trees, pulled up through capillary action to energize the heartwood.

Celli felt her vision diminishing, but also expanding. As a green priest, she had been able to peer through the verdani mind, but now she became part of it in a more intimate way.

She had always been a slip of a girl, wiry and athletic, able to treedance across the fronds. She had leaped into the air, and strong Solimar was always there to catch her without any effort at all. He would swing her up, throw her to another branch, and she would swing around and bound back to him.

Now she felt enormous and powerful. She had many arms, count-less branches and fronds—a hybrid worldtree form that encom-passed not just her small figure, but also the giant tree. Her new body still ached, having been bent over for too long, nearly broken. Now, though, she was free.

Finally, as she and Solimar both transformed into verdani tree-ships, Celli knew it was time. She was wental and she was verdani . . . and she was also still very human. The surge of strength came with a rush of joy, and she straightened her long-stunted body, stretched her magnificent tree form so that she stood upright at last.

Celli reached out many wooden arms with countless fingers made of green fronds. It took almost nothing to shatter the crystal terrar-ium dome, break apart the support beams, and knock aside the partially constructed new dome. Solimar did the same.

The two newborn verdani treeships, with Celli and Solimar inte-grated as pilots, sprang free. Beneath them, the tree roots broke through the lower deck and the base of the terrarium, and the mas-sive branches pushed upward, outward. They tore free of the chains that had bound them for far too long.

It was glorious! In the flood of nourishing light from the Fire-heart nebula, her arms and branches grew and grew. She could feel the strength pouring into the tree's heartwood and what remained of her mortal cells, but also the energizing sunlight from the hot core stars in the nebula.

The two new verdani ships soared out into the chaotic battlefield of Fireheart, and Celli felt exhilarated and free.

ELISA ENTURI

Garrison's ship was offensive in so many ways. The *Prodigal Son* was originally an Iswander ship that he had stolen from Sheol and used to kidnap her son. Elisa knew he didn't possess enough weaponry even to force Lee Iswander to turn down a thermostat, yet he flew here making arrogant demands.

She watched Iswander's face when Garrison's companions blithely commanded him to cease all ekti-X extraction operations. The arrogance! As if Lee Iswander hadn't already been hammered enough? Her rage extended beyond what she saw in his expression, but she knew Iswander felt it inside his heart too. She was attuned to him. She felt for him, and she had often made the hard decisions and performed the dark tasks that he wouldn't admit he needed.

In the control center, Iswander stood in front of the comm screen. He scowled at Garrison. "Let me get this straight, Mr. Reeves. You flew here to demand that I shut down my operations and cease all ekti-extraction work? And everyone else in the Confederation has received the same demand, thereby cutting off the supply of stardrive fuel throughout the Spiral Arm? That's ridiculous—how is civilization supposed to survive?"

"Right now we're focused on letting the *universe* survive," Garrison answered in a cool voice. "We have to think bigger than one industry. Bloaters are the brain cells of a cosmic mind powerful enough to fight the Shana Rei."

"Preposterous," Elisa said.

"It's true, Mother," Seth said. "We saw it ourselves." When he appeared on the screen, her heart skipped a beat. Garrison had brought her son to use him as emotional blackmail, no doubt placing him in harm's way. There were no depths to which that man wouldn't stoop.

With the *Prodigal Son* hanging amid the bloaters, the extraction operations had ground to a halt as the workers waited to hear an answer. Alec Pannebaker moved around the control center looking flustered and confused.

Princess Arita transmitted a harder warning. "You are still part of the Confederation, Mr. Iswander. All operations received the same command. If you wish to file a complaint with the King and Queen, you can go to Theroc."

"And bring Elisa with you when you do," Orli said with an edge in her voice. "The Confederation courts want to have words with her."

Elisa turned to Iswander. "You can't let them walk all over you, sir."

"No, Elisa. No, I can't. They have hounded me enough already." He pounded his fist on the comm deck and opened a channel across his ekti operations. "Attention Iswander Industries personnel. I'm giving you a clear directive to continue your work. Ignore the threats of these intruders. This is a private facility outside of Confederation jurisdiction, and my business is my own. You've stood with me for this long. Thank you for having faith in me a little longer."

Though obviously uneasy, Pannebaker nodded. "We're with you, Chief."

Garrison transmitted back, "Mr. Iswander, the bloaters have to be protected. We can't let you harm any more of them—you're damaging Eternity's Mind."

"This is my company," Iswander shouted back, and Elisa was proud to see the emotions rising inside him. "I'm trying to provide for my people—and I have had *enough*. The Roamer clans have disrespected me again and again. I've been beaten down, yet I pulled myself back up. I have played by the rules. I have fought, and I have succeeded—only to have someone come and take it from me again. No more!" He yelled at the screen. "No matter what I do, someone finds a way to turn it against me. You cannot take everything. Do you hear me? You cannot take everything." Sweat appeared on his forehead.

Now Elisa grew alarmed at the intensity. Iswander was actually shaking, and she worried that he might suffer a breakdown. "You can't take everything," he repeated in a quieter voice.

Elisa understood what he needed her to do. She had always understood. He didn't just need her as his adviser and as his deputy; he needed her personal strength. He needed her to take necessary action—he always had, even though he wouldn't admit it. Elisa had to do what he wouldn't: that was why she was so important to him. That was why she was a part of Iswander Industries in a more intimate way than any other employee.

Iswander hadn't meant it when he claimed that he didn't know what she was capable of, to pretend that he hadn't realized what instructions he implied, when his instructions had been perfectly clear to her.

She heard what he said now, and she knew what his heart meant. Lee Iswander demanded to be the one in control of his own fate, when too many cosmic vagaries had knocked him back and forth. He was through being pummeled. Elisa had seen it happen again and again. She had to save him. No one else could.

She slipped away from the admin center as Garrison and his companions continued to argue over the comm, trying to make Iswander "see reason." But they weren't going to see reason. Elisa would make them understand just how determined Lee Iswander was, however. She would make *him* see just how determined he had to be. Some things could not be done by half-measures.

Racing to the launching bay and her waiting ship, Elisa knocked workers aside, paying no attention to their surprised shouts and questions. She had the engines prepared within moments. She didn't ask permission to launch, didn't bother with safety checks or interlocks.

Using the emergency-release system to open the launching-bay doors she dropped her ship out and away, and soon she was among the bloater operations: the protected clusters of nodules, the pumping stations, and the fuel-tank arrays full of stardrive fuel even though there was no current market for it.

Elisa saw the *Prodigal Son* and headed straight for it.

Garrison had brought that ship here to poke a sharp stick in her eye. He had brought Seth to flaunt the boy in front of her—but this was a necessary action, and it would be Garrison's fault. He had dragged the boy into danger, so he would be responsible for how these next few minutes played out.

They might claim that the nodules were living cells in a bizarre space brain, but Elisa also knew how dangerously volatile the bloaters were. And so did Garrison.

She powered up her weapons and positioned her ship among the nearest bloaters, within clear view of the *Prodigal Son*. Garrison would have noticed her by now; maybe he would even guess what she intended to do. This standoff was in her control.

Garrison transmitted, "Elisa, what are you doing?"

"I'm doing what I have to. You forced us to this. No one is going to disgrace Lee Iswander again. No one will take these operations away from him. He will sacrifice them all, and you, before he lets that happen."

Orli shouted on the comm. Even Seth cried out, "Mother, what are you doing?"

Steeling herself, Elisa broadcast on the open channels so that everyone in the extraction field, including Lee Iswander, could hear her. "You need to back away, Garrison. Withdraw and leave us alone. One blast from my jazers will ignite the bloaters. This whole cluster, all these ships, your ship, mine, and the administration hub, will go up in a flash. You know what'll happen."

"You can't," Orli cried. "You'd wipe us out, including yourself."

"And you'd kill a whole section of Eternity's Mind," Arita said. "You can't do that!"

"And I can't let you crush Mr. Iswander again. I know what he wants."

"But we're trying to stop the Shana Rei," Garrison said.

"I have more personal concerns than that. One shot, that's all I need." Elisa's voice had a ragged edge. "I'll do it, Garrison. You know I will."

Lee Iswander broke in. "Elisa, you must stop this. It isn't what I want."

She just smiled and muted his transmission. She knew he didn't mean it. Instead, she put her fingers on the firing controls.

RLINDA KETT

Abandoning Celli and Solimar tore her heart, but as soon as the two green priests had the wental water, Rlinda seemed not to exist for them. They were absolutely certain of what they intended to do.

She had no choice but to trust them. Rlinda had to get the hell out of there.

Believing that the two green priests were as good as dead, she flew off, complaining about the *Declan*'s sluggish engines and wishing she were back in her beloved *Voracious Curiosity*. She accelerated away for all she was worth.

When she looked behind her, she saw the glowing greenhouse under fire by a squadron of black robot ships. Then something wondrous happened.

The terrarium dome shattered like a hatching egg, and two enormous verdani treeships emerged: worldtrees infused with wental water that grew into titans, spreading their boughs wide. Huge thorny branches reached out to embrace the universe.

Three black robot ships blasted at *Declan's Glory*, and Rlinda was thrown to one side. The shields vibrated as she corkscrewed into evasive action while the marauders swooped after her. As she tried to get away, the new verdani battleships were huge and exuberant, and with one sweep of their thorny boughs they smashed the robot attackers. Unhindered now, Rlinda accelerated away with a loud whoop.

Back during the Elemental War, she had seen the hybrid treeships, some of which were still guardians in orbit around Theroc. Her heart swelled with wonder as she realized that Celli and Solimar must be inside those trees. That was how they got away! That was why Jess and Cesca had sent the wental water.

In their verdani forms, the transformed green priests flew from the debris of the shattered terrarium, and Rlinda could sense their joy, their newfound energy. The stunted trees that had been confined for far too many years were now liberated. They could fly free, and the green priest pilots, no longer human, could imagine the places they might go. They should have soared across the Spiral Arm exploring empty spaces and unknown star systems—but now, at the moment of their birth and creation, the treeships could barely escape from the Fireheart nebula.

The verdani battleships expanded as they flew into the sea of gases, doubling and tripling in size from the vivifying energy of the core stars. Robot vessels swirled around the verdani battleships, foolishly attacking them, but the thorny boughs struck back, smashing hundreds of robots at a time.

Ahead of them, the other Shana Rei cloud oozed in through the ionized gas, implacable tendrils reaching for the treeships.

Another explosion slammed against Rlinda's shields, and the *Declan's* control panels sparked. Several systems went dark, and she raced to reconfigure her backups, adding power to the front shields because the bombardment was most intense there.

She concentrated on flying instead of gawking at giant trees, but she could not shake off her dread as the last shadow cloud encroached, swelling up to block the escape of the treeships.

Suddenly, robot marauders closed in on Rlinda, opening fire all around. Cursing, she dodged again and again, but they kept targeting her. The shields began to fail. Her lone ship was insignificant in this nebula battlefield, but there were so many hunting robots that a swarm noticed her—and targeted her.

She used every trick she knew, pressed every system beyond its limits, but the robots were relentless. Another hundred angular black vessels closed in. Rlinda swallowed hard. Her shields wouldn't last much longer.

"You don't know who the hell you're dealing with, bugbots," she said. It was ridiculous defiance, but it felt good. Her left hand strayed to the capsule in her pocket for consolation and comfort. "We'll get out of this, BeBob." She had always wanted her ashes to fly through space with his when she died—that just might be the case here.

BeBob had been a damn good evasive navigator himself, but Rlinda was on her own. "Wish you were here."

Her ship raced alongside the towering verdani treeships. They might get away together, or they might all be vaporized right here inside the nebula.

119

MUREE'N

After the Mage-Imperator had nearly bled himself to death, the medical kithmen tried to save him, connecting him to Gale'nh in a desperate transfusion. Yazra'h, Nira, and Prime Designate Daro'h hovered over the dying leader, hoping Jora'h could cling to his strength, hoping the *thism* could save him—and, more than anything, hoping he had purged the shadows from himself.

But Murce'n felt the danger and the darkness spreading much farther. Right now, all of the focus was on the Mage-Imperator, but she sensed another vulnerability. There were more threats just waiting to strike. Yes, the Shana Rei meant to contaminate and possess Jora'h, but they also needed to destroy anything else that might hurt them.

Others were vulnerable.

Muree'n knew not to let down her guard. The shadows had already converted numerous Ildirans into mindless killers. She had seen what they could do. The mobs had tried to kill Nira, Prince Reynald, Anton Colicos, and many more. More than once, they had attempted to slaughter the misbreeds, who remained unprotected.

Mungl'eh had sung her enchanting song, and when the rest of the misbreeds added their unusual *thism*, they had been turned into a powerful weapon. Muree'n realized that the misbreeds were more than they seemed—not disappointments, but unexpected resources. And when Mungl'eh's heart-wrenching voice had resonated through the cosmos, that power awakened something . . . something powerful and wonderful.

Muree'n wouldn't abandon the misbreeds now. They might be at risk, even now.

As the Mage-Imperator received his lifesaving transfusion and the guard kithmen, bureaucrats, and doctors were focused on him, Muree'n left the Mage-Imperator in good hands and ran to defend the misbreeds—in case they needed it.

Shawn Fennis and Chiar'h were with them, both distraught and tense. Chiar'h's face and arms were covered with medical bindings from the slashes she had suffered in the previous attack. On guard, she and Fennis held makeshift weapons, just in case. Muree'n doubted they knew how to use them, but the two were clearly ready to fight to the death, regardless.

The surviving misbreeds huddled in a protected recovery chamber with soft beds and bright, restorative lighting. Ildiran guard kithmen stood outside the room, but Fennis had refused to let them come close.

Muree'n, though, was different. She entered the chamber and said, "I will do my best to protect you."

"Will that be enough?" Fennis asked.

She grasped her crystal katana. "It is all that I can give."

Chiar'h nodded with visible relief. "That may well be sufficient."

Mungl'eh lay back with her flipper arms raised. Her mouth was open, and her torso inflated as she drew a deep breath to sing. She produced another beautiful melody that vibrated the walls and drew the misbreeds together, pulling them, uniting them. Strengthening them.

Gor'ka and Har'lc added their synergy, and her singing became louder.

Muree'n's heart felt lighter. Her pulse raced, and she experienced a new emotion alongside the dark determination that had filled her for a very long time. It was hope. It was the melody of possibilities. It was the energetic song of a future with no boundaries. And when the song was over, the misbreeds heaved a sigh and settled down.

Muree'n steeled herself to be alert, to be protective.

The misbreeds blinked, and in unison they turned to Fennis and Chiar'h, then to Muree'n. "We wish Tamo'l were with us. But she's gone now."

"We could sense her before on a faraway planet," said Gor'ka. "But the Shana Rei have her now."

Har'lc said, "She is swallowed up in a black nightmare, trapped and drowning."

"I have sensed my sister, too," Muree'n said. "And Rod'h. They are together. Perhaps we can find a way to rescue them."

"No, nobody can," said Gor'ka. "We've called for her with all we possess, and we have touched her mind. She and Rod'h are both still alive."

Har'lc said, "They are fighting together, searching for a way to free themselves. Even here, at such a distance, we can pool our thoughts to give them strength, to give them hope, to beg them to rejoin us."

"I would fight along with them," Muree'n said. "And with you. Can I help?"

"You can join us," said Mungl'eh. "We don't know if there is a way, but we are trying."

"We are all trying," said Gor'ka.

Muree'n took a step in among the misbreeds and closed her eyes. She reached out, not just with her *thism* but with her tight sibling connection. "If there is a way for me to help Tamo'l and Rod'h, then I will do so."

"None of us knows," said Har'lc, "but we all try."

CHAPTER

120

MAGE-IMPERATOR JORA'H

When he woke, the Mage-Imperator felt disoriented—yet strong. Surprisingly strong! His heart was beating, his thoughts were racing, and his pulse had a power that he hadn't felt in a long time. An energy surged through his bloodstream, a clean vibrancy that he could barely remember—and he realized with a sharp intake of breath that he did not feel the shadows inside, not anymore. His blood was clean, the *thism* was pure. All the entangled strands were under his control again.

A sharp pain throbbed in his arms from where he had slashed open his blood vessels, but those were mere physical wounds, and the pain was just physical.

Something was definitely different about him now. He had been purged, and as thoughts swam in his head, he recalled his despair. He had attacked Nira and so many others when he fell under the influence of the Shana Rei. As his last hope, he had bled himself out, just like the Ahlar Designate had. He'd meant to spill all the darkness, drain the taint out of him and out of the *thism*. He had intended to die.

As he became aware again, he blinked his eyes and focused his vision. Medical kithmen surrounded him—but more importantly, he saw Nira, with her beautiful features, smooth green skin, and sparkling eyes. "Jora'h!" She let his name come out with a relieved sigh. "Oh, Jora'h."

He lifted a hand to grasp hers, but he could barely move with all the bandages and tubes. He turned his head and saw a familiar young man in the bed beside him. Gale'nh! "What happened? Why am I here?"

"We saved you, Jora'h," Nira said. "The Ildiran people need you.

They need your *thism,* and they need your leadership. And I need you."

Prime Designate Daro'h also came close. He clutched his father's shoulder. "You succeeded in purging the shadows, and you're still alive."

"But how?" Jora'h said. "How am I alive?"

On the adjacent bed, Gale'nh looked as cold and still as a statue. His already pale skin looked even grayer than before, drained of life. Medical apparatus was connected to him as well, and Jora'h saw that tubes joined the halfbreed man directly to him. Their blood was intermingled. The Solar Navy officer had surrendered his blood, his essence, his immunity that had once been strong enough to resist the Shana Rei. Gale'nh had given of himself, and he had saved the Mage-Imperator, but apparently at a tremendous cost.

Jora'h tried to sit up, felt dizzy.

Nira leaned close. "Gale'nh gave you his blood. You had drained most of yours, and he offered himself. He believed that with his immunity you might stay pure of the Shana Rei."

Feeling the energy inside him, Jora'h pushed himself up. "But what about him? Will he live?"

"He is strong," said Prime Designate Daro'h.

Jora'h narrowed his eyes, not hearing the answer he wanted. "But will he survive?"

"He is strong," Nira repeated. "And we think he is strong enough to live. And you will live as well. Can you feel the difference inside yourself?"

He definitely could. The strands of the *thism* were no longer just frayed spiderwebs; now they were tight, unbreakable cables, woven together and connecting every Ildiran: all the kiths across all the planets in the Empire.

He clenched his fists, and his injured tendons shouted with pain. The sutures in the slashed skin tightened, and bolts of sharp agony ran up his arms and into his shoulders and chest. But at least the jolt made him feel alive. He looked over at Gale'nh. "How much blood did he . . . ?"

"As much as you needed," Nira said. "And now you've expelled all the shadows. You're pure again."

"You are the Mage-Imperator, Father," Daro'h said. "You are the strength we need."

"Yes." Jora'h gritted his teeth and summoned up his own inner fire. "I am the strength we need. I am the strength Ildira needs."

He did feel energized, even though he was weak and drained. This was a different kind of power. The *thism* web had been reconnected, and he could withstand the creatures of darkness now. The shadows could no longer penetrate him. With his added immunity, they could not steal other Ildirans either, could not possess them and turn them into a murderous mob. The people belonged to Jora'h now. The *thism* was his defensive shield, and it was also his weapon.

He could feel Gale'nh's blood surging through his circulatory system. His head ached, but the throb was invigorating. He could pull it all together. He controlled the *thism,* and he reached out to touch the members of all kiths, and in return his people gave him a strength that he had always possessed, but hadn't previously known how to tap. It was a joyous thing. He had not expected to feel such excitement and hope, but there it was inside him, all the strands under his control.

Through the *thism* bond, he saw his people and his Empire, saw the spreading shadow clouds, some of them collapsing into newborn stars, while others closed in on populated worlds. In the Fireheart nebula, he connected with Adar Zan'nh, was shocked to see the Solar Navy ships struggling against impossible odds. Over half of the Adar's maniple had been wiped out already—while *he* had been gone from them.

But the Mage-Imperator could help them now. He felt the entire Ildiran race waking up, coming together, and *he* was doing it. But he could do more, so much more.

So he did.

Jora'h called upon his allies, and he made his demands. Before, he had begged them, but haphazardly, weakly. Now the Mage-Imperator was no longer weak. He needed help on behalf of the universe itself, and he had allies who could fight in ways that no Ildiran could imagine. He needed them now. He reached out with his mind, remembering the brief contact he had felt, the searing fire that coursed through the *thism* strands.

In the adjacent bed, Gale'nh twitched. The young halfbreed lifted his head. His eyes were dull and weak, but he was overjoyed with what he saw. Gale'nh let out a long weak sigh as he nodded.

Jora'h pushed forward even harder. He sent out the call—an urgent *demand* that he knew nothing could resist.

From out of their hiding places, Mage-Imperator Jora'h summoned the faeros.

LEE ISWANDER

He did not intend to lose everything—not through misfortune, not through his own bad decisions, and certainly not through Elisa Enturi's rash stupidity. No matter what Iswander did, no matter how hard he worked, no matter which ingenious plans he developed, he faced setback after setback.

In the past, he'd been appalled by what Elisa did in his name. A disaster brought about by misguided loyalty was still a disaster.

He had nothing left but these bloater-extraction operations, and he clung to them with a desperate possessiveness. He'd lost the respect he had built up over years of being a brilliant investor, a talented industrialist, someone whose innovation changed the Confederation. He should have been a Roamer's Roamer, but now he was holding on by his fingernails. But he refused to let go and plunge down into the black hole of obscurity.

And yet, Elisa was dragging him down that black hole with the ball-and-chain of her good intentions. When he saw her fly out and make her outrageous bluff—he hoped it was a bluff—to explode all the volatile bloaters, he clenched his fist so hard that he heard his knuckles crack. "Damn her!" He turned to Alec Pannebaker. "Stay here and monitor the operations, but don't take any preemptive action. There may still be a way to salvage this."

His employees needed to hear that there was a chance, but his mind spun as he tried to think of a solution. Lee Iswander was a man with impossible dreams and unlikely solutions. Maybe he could pull it off just one more time.

He ran down into the launching bay, hoping that a ship would be ready and waiting. The crews were out in their work shifts and many company vehicles had been deployed. Most of the bay was empty, but he spotted an inspection pod parked and available. It was a small, slow, unshielded ship, a little vessel built to hold one or two people. He rarely flew such things himself, but it was exactly what he needed now.

Elisa's ship hung among the bloaters, threatening to blow them all up—which would destroy his industrial operations along with the bloaters and everything else. Iswander had to stop her. His inspection pod looked ridiculously insignificant as it moved away from the admin hub, and he knew it.

It was the same sort of vessel that Aelin had flown out to marvel at the mysterious bloaters. The green priest was eccentric, damaged, and he had believed his contact with the bloaters let him connect to a vast consciousness. The idea that there might be some pulsing intelligence inside the gas bags seemed absurd to Iswander, but considering what Garrison Reeves and his crew claimed, maybe Aelin had been right.

Or more likely they were all insane. Certainly Elisa was on the edge of madness herself, and he had to stop her before she did something even more destructive.

He flew the inspection pod out toward the bloaters. Elisa had stopped answering his transmissions, but if he dropped directly in front of her ship, she would be forced to respond. He was sure he could convince her to back off. She needed to listen to him—he would make her listen to him.

In the small pod, he felt unprotected and vulnerable . . . but that was what he needed. He had to tap into Elisa's feelings for him, had to make her see that he relied on her protection. If she detonated the bloaters and ignited all that pure stardrive fuel, then they would all die. But if he approached her in just a little, nonthreatening inspection pod, maybe she would hesitate. Maybe she would withdraw.

Or maybe she wouldn't.

As he flew out to the standoff, he transmitted his message again, whether or not Elisa was listening. Her ship faced the *Prodigal Son,* and her weapons ports glowed. Garrison's ship hung there in surrender, but did not back away.

The bloaters drifted around like silent bombs. Iswander flew toward them, broadcasting on all bands. He hoped Elisa was still listening. He doubted she would cut him out entirely.

He imagined her rationale: Elisa would believe that her actions were for the best. She thought she was making a hard decision that he didn't have the stomach to make. She believed she was doing the right thing for him.

And she had been wrong so many times before.

Iswander knew he was a difficult man, that he pushed people and insisted on getting his way. He'd invested vast fortunes, had taken risks; he had nerves and he had hopes.

"You've got to stop this, Elisa. That's a direct order. It's not what I want. I need you to hear me."

He flew closer. The pod was just a tiny speck among the huge mottled bloaters. Many were already drained, and their shriveled husks had been towed to the edge of the cluster. Bright lights marked the pumping stations and the tank arrays, but everything would be wiped out if the bloaters exploded. Iswander was in the thick of it now.

A flicker of light twinkled inside a distant bloater, like a brief newborn star, and then it went dim again. All of the nodules seemed hushed and silent, as if waiting to see what would happen next.

Garrison transmitted, "Elisa, if you open fire on the bloaters you'll kill us all, and you'll kill Seth—and you're going to harm the only thing that can save the human race from the Shana Rei. Even you wouldn't do that—I know you, Elisa."

"You don't know me at all," she retorted. "You thought you did, and I thought I knew you, but you just fooled me. Mr. Iswander needs me, and I'm going to save his operations."

Iswander broke in. "Not this way you aren't! I will be dead, and my memory reviled across the Confederation. Even if we get out of this, I'll be punished. I'll be more of an outlaw than I am now."

"Only if I fail, sir," Elisa said.

At least now he knew she was listening on his channel. "I forbid it! There's been enough done in my name. Yes, I made mistakes, but I made them on my own. I don't need other people to make them for me—and you are making a mistake, Elisa."

"I will not let you be weak, sir."

Iswander summoned all the command he could put into his voice and burned his gaze into the comm screen. "How dare you suggest I'm weak. You have been loyal, and you've followed my orders, but you do not understand every aspect of my business, or all of my plans. What you're doing right now is damaging my future." He drew a breath and spoke each word as if he were firing a weapon at her. "*I need you to back down!*"

"No! Then we'll lose."

"You've already made us lose, Elisa. Now I'm just trying to salvage what I can."

She remained silent, her ship hanging there, her weapons ports glowing. Even though he had her attention, even though he knew she was listening, part of him realized this was the most dangerous moment of his life. One twitch could make her open fire. If she felt despair, if she refused to surrender, they would all vanish in an expanding ball of ignited stardrive fuel.

"But . . . sir!" she beseeched him.

Two of the nearby bloaters sparkled, bright flashes strobing from their cores. Iswander let out another slow breath.

Wisely, Garrison Reeves and Orli Covitz remained silent, just waiting.

Elisa's voice was filled with anguish. "*Sir!*"

As his scout pod drifted close to one of the nodules, the patterns across its outer membrane flexed like some strange and incomprehensible map, and its interior lit up like a tiny nova, a flash of intense light as a chain of thought cascaded along the ganglia of the cosmic mind.

The nucleus of the nearby bloater flared into blinding light, and the flash slammed into Iswander's scout pod. Energy flooded through the craft, shorted out all the control circuits, but it kept throbbing, overwhelming him.

Iswander howled as his cells and his thoughts and his mind exploded in an unbearable surge of power, but his comm systems were eradicated, so no one heard him scream.

SHAREEN FITZKELLUM

The maneuvers threw Shareen from side to side as Tasia and Robb raced like maniacs away from the Fireheart central complex. The robot attackers could blast the *Curiosity* into molten debris at any moment.

The nebula battlefield sparkled and flared with the constant firepower. The Solar Navy ships suddenly rallied as if the Ildirans had snapped out of their stupor, and now the remaining warliners were all flying together in perfect coordination. They lashed out with their laser cannons, deployed their last few sun bombs. General Keah's Juggernauts and Mantas had depleted all their major weaponry, but they continued to use conventional jazers as they retreated from the nebula.

"Obviously, they see no point in staying here," Robb said aloud.

"Neither do I," Tasia said.

On the screen, moments after Shareen saw *Declan's Glory* fly away from the terrarium, the dome burst open to release a pair of enormous verdani battleships that soared into the sea of gases, their boughs outstretched. But the remaining shadow cloud expanded like a suffocating blanket, growing thicker and blacker as the Shana Rei filled the ocean of ionized gases.

"Where do we go now?" Howard said, grabbing a console to keep his balance.

"As far away as possible." Robb answered as he tried to coax even more acceleration from the engines. "Heading there now."

More than a hundred black robot ships were closing in on them from all sides. No matter how Tasia tried to maneuver, the marauders blocked them off, opening fire. Their shields were about to fail.

With a sick heart, Shareen remembered how her grandfather had insisted on sending her here so she could study under Kotto Okiah. "It's a great opportunity," Del Kellum had said. And she had certainly learned a lot.

"I'm glad we could be together, Howard," Shareen whispered.

"School certainly wasn't boring," he answered. "Though I would have preferred a different end."

"Don't distract me, you two," Tasia snapped. "It's not over yet."

The blue supergiants at Fireheart's core had begun to pulse and flare. "Look at the core stars!" Shareen said. "Something's happening to them."

They had been so intent on escaping the Shana Rei and the robots that they paid no attention to the heart of the nebula. Now Shareen took over the *Curiosity*'s sensor package and used the controls to expand the view and zoom in. From the back, the other passengers yelled as Tasia took rough evasive action from a flurry of robot potshots, diving and corkscrewing with nauseating finesse.

Fighting to keep her balance and focus the image, Shareen gasped at what the sensors showed when she enlarged the view. "Look at that!"

On the screen, the nebula's central stars were swarming with faeros! Tens of thousands of the ellipsoidal fireballs emerged from within the hot supergiants.

Howard was at her side. "All those faeros . . . what are they doing?"

Robb said, "The main question is whether it's a good thing or a bad thing."

"They must be trying to help us," Shareen said.

Tasia could barely spare a glance at the screen. "How do you figure?"

Shareen looked at her, swallowing hard. "Because if they're *not* trying to help, then we may as well just hit the self-destruct right now."

The shadow cloud kept filling the rarefied gases, but the supergiant stars brightened, as if the countless fire elementals were adding fuel, making the central nuclear reactions unstable. The already unstable stars flared brighter, noticeably increasing in magnitude. The faeros plunged into the suns like hornets around a large hive; then they swam around, building up nuclear reactions. They manipulated gravity.

On a scale of incomprehensible distance and speed, the faeros pulled the already packed stars closer. The fireballs dragged two smaller companion stars into one of the supergiants, pulling them together. The smaller stars swirled around in ever-tightening orbits until they fell into the supergiant's gravity well. The outer veils of their chromospheres were torn away, large amounts of fuel feeding the monstrous star. The faeros pushed and pulled and dragged in more stellar material. The huge, hot star swelled and flared.

"They're doing it on purpose," Shareen whispered.

"Are they trying to create a super-supergiant?" Tasia asked. "For what?"

"No, not that," Howard said.

Shareen suddenly caught her breath. "Once they increase the material, when the main star has more mass than its nuclear reactions can support, the core will collapse catastrophically."

"And then what?" Robb asked.

Howard yelled. "We'd better get out of here!"

"What?" Tasia cried, flying straight toward the flurry of robot ships converging in front of them. "*What?*"

"Supernova!" Shareen said.

"The core will collapse and throw off all the outer layers in an explosive reaction—the largest explosion in the known universe," Howard said. "And when that giant star goes supernova, it'll trigger the other core stars and ignite a chain reaction of supernovas. That's what the faeros are doing. It'll wipe out the entire Fireheart nebula, and all of us!"

Shareen steeled her voice. "And quite possibly the Shana Rei. Much more than a million sun bombs all at once—that's what they're trying to do. And I hope it works."

The two newborn verdani treeships flew away, catching up with *Declan's Glory* as they soared toward the fringes of the Fireheart nebula. Rlinda's ship was much too close to the core and the faeros. The blue star throbbed, clearly reaching its critical instability.

"Run!" Shareen said. "The situation just got a thousand times worse."

"We haven't exactly been dallying." With an even more frantic edge, Tasia and Robb hurtled between several black robot ships, barely missing one, then flying away at all possible speed.

At the nebula's core, the faeros finally achieved their goal. The blue supergiant swallowed up the companion stars and pulled in even more stolen stellar material. It was all happening so fast. The gigantic star throbbed, throwing off great shock waves of building radiation. The faeros seemed to revel in it.

And then it all changed. As the heart of the nebula detonated, the star exploded with a thunderclap loud enough to awaken the entire universe.

The CDF battleships and Solar Navy warliners were already retreating, nearing the edge of the nebula.

The *Voracious Curiosity* fled with as much acceleration as their bones could tolerate—and still, they were overtaken by the violent slap of the shock wave. All of their systems flared, nearly overloaded. The shields were at maximum, but weakened from the constant hammering of robot weaponry. Their ship was buffeted about like a bit of pollen fluff in a hurricane.

Under the impossible photonic and radiation flood, the Shana Rei shadow cloud curled back, torn into black shreds as the shock wave from the multiple supernovas expanded and expanded, rolling along in intense walls of radiation.

Just before their screens failed, Shareen saw *Declan's Glory* trying to keep up with the huge verdani treeships, but the flare of light engulfed Rlinda's ship.

Tasia screamed. "No! Rlinda!"

Then the secondary shock front slammed into them as more of the core supergiants exploded, tearing a gigantic hole in the nebula. The *Curiosity*'s systems overloaded into static. The ship's interior lights dropped out, then reawakened as dull red emergency systems.

The *Voracious Curiosity* spun about until Shareen was sick, confused and lost, barely holding on to consciousness. Then even the emergency lights went black.

ROD'H

Trapped inside the entropy bubble in the void, Rod'h and Tamo'l watched the faeros inflict a tremendous blow on the Shana Rei, bombarding them with more light and cleansing radiation than even the creatures of darkness could withstand.

But still they needed more.

Previously, when the faeros attacked the shadow clouds, they had only been able to hurt the darkness by sacrificing themselves—but the multiple supernovas caused far more harm. The fiery elementals had combined their powers to drive the unstable stars over the brink, and now the faeros struck back using the weapons of physics and the secrets held within the nuclear reactions of the universe itself.

Inside the core stars, the fireballs had changed nuclear chemistry, unleashing a supernova reaction like a scream of defiance in the face of the shadows—as devastating as the cosmic mind crushing their shadow clouds, as damaging as the sun bombs unleashed inside the dark void against the vulnerable flank of the Shana Rei.

Within the prison of their entropy bubble, angry dark inkblots appeared before Rod'h and Tamo'l, as if they blamed their captives for the damage. Rod'h wished he could have taken credit for such a blow. He didn't have the power, but now he had the inspiration. And he had Tamo'l.

The blazing eyes inside the inkblot smears flared. Shana Rei voices roared out, "The light! Burning light!"

"Then burn more," Rod'h growled. "Tamo'l, they are weakened!"

Out in the nebula, the faeros were no longer afraid of the creatures of darkness, and they plunged into the expanding supernova flare as if overjoyed. Bombarded with such intense damage from the real universe, the walls of the entropy bubble rippled.

"It's collapsing," Tamo'l said. "Will we escape?"

"No," Rod'h answered, because he did not want to lie to her. "But maybe we can help. Maybe the faeros can help us."

Her voice carried the faintest tremor. "How?"

Rod'h remembered when he and Osira'h had sought out the elementals around the unstable star of Wulfton, begging them for assistance. The two siblings had used their telepathic powers to link with the faeros. Rod'h had strained his innate abilities and used his mind to pull on them, to plead with them as he had been *born* to do.

Rod'h had always tried to compete with Osira'h, struggled to be as strong, sure that with his superior halfbreed genetics he should be able to draw on the same strengths that his sister could. Together, they had touched the faeros, opened a channel . . . and the fiery elementals had fled in fear, refusing to help.

But now the situation had changed. Osira'h wasn't here, and it was entirely up to Rod'h. No, he had Tamo'l, his sister—both of them halfbreeds, both of them with incredible potential thanks to the breeding program. She could help.

"I need you, Tamo'l," he said.

Within their shadow cloud, the Shana Rei squirmed and flickered. Their symbolic eyes swelled wider, blazed brighter, then turned red as if they were being torn apart by agony. Rod'h saw that the creatures of darkness were suddenly vulnerable, and he knew how to destroy them—if only he could make the connection, if only he could prove himself one more time.

If only the faeros would listen and realize what he was offering them.

"We cannot let the shadows control us, Tamo'l." He reached out to her, but because of the dimensional folding, she drifted just a hairsbreadth from him, yet a universe away.

It didn't matter. They were together in the way that counted. He could look into her eyes, and somehow she understood.

"I can sense you, and that is enough," Tamo'l said. "And I can sense the misbreeds watching, sharing their strength with us, too. They will give us what we need."

Rod'h knew what they needed. "The faeros are out there, but we need to bring them in here. Because of what we are, you and I have a connection to them. That is why we were bred in the first place, and now the faeros can put an end to this whole war. If they could get inside here—if they could come into the shadow cloud." He allowed himself a bitter grin. "The Shana Rei believe they're safe and protected in their void. But they will be the cause of their own downfall."

Tamo'l nodded, accepting, willing to do anything that was within her power. "Draw on me. Use whatever you need. We have to do this."

Rod'h opened up his mind. He yearned; he connected. He sought out the faeros. The fiery elementals were close, swirling in the expanding Armageddon bubble of the supernovas they had triggered.

Suddenly, nearly fifty black robots appeared with them inside the entropy bubble. Their carapaces split apart, their jagged solar-power wings extended, as well as clawed pincers, sharp implements they had used to torture and experiment on Rod'h. They came close with murderous intent. Somehow, they knew what Rod'h and Tamo'l were trying to do.

But he was beyond fear. His captors had done every terrible thing they possibly could, and nothing remained for him to be afraid of. Now, he was only afraid of failure.

The Exxos counterparts buzzed in unison. Numerous robots suddenly grew alarmed, fearing what the two halfbreeds were about to accomplish. Rod'h reached out, and Tamo'l reached out with him. She spoke with a whisper of wonder. "Can you hear it? In the back of my mind—it is Mungl'eh . . . singing."

There, in the vast empty sea of unreality, they linked with the faeros, and the elementals recognized them, catching their thoughts . . . and they understood where the two halfbreeds were, what they were offering.

With all of his being, surrendering every last scrap of his heart and mind, his *thism,* his thoughts, his soul, Rod'h invited the faeros inside. He drew the fiery elementals through him, through Tamo'l, and into this cavernous sheltered bubble of the shadow cloud.

Rod'h felt a purifying blaze of fire, a heat that did not, in fact, contain any pain, but simply relief and victory. Tamo'l was with him, and he could feel her thoughts, too. His mind shouted outward with victory and exhilaration, a flood that poured outward to his siblings, throughout the Ildiran *thism* . . . and even to their mother, far away in Mijistra.

The faeros came through them like a meteor storm. In a searing flash, the fireballs roared inside the shadow cloud through him. Rod'h opened a channel and became a living transportal that disintegrated his body before he knew anything else, and thanks to his connection to Tamo'l she was able to do the same.

In doing so, they let a wildfire of elementals enter the core of Shana Rei entropy. For the first time, the faeros could come directly *inside* the most vulnerable heart of the shadows, erupting with fire and light. Incandescent and growing stronger, they blazed through the last remnants of Rod'h and Tamo'l to destroy the creatures of darkness and their monstrous shadow ships from within.

124

OSIRA'H

With Prince Reynald still in a coma and fading away in the last stages of his mysterious sickness, Osira'h struggled to find a solution—something they hadn't yet tried. But hadn't they tried everything? Neither the green priests nor the Confederation's best doctors knew what to do. It was not through lack of effort. Reyn was dying.

Osira'h had spent days at the Prince's bedside, but he never opened his eyes, never whispered a word to her. His pulse remained steady but weak, and his skin had lost much of its color. She stayed with him because she believed that her presence gave him strength. Reyn had always said so.

"We're supposed to see the ice geysers on Edilyn," she said to him, "and the fossil canyons on Fornu."

Back on Ildira, medical kithmen had run every test and devoted tremendous resources to finding a cure. Confederation pharmaceutical labs had synthesized drugs similar to the kelp extracts from Kuivahr, but they no longer proved effective. Research teams had made partial progress, thanks to the Pergamus data, and they knew a chemical template that would block the debilitating microfungus . . . but they had to find it among millions of Theron native specimens.

It was not enough.

Osira'h could think of only one other place where she might make a demand. It was a very slim hope, but right now it was her only one. Though it meant leaving Reyn's side, she had to take that gamble.

King Peter and Queen Estarra came to stand beside the Prince's bed. Under any other circumstances, their dying son should have been the only thing they were worried about, but the crisis sweeping the Spiral Arm also demanded their attention. The green priests provided them dire updates about the battle taking place in the Fireheart nebula, but their descriptions were erratic, disorganized, as if none of their counterparts aboard the battleships had clear knowledge of what was actually happening.

The Shana Rei were tearing apart the Confederation and the Ildiran Empire, and nothing could stop them. Earth had been destroyed, the CDF and the Solar Navy decimated. And her brother Rod'h was trapped among the shadows, beyond any hope of rescue— joined now by Tamo'l. Osira'h agonized over that, but she could not help them, no matter what she tried.

For Reyn, though, she had an idea, another desperate chance. . . .

Osira'h said to Peter and Estarra, "I have to make the attempt. Even if it fails, I need to try. I'm going—by myself. I think maybe the Onthos can help. Their disease, his disease—different, but both are connected to the trees."

Estarra scowled. "They murdered my sister, and they're killing the trees. They won't be inclined to help."

Osira'h couldn't articulate her reasoning or her hope. She could only say, "I've asked everyone else. Your green priests insist on preserving the Gardeners, and the verdani won't let them die. They must have something to offer."

She felt isolated and alone as her private flyer crossed the narrow sea to the other continent. Though she was far from the gigantic struggle taking place, Osira'h could sense great turmoil throughout the Ildiran Empire. Mage-Imperator Jora'h was under impossible strain, and his anguish was like a high-pitched wail in her mind. With her closer sibling bond, she experienced similar desperation from Gale'nh, as well as Muree'n.

Building in intensity, she felt a smothering struggle tempered by a desperate hope: Tamo'l and Rod'h were doing their best to resist the Shana Rei inside their void prison. So many wildfires of crisis building to an out-of-control blaze, so many people pulling on their last energy to make a final stand. So many . . .

Osira'h knew she would be on her own to help Reynald. She was cut off from the other battles against darkness, but she could fight for *him*.

She landed her flyer outside the miles-wide swath of dead trees. Up to the blight's boundary, the dense worldforest seemed lush and peaceful, although she was aware of the dark disease churning beneath its surface. The Theron home guard and green priests had fought against the Gardeners, and they had begun blasting away the already-dead trees where the Onthos had built their fortress. But when General Keah had arrived announcing the destruction of Earth, King Peter had rushed back to the capital, leaving only a contingent here to contain the Onthos. The Gardeners hadn't made any further moves.

Emerging from her ship, Osira'h met a haggard-looking military commander and the green priest Zaquel, both uncomfortable with the standoff. The commander said, "They haven't tried to attack, but we know they're breeding in there. They'll infest the whole worldforest."

Zaquel said, "The Onthos spore mothers need healthy worldtrees to reproduce. By bottling them up in the dead section, we can stop them from multiplying further—for now." She sighed. "But the worldforest is still dying. The blight that afflicts the trees and the Gardeners afflicts the entire universe."

"And Prince Reynald, too. We need to cure one piece at a time," Osira'h said. "If we can."

She walked past the barricade line, and no one tried to stop her. She stepped in among the fallen brown trees, the smashed branches and splintered wood. She picked her way carefully into the desolate area. Osira'h heard a rustle in the branches and saw that the Onthos were all around her. The smooth-skinned aliens peered down at her, seemingly frightened and angry.

"There's a disease inside you," she shouted. "You know it. You can feel it. Why do you choose not to cure yourselves?"

The Gardeners chittered. More of them came, as she waited for an answer. Finally one of the aliens stepped forward. "The darkness is in us, and it is integral to us."

"My friend is dying of a similar thing," she said. "But you're not dying. How do you still function? How can I save him?"

The spokesman—Ohro, she assumed, or another just like him—

said, "Would you save your friend if the cost was to let him suc-
cumb to shadows?"

Osira'h wasn't sure how she would respond to that terrible
choice. "Others are fighting. You have surrendered, but the people
of Theroc, the human Confederation, the Ildiran Empire, the green
priests, the verdani, the faeros—" Inside herself, she felt a rush of
heat, a burning urgency. She linked tightly with her siblings, Gale'nh
and Muree'n both adding strength, making a clear connection . . .
to Rod'h! And Tamo'l!

Deep inside the smothering blackness, she suddenly felt fire, a
welcome blaze of light. Rod'h had done it. He had called the faeros.
Osira'h gasped. The searing light raced along her mental connection
with her siblings. They smashed open the floodgates and used their
own special abilities to let the fiery elementals inside.

Osira'h experienced a swelling wave of triumph from both of
them. She sensed what her siblings had done, and she knew they
were gone in an instant. She could experience the fire, the exhilaration, the pain . . . and she knew the incredible blow they had dealt
to the Shana Rei. She was proud of what they had done, and grief-
stricken to know they were gone.

As the incandescent pain burned and broke the telepathic connection between them, Osira'h's body hunched over, as if a seizure
had shaken her entire being.

The Onthos reacted as well, but their agony seemed different and
deeper—and it went on far longer. Tamo'l and Rod'h had been consumed in an instant, and their psychic cry fell silent inside her mind,
but the Onthos continued to gasp and hiss. Something fundamental
had been ripped out of them.

They began to drop from the high branches like rotting fruit, falling from the brown boughs of the worldtrees they had killed. One
struck the ground beside her with a loud thud and snap of bones.
Many crashed down from great heights, while others were impaled
on the broken wood they had left strewn around. Dozens lay dead
from the fall, while others slid down from the trees, bleeding,
exhausted. Broken.

Even as Osira'h tried to comprehend what had just happened,

she listened to the dwindling agony of the Gardeners. Their wails became whimpers.

Finally, one of the creatures picked himself up, stunned, barely able to maintain his balance. "I did not think we could be cured or saved, but the shadows are burned out of us now. The blight has been extinguished within."

Other Onthos came forward shaking and confused as if they had just awakened from a deep slumber. "We surrender," said Ohro. "Take us back to Father Peter and Mother Estarra. We have many things to tell them."

Though she could feel the raw wound inside herself after what Rod'h and Tamo'l had just done, Osira'h also had another urgent need. "And Prince Reynald?"

Ohro looked at her, pondered for a moment, and said, "He has a different disease, but we will see what we can do."

125

ELISA ENTURI

The bloaters in the cluster sparked like fireworks, their nuclei flaring bright in random signals—but Elisa cared only about the damage they had done to Lee Iswander's scout pod. She had watched him on the comm screen, heard him begging her—and then the energy burst slammed into the vulnerable craft. All his systems had failed, and now his pod drifted dark and silent, showing no energy signature whatsoever, no engines, no comm, no life-support readings.

Elisa sprang into action. She forgot her ultimatum to Garrison because none of that mattered. Iswander was in trouble! She activated her engines and raced toward the tumbling pod, hoping he wasn't dead. His life-support systems had been knocked offline, but he should be able to survive for a while at least . . . long enough for her to save him. She had to save him.

Even though Elisa's ship wasn't a large vessel, its cargo bay was sufficient to receive the small scout pod. As soon as she had sealed the bay doors and cycled the atmosphere, she ran to extract him from the tiny ship. His electronic systems were down, and if she couldn't activate the hatch, she would cut through the hull itself, break open the pod, and release him. She would find him inside, glad to see her, exuberant and forgiving. Together, the two of them could stand against the arrogant fools who ordered him to shut down his industries. She had devoted so much of her energy to this man, hitching herself to his star. If he failed, then she would fail. He was her last chance.

The pod's hatch wouldn't open, no matter what she tried. She pounded on it, but heard no response from inside. He should have

been able to use a manual release, unless he was hurt or unconscious.

From the piloting deck, she could hear voices over her ship's
comm system, people demanding to know what was happening, but
she didn't have time to answer them. She had other priorities.

She ran to get a set of laser cutters and sliced into the control circuitry so she could use the external lock. When Elisa finally breached
the pod's seal and accessed the manual release, she managed to open
the hatch, which sighed open.

"Sir! Can you hear me?" She wanted him to help her, but she
received no response. He wasn't moving in there.

She found Iswander inside, slumped and motionless. He wore no
protective suit, didn't even have an oxygen mask—just his business
attire, as if he had meant to attend a meeting. He must have rushed
out to talk her down, and now she recalled everything he had said,
how he'd commanded her to reconsider her course of action.

Elisa had only meant to do what was necessary, assuming that
her edgy defiance would make Garrison back away, because
Garrison Reeves, of all people, would have known that she was
not bluffing.

What had she done?

She shook Iswander by the shoulders, but got no response. His
skin was pale, his eyes closed, his mouth slack. She placed her ear
against his chest, touched his neck and found a pulse. He was breathing, still alive—but unresponsive.

She remembered when Aelin had been caught in one of the bloater
surges. He had been rendered temporarily catatonic from the neural
overload, but the green priest had been connected to his treeling at
the time, hence the destructive surge in his mind. Aelin had been
broken afterward, somewhat insane, his head filled with delusional
visions. Stray thoughts from Eternity's Mind?

She could not let that happen to Iswander.

"Sir!" She touched his face, she shook him. With her thumb, she
peeled back his eyelid, but his eyes were rolled back. She pulled him
out of the scout pod and dragged him to the cabin of her ship. She
laid him out on the bunk, tried to make him comfortable. Her heart
was pounding, desperate to do something else.

Determined, she flew her ship back to the admin hub, broadcasting a distress call. "Prepare the doctors! I need medical attention right away. Mr. Iswander is injured." She swallowed hard. "He needs treatment—now."

As soon as she docked and shut her systems down, the doctors hurried forward into the launching bay to take the patient. Back when a catatonic Aelin had been brought in, they had tried everything possible, and none of their efforts had worked. With Elisa following close behind them, they rushed a gurney pallet along as they attached monitoring systems and electrodes to Iswander's head.

Pannebaker also came in, deeply concerned, but from the flare behind his narrowed eyes, Elisa could see that the deputy blamed her for what had happened. "He went out to stop you, Elisa. If you hadn't been so stupid, if you'd just listened when he—"

"Shut up. While you just sat here ready to surrender, I tried to save us all. Mr. Iswander was caught in a bloater discharge, and I could do nothing to stop that, but at least I tried to keep him from losing everything." She gritted her teeth and drew a deep breath. "And we're going to keep trying to protect this facility."

To add insult to injury, the *Prodigal Son* also flew to the admin hub. Garrison and Orli brought Seth in with them. Princess Arita's green priest friend carried his treeling and dispatched reports of what was happening there.

Elisa gritted her teeth to see the green priest. Thanks to him, now everyone across the Confederation knew about their face-off, knew that the great industrialist had resisted these capricious demands, and now lay helpless. Rage swelled within her, and there were so many targets for it.

"It's over, Elisa," Garrison said. "Time to make amends and try to salvage your life and your relationships. You have to face what you've done—to clan Duquesne, to Seth, to everyone else you've hurt."

She stiffened. "What I've done to *Seth*? I only ever wanted the best for Seth." Her own son looked at her with disappointment. She realized that only a few hours ago Seth had seen her ready to blow him up along with everyone else, just to make a point. Earlier, he had watched her threaten Jess and Cesca at Academ when she had tried to steal him away.

Elisa struggled with an unfamiliar backlash of guilt, and she turned to the boy. "I haven't done right by you. I know that, and I apologize." Then she faced Garrison, hardened her voice. "But for you and for everything else, I had my reasons. If you'd had your head on straight from the start, you and I could have gone far. We could have been important. But you made me do it by myself. See what I accomplished—imagine what else I might have done if everyone hadn't interfered."

"We can see what you accomplished," Garrison said, his expression dark. "It's nothing to be proud of."

She wanted to lash back at him, but the doctors interrupted her. "We finished our scans." They issued their report indiscriminately, so that everyone could hear. "His mind is unresponsive. It's worse than what we saw with the green priest. There is only a very small chance Mr. Iswander will ever recover."

Collin said, "It's like what happened to Kotto Okiah at Fireheart Station. When he connected with Eternity's Mind, it was too much for him." He shook his head. "He never came out of it, and his body died a few days later."

Elisa showed her disappointment to the doctors, realizing that she'd always known they couldn't do anything. From the moment she had seen Iswander's unconscious form inside the blasted pod, she understood his prospects.

"The green priest recovered, though," she said. "Even after Aelin was damaged, he flew out and immersed himself inside a bloater. That changed him, brought him back." She whipped her gaze to Orli Covitz. "And you too! You came here dying. You should be dead from that Onthos plague, but you went inside a bloater, and you came out healed."

"That was a desperate circumstance," Orli pointed out. "And the bloaters are different now, more aware—"

"What other chance do we have?" Elisa demanded. She turned to the doctors. "I'm getting an exosuit. I'll fly him out to the nearest bloater."

"That's not wise," said the doctor.

"You said yourself, there's little other hope." She turned to glare at Pannebaker, Garrison, Orli. She didn't care what they all thought, and she certainly wasn't interested in Arita or their pompous warnings. "Do I need to threaten you?" She waited for someone to argue, but Iswander was completely catatonic, and they could all see he had very little chance. "I'm taking him."

Pannebaker gave a brief nod. "In the meantime, since I'm in charge of operations, I'm calling a full halt in compliance with the moratorium imposed by the King and Queen. The bloaters are clearly hazardous, and we will reassess the dangers. There will be no more ekti extraction for the time being."

"Thank you," Arita said, in a low whisper.

Elisa couldn't be concerned with that. She took the motionless Iswander and carried him back to her ship with very little assistance from the others. She didn't bother to look back at them as she propped him in the second seat in the piloting deck, activated her engines, and flew out into the bloater cluster.

The drifting nodules sparkled with erratic pulses of light, as if the space brain were filled with furious thoughts. One such outburst had damaged Iswander's mind, and she hoped that the so-called blood of the cosmos would also save him.

In the complex around them, she looked at the industrial operations that had now gone dark, just waiting. The exosuited workers, the ekti extractors, the cargo ships did nothing, paralyzed without a bold and decisive leader like Iswander. Elisa wished they all had the same dedication she did. How did they expect to get ahead in their lives and in their careers? How did they intend to make progress without putting in the effort, without taking the risks? Iswander had taught her that all along, and she understood full well that one had to be willing to fail spectacularly in order to hope for success.

Of course, Elisa would take the risk.

She flew directly to the closest bloater, hoping that another discharge would not strike her vessel and leave her as brain-damaged as Iswander. She couldn't count on anyone else to do what was necessary, and Elisa knew exactly what actions were required.

She brought her ship close to the nodule, whose mottled outer membrane bore indecipherable patterns. She saw flickers of pulsing energy deep inside the swirling murk. That fluid inside the bloater was more than just stardrive fuel; it was protoplasm in a giant brain cell. It was *hope,* maybe even a miracle.

She stabilized her ship and then spent a tedious half hour putting an exosuit on Lee Iswander. His arms were loose, his legs floppy, his eyes still closed. She sealed the helmet, then donned her own suit. Together, they would go inside the bloater, immerse themselves. It was the only chance they had.

Tethered to him and holding his limp arm, she opened the airlock hatch, and the two drifted into space. She held Iswander, spoke to him over the comm, but of course he didn't respond. Not yet. But she held on to hope. The bloater would save him, she was sure of it.

They drifted up against the giant, soft membrane. Elisa had to have faith and determination.

Cutting through the membrane was easy, and they climbed inside as protoplasm spilled out into space around them. Aelin had done this. Orli Covitz had done it. Surely Elisa could do better.

The two suited figures were drawn into the cell of the awakening space brain, sinking into the blood of the cosmos. Elisa immersed herself completely as the nodule crackled and pulsed with burgeoning energy. She pulled Lee Iswander deeper inside with her, and the membrane quickly sealed itself.

They never re-emerged.

Hours later, Elisa's silent and empty ship drifted away while the bloaters continued sparkling and flashing. The thoughts of Eternity's Mind continued to impose order on the universe and strengthen the laws of physics against the Shana Rei.

But Lee Iswander and Elisa Enturi were no longer part of the equation.

126

EXXOS

The Shana Rei were blasted and battered by the titanic counterattacks that struck them from the Fireheart nebula and from within the void itself. Even as Exxos rallied, countless black robots had been annihilated; worse, he saw the creatures of darkness crippled and broken, unable to fight back and unable to flee.

The shadows had wanted to unmake the cosmos, to eliminate all life that caused them pain. But the human and Ildiran forces had attacked and wounded them in their dark dimension, unleashing so many sun bombs that they caused considerable harm.

At the same time, across the Spiral Arm the awakening Eternity's Mind strengthened the fabric of the universe, building invisible cages of structure and life that could withstand the flailing chaos of the Shana Rei. Their shadow clouds were collapsing into newborn stars, driven by the clusters of gigantic ganglia.

As the shadows reeled from that, the chain of supernovas erupting inside the nebula was orders of magnitude more devastating to them—and now the faeros had found a channel directly into the deepest black corners of the void, flooding in to destroy countless more Shana Rei, incinerating them from within.

Exxos and all his counterparts would be annihilated along with the creatures of darkness—and he could not allow that to happen.

The last remaining Klikiss robots had been painted into a corner by the Shana Rei, and they were treated as captives as much as allies. The shadows had destroyed many of the original robots by capricious whim, but they had also created millions of duplicates with their manifested dark matter.

Although Exxos had once considered the Shana Rei to be an

undefeatable enemy, his robots had combined millions of processors to prepare an illicit weapon that would beat the monstrous shadows. Even so, he had not intended to use it—not yet. He had hoped that if they cooperated and helped to eliminate the humans and Ildirans, just as they had eliminated the progenitor Klikiss race long ago, then the shadows would grant them their promised reward. But Exxos had never truly believed their promises.

On the other hand, he had never believed the Shana Rei could be defeated by outside forces either. And now they were obviously wounded and reeling.

It was time. One last chance.

The harm the shadows had already suffered was immeasurable. More than half of the Shana Rei were gone, unable to comprehend their own near-mortal wounds. Right now, the creatures of darkness were the weakest they had been since reemerging into the universe. Now, the last of them retreated into the sanctuary of their protected void. They were unfocused, confused—and vulnerable.

Exxos and all the identical black robots came to the same conclusion instantaneously. Over millennia, the robots had always been willing to turn at a moment's notice, to find a vulnerability and strike. Now was their perfect chance.

Exxos gambled. He surmised that the Shana Rei might recover and grow strong again. If the robots fought alongside the creatures of darkness, helped them to escape, rebuild, and come back, then they might eventually strike the Spiral Arm again. It was a possibility . . . and, oh, how Exxos wanted that!

But if the Shana Rei did become powerful once more, then the robots would be mere playthings and slaves all over again. Exxos would never trust the shadows, and the robots would never escape.

Yes, this was their best opportunity.

For months, the combined processing power of millions of robot minds had developed their unorthodox entropy nullifiers, the reality-crystallization effect that required the highest-order calculations of exotic physics. Unable to guarantee that it would work, the robots would have only one chance, only one test.

Now that the Shana Rei were battered, this was an opportunity he could not ignore. The robots simultaneously put the plan into effect. They would annihilate the Shana Rei, and then they would all escape.

The pulsing inkblots with angry glowing eyes were all around them, but the shadows were desperate and paid little attention to the numerous Exxos copies that remained. He knew the Shana Rei would sacrifice every one of the robots if such a massacre would give the shadows one more moment of continued existence.

Exxos meant to take that away from them.

As the creatures of darkness retreated into their empty void, the swarms of robot copies manipulated physics, activated their calculated algorithms, and triggered the net that changed reality around the Shana Rei. The process nullified the entropy that formed their very being.

The swelling, shapeless black smears shuddered, squirmed. Their representational eyes blazed, then went dim as the inkblots fossilized. Their framework of existence crystalized into sharp order—and they shattered.

In the emptiness between dimensions, all of the Shana Rei ceased to exist—in exactly the way they had wanted to uncreate the real universe.

Exxos watched what was happening, unable to believe his perfect and complete success as the creatures of darkness simply evaporated, as if they had never existed at all. He experienced a moment of total victory.

But when the Shana Rei faded, all of the new dark matter that they had manifested out of the chaos was also erased. The atoms they had created through sheer force of will dissolved and returned into the energy of the void.

Thus, every one of the black robots they had assembled with such dark matter were similarly erased. Hundreds of thousands of Exxos copies simply vanished—every one that the Shana Rei had manifested.

After so many devastating battles, so many sacrifices in the great combat zones in space, only a single original Exxos remained.

Exxos, the last one, was left floating alone in the infinite void, an impossible speck in a universe of nothingness. . . .

TOM ROM

The symptoms of the Onthos plague manifested in Zoe with devastating swiftness. Tom Rom was all too familiar with the disease's progress.

After everything he had done to save the two of them from the black robots and the Shana Rei, after he had sacrificed the researchers on Pergamus, using every last trick just to get away, just to rescue Zoe—now this.

"Remember when I had Conden's Fever?" Zoe said, clearly trying to keep her voice strong, which Tom Rom knew was more for his benefit than her own. "How far you flew in search of a cure, everything you did for me? You took me to Rakkem, and you got me the treatment I needed."

"I'd do it again," he said. "But Rakkem is empty, and any possible cure was destroyed on Pergamus."

"That cure wouldn't have worked on the new strain anyway," Zoe said. "I ran the test myself. The Klikiss royal jelly is no longer effective. I'm glad it saved you, though."

She looked up from her bed in the back compartment. She was sweating, her skin gray except for where it was mottled with darkening spots. "And you? Any symptoms yet?"

"Nothing," he said. "I feel fine. I'm capable of taking care of you."

"You would take care of me no matter how you felt," she said, and added a faint smile. "I'm glad you're still immune. It was my stupid mistake. All my life I knew that if I dropped my guard, some disease would get me. It's almost as if the viruses were planning revenge for everything I did to wipe them out." She tried to prop herself up on the bunk.

As the ship flew onward into the emptiness of nowhere on autopilot, Tom Rom knelt beside her. "Can I get you anything?"

"Just stay here. I think I might like to review the records of the old plague after all. I never much cared about those maudlin last messages from clan Reeves, but would you watch them with me now? I want to see how those people said farewell as they faced the same disease."

"I don't think that's wise," said Tom Rom. "You're different from all of them. Stronger than all of them. They were just Roamers, afraid of their own shadows. They ran into hiding because they couldn't face society. You're nothing like that."

Zoe raised her eyebrows. "Really? We hid on Pergamus. We kept ourselves away from the rest of the Confederation."

"You weren't hiding. You were isolating yourself. You were protecting your specimens and your research. There's a difference."

"You're just rationalizing," she said. "I was keeping my work away from everyone else in the Confederation. I didn't think they deserved any of it after what they had done to me."

Tom Rom nodded. "It was your decision to make. It was your research, your discoveries."

He thought of how the two of them had tended Adam Alakis during his slow death from Heidegger's Syndrome, how they had gone to the biomerchants on Rakkem, seen the hideous profitability of cures and vaccines, as well as crackpot treatments.

Even with her huge research facility, Zoe had never preyed on other people, had never taken advantage of the sick and dying. She just wanted to build her own collection. Was that so terrible? A wealthy man who collected antiques wasn't obligated to share them with anyone else who wanted them. Why should Zoe's collection of disease specimens and cures be any different? She had paid for it. She had monitored her scientists, who produced magnificent work, and Tom Rom was proud that he had contributed to the Pergamus effort. He had obtained so many of those specimens. For her.

Even though Zoe didn't ask for it, he brought her water and an energy infusion, which she needed despite claiming she didn't want it. "Do it for me," he said. "I need you strong, and I need you to fight. We'll find some way to treat this plague, just the way you saved me. You devoted everything to curing me when it was obvious I was going to die. We'll find a miracle for you, too."

She reached out to touch his arm. "That's no better than the platitudes the cure-sellers on Rakkem gave to desperate dying people. Those patients believed anything, but I'm not so gullible. We know how dangerous the Onthos plague is. We know we can't let it come into contact with any other human. Even if you're still immune, you're exposed." Her gaze was hard and strong. "A carrier."

"I know I can never go anywhere," he said. "I'll just stay here with you—but I won't stop trying to find a cure. I have all the Pergamus records. I can comb through the research. Maybe I'll find something."

"It's just data," Zoe said. "No matter what you find, you don't have the facilities to produce any sort of treatment. And I've read all the records myself. I know more than you can ever learn in time, Tom Rom. Believe me, this strain is worse than the one that infected you and Orli Covitz."

Tom Rom was surprised Zoe knew all the details. He had been careful about how much he revealed to her. He had never told Zoe what he'd done in order to obtain the specimen from Orli Covitz, how he had hunted her down and been accidentally infected.

Now, despite all of Zoe's precautions, she was in the same situation. This new strain was even more virulent than the original, and the progress of her illness seemed swifter. From the way her symptoms were manifesting, he could see she was four days ahead of where he had been in this point of his infection.

She wasn't going to last long, but he couldn't tell her. In Zoe's eyes though, he could see that she understood it herself.

He wanted to rail at her in misplaced frustration, demand to know why she had felt it so important to take that one specimen out of storage when he'd made the data available to her anyway. The rest of her disease specimens had been destroyed on Pergamus. She should have left this one behind, too.

This specimen was the one that had almost killed him. He knew that was what had so fascinated her.

But there would be no point in scolding her. She was already blaming herself, and he didn't want to ruin a single moment of the few days they had left.

"I have one more mission for you, Tom Rom," she said, surprising him. "You saved the complete data library of Pergamus. All along, I refused to share it with anyone, but now . . . it doesn't matter. Those cures could save countless lives. After I die, I want you to take our data somewhere. Transmit the whole library to a research center—in fact, give it to King Peter and Queen Estarra. They did a good job wiping out Rakkem, didn't they?"

"Yes, they did," Tom Rom said. "But are you sure? This goes against everything you've commanded for so many years."

Her face looked determined. "Think of it as another way to strike against all the other biomerchants and cure sellers that are bound to crop up. If you can offer the real cures, then we'll hamstring those charlatans." She let out a quick, painful laugh. "Yes, that'll be another form of revenge, and it makes me glad. I'll be content with that." She looked up at him. "Promise me you'll do it."

"I promise."

She knew she could count on his promises. He would transmit the entire medical library to a worthy recipient, and then he would fly off. When Zoe was dead, his purpose in life would be over anyway. Tom Rom just needed to spend his time in peace at last with Zoe, so they could be close, talking, facing each other without decontamination walls and comm screens between them.

"I'm sorry this is all there is," he said. "I've failed by letting you die here all alone in the ship."

She sat up and squeezed his hand so hard it hurt. "No, Tom Rom, not alone. I'm with you. Always you."

Zoe looked at him with a burning intensity that gave her energy even with her last threads of strength. "And after I am dead, Tom Rom, I want you to do another thing for me."

"You know I will."

"Your previous antigens seem to be keeping you safe, and that means you have time, even if you are a carrier. I want you to find a medical research center and make them work to cure you, make you clean again so you have a real life. Pay them every last prisdiamond on Vaconda. Do the impossible—you're good at that." She heaved a long, trembling breath. "I want you to live, Tom Rom. Find a way to save yourself."

He squeezed her hand again, sitting at the edge of her bed. "I will do my best, Zoe."

"Not good enough. Promise me!"

"Of course, I promise."

But he knew that the plague had lain dormant in the derelict Onthos space city for thousands of years, then became virulent again as soon as the humans encountered it. Even if his new exposure to the disease did not kill him, it still resided in his cells, whether or not he showed symptoms. He could never guarantee that some person he encountered might not be infected, then pass it on to another person, and another. He could never risk that.

This entire ship was contaminated, as was Zoe's body, and his own. He could never guarantee that the most rigorous cleansing routines could sterilize him. He had already made up his mind that after he transmitted the Pergamus data, he would choose his place—maybe somewhere quiet and alone, or maybe somewhere spectacular like the Fireheart nebula or a black hole. Then he would self-destruct his ship.

No matter what Zoe insisted, Tom Rom could not be sure, and he would do what was necessary, as he always did.

It was the only promise to Zoe he would ever break.

As the ship drifted, she grew progressively sicker, delirious, in agony. Her fever spiked, and blotches covered her skin as the plague ate away at her. But Zoe held on, and Tom Rom didn't feel the slightest bit sick. That was the worst part, he realized—that he remained immune and alive while she died next to him.

He held her hand and sat at her side, stroking her sweaty, fevered forehead and clasping her fingers until they finally fell limp.

And then he was truly alone aboard the ship, flying nowhere.

128

OSIRA'H

Osira'h felt uncomfortably hopeful as she led the Gardeners to the fungus-reef city. She still felt the ache from knowing she had lost Rod'h and Tamo'l, but she also knew the damage they had inflicted on the Shana Rei, how they had weakened and possibly even destroyed the creatures of darkness.

The defeated and despairing aliens also knew exactly what they had done. Fully aware now for the first time in many lifetimes, their guilt clawed within them, as apparent as the insidious shadows that had resided there for so long.

She recalled how the possessed Ildiran mob members back in Mijistra had died from the appalled realization when they recovered and saw what they had been forced to do. The Onthos, though, had lived with their inner shadows for much longer—for generations, in fact. Now they were hollow, but still anguished at what they had done.

Ohro abased himself before the throne, but Osira'h took no satisfaction. Right now, she wanted to see Reynald, to hold his hand and give him strength. She had not been away for long . . . but she didn't know how much longer he had left. Unless the aliens could do something.

The Onthos representative said, "We have caused great harm to the worldforest. We should have been stewards of the verdani mind, but we lost our own trees and then wandered for millennia until we encountered Theroc. We brought the blight here. We made the trees suffer when we should have cared for them." Ohro looked up, directed his intensity to Queen Estarra. "We killed your sister Sarein."

They all swayed, muttered, clustered together. "We absorbed Kennebar and his green priests. We have caused irreparable damage."

Zaquel and five other green priests stood tensely around the edge of the throne room as the King and Queen stared at the groveling aliens. The priests did not offer further accusations, but they listened intently.

Ohro hung his head. "We have betrayed the verdani mind. Those of us who survive will now depart from Theroc. We will no longer have any contact with the trees. We are not worthy."

"And that will be punishment enough?" Estarra asked in a cold voice. "For all the harm you caused?"

The green priests muttered among themselves, and what Zaquel said surprised Osira'h. "You must not go. The trees still want you here. They say you are an integral part of the verdani mind—a missing part. They need you to help Theroc recover. They say there is more that you can do."

King Peter angrily rose from his throne, but Zaquel continued before anyone else could make a sound. "You can help Prince Reynald."

The Gardeners, fundamentally altered from within now that the Shana Rei had been eliminated, gathered around Prince Reyn in his sickbed in the fungus-reef city. Osira'h would not think of it as his deathbed, though that seemed to be the unspoken consensus among those tending him, even his parents.

Osira'h had rushed here to be with Reyn. After she had seen the aliens recover from their internal blight, part of her had naïvely hoped that Reyn would improve as well, but there was no miraculous cure. He lay unchanged, clinging to a thread of life; if anything, his coma seemed to have deepened. He was gaunt to the point of looking skeletal. Nutrient fluids were pumped into him, because he could no longer awaken to eat.

But Osira'h still refused to believe that there was no way to save him.

The Onthos representatives stood around the bed, quietly chittering. Ohro said, "The disease that afflicts him was known to us in ancient ages, but when our worldforest died, we lost all those memories—or so we thought."

Zaquel nodded. "The green priests can feel the emptiness in the verdani mind. All that knowledge is gone, lost when the Onthos trees were eradicated."

"But our race reproduces by using the trees. We are an integral part of them, down to our cells, down to our chromosomes," Ohro said. "The Gardeners are different from human green priests. Our spore mothers enter a dying tree and in a symbiotic reaction, the trees give birth to other Onthos."

He looked around at the audience, waiting for them to understand. "Our own *cells* grew out of the ancient worldtrees before we fled our homeworld. Our bodies contain DNA from that ancient worldforest. The original worldtrees that we tended and nurtured are *part of us*. Just as the shadow blight was intrinsic to us, so is that lost verdani knowledge." The alien looked at Zaquel. "The Gardeners know how to recover those long-lost memories. There is a ceremony we can undertake."

Osira'h gasped at the possibility. She bent over and squeezed Reyn's hand, wondering if those ancient memories might contain a secret that could help him. If the Gardeners had already known about a disease like Reynald's, if they had prior experience with it . . .

King Peter and Queen Estarra straightened, filled with questions. "And what do you need to do?"

Ohro looked around at his companions. "We must go outside under the trees, amidst the fronds and the roots." He paused, and Osira'h thought he seemed tense and afraid. "And it must be me."

The Gardeners chittered and agreed.

On the worldforest floor, the group of Gardeners moved away from the fungus-reef city, accompanied by an entourage of green priests, the King and Queen, and Osira'h.

Ohro touched stray fronds as he walked past, and he let his pale fingertips brush against the gold-scaled tree bark. He seemed to be searching for the right place, and he finally chose an appropriate clearing. When he stopped, his pale alien companions encircled the area. The worldtree fronds drooped nearly to the ground. Branches were dense all around, and exposed worldtree roots protruded from the soil. His companions picked up small sharp sticks they found among the forest debris.

Ohro knelt down and stroked the exposed roots to initiate contact. After a long pause, he nodded to the other Gardeners.

Zaquel seemed concerned, picking up on the tension in the aliens. The rest of the green priests didn't know what the Onthos intended to do.

"The memories of the old worldforest are deep inside me," Ohro said. "And inside all the members of my race. As we are symbiotic allies of the trees, we have drawn from the verdani, and now we give back. I will surrender everything I possess to the forest mind." The leader of the Onthos stood, spread his arms, and closed his large black eyes.

The other Gardeners swarmed forward and fell upon him with their sharp sticks, stabbing swiftly and repeatedly.

Osira'h gasped. Peter and Estarra cried out, but they could do nothing to stop the murder.

The alien leader made no sound, and it was over swiftly. Their pale flesh stained, the other Gardeners poured Ohro's blood onto the upraised roots, smeared it on the scaled tree bark, moistened the soil, where it was swiftly absorbed. The alien hands were covered with red. Ohro's body lay drained, torn, and motionless on the forest floor.

Estarra shouted, "This was necessary? You killed him!"

The other Gardeners nodded. "It was the way to extract what we needed. What the worldforest needed."

"Now the verdani can draw all the locked secrets directly from his blood, his DNA."

"The lost verdani memories are restored."

Shaking and hesitant, Zaquel went to the nearest tree and pressed her palms against the bark scales. The tree no longer showed any sign of the blood, having absorbed it all into its own cells. Other green priests came forward and did the same. Their eyes went wide with wonder as they drank in the new knowledge.

"There is so much more inside the trees now," Zaquel said.

"Before, the verdani mind was incredibly vast, but now there's a whole new era of history, as if a huge additional library opened up." She looked around, trying to share her amazement with the others. "Those more ancient trees understand themselves and what they knew, and now our own worldforest understands more than it ever did."

More green priests gathered around, rushing forward to press themselves against the nearby trees, and they plunged their eager minds deep into the worldforest. They meditated, concentrated, while Osira'h waited tensely for an answer. Just having more knowledge was not good enough for her.

When Zaquel emerged, her face was filled with indescribable wonder. Her breathing was fast, and she stared at Osira'h and the King and Queen. "Yes—it is here. The knowledge is here! The trees understand exactly what afflicts Prince Reynald. And how to cure it."

GENERAL NALANI KEAH

Even though half of the *Kutuzov*'s comm systems were down after the supernova blasts, Keah's crew jury-rigged enough of a signal to transmit to the remaining CDF ships, calling a rendezvous point outside the nebula. The two Juggernauts and the remaining Mantas limped to a safe distance.

Adar Zan'nh intercepted the transmission and called his warliners to join General Keah at the same point. The ships converged beyond the dust boundary, while inside the nebula the new supernovas poured out light like a fire hose of radiation.

The last shadow cloud was being dissolved by the stellar eruptions, torn to shreds. As the surrounding dark veil was stripped away, the hexagonal cylinders also began to crumble, turning to brittle crystal that shattered and fell away like ashes. "That's a lot more than a 'setback,'" Keah said.

Her crew cheered, confused but exuberant. Keah wasn't sure what she was seeing, but she didn't want to complain about it.

She stood on the *Kutuzov*'s bridge, arms crossed over her chest as she paced back and forth in front of her command chair. She couldn't be expected to sit still. Her long dark hair had come undone and hung in a decidedly nonregulation tangle, but she didn't care. Although the events certainly warranted it, she was not posing for the history books.

And then, equally miraculous, as soon as the hex cylinders broke apart and dissipated, the thousands of remaining bugbot battle vessels also vanished, as if they had never even existed. All of them, even the wreckage.

Nadd was still shaking. How could a hairless man clad in a loin-cloth manage to look disheveled? Keah asked, "Mr. Nadd, have you informed the network that we are still alive?"

"Yes, General," he said, shivering. "I tried to keep a running commentary through my treeling during the battle, but sometimes I got distracted."

"A lot of us did, but now you can catch up. Fill them in, and tell them that to the best of our knowledge, the Shana Rei are defeated." She stared out at the images, reveling in the supernova blaze. "Now isn't that a glorious sight?"

The remaining Ildiran warliners gathered around. Their solar-sail fins had been torn to tatters, and their hulls were blotched and streaked from energy impacts. "It appears we have survived," said Adar Zan'nh.

"Stating the obvious, Z." Then her voice grew heavier. "Plenty of us didn't survive, though, and it'll be a while before we can tally our casualties, both among the CDF and at Fireheart Station. Right now, I just want ten minutes to digest the fact that we won. I mean, really won!"

"That was our objective, General," said Zan'nh.

"If I didn't know better, Z, I'd accuse you of being sarcastic."

"Sarcasm was far from my intent," he said.

The ships in her battle group transmitted their ID beacons, and her officers took an inventory, beginning the grim task of compiling a list of casualties from each ship. After the annihilation of Relleker and Earth, though, even huge casualties no longer had any real meaning. There was no way to grasp the harm that the Shana Rei had done to the Confederation and the Ildiran Empire.

As she stared out at the roaring sea of gases, Keah nodded slowly to herself. "Fireheart is going to be an even more impressive nebula—a fitting memorial for everyone killed by the shadows. In fact, I'd venture to say that's the most spectacular graveyard in the Spiral Arm."

"It is better than medals or ribbons," Zan'nh said.

The human historian appeared on the screen beside the Adar. "I recorded everything—and it is definitely something for the history books." Anton shook his head. "It was a rough time there when you all were out of commission because you thought the Mage-Imperator had died. I was the only one with his wits about him!"

"Before the next expedition, I will have to teach you how to pilot a warliner," Zan'nh said to the man. "Just to be sure."

Now Keah was convinced she heard sarcasm. Once they got back to a safe, calm situation, she promised herself that she would host the Adar for a fine dinner aboard her Juggernaut, regardless of whose turn it was.

"I'm not sure we'll ever understand all the factors that came together at the right time," Keah said, "but we kicked the butt of the undefeatable enemy—that's good enough for me. Would you like to shuttle over for a celebration, Z?"

The Adar considered, gave her a considerate bow as he faced her on the screen. "I would like that very much, but I need to return to Ildira. Too much remains unsettled, and I need to know exactly what happened. The Mage-Imperator is still alive, and your green priest has provided enough basic information to reassure us, but there are still many vital questions."

She smiled. "We'll have plenty of time later, Z. Make your own celebration in whatever way Ildirans prefer to celebrate. The shadows are gone, the bugbots are gone—all in all, I'd say that's a good day."

"Yes," the Adar agreed. "All in all, a good day."

130

TASIA TAMBLYN

The *Voracious Curiosity* spun wildly out of control. How many of the CDF, Solar Navy, or Roamer ships had failed to escape the blast? Robb tried to stabilize their flight, increasing shields against the torrent of radiation. Tasia held on, but she felt a rip in her heart knowing that Rlinda Kett and the *Declan's Glory* were among the lost.

The multiple new supernovas unleashed millions of times more starlight than even the original core supergiants. The remnants of Fireheart Station and the Roamer operations had been vaporized in an instant. Fierce cosmic radiation slammed into the dust barrier at the edge of the nebula, plowing the gases and building up a steady shock front.

Continuing their glorious flight away, the two newborn treeships spread their branches wider. Furious light from the supernovas provided all the nourishment they needed. Tasia realized that Rlinda's delivery of the wental water had allowed the verdani treeships to come into being, saving Celli and Solimar. Jess and Cesca had somehow known, and Rlinda had given her life to make that happen. . . .

"At least Rlinda got to see what she accomplished," Robb said, thinking the same thing as Tasia. "Now her ashes and Captain Roberts's are intermingled out in the universe, just as she wanted."

Tasia's heart was too heavy for her to answer.

As the supernovas let out a victorious shout of light into the nebula, they watched the shadow clouds disintegrate, the hex cylinders crumble into nothingness, the black robot ships vanish.

Shell-shocked, Station Chief Alu kept staring through the heavily filtered windowports while Robb worked on emergency repairs to the *Curiosity*'s overloaded systems. Alu shook his head. "My whole facility is gone."

"I hope you had insurance," Tasia said.

"The Roamers will hold together," he said with a long sigh. "I'm sad about the destruction, but we can start again and build somewhere else—it'll be a lot easier now that the Spiral Arm is free of the Shana Rei."

Howard suggested, "You might not have to go far. There are still opportunities right here. We've never had the chance to study a brand-new supernova so soon after the blast."

Shareen also brightened. "It's a giant laboratory. Think of the tests we can run, the information we'll gather."

Alu pursed his lips as the possibilities dawned on him. "Not just a laboratory, but a *factory*. Imagine how many exotic isotopes and ions were created in just the past hour? All those treasures have been flung out here for the taking. We can build another Fireheart Station to harvest them."

Howard and Shareen were both grinning. Shareen said, "Kotto Okiah would have been proud."

As Tasia accelerated the *Curiosity* away, she suddenly swerved, yelping as her collision-avoidance detectors sounded loud alarms. With their overloaded sensors they nearly crashed into another ship that was lumbering along, battered and mostly dark. In an instant, Tasia recognized it.

A burst of static came over the comm along with a weak transmission, barely discernible words—and a familiar voice. "Glad you found me! I'm busy trying to do repairs here, and that's hard to accomplish with glue, chicken wire, and duct tape." The screen flickered, and a poorly resolved image of Rlinda Kett appeared. "I could use some help, if you're not too busy trying to run me over."

Tasia cried out, "We thought you were killed in the supernova blast!"

"Outrunning an exploding star is certainly within my abilities. The *Curiosity* would have done better, no doubt about that, but *Declan's Glory* is a decent ship." She chuckled. "Actually, the tree-ships shielded me. Both Celli and Solimar enfolded me in their huge branches at the last instant and blocked the worst of the radiation blast."

Tasia felt overjoyed as she docked against *Declan's Glory*. Many of Rlinda's systems had been blown, and the hull was severely damaged. The big trader woman met Tasia and Robb at the airlock, giving them an enormous hug. The two had donned exosuits for protection, but Rlinda wore a regular ship suit.

Robb said, "I'm sure you received a substantial dose of radiation with shields as bad as these."

"Probably so," Rlinda said. "But I'm alive, and I can undergo treatment for the exposure. Now get over here, you two."

"You should have your own suit on now," Tasia chided. "Your exposure is accumulating."

"You're right, I should . . . but when we escaped from Earth, we flew away so fast I didn't have time to double-check the emergency locker. I only had two suits aboard, one medium and one small." She gave a wry smile. "I doubt they'd fit me even if I somehow figured out how to combine both of them."

Robb carried the *Curiosity*'s extensive repair kit, ready to check what sort of shape the ship was in. He looked around in dismay at the flickering interior lights. Several system banks still spat out cascades of sparks. "Go over to the *Curiosity* while we check out repairs," he said. "It's more sheltered there."

"Shizz, why bother?" Tasia pointed out. "There's not much left of *Declan's Glory*. It would take a month to complete repairs, and we should get out of here pretty damn soon. Leave it behind with all the other wreckage in the nebula."

"Not a chance. I've grown rather fond of this ship, after all we've been through together," Rlinda said. "And I need a ship of my own, unless you want to give me the *Curiosity* back? I didn't think so." She led them toward the engine compartment. "Let's spend a day at least fixing my stardrive and setting my shields back up. If we get *Declan* moving, I can take some of your passengers, lighten your load." Rlinda frowned. "And don't tell me you've got enough elbow room and life support to hold them for very long."

"Not really," Tasia admitted.

Robb got back to the point. "Even so—Rlinda, *you* need to be in shelter. Right now. You've received a substantial dose already, and we can find someone to wear your two spare exosuits and help us with repairs."

Tasia grudgingly agreed. "But I'll allow only eight hours. If we can't get your ship functioning by then, we just leave it behind. These people have to get to Newstation."

Rlinda looked around at the nearly destroyed ship. "Eight hours is well within my repair estimate."

Tasia let out a lighthearted laugh, then suddenly found herself choked up. Tears welled in her eyes, and she gave Rlinda a furious bear hug. "We saw the shock wave wash over your ship. We thought you were gone!"

Rlinda patted her on the back, then dismissed the dire situation. "Heroic deaths are fine, dear girl, but I would rather die of old age in a bed with a nice dessert in front of me."

ARITA

Human settlers had lived in the worldforest for mere centuries, and with the extreme rarity of the microfungus infecting Reyn, the Therons simply did not have enough experience to know how to treat it. But the old verdani knew about the debilitating disease.

The Gardeners had tended their separate worldforest for countless generations, and a similar illness had struck them intermittently over all those millennia. The ancient memories retrieved from the lost verdani mind held the key—a rare and transient plant that hid in the worldforest ecosystem. With the flood of old memories released by Ohro's blood, the Theron green priests could now see the plant, could share the images from the Onthos recollections. They knew what to look for.

Far out in space, Collin rode with Arita in the *Prodigal Son* as they departed from the Iswander extraction field. Delighted to receive the message through telink, the young green priest grabbed Arita. "They know how to cure Reynald! The Onthos memories showed us the right plant—an extract to be used as a molecular block against the microfungus inside of your brother." He grinned.

Arita was so delighted that she threw her arms around him. "What is it? What did we miss before?"

"We didn't miss it. It was right in front of us—an elusive plant, but the researchers had so many possibilities to test. Now they just need to find a sample. Where are your botanical record books?"

Arita called up images in her logs, all the specimens she had catalogued in her many years of studying the worldforest. She and Collin scrolled through countless plants, and Arita guided him through her personal organization structure, searching for the correct white flower. Collin pointed vigorously. "That one. That is what the Gardeners say we need to find for Reyn."

It was a creamy white vine orchid that the original settlers had named a starflower. It was ethereal and transient, blooming for only a day and then disappearing, though its root systems lay hidden for years. "I know that flower."

All the information that Zoe Alakis had given them from Pergamus had sent the medical researchers on the right track, but it was the Gardeners' restored knowledge that had brought out the singular answer.

"The medical researchers need to extract the cure from a starflower root," Collin repeated what he learned through telink, "but unless the plant is blooming, a starflower is impossible to find." He frowned. "And starflowers rarely bloom. . . ."

Arita brightened. "Wait, at the funeral for Father Idriss a year ago, starflowers bloomed over his fresh grave. They are long gone now, but the roots will still be there until the next blossoming. The green priests know where it is, my parents know where it is! They can get the roots from there and save Reyn."

She beamed. "Send the message, tell them how to cure him." She looked up, called to Garrison in the cockpit. "Can we go back to Theroc? I want to be there as my brother recovers."

Garrison smiled. "We'll take you home."

The *Prodigal Son* landed on the treetop canopy, and Osira'h hurried out to greet the ship, leaving Reynald's bedside for the first time in days. Arita embraced the Ildiran halfbreed, exuberant with their news about how they had discovered Eternity's Mind and how the shadows were finally defeated.

But she had other business first. "Let me see Reyn. How is he recovering?"

"Follow me," Osira'h said. "He wanted to come see you himself, but he still doesn't have all his strength. I would not let him get out of bed." She gave a small smile. "I tend to be very protective right now. But the doctors say that the new treatment has cleansed the contamination from him. If you hadn't told us where to find the starflower . . ." Osira'h looked tired, but happy. "I haven't felt this joyous or mentally exhausted since the end of the Elemental War."

Osira'h led them to Reyn's recovery chambers in the fungus-reef. Her brother had gotten out of bed and sat at his desk. Arita hurried over to sweep him into a hug as he rose to his feet.

Osira'h grabbed his shoulder. "Not so fast. Do not strain yourself."

Arita felt just as concerned. "You should be in bed resting."

"I've already spent too much time in bed," Reyn said. "I feel stronger than I have in a year. Just let me bask in my health."

Osira'h put her arms around him. "I plan to take most of the credit for your recovery."

"A lot of people can share that credit."

A thin pinch-faced man appeared in the doorway bearing a tray of food and surrounded by an aura of officiousness. The aromas of the dishes surrounded him like tantalizing, mouthwatering music. "Excuse me, I have a delivery of food for the Prince—and his companions." The man looked around the room, as if disappointed at how many mouths there were to feed. "I am Zachary Wisskoff from the Arbor restaurant."

"We didn't order any food," Reyn said. "But it smells delicious."

"It's supposed to smell *invigorating*," Wisskoff said. "I chose the items after careful consideration. Rlinda Kett sent a message informing me that I was to take care of you until she arrives."

Reyn brightened. "Rlinda's on her way?"

"Yes, apparently she intends to take a more active role in restaurant management. She just survived the Shana Rei in the Fireheart nebula, but now for some reason she is worried about Arbor. Her ship is on its way to Handon Station for repairs, but she will be here soon to look over my shoulder." He added in a cool, deadpan voice, "As you can tell I am thrilled at the prospect." He heaved a noisy breath, let it out. "She instructed me to make the best possible meal for you, so you can regain your strength."

Osira'h, Arita, and Collin cleared the desk so they could set out the meal Wisskoff had brought. The man bustled about with unnecessary attention to detail to make sure that all the dishes were served with the proper perfection. When the meal had been laid out, he stood back and watched as they ate with great gusto. The smells were wonderful.

Wisskoff seemed to be waiting for something. "Although Rlinda did not specify, I believe she does not intend for there to be a charge for the food."

Reyn looked up. "Thank you very much."

The man's smile was as thin as a sheet of paper. "I'll be sure to let Rlinda know, so she can add your gratitude to the account. If there is nothing else?"

Osira'h was enjoying a dish of stewed pollen-filled stamens from treelilies, while Arita and Collin ate roasted butterbeetles right out of the shells. They all remarked on the delicious tastes.

"Thank you again," Reyn said. "We'll be certain to tell Rlinda when she arrives."

"You're welcome, I'm sure." Wisskoff departed.

When he finished eating, Reyn picked up the documents he had been reading. "Summaries of the recent events in the Spiral Arm. If I'm going to be the next King, I have to learn how to lead people."

Osira'h hugged him again. "One of the most important things you can do as King is make sure you have a solid alliance with the Ildiran Empire. Therefore, you should stick with me."

Reyn hugged her back . . . and then Arita wanted part of it, and then Collin was hugging *her*. Osira'h didn't need the light of the seven suns to know how bright the future was.

132

XANDER BRINDLE

Back at the site of Rendezvous—*Handon Station,* Xander corrected himself—more ships came in every day. Finally one brought the long-awaited medical-analysis reports that Xander had secretly requested.

He compiled his full case for Terry, wanting to be sure he had all of the options and all of the risks. Xander had to be as convincing as possible, although he wasn't sure Terry wanted to be convinced.

After their side trip to Theroc to bring Arita and Collin home, the *Prodigal Son* had flown back to Rendezvous, and Garrison resumed his admin duties. He got to work organizing all the new arrivals and ranking the necessary repairs, assigning teams to the vessels that could be most quickly returned to service. Even with the cessation of bloater harvesting, the market for new and repaired ships was going to be huge. Xander had no doubt that Handon Station would thrive, and the two of them would triple their fortune.

Orli set up her shop for compy maintenance and program upgrades. She was quite content to be with Garrison. DD was her ever-faithful companion, and Seth Reeves seemed to be a budding genius himself, eager to help Orli with the compies. Xander was glad Handon Station could provide the opportunity.

He looked out at the screens on the control center walls. The souped-up *Verne* was docked in the thick of all the busy traffic. Omar Selise returned with another haul of salvage from Relleker, clearly impatient. "Do you have it yet, Brindle?" he said in an open transmission while they were inside the main control center. "I've got to know."

Xander drew a breath and replied to the old clan leader on the

540 KEVIN J. ANDERSON

comm. "I compiled a full report for Terry to consider. You can look it over and make your own decision."

"I want to be damn sure. This is my grandson we're talking about."

"I understand completely. Here it is." Xander transmitted the data while Terry stared at him wide-eyed.

"What is he talking about? What are you two scheming? You and Omar aren't even friends."

"We have some things in common." He straightened. OK stood silently by. Xander had taken a lot of time to convince the compy to keep the secret, and OK had admirably kept the confidence. But now it was out in the open.

"All right, explain it to me!" Terry said, sounding exasperated. "If it's good news, go ahead and ruin the surprise. If it's bad news, I can handle it."

"What if it's just something serious I want you to consider?"

"Of course I'll consider it. We're partners. You and I have been through enough. I'd just like to get back to normal and have some calm stability so that the only headache I have to worry about is running our new station."

Xander swallowed hard and began to explain. "Omar has a grandson with a degenerative spinal condition very similar to yours. That's what this is about. I've got something to ask you. Come with me to the galley—I hope you keep an open mind."

Terry maneuvered very well without the use of his legs in the asteroid's low gravity. The analysis reports he had received were a mixed blessing; some touted enthusiastic successes, some failures, some extremely happy customers (which may have been faked or otherwise solicited), and some disappointments. There were clearly risks. It would have to be Terry's decision.

OK said to him, "I wish you the best of luck, Xander Brindle."

Terry had taken a seat at the galley table, fidgeting with his fingers. Xander activated a screen, called up his files, and jumped right in. He had put this off long enough already. "I'm going to present you with a medical possibility for restoring your legs. It's expensive, and it's risky. There are possible side effects." Xander turned to look at his partner. "And I think it might be real."

Terry frowned. "There's no cure for my condition. I've been through all that, had every one of the tests. And I moved on a long time ago."

"But something's changed—two things, actually. There's been continuing research in a new treatment process that shows promise. The other thing that's changed is that we can *afford* it now, no matter how much it costs."

"How come I haven't heard about this research before?" Terry asked.

"It's not exactly orthodox. I won't kid you, the primary researcher had some connections to Rakkem."

"*Rakkem?* Then the answer is no."

"Everything about Rakkem wasn't corrupt or useless." He displayed the report. "I tracked down several patients who have had the procedure, people who suffered from a similar condition . . . the same one Omar Selise's grandson has. The treatment didn't always work—I won't lie to you—but the success rate is better than fifty percent. I want you to be realistic about the pain and the recovery."

"And what if it fails?" Terry said.

"Then you'll be in the same condition you are now, and at least I'll know that we tried everything."

"Side effects?"

"Serious tremors, possibly. Loss of vision in a few rare cases. It's not a walk in the park." Xander winced as he realized how blithely he had mentioned "walking."

Terry skimmed through the files, but didn't seem to be interested. Instead, he was frustrated. "We've talked about this over and over again. I'm excited about the good things happening here, but I don't understand your obsession to fix me. Have I led you to believe that I'm unhappy? That I'm somehow desperate enough to take risks like that?"

"I just thought that you'd want it," Xander said. "I keep trying to think of something I could do for you, something you could do for yourself, with all the money from Maria."

"I'm happy with who I am." Terry gestured generally toward the walls of the room. "And when I'm out there, with the salvage yard and the repair facilities, I'm just as capable as anybody else. Does it bother *you* that I can't walk?"

"No!" Xander felt he was tied in knots, and he realized he was crying. "I was just doing it for you."

"I'm fine, really." Terry reached out to clasp his forearm. "I don't feel like I'm any less of a person. I wouldn't risk the pain, the recuperation time away from you, and what if something went wrong with the treatment? Tremors or blindness? Honest, I'm happy as I am." He looked up. "Aren't you?"

"Yes, I'm perfectly happy, and I'm happy with you." He gave Terry a tight embrace, and they held on to each other for a long time.

Xander explained about Omar's grandson, who was considering the same treatment, waiting for the more thorough investigation in light of the huge expense involved.

Terry said, "Then I'll pay for it. If that's what Omar and his grandson really want to do—once they've reviewed all the possibilities and drawbacks—we'll give them the funds."

Xander felt a rush of happiness. "That would be wonderful. But it has to be their decision."

"It will be," Terry said, and responded with an unexpected quirk of a smile. "Now, it may surprise you that I haven't been entirely ignoring my situation either. I've been thinking of a few other options myself." He called for OK to come in to the galley. "I've got some news of my own, Xander." He grinned. "I guess it shows just how much you and I understand each other. But I found an alternative solution."

OK trudged in carrying a long cybernetic apparatus in his outstretched arms. Xander could see the adhesive straps attached to leggings, embedded flexmesh tendons and pulleys.

"Since Orli Covitz is so good with compies," Terry explained, "I had her develop these for me. I think they just might work."

Xander reached out and took the apparatus from OK. "What are they?"

"Compy leg augmentations. I can strap them on and be able to walk just like a compy does. I won't wear them all the time, because I can still get around faster than you." He grinned. "But under other circumstances I won't need to hold OK's shoulder anymore, and I can go into gravity environments just like other people."

Xander turned to the compy. "You knew about this?"

"Yes, Xander Brindle," OK said. "He made me promise not to say anything. You yourself taught me how to keep secrets."

"But I thought . . ." Xander said, then he burst into laughter, as did Terry.

"I believe they'll work out exactly as planned," Terry said.

CHAPTER

133

MAGE-IMPERATOR JORA'H

He had not seen shadows in his dreams for days, and Jora'h knew that the Shana Rei were indeed gone from the universe. He still felt incredibly weak from having nearly bled to death, but he had pulled through, thanks to the sacrifice of Gale'nh. At the critical moment, the Mage-Imperator was strong enough to call the faeros to the last battle.

And they had won.

For the first time in days, he felt strong enough to go to the sky-sphere audience chamber. Taking his rightful place, he sat in the chrysalis chair under the projection of his smiling visage on the mists overhead. Beside him, Nira rested her hand on his arm.

The Ildiran people had sensed when their Mage-Imperator was on the brink of death, and now they needed reassurance. For so long, they had lived with a shadow inside the *thism*; they hadn't noticed its debilitating power until it was gone. Now, the entire Ildiran race seemed revitalized. People of all kiths made the pilgrimage to Mijistra by the thousands, wending their way up the ellipsoidal hill to the Prism Palace. Just to see him. One after another they came forward to give him their good wishes, to reaffirm their loyalty, or perhaps just to see with their own eyes that he was still alive and well.

Gale'nh had also recovered, and he stood proudly in his fine Solar Navy uniform next to Muree'n and Yazra'h. Nira's son was as strong as she claimed he would be. He had clung to life and helped pull Jora'h back. Osira'h was still on Theroc with the recovering Prince Reynald, but she had contacted her mother through the green priests.

After the battle in the Fireheart nebula, Nira had only three children now, but Jora'h would honor Rod'h and Tamo'l, knowing what they had done, how their sacrifice was one of the most important death blows to the creatures of darkness.

That shock had thrummed through Gale'nh, nearly killing him as he recovered from giving so much of his blood. As the doctors struggled to save him from that terrible setback, Muree'n had also stumbled into the medical center, looking weak and shaken. She had grabbed the medical kithmen. "Take my blood, give it to my brother. We have to share strength." And the doctors had drained as much from her as they needed to stabilize Gale'nh, strengthening him, saving him.

Now in the audience chamber, Nira rested her hand on Jora'h's arm. She leaned close to whisper, "Thank you for helping to save us all. Rod'h and Tamo'l know how much we appreciate what they did—I can sense it."

She had been connected to the verdani mind, listening to reports, when Rod'h had uttered his last mental outcry. Though telink rarely let her connect with her halfbreed children, this time she had sensed him and Tamo'l. They had been her children, after all. Nira had been quite shaken by the experience, but also glad that she'd had a last moment of contact. She believed that Rod'h and Tamo'l had sensed her for the briefest fraction of a second before the faeros engulfed them. . . .

Now the shadows were gone. The Ildiran people would not transform into mindless killers—nor did Jora'h have to worry about the corruption inside himself. He shuddered to recall what he had done in the banquet hall.

But that blackness was behind him now, and the seven suns shone bright in the skies of Ildira.

Many pilgrims insisted on providing a small sample of their blood to be added to the Mage-Imperator's next transfusion. As the nexus of the entire race, Jora'h could receive blood from any Ildiran of any kith. They all wanted to help, and as a symbolic gesture, he ordered that every one of the samples (after testing pure) be mixed together in a large sample, and he would take it into his veins to reaffirm himself to all of his people. His blood flowed through the entire Ildiran race, and now they would know that their blood flowed in him as well.

The Ildiran Empire was strong, as Jora'h was strong.

A lens kith pilgrim bowed before the dais. "Thank you, Liege. Thank you!" Then he moved away, and a miner female took his place; she, likewise, bowed and expressed her gratitude. They needed to say it, and he didn't ask them to explain.

Then a murmur of alarm and excitement rippled through the court, and Jora'h felt an ominous thrum through the *thism*. Looking up, he saw the light brightening overhead through the skysphere dome.

Prime Designate Daro'h drew in a quick breath, pointing upward. "It is the faeros! The faeros have come back."

This time, though, Jora'h felt no panic or dismay. He could sense that the fiery elementals had not come here to destroy. "Let us go to the rooftop. We need to thank them."

Reaching the top of the Palace, they watched a parade of fireballs come down like shooting stars. The faeros swirled overhead, circling the Prism Palace like ignited comets. The Ildirans gasped, and Jora'h raised his hands in acknowledgment. The flaming ellipsoids rippled past, making the air shimmer with their heat. Their erratic patterns seemed to salute the Mage-Imperator.

Jora'h could no longer control the elementals, of that he was certain. The faeros did not wish to remain connected with the Ildiran Empire. They could return to live inside their suns, never needing to come out. Now that the Shana Rei were firmly defeated, the fiery elementals were safe, as was the rest of the Spiral Arm.

The people stared in awe as the sky filled with fireballs. The rememberers drank in the sight, as if deciding which words they would use to record this in the Saga of Seven Suns. Anton Colicos was with them, and his eyes sparkled. "This will make an excellent story," he said, then paused to consider. "In fact, all of this will. I have a lot of writing ahead of me."

The faeros hovered in silence, as if communicating, and then they streaked away, leaving smoky vapor trails crisscrossing the sky.

Out in the open air, Jora'h took Nira's hand. "We should hold court up here, where the whole universe can see us."

Soon, with much assistance from medical escorts, Chiar'h and Shawn Fennis came up to join the Mage-Imperator, leading the misbreeds that had been rescued from Kuivahr, in all their shapes and forms. "We know what Tamo'l did at the end," Chiar'h said. She had many bandages on her face and arms.

"We all know what she and Rod'h accomplished, and I also know what the misbreeds did," said Jora'h. "You will all be honored for your part in helping to win this war. You awakened Eternity's Mind, and that force was instrumental to defeating the Shana Rei. We are grateful for you as well. All of you."

Nira added, "If there is anything you need, any request you'd like to make of the Mage-Imperator, he will grant it."

"We already have what we need," said Shawn Fennis.

"Then there is one thing I would ask of you," Jora'h said, looking at the group of misbreeds. He saw their mismatched genetics, their odd adaptations, and although he remained sad for the breeding program that had created them, he was not disappointed that they existed. They had much to share.

"How can we help, Liege?" asked Har'lc, one of the most hideously deformed misbreeds. His skin was a canvas of rashes and peeling patches. "We will serve, if we are able."

"I know you are able," he answered with a smile. "I would ask Mungl'eh to sing, and all of you to sing. I already know how beautiful it sounds, but the rest of our people should hear it." He looked over at Nira. "It will move you."

"I do so with great pleasure," Mungl'eh said. The other misbreeds joined her.

The woman's misshapen face formed into what was clearly a grin. With her voice that could—and did—change everything, she and the other misbreeds sang a song of joy to the Mage-Imperator.

ZHETT KELLUM

It was exhilarating to feel the wind on her face and stirring her long black hair. Zhett drew a breath, inhaling the scents of odd chemical mixtures that wafted from the cloud layers below. She extended her arms to either side, splayed her fingers to revel in the infinite sky.

"Enjoying yourself, I see," Patrick said.

She closed her eyes and turned slowly around. "Absolutely." The wind picked up, whistling around the upright antennas that studded the dome of the cloud harvester. On the underside of the structure, kilometers-long whisker probes snaked down into different layers of the cloud deck, analyzing and sending signals to guide the skymine where the ekti concentration was heaviest.

Patrick came up from behind and slipped his arms around her waist. They stood close in a hug. "I can't let you fall."

"I don't think I was at risk," she said as she snuggled up against him, "but you're welcome to keep holding me steady."

A noisy skimmer zoomed out and around the cloud harvester, an airbike that did tricky barrel rolls and loops in the sky. Zhett recognized Kristof flying the thing. "Those stunts are completely unnecessary."

"And dangerous," Patrick added. "But you have to admit, he's good at it."

Kristof swooped along, then dove at a steep angle into the clouds, where he disappeared into the mists.

"I was better at his age," she said. "We should make him keep practicing."

"That won't be difficult."

A cargo ship came in with goods they had ordered from the various Roamer clans, then dispatched here to the gas giant Qhardin, where the Kellums had set up their new cloud harvester.

Del Kellum came up to the rooftop, interrupting their quiet moment, as Zhett had known he would. She knew to relish every bit of peace with her husband, but there was also business to be done. "He says he won't extend our credit, by damn!" said Del. "Who does he think he is?"

"A conservative businessman, probably," Patrick said.

"Our credit's been stretched to the breaking point, and it's been tied and reknotted." Zhett turned to follow her father. "I'll have words with him. We need another month before this skymine is producing surplus ekti."

Del snorted. "The man says with ekti prices so low, it'll take us five generations to harvest enough fuel to pay off the debts we've already incurred!"

"He should go back to Academ and see if Jess and Cesca are still teaching math. Any fool knows that the Confederation's stockpiles will run out soon enough, now that we've stopped harvesting bloaters. Half of the clans had already given up skymining, and now they'll have to ramp up fast again." Zhett was starting to feel annoyed. "But we're ahead of the game. This skymine will be one of the first to bring regular ekti to market."

Del snorted. "I'm inclined to tell him just to take his cargo and fly somewhere else."

"Let me talk with him first before you have a tantrum, Dad."

Patrick made a wry smile. "Well, that's it, then—how could anyone ever say no to her?"

Del commiserated. "You know my daughter as well as I do. You better go along, too, Patrick—just in case she needs backup."

Zhett sniffed. "You think I can't handle it myself?"

Del shrugged. "No, I just wanted your husband to think he was useful."

After helping to spread the news about the bloaters and Eternity's Mind, Del had overseen the dismantling of the Kellum ekti-extraction operations out beyond Ikbir, but they had already harvested enough stardrive fuel that Zhett and Patrick sold it at

Newstation for a decent price. Then they'd tracked down the surviving members of clan Duquesne.

A few months ago, Aaron Duquesne had come to their distillery on Kuivahr, trying to unload his family's cloud harvesters; he claimed they wanted to get out of the skymining business. At the time, the Kellums were content running their quiet but modestly successful brewing operations, and Zhett had seen how Iswander Industries was able to produce stardrive fuel far more cheaply than any traditional Roamer operation. Zhett missed their Golgen skymine and had been sorely tempted to make the business deal, but the prospect of competing against Iswander seemed a sure road to bankruptcy.

Not long afterward, though, they had lost the Kuivahr distillery, too, so they were no better off. *Circumstances beyond our control.* When the family jointly decided to go back into traditional skymining, Del remembered that the mothballed clan Duquesne skymines were still on the market. They had scraped together enough investors and a down payment to purchase the old cloud harvester. Now the Kellums were established again on a new gas planet.

Zhett knew this was where she belonged. The Kellums were meant to do skymining. This was where she felt most at home.

As she and Patrick followed her father down from the upper observation deck, her mind was preoccupied with business concerns. Ready for a debate with the intractable trader, she considered arguments about the increasing price of ekti, the significant investments she had here, the historic reliability of clan Kellum—no, scratch that, she thought. She didn't want to call attention to how many businesses they had operated and how many disastrous failures they had suffered (through no fault of their own).

When the three finally reached the landing bay, she had all of the salient points lined up in her mind and had worked herself into a mood that would surely win any debate. Then she realized that her father was grinning. "What's wrong with you, Dad? You're smiling."

"Oh, nothing, my sweet. Just glad I managed to hide it this long." With a grand gesture, he opened the sliding door and they stepped through the personnel access to the wide landing bay.

Shareen and Howard were there waiting for them.

Zhett was taken completely aback. Patrick let out a loud laugh. "You knew all along, Del!"

"Yes I did, by damn. I wanted to see the look on your face."

Zhett let him enjoy his practical joke while she ran forward to their daughter. "When did you get back?"

"We came through Newstation and hitched a ride aboard the cargo ship."

Del frowned, seeming embarrassed. "I feel terribly guilty I sent you both to Fireheart Station. I thought it would be a good experience. I thought you'd learn a lot but—what a disaster!"

"A disaster perhaps, sir," said Howard, "but we certainly learned a lot. As you promised we would."

"Sounds like there was just as much of a disaster if we had stayed with you on Kuivahr," Shareen pointed out. "And this way we were the last ones to work with Kotto Okiah."

"It was a great honor," Howard said.

Zhett draped her arms over both their shoulders, "You're back here now in a skymine in the clouds. In my opinion, this is just how it should be."

Shareen mused. "Howard and I will stay here to make sure your new skymine is up and running properly, but there's talk of building a new research station at Fireheart to study the supernovas."

Howard added, "It offers a great many scientific and industrial possibilities. We'd like to participate at the beginning."

"So, Howard's staying with you, then?" Patrick asked. "Shouldn't we take him back to his family?"

"Wait, weren't they on Earth?" Zhett said with sudden alarm.

Howard shook his head. "They just lived there temporarily for a contract job my mother took. They moved back to New Portugal a week after I first came here with Shareen."

Shareen said, "We sent a message to them to let them know he's all right. Howard's old enough to make his own decisions, and we've decided that he's staying right here with me." When she took his arm, Howard blushed furiously.

Zhett smiled at the two. "Like I said, just the way everything should be."

RLINDA KETT

Flying carefully so as not to strain the ship's frayed systems, Rlinda brought *Declan's Glory* to the Rendezvous asteroid cluster. "If Handon Station is open for business," she transmitted, "then I've got some business."

Xander and Terry were both delighted to see her, and they hurried out to greet the scarred and battered ship in the main bay. Rlinda emerged and swept them into big bear hugs. Terry was wearing contraptions on his legs that let him walk better, even in the low gravity.

Running his gaze over the hull, Xander made a scornful noise. "Not sure how much we can pay you for that salvage, Rlinda . . . if there's anything salvageable."

"Salvage? Not on your life, dear boy. You're going to make *Declan's Glory* even better than new. Spare no expense—I want *Declan* to be as fancy as the *Verne*."

"That's a tall order," said Terry.

"And we're going to do it." Xander rubbed his palms briskly together. "We'll take Before and After images to use in our advertising—'Handon Station can do the impossible!'"

Rlinda just snorted again.

"Save room for us in the bay," Tasia called as the *Voracious Curiosity* cruised into the Roamer center only moments later.

Both ships had dropped the Fireheart refugees at Newstation. Many—including Rlinda—had to undergo treatment for heavy radiation exposure, but even though the medication caused a constant queasy nausea and (worse) a loss of appetite, it was better than dying from radiation sickness. And far better than being wiped out by bugbots or the Shana Rei.

As Tasia and Robb got settled, Rlinda chose the best available quarters in the main Rendezvous asteroid, since it would be a while before *Declan's Glory* was repaired. She took the time to assess the many things she had to do: Her fine restaurants on Relleker and Earth were wiped out, but she still had her favorite of the three, Arbor, on Theroc. She had already made up her mind that it was time for an expedition to Theroc, especially since hearing the news about Prince Reynald's unexpected treatment from the Onthos.

She had sent Zachary Wisskoff instructions for him to see that Raindrop was properly fed, but before she could leave she had other important business to attend to. The headquarters of Kett Shipping had been destroyed on Earth, but much of her fleet was still intact, having been out on trading runs across the Spiral Arm. Her pilots were good people and her ships in great demand, but she didn't dare let her ships manage themselves, though—it would be like herding cats. Rlinda liked cats, but one had to be realistic with expectations for their cooperation.

Terry and Xander sent Roamer repair crews to work on the *Declan's Glory*, giving her ship priority. Handon Station was already a bustling place, with many salvaged starships and more scrap components than they could use in a decade. Rlinda was sure that very soon this place would be just as vital and profitable as Ulio Station had been. Considering the connections Tasia and Robb already had through their son, Rlinda decided that this was where she wanted to hitch her star.

Later that day, Rlinda made her proposal to Xander and Terry, while Tasia and Robb sat in on the meeting. Since it wouldn't be a proper meeting without refreshments, she had taken care to make a custard-filled Napoleon and extra-sticky baklava.

She put her elbows on the table. "I want to buy one of these asteroids, set up new Kett Shipping headquarters. It makes sense. Handon Station will be a trade center, a repair yard, and a refueling station, everything my ships could need. I may as well bring business to you."

Xander laughed. "Terry and I talked about that yesterday. We wholeheartedly agree. By the Guiding Star, this is where Kett Shipping should be."

Terry said, "But we won't let you *buy* one of the asteroids. You've earned it. Just set up shop here, claim one of the abandoned complexes, make it your new headquarters."

"I won't take advantage of your kindness, dear boy," she said, tapping a stern finger on the tabletop. "This is Handon Station. You're in charge. I appreciate the gesture, but I expect to pay for it—at a fair price."

"We were prepared for that, too." Terry gestured to OK, who called up numbers on the table's filmscreen. "After agreeing on a price, we'll sell the asteroid to you on credit. We expect you to pay us back over time."

"Yes," Xander grinned. "Terry and I already decided on terms—take them or leave them."

Rlinda had never expected these two to be hard negotiators. "And what are the terms?"

"We want you to pay us back at a rate of ten credits per year," Terry said, "over the next million years or so. That should be sufficient."

Rlinda blinked. Tasia and Robb both burst out laughing. Rlinda extended a large hand. "Deal."

"We have a lot of good news to celebrate," Tasia said.

"Then let's get on with celebrating," Rlinda said. "I'll cook."

She returned to her private quarters—quarters that she decided would be her permanent ones, to be remodeled and expanded to her specifications. For now, they were cozy and comfortable enough.

She removed the silver capsule of ashes from her pocket, held it between her fingers, and smiled wistfully. She set the capsule on a stand inside one of the rock alcoves in the wall. She still dreamed of a romantic ending someday, having her ashes sent off with his into open space, but for now the capsule would stay right there on the shelf.

"I won't be needing to move you for a long, long time, BeBob. Get used to staying here."

CHAPTER

136

ARITA

In their new treeship forms, Celli and Solimar came to Theroc, look-ing even more intimidating than the verdani battleships that re-mained as sentries in orbit. Collin led Arita up to the canopy so they could watch the arrival together. "I want to be with you to see this."

They climbed into the open air and sat among the rustling fronds. Though Arita had prepared herself, she was still astonished when the immense forms drifted down through the blue skies like thistles each the size of a space station.

"Celli and Solimar are inside those?" she whispered.

Collin turned his face to the hazy sky, extending his hand both to point at the trees and to welcome them. "They aren't *in* those trees. They *are* the trees, one and the same. Celli and Solimar are part of the heartwood."

Arita saw the sheer wonder on his face. "You wouldn't ever do that, would you?"

He gave the question serious consideration. "No, because then I would have to leave you behind." Collin continued, "Through telink, I know everything that Celli and Solimar feel, what they've experienced, how they've grown together with the trees. I'm sorry you can't sense it in the same way."

Arita said, "I used to feel disappointed about that, and I still wish I could become a green priest, but I have something else that makes up for it."

Although Eternity's Mind had quieted now that the Shana Rei were eradicated, she could still hear those immense thoughts throb-bing through the universe, whispering in the back of her mind. She understood that she was touching something incomprehensible, and she was part of it. "Don't feel sorry for me. I have all the sense of wonder I can handle."

Many others arrived in the canopy to stare and wave at the new treeships, including the King and Queen. The crowds gathered, representatives from various Confederation planets, Roamer traders who had pulled back from bloater harvesting.

Collin stood up. "We can join the others now. Look, Reynald is stronger than ever."

Arita's brother had climbed up to the canopy on his own, although he often leaned on Osira'h's arm. Oddly, he never seemed to need the help of anyone else, Arita thought with a smile. She and Collin joined them, and they all watched the sentient trees hang in the air.

Queen Estarra had a wistful look on her face. She spoke aloud, as if the treeships could hear—and maybe they could. "Little sister, I remember you catching condorflies and spending your days climbing trees. Now look at you. I hope you're happy."

In an eerie unison, ten nearby green priests spoke in harmony. "She is."

Arita couldn't stop herself from laughing out loud. "Of course she is."

Collin nodded to her. "And all the green priests are happy for her."

Reyn still hung on to Osira'h's arm, though he seemed perfectly steady. Osira'h said, "I miss my mother and my brother and sister." She heaved a sigh. "Gale'nh and Muree'n are the only two left."

"You should go home," Reyn said, "at least for a while. They need you there."

"I'm waiting for you to get well enough to accompany me."

"I'll be well enough to go soon," he said, "as long as you take care of me."

"It would be a responsibility I take seriously," Osira'h said.

Estarra looked concerned, but Peter seemed much more understanding. "I think you're well enough to represent us to the Mage-Imperator."

Osira'h smiled. "My father will send an entire Solar Navy septa to escort us home." Arita could tell that she meant it.

Now that the blight was gone from the Onthos, the surviving

Gardeners had gone to the Wild, where they were working with Theron teams to clear the fallen wood from the dead zone. Meanwhile, green priest acolytes climbed among the healthy worldtrees in the main forest, harvesting seedlings from gaps in the bark scales. Teams of volunteers would replant the entire dead zone with a new grove so the worldforest would thrive again.

She and Collin intended to go there to help, and she would continue her studies of Theron biology as well. That was what she had always wanted to do, and now she would have her chance without other obligations or distractions. Her work had helped find the right cure for her brother.

Overhead, several spacecraft arrived, cargo ships filled with goods to disperse and sell; all the vessels bore the Kett Shipping logo. Arita looked up as the trading ships darted around the enormous verdani treeships. Even though Earth and Relleker were both gone, the rest of the Confederation continued to thrive. The human race would keep growing and spreading.

Eternity's Mind seemed to be dreaming and content. She could feel it in the back of her thoughts. Arita inhaled deeply of the moist forest air and leaned against Collin. The sun and the stars seemed very bright indeed.

GLOSSARY

ACADEM: Roamer school inside a hollowed-out comet, near the Roamer complex of Newstation. The school is run by Jess Tamblyn and Cesca Peroni.

ADAR: highest military rank in Ildiran Solar Navy.

AELIN: Iswander's former green priest, with a special connection to the bloaters. Killed at Ulio Station.

ALAKIS, ADAM: researcher on Vaconda, father of Zoe Alakis, died of Heidegger's Syndrome.

ALAA'KH: one of the misbreeds in the Kuivahr sanctuary dome.

ALAKIS, ZOE: wealthy head of the Pergamus medical research facility.

ALU, BEREN: station chief of Fireheart Station.

ANNIE D: Roamer salvage worker at Relleker.

ARAGAO, OCTAVIO: communications officer aboard the *Kutuzov*.

ARITA, PRINCESS: daughter of King Peter and Queen Estarra, a budding naturalist.

ATOA: Confederation world, known for hanging kelp-vine gardens.

ATTENDER: servile Ildiran kith.

AURIDIA: sparsely inhabited planet over which Newstation and Academ orbit. Auridia contained a Klikiss transportal, which was destroyed by Tom Rom.

BEBOB: Rlinda Kett's pet name for Branson Roberts.

BIG RING: Kotto Okiah's large experimental accelerator at Fireheart Station. The first test run failed and tore a hole in space.

BLACK ROBOTS: intelligent and evil robots built by the Klikiss race; most of them were wiped out in the Elemental War, but now they have been resurrected by the Shana Rei.

BLOATERS: strange organic nodules found in deep, empty space, the source of ekti-X.

BRINDLE, ROBB: administrator of Kett Shipping, married to Tasia Tamblyn, father of Xander.

BRINDLE, XANDER: one of the pilots of the Kett Shipping vessel *Verne*, son of Robb Brindle and Tasia Tamblyn.

BUGBOT: deprecating slang term for a Klikiss robot.

CAIN, DEPUTY ELDRED: former deputy of the Terran Hanseatic League, now an administrator of Earth, loyal to the Confederation.

CELLI: green priest, married to Solimar, who tends a terrarium dome in Fireheart Station. Celli is the sister of Estarra and Sarein.

CHAIRMAN: leader of the former Terran Hanseatic League.

CHIAR'H: Ildiran woman of the noble kith, volunteer worker on the Kuivahr sanctuary domes tending misbreeds, married to human Shawn Fennis.

CHRYSALIS CHAIR: reclining throne of the Mage-Imperator.

CLINTON, RAJESH: interim supervisor at Handon Station.

COLICOS, ANTON: historian, known for his work with Ildiran records, first human to translate portions of the Saga of Seven Suns.

COLLIN: young green priest, friend of Arita's.

COMPETENT COMPUTERIZED COMPANION: intelligent servant robot, also called a compy, available in Friendly, Teacher, Governess, Listener, Worker, and other models.

COMPY: nickname for competent computerized companion.

CONDEN'S FEVER: deadly human disease.

CONFEDERATION: new human government replacing the Terran Hanseatic League, loose alliance among Roamer clans, independent planets, and remnants of the Hansa. Ruled by King Peter and Queen Estarra, capital on Theroc.

CONFEDERATION DEFENSE FORCES (CDF): military serving the Confederation, headquartered at Earth with its main base in the rubble of the Moon, the Lunar Orbital Complex. Commanded by General Nalani Keah.

COVITZ, ORLI: strong advocate for compies, former pilot for Kett Shipping. She recovered from the Onthos plague. She is the owner of DD and in a relationship with Garrison Reeves.

DARO'H, PRIME DESIGNATE: oldest noble-kith son and successor to Mage-Imperator Jora'h.

DD: Friendly compy owned by Orli Covitz.

DECLAN'S GLORY: Kett Shipping vessel often flown by Rlinda Kett.

DENVA, MARIUS: line supervisor at Del Kellum's distillery on Kuivahr, presumed lost in the Shana Rei attack on that planet.

DOBRO: Ildiran splinter colony, former home of the secret breeding program where many humans were held captive.

DOMINIC, KELLIDEE: student at Academ, daughter of an ekti-harvesting clan.

DOMINIC, SEYMOUR: head of a Roamer ekti-harvesting clan, father of Kellidee.

DREMEN: cloudy Confederation planet primarily known for fungus harvests.

DRE'NH, SEPTAR: leader of a Solar Navy septa.

DUQUESNE: Roamer clan, victims of Elisa Enturi's attack on their bloater operations.

DURRIS-B: one of the seven suns of Ildira.

EARTH DEFENSE FORCES (EDF): former military for the Terran Hanseatic League, precursor to the Confederation Defense Forces.

EDILYN: Ildiran planet known for its beautiful ice geysers.

EKTI: exotic allotrope of hydrogen used to fuel Ildiran stardrives.

EKTI-X: stardrive fuel with higher energy potential than traditional ekti, harvested from bloaters.

ELEMENTAL WAR: conflict across the Spiral Arm involving the human race, the Ildiran Empire, the hydrogues, faeros, wentals, verdani, as well as the Klikiss and their black robots.

ELJIID: abandoned Klikiss world where Tom Rom obtained his first samples of Klikiss royal jelly. Eljiid and its small research colony were wiped out by a malicious attack from the Shana Rei and the black robots.

ENTURI, ELISA: former wife of Garrison Reeves and mother of Seth, deputy of Lee Iswander at the Sheol lava mines. Once went by her married name of Elisa Reeves.

ESTARRA, QUEEN: ruler of the Confederation, married to King Peter, with two children, Reynald and Arita.

EXXOS: leader of the surviving Klikiss robots.

FAEROS: sentient fire entities.

FENNIS, SHAWN: human born on Dobro, volunteer worker in the Kuivahr sanctuary domes to take care of the misbreeds, married to Ildiran woman Chiar'h.

FIREHEART STATION: Roamer research and industrial station at the heart of a nebula, specializing in energized films. Site of Kotto Okiah's Big Ring experiment.

FITZKELLUM, KRISTOF: thirteen-year-old son of Zhett Kellum and Patrick Fitzpatrick III, also called Toff.

FITZKELLUM, REX: two-year-old son of Zhett Kellum and Patrick Fitzpatrick III.

FITZKELLUM, SHAREEN: seventeen-year-old daughter of Zhett Kellum and Patrick Fitzpatrick III.

FITZPATRICK, PATRICK, III: husband of Zhett Kellum, one of the managers of the Kellum skymine on Golgen.

FORAY PLAZA: gathering area in front of the Prism Palace.

FORNU: Ildiran planet known for its colorful fossil canyons.

FUNGUS-REEF: large inhabited fungal growth on the worldtrees of Theroc.

GALE'NH, TAL: halfbreed son of the green priest Nira and Ildiran war hero Adar Kori'nh, a tal in the Ildiran Solar Navy. Gale'nh was the captain of the exploration ship *Kolpraxa* and once captured by the Shana Rei.

GARDENERS: ancient, original tenders of the worldforest, also called the Onthos.

GOLGEN: gas-giant planet, former home of the Kellum skymine before it was destroyed by the Shana Rei.

GORHUM: transportal nexus world.

GOR'KA: one of the misbreeds in the Kuivahr sanctuary domes.

GREEN PRIEST: servant of the worldforest, able to use worldtrees for instantaneous communication.

GUIDING STAR: Roamer philosophy and religion, a guiding force in a person's life.

GUPTA: Roamer clan.

GWENDINE, LYNNE: assistant manager at Dr. Krieger's sun-bomb-manufacturing facilities.

HANDIES, EDGAR, ADMIRAL: CDF Admiral, one of the "Three H's."

HANDON STATION: new repair complex established by Terry Handon and Xander Brindle at the former site of Rendezvous.

HANDON, TERRY: one of the pilots of the Kett Shipping vessel *Verne*, partner of Xander Brindle.

HANSA: Terran Hanseatic League.

HAR'LC: one of the misbreeds in the Kuivahr sanctuary domes, son of swimmer and scaly kiths.

HAROUN, SHIMAL, ADMIRAL: CDF Admiral, one of the "Three H's."

HARVARD, PETROV, ADMIRAL: CDF Admiral, one of the "Three H's."

HEIDEGGER'S SYNDROME: fatal degenerative neurological disease, thought to be incurable. Adam Alakis died of Heidegger's Syndrome.

HILTOS: Ildiran shrine to the Lightsource, destroyed by the Shana Rei.

HYDROGUES: alien race that dwells within gas-giant planets, the main destructive antagonists in the Elemental War.

IKBIR: Confederation colony world.

ILDIRA: home planet of the Ildiran Empire, under the light of seven suns.

ILDIRAN EMPIRE: large alien empire, the only other major civilization in the Spiral Arm.

ILDIRAN SOLAR NAVY: space military fleet of the Ildiran Empire, commanded by Adar Zan'nh.

ILDIRANS: humanoid alien race with many different breeds, or kiths.

ISWANDER, ARDEN: thirteen-year-old son of Lee Iswander.

ISWANDER INDUSTRIES: company owned by Lee Iswander, prominent producer of ekti-X.

ISWANDER, LEE: Roamer industrialist with numerous operations, including the Sheol lava mines and now ekti-X extraction from bloaters.

ISWANDER, LONDA: wife of Lee Iswander.

JAZER: energy weapon used by the Confederation Defense Forces.

JORA'H: Mage-Imperator of the Ildiran Empire. He is the father of numerous important Ildirans, including Adar Zan'nh and the halfbreed Osira'h. His consort is the green priest Nira.

JUGGERNAUT: largest battleship class in the Confederation Defense Forces.

KEAH, NALANI, GENERAL: commander of the Confederation Defense Forces.

KELLUM, DEL: former Speaker of the Roamer clans, successor to Cesca Peroni, father of Zhett Kellum. He ran a distillery on the Ildiran ocean planet of Kuivahr before it was destroyed.

KELLUM, ZHETT: daughter of Del Kellum, married to Patrick Fitzpatrick III. She ran a large skymine on Golgen, then helped with the Kuivahr distillery, both of which were destroyed by the Shana Rei. She and Patrick have three children, Shareen, Kristof, and Rex.

KENNEBAR: leader of an isolationist faction of green priests on Theroc, possessed by the shadows.

KETT, RLINDA: trader and former Trade Minister of the Confederation, now owner of Kett Shipping. She also owns several high-end restaurants.

KETT SHIPPING: Rlinda Kett's shipping company, managed by Robb Brindle and Tasia Tamblyn.

KLANEK, TONY: operations worker at Newstation.

KLEE: a hot beverage made from ground worldtree seeds, a specialty of Theroc.

KLIKISS: ancient insectlike race, creators of the black robots, long vanished from the Spiral Arm, leaving only their empty cities. After their resurgence in the Elemental War, they departed through their transportal network and are considered lost or extinct.

KLIKISS ROBOTS: intelligent and evil beetle-like robots built by the Klikiss race; most of them were wiped out in the Elemental War. Also called black robots.

KRIEGER, JOCKO: human weapons scientist who developed modifications to the Ildiran sun-bomb design.

KOLPRAXA: Ildiran exploration ship that ventured beyond the Spiral Arm, led by Tal Gale'nh; destroyed by the Shana Rei.

KUIVAHR: Ildiran planet with shallow seas and strong tides, site of Tamo'l's sanctuary domes for misbreeds and Del Kellum's distillery; was completely englobed by the Shana Rei and destroyed.

KUTUZOV: flagship Juggernaut of the Confederation Defense Forces.

LENS KITH: one of the Ildiran breeds, religious philosophers.

LIGHTSOURCE: higher plane of existence above normal life, an Ildiran version of heaven.

LUNAR ORBITAL COMPLEX (LOC): military and civilian base established in the rubble of Earth's Moon.

MAGE-IMPERATOR: the god-emperor of the Ildiran Empire.

MANTA: cruiser-class battleship in the Confederation Defense Forces.

MIJISTRA: Ildiran capital city.

MUNGL'EH: one of the misbreeds in the Kuivahr sanctuary domes, a powerful singer.

MUREE'N: halfbreed daughter of Nira and a warrior kithman, a skilled fighter, student of Yazra'h.

NADD: green priest serving aboard the *Kutuzov*.

NEW PORTUGAL: Confederation planet, home of a university and also known for its wines.

NEWSTATION: large orbiting station above planet Auridia, the new Roamer center of government. The Roamer school Academ is also nearby.

NIRA: green priest consort of Mage-Imperator Jora'h, mother of five halfbreed children: Osira'h, Rod'h, Gale'nh, Tamo'l, and Muree'n.

OHRO: spokesman for the Onthos on Theroc.

OK: compy owned by Xander Brindle.

OKIAH, KOTTO: renowned but eccentric Roamer scientist, designer of the failed Big Ring experiment, which tore open a hole in space.

OKRUN: CDF Juggernaut commanded by Admiral Haroun.

ONTHOS: alien race, also called the Gardeners.

ORBITAL RESEARCH SPHERE (ORS): isolated medical research satellite orbiting Pergamus, where the deadliest disease specimens are tested.

OSIRA'H: daughter of Nira and Jora'h, bred to have unusual telepathic abilities.

OSQUIVEL: ringed gas giant, former site of Kellum shipyards.

PANNEBAKER, ALEC: one of Lee Iswander's deputies at the bloater-extraction fields.

PATTON, DILLON: weapons officer aboard the *Kutuzov.*

PERGAMUS: secure medical research facility owned by Zoe Alakis.

PERONI, CESCA: former Roamer Speaker, wife of Jess Tamblyn; together they run the Academ school complex for Roamer children.

PETER, KING: ruler of the Confederation, married to Queen Estarra, with two children, Reynald and Arita.

PLUMAS: frozen moon with deep liquid oceans, former site of Tamblyn clan water industry, destroyed by the Shana Rei.

POL'UX: one of the misbreeds on Kuivahr.

POWER BLOCK: energy source made of a charged film folded and packed inside a container.

PRIME DESIGNATE: eldest noble-born son of the Mage-Imperator, and successor.

PRIMORDIAL OOZE: trade name of one of Del Kellum's distillations from Kuivahr.

PRISDIAMOND: rare precious gem found on several Confederation planets; a large vein of prisdiamonds on Vaconda provides all of Zoe Alakis's wealth.

PRISM PALACE: crystalline palace of the Ildiran Mage-Imperator.

PRODIGAL SON: Garrison Reeves's ship, formerly an Iswander Industries vessel.

QHARDIN: Conferation gas giant, site of new cloud-harvesting activities.

RAFANI: CDF Juggernaut captained by Admiral Handies.

RAINDROP: Rlinda Kett's pet name for Prince Reynald.

RAKKEM: planet known for unregulated black-market medical services, shut down by the CDF as part of an agreement with Zoe Alakis.

REEVES, ELISA: wife of Garrison and mother of Seth, deputy of Lee Iswander. Also goes by her maiden name of Elisa Enturi.

REEVES, GARRISON: Roamer worker formerly at the Sheol lava-processing facility. He was married to Elisa; father of Seth. He is the son of clan head Olaf Reeves. Now in a relationship with Orli Covitz.

REEVES, OLAF: gruff clan leader of isolationist Roamers who died of a plague on the derelict Onthos city; father of Garrison Reeves.

REEVES, SETH: ten-year-old son of Garrison Reeves.

RELLEKER: Terran colony planet, former home of Orli Covitz's compy laboratory.

REMORA: small attack ship in the Confederation Defense Forces.

RENDEZVOUS: asteroid cluster, former center of Roamer government. Destroyed by the Earth Defense Forces, but clan Reeves attempted reconstruction for years.

REYNALD, PRINCE: son of King Peter and Queen Estarra, in line to be the Confederation's next King, suffers from a fatal debilitating disease caused by a rare Theron microfungus.

RICKS, SAM: current Speaker of the Roamer clans.

ROAMERS: loose confederation of independent humans, primary producers of ekti stardrive fuel.

ROBERTS, BRANSON: Rlinda Kett's favorite ex-husband, affectionately called BeBob, now dead.

ROD'H: older halfbreed son of Nira, fathered by the Dobro Designate as part of the secret breeding program; he was captured by the Shana Rei at the Onthos home system.

ROHANDAS, HOWARD: fellow student with Shareen Fitzkellum, works with her as a lab assistant to Kotto Okiah.

RUSKIN, BOWMAN: Roamer worker at Fireheart Station.

SAGA OF SEVEN SUNS: historical and legendary epic of the Ildiran civilization.

SALIBA, SHARON: sensor technician aboard the *Kutuzov*.

SAREIN: sister of Estarra and Celli, lived in self-imposed exile in the Wild, but was killed by the Onthos.

SELISE: Roamer clan.

SELISE, OMAR: clan leader working salvage at Relleker.

SEPTA: Ildiran battle group consisting of seven warliners.

SHANA REI: fearsome creatures of darkness, chaos incarnate, who wish to destroy all life.

SHEOL: lava planet, site of a disaster that wiped out operations led by Lee Iswander.

SHIZZ: Roamer expletive.

SKYMINE: ekti-harvesting facility in the clouds of a gas-giant planet, usually operated by Roamers.

SKYSPHERE: audience chamber of the Prism Palace.

SOLIMAR: green priest, married to Celli, who tends a terrarium dome in Fireheart Station.

SPEAKER: leader of the Roamer clans.

SPIRAL ARM: the section of the Milky Way Galaxy settled by the Ildiran Empire and Terran colonies.

STARFLOWER: rare, transient white vine orchid on Theroc.

SWIMMER: otterlike Ildiran kith that spend most of their time in the ocean.

TAIT, MATTHEW: tactical officer aboard the *Kutuzov*.

TAL: military rank in Ildiran Solar Navy, cohort commander.

TAMBLYN, JESS: one of the heads of Academ school, married to Cesca Peroni.

TAMBLYN, TASIA: administrator of Kett Shipping, married to Robb Brindle, father of Xander.

TAMO'L: one of Nira's halfbreed children, daughter of a lens kithman. She ran the sanctuary domes for misbreeds on the planet Kuivahr.

TAVISH: Roamer clan.

TELINK: instantaneous communication used by green priests via the worldtrees.

TERRAN HANSEATIC LEAGUE: former commerce-based government of Earth and Terran colonies, dissolved after the death of Chairman Basil Wenceslas at the end of the Elemental War.

THEROC: forested planet, home of the sentient worldtrees, capital of the Confederation.

THERON: a native of Theroc.

THISM: faint racial telepathic network, centered on the Mage-Imperator, that binds all Ildiran people.

THREE H'S: Admirals Handies, Harvard, and Haroun in the CDF.

TOM ROM: guardian and majordomo of Zoe Alakis.

TRANSPORTAL: Klikiss instantaneous transportation network.

UGRU: sluggish Ildiran combat beast.

ULIO, MARIA: founder of Ulio Station who left to wander space by herself, giving her entire fortune to Terry Handon.

ULIO STATION: large trading complex in open space, frequented by traders of all sorts, destroyed by the Shana Rei.

VACONDA: wilderness planet where Zoe Alakis lived for years before departing with Tom Rom.

VERDANI: organic-based sentience, manifested as the Theron world-forest.

VERNE: cargo ship flown by Xander Brindle and Terry Handon.

VOIDPRIESTS: Kennebar's isolationist green priests, possessed by the shadows.

VORACIOUS CURIOSITY: Rlinda Kett's private ship, now primarily flown by Tasia Tamblyn and Robb Brindle.

WARGLOBE: crystalline sphere used by hydrogues.

WARLINER: largest class of Ildiran battleship.

WENCESLAS, CHAIRMAN BASIL: former leader of the Terran Hanseatic League.

WENTALS: sentient water-based creatures, now mostly dormant.

WILD, THE: unexplored continent on Theroc.

WINGO, MERCER: first officer aboard the *Kutuzov*.

WISSKOFF, ZACHARY: manager and maître d' of Rlinda Kett's Arbor restaurant.

WORLDFOREST: the interconnected, semisentient forest based on Theroc.

WORLDTREE: a separate tree in the interconnected, semisentient forest based on Theroc.

YAZRA'H: daughter of the Mage-Imperator, skilled warrior and bodyguard. She is the mentor of Muree'n.

YODER, DANDO: trader pilot who works for Kett Shipping.

ZAN'NH, ADAR: Ildiran military officer, eldest son of Mage-Imperator Jora'h, Adar of the Ildiran Solar Navy.

ZAQUEL: female green priest under whom Arita and Collin served as acolytes.